Double Bound

NICK NOLAN

DOUBLE BOUND
A NOVEL

LITTLE EDEN PRESS
2008

Double Bound

ACKNOWLEDGEMENTS

First and foremost, thanks to Jaime—my partner of twenty-one years. How could I have been so lucky to have found you? Aside from being my best friend and lover, you helped me hone both stories, and supported me through their conceptions, as well as their protracted births. I can't thank you enough for listening to me drone endlessly about this all. No one but we will ever know what this journey was like, and I'm so happy to have shared this all with you. Thank you for arguing with me and making me see your point, although in my head they'll always be together...

Thanks to my dear friends Arlet and Margo, once again, for their tireless cheerleading. I hope you like the story, and you felt it was worth the wait. I love you both, dearly. Batcheeks!

Big thanks to Art and Claudine, my beta readers and our alpha friends. Sometimes fate is a wondrous thing. Thank God for that old ping pong table!

Once again I need to acknowledge groundbreaking author Kathleen McGowan, who already sees me as the successful writer I aspire— humbly—to be someday, and who has shared so generously every resource at her disposal. They were lucky stars, indeed, my dear. And speaking of Kathleens, I am forever grateful to my wonderful sister who, after an arduous workday and caring for her kids, drove across Los Angeles to my book signing and got lost, but still managed to walk in the door smiling, even as the tables and chairs were being carried away. No one but you knows the truth on these pages.

And thanks to Kirk Frederick for championing *Strings* to everyone he knew, and for suffering through that early unedited version of *DB* (sorry about that!); and thanks to Joe Clapsaddle, who fortified my confidence. Also thanks to Jim Fain for providing suggestions for the 'zombie' drug used on Ryan and Jeremy.

Thanks to my editor, Eileen Chetti, for her invaluable input on these sentences and dots and dashes and apostrophes. Thank you for your hard work and sparkling expertise, as well as your open mind.

And where would we be without our friends David and Larry, Judie and Marty, Lee and Andre, wonderful Courtney, newlyweds Mark and Gordon, Michael and Kelly, John and Jennifer, Henry, Brian and Rose? And especially Kalua and her husband Celso, who provided me with the Brazilian Portuguese phrases. (What would I have done without you?) And I haven't forgotten you, Jason, and what you did for me with the photo on *Strings*. We both wish you the best.

I'm always grateful to my author friends DC Elmore, who is as charming as she is talented and beautiful, and fellow *ForeWord Magazine* award winner Nick Poff, whose *The Handyman's Promise* stole my boyfriend from me one weekend.

I also want to acknowledge those who wrote such wonderful reviews of *Strings* on Amazon, most notably Amos Lassen of *Literary Pride*, Paul Minafri, Bob Lind, Elton Elliott, R. Rutar, Michael Brown, Jerome Lowe, T. Cullens, Foster Corbin, Lawrence Coles, Matthew Boger, David Means, our friend Jonathan Taylor, and Jeffrey Schmidt. Huge thanks go to my hero Richard Labonte, and Rich Wiesenthal, for their glowing press reviews. Your effort and praise will be appreciated by me until my last day on this earth. And thanks to Stan Thompson, who provided me with a comprehensive list of errata from *Strings*, and volunteered to proofread this manuscript.

And last but not least I thank Pam Castle, my cyber best friend. You have been a continuous source of love and support through this process. I treasure your input, your intimacy, and your trust. You know the magic of the written word better than anyone.

Finally, to our darling Emma Lou, who passed away during the writing of this story, a year to the day after our beloved Margaret left us. You were here for me the way you are there for Arthur. We had such a short time together, but you touched my heart so much that I have tears in my eyes as I write this. I am so glad to have been able to give you some new life in these pages. I look forward to seeing your sweet brown eyes and happy grin again, while feeling your hot breath on my chest, once I cross over that proverbial "rainbow bridge."

Thank you, dearest readers, for taking a chance on my work.

Nick Nolan
August 2008
nick@nick-nolan.com

*For a complete explanation of the symbolism underlying **Double
Bound**, please visit nick-nolan.com*

"No matter how old our eyes may look on the outside,
on the inside they are always seventeen."
-Arthur Blauefee

"I have found the paradox that if I love until it hurts,
then there is no hurt, but only more love."
-Mother Teresa

"Quien engaña no gana."
-an old Spanish proverb

"He that believeth in me, as the scripture hath said,
out of his belly shall flow rivers of living water."
-John 7:38

Author's note:
English translations of foreign phrases are listed on the final pages.

For Jaime—My Partner, And My Best Friend.
Thank You, My Love.

PROLOGUE

The rain soothed his ears, even as it called him gently from his sleep.

He opened his eyes.

Had it really happened? He didn't need to look over at the sleeping form next to him to know it had. He'd been dreaming about it even before he'd awakened; his mind had been running it over and over the same way it did a beautiful song while it's playing, and then even after it ends, with a melody so sweet that you can't let it go—you keep humming and humming it until you get tired of it.

But he knew he wouldn't get tired of this.

Tired of him.

He was a song he'd been singing all his life, even before he knew the melody. Before he knew the words.

For so long now, he'd been harmonizing with silence.

Until tonight.

He smiled in the darkness, then reached over to smooth his warm, muscled shoulder.

His lover shifted, and rolled onto his back.

Then he sighed.

A sigh of contentment is what it sounded like.

No, a sigh of *elation*—like the sigh you make when you see the grand finale at a fireworks show. Or maybe it was the kind of sigh like wind winding through a cave...the sound of emptiness filled with God's breath.

He'd never heard a sigh like that before.

Or had he?

Yes, he had.

Once, a long time ago.

CHAPTER 1

The dirty yellow and blue cab rolled to a stop at the curb, idling noisily.

"Are you sure about this?" the blond one asked his friend.

"Don't be a dick, Ryan. We talked about this already. You said you wanted to do this, so let's do it. We'll just look around for a while, and then grab another cab outta here. I've got it with me," he said as he patted his belt where the revolver was tucked, "so we're safe. Everyone here's fucked up on drugs anyhow, so what could happen?"

"Ten minutes," Ryan demanded, staring him down. "We look around for ten minutes, and then we're gone."

"Twenty," Kris replied.

They nodded at each other, and then Ryan slipped a black ski cap over his yellow hair as Kris paid the driver and they scooted out of the car.

The city on the hill looked almost welcoming at night; the sparkling lights higher up, as well as the yellow glow coming from some of the nearby windows, beckoned the young men up from the street. And the darkness did a pretty good job of hiding the debris and the filth and the poverty and the ramshackle state of the shelters and cheap structures jammed together like some crazy urban jigsaw puzzle, as well as the suspicious stares of the dark faces that followed their trajectory up the stairs.

"I can't believe people actually live like this," Ryan nearly shouted over the din of Portuguese rap music, combined with dogs barking and people yelling and traffic honking in the street below.

"What the fuck is that smell?" Kris asked. "Jesus Christ, it smells like someone's cookin' shit for dinner."

"Maybe they are." Ryan laughed nervously. He glanced at his watch: they still had fifteen more minutes before they could flee. But then at least he could say that he'd been in the heart of a favela. He considered that for some American college students like himself, the exploration of the slums of Rio de Janeiro had become the bungee jumping of their generation. And he could see why. The fear he was experiencing at this moment was better than the thrill he got watching some slasher movie; his heart pounded and his flesh was crawling and every sense—especially his sight, hearing and sense of touch—was heightened. It was like those few times in high school when he'd done meth, but without the phantom skin bugs.

He felt as terrified as he was giddy.

The unmistakable *thump-diddi-thump-diddi-thump* of faraway reggae music met their ears, as well as some raucous laughter. The boys turned to each other. "Ever been to a party in Rio, my friend?" Kris asked.

"I'm not so sure if we should—" Ryan began to protest.

"Life is short," Kris cut him off. "We'll stick our heads in and say hi, smoke some ganja and then leave. Just so we can say we did."

"You are so fuckin' crazy," Ryan told him. And with that, they began picking their way along the labyrinth of paths toward the music.

Thump-diddi-thump-diddi-thump. It grew louder and louder until they could tell that the party was just over a wall.

"How do we get over that?" Kris asked, pointing to the peeling plaster with the broken bottles set into cement on its ridge. "There's no fuckin' way."

Ryan looked at his watch. They were already way past their agreed-upon twenty minutes. "Kris, let's go."

"No way, man. We've come this far. Let's go back how we came and see if we can find a way around this wall."

They made a U-turn and began their descent down a flight of stairs, where Kris discovered a path leading off to the right. "Let's try this one." He pointed excitedly into the darkness.

"I'm leaving," Ryan replied. "You do whatever the fuck you want, but I'm outta here."

"Ryan, *come on!*"

He shook his head and began making his way down to the street, walking at first and then nearly running.

"Ryan!" Kris yelled after him, but when his friend didn't turn around he began following him down. "OK, OK—just slow up!"

Ryan kept running.

"Wait! It's not that way; it's over this way!"

Ryan sprinted, terrified—there were no thrilling goose bumps or mild euphoria or anything even remotely good about this; he felt like a lost dog with its tail down running along a busy highway.

And then something tripped him. He flew chin first through the air, landed with a *whump* on his chest and then skidded headfirst along the ground and came to a rest just as something sharp dug into his forearm. He couldn't breathe. *Wind knocked out*, one part of his scrambled brain reported to the other. And in a moment, Kris was behind him, kneeling down.

"Jesus, are you OK?" Kris asked, suddenly panicked.

"Ow, oh," Ryan answered from the ground, rubbing his arm.

"He'll be OK," a woman's voice advised. *Or was it a man's?*

Kris heard the flick of a lighter, and then at once a masculine face adorned in heavy drag makeup—painted arching eyebrows, spider's legs eyelashes, darkly rouged cheeks and scarlet lips—emerged from the darkness. The creature held the yellow flame to what looked like a cigarette, and then he caught a whiff and realized that it had just sucked down a huge toke, which it held in its lungs for what seemed an eternity, and then blew out in a foglike plume.

Then Ryan looked up from where he was sprawled to see what was clearly a frail man dressed in tight jeans and a halter top and wearing a long, frizzled, black Disco Diva wig. *This is a nightmare*, he thought as he touched his forearm and felt the warm, sticky wetness of his blood emanating from the raw, throbbing skin. *This is a shittin' nightmare.* "What do you want?" he demanded.

Kris leaned over and held out his hand. "Come on, *let's go!*" he whispered. "*Get up! Now!*"

"*Meninos?*" it asked in its creepy, sultry voice, and then Ryan's eyes made out the silhouettes of four young men as they emerged from the darkness.

"Stand back!" Kris turned and shouted at them as he pulled the gun from his belt.

But he didn't shoot—he intended only to scare them.

POP-POP-POP—accompanied by triple flashes of light—issued from a gun held by one of the young men, and Kris jerked and spasmed as the bullets tore tiny, ragged tunnels through his body.

He slumped down beside Ryan, and then his head hit the cement with a sickening crack.

Ryan's chest heaved and he nearly hyperventilated as he threw his hands in the air and yelled, "*Don't shoot me! Please don't shoot me! Don't shoot me! Please, don't!*"

"You have the gun?" the creature asked him gently.

"No, no, no!" he exclaimed, waving his hands wildly and shaking his head.

It held out its hand. "Then come with us," it offered.

Ryan refused the hand, and shook his friend's shoulder instead. "Kris? Kris!"

The boy's head only jiggled limply, while his blank eyes stared at nothing.

Jesus Christ, he's dead!

Ryan pushed himself up off the ground. "Where are we going?"

"You are losing blood," it answered. "You must not lose the blood." Then it began to pick its way slowly down the path into the darkness, limping as if one of its high heels had broken off.

Ryan followed behind it, his hand applying pressure to the wound on his arm, while the *meninos*—mumbling cheerfully in their velvety, completely unintelligible tongue—followed right behind.

CHAPTER 2

"Where are you taking me?" Ryan asked the creature, trying not to sound panicked. "Please, I haven't done anything to you. Just tell me what you're gonna do." He looked around for someone who might be able to help him, but anyone who materialized either ducked into a doorway or skittered away at their approach.

It laughed casually. "Do not worry, if you do what we say. You should be much honored to have been chosen."

Chosen?

They made their way down a set of stairs, past a shack where some girls were screaming with laughter, and then stepped out onto a busy street. There Ryan spotted a big white Mercedes amidst the tiny cars, looking like a cruise ship amongst dinghies. Leaning against the car was a heavily muscled black man, with bulging arms crossed over his massive chest. When they got closer he jerked to life and pulled the doors open for them.

The gun pressed into Ryan's back, as well as the image of Kris lying dead, forced his cooperation. So he sidled into the rear seat between the creature and two of the boys. After the other two climbed in front, the driver pulled away and began threading his way into Rio's crazed nighttime traffic.

"I'm so sorry," it told Ryan at last, while withdrawing some bandages from a purse and handing them over. "I am Rosa." She held out her gloved hand and Ryan shook it weakly. As she smiled at him disingenuously, he saw that she wore badly stained dentures, and the exaggerated crust of makeup on her skin made her look half silent film star and half mummy. "What is your name?"

"Ryan," he mumbled icily, peeling the paper cloth from the adhesive. Then he pressed the bandages carefully to his wrist.

"You are *very* handsome, Mr. Ryan," she said, and then withdrew a black, Spanish-style lace fan from her purse, unfurled it with a *zzziiip* and began fanning herself exaggeratedly with it.

"Where'm I going?" he demanded once again.

She parted her lips in what had once been, centuries ago, a good imitation of a coquettish smile. "You will meet my good friend. He is very fond of such handsome boys like you."

He squinted disgustedly at her. "I'm not a queer!"

She shrugged her shoulders. "It no matter," she said, withdrawing her cigarettes and lighter from her purse. "You make everyone so, so happy."

"*I'm an American!* You can't do this to me!"

"We all *American*, Mr. Ryan," she said, placing a cigarette between her lips. "You *North*, we *South*; no difference—we all laugh at the same Jim Carrey."

The driver raced the Mercedes through the crush of nighttime traffic toward the outskirts of the city, where the favelas and apartment buildings and businesses and hotels gave way to high-rise condominiums, and then merged into sprawling houses behind gates reinforced by lush tropical overgrowth. Then Ryan felt the road begin to climb and twist and bank from side to side as they came to a place where the land dropped precipitously on one side all the way down to the water, while on the other only a tall stretch of iron fence ran parallel to the street in either direction as far he could see.

The Mercedes slowed before making a sharp left into a driveway, where three men holding Uzis stopped them. The driver put down the back window; then, with a reassuring nod from Rosa, the twin gates parted for them.

As they motored upward, Ryan saw the shimmering crescent September moon reflected upon the black bay far away to his right, as well as the gargantuan Cristo Redentor lit up like a psychotic hallucination just beyond them—on the mountain peak to the left. Finally an immense, bland white structure loomed, and the Mercedes ascended the last section of steeply inclined driveway before stopping under a porte-cochère at the top.

Rosa opened her door and got out, as did the silent henchmen. But Ryan didn't budge. "Come," she demanded. Reluctantly, he scooted out of the seat and stood, secretly relieved to stretch his tension-cramped legs.

He looked around.

This mansion or compound or abandoned library reminded him of that place he'd visited once with his parents while on vacation in Los Angeles—what was it called? The Music Center. Those three huge white buildings: the Someone's First-and-Last-Name Pavilion and that cool round forum place and then that other theater—with the fountains and the shallow reflecting pools and the brilliant up-lights and those dizzying concrete colonnades that surrounded the place like a rectangular aerial racetrack. That's kind of what this looked like. Only smaller. *And dirtier.* The once shimmering reflecting pools were now olive green with algae, and vines crept up the chipped white walls; where there were rows of lights at the base of the buildings, many were burned out, the concrete below his feet was buckled in places and weeds flourished between the cracks.

He could tell the place had been grand once. Elegant, even.

But now it just looked spooky.

He followed Rosa through a pair of glass doors into a great terrazzo-floored entry hall, where he saw a trio of dusty, half-lit chandeliers overhead. Then his eyes traced the ceiling over to a cantilevered stairway, which appeared to defy gravity as it zigzagged down three stories over a burbling indoor reflecting pool.

"Dear Rosa," came a robust baritone from high up. Ryan craned his head back to see, standing at the top of the staircase, a tall man wearing a white robe. He was overly tanned and perfectly bald and wore a series of gold chains with medallions around his neck. "I see that, once again, your unerring eye has found another treasure," he said. And then he practically floated, smiling broadly, down the stairs.

Another treasure?

Ryan looked away, feigning casual disinterest. But as the man drew nearer he found himself backing up—he was huge.

"Don't be afraid, handsome one," he told Ryan, and then grasped his chin and tipped his head back gently, so they were eye to eye.

Ryan tried to look away, but something about the man's friendly, tobacco-colored eyes intrigued him.

"A blond?" he asked Rosa without taking his gaze from Ryan's. "Never have we had a blond Januário."

Rosa pulled at her own black hair. "The color is no problem, Dom Fabiano."

"Then you must work quickly," he instructed soothingly. "Our wonderful celebration is only hours away."

7

CHAPTER 3

O nce Ryan, Rosa and two of the gun-wielding *meninos* were shut
inside what appeared to be an ancient jail cell—with its chiseled
granite walls, uneven rock floor and medieval-looking wooden
door—she directed him over to a short, backless bench.

After huffing in protest and rolling his eyes, he sat.

She retrieved a big, dirty purse from the corner of the floor. From
inside this she withdrew an extensive assortment of vials and tubes and
brushes, which she organized on a table in front of him with as much
precision as a surgeon preparing her scalpels.

"Stop moving your face," she told him. Then from a tube she
squeezed into her hand a string of white paste, which she wiped onto his
face and neck, and then smoothed evenly.

"Are you making me a bitch?" he asked her, feeling his dread
building.

"Oh, no!" She laughed and then shook her head. "I am only making
you more like our beloved Januário."

"Who the fuck's Januário?"

"He is you, my sweet. And you are he. Don't blink." She took the
eyeliner and began tracing his eyelids with it.

His eyelashes batted despite her instructions—not from the pressure
of the instrument on his skin, but rather because her breath stank.

Then she took some charcoal and contoured his face with it—his
cheekbones, under his eyes and chin—and then finally she encircled his
lips with ruby lipstick.

She told him to stand.

He stood.

She pulled over his hair a short black wig that itched his scalp and
tickled his ears. Then she handed him a pair of black slippers that were so
small they curled his feet. After this she took from a stand in the corner
numerous undergarments—ancient-looking lacy, dressy, girly-looking
things—which she fitted him with, one atop the previous. Finally, she

slipped his arms into a white silk robe with a high, stiff collar and cuffs embroidered with gold and scarlet filigree.

He looked down to see his wiry athlete's frame buried so deeply in the garments that he looked like a hefty peasant bride all dressed up for her Slavic wedding.

"And for the most beautiful touch," she murmured, unfolding an extravagant crimson cape, which she wrapped around his shoulders and buttoned at his neck.

"Would you like to see?" she asked him at last.

He shook his head *no.*

"You'll like; you see." She smoothed the blood-colored silk down along his shoulders and tugged at his cuffs. *"Finis!"* she said, and then stepped back as her mouth split into a ragged smile of satisfaction. Then she turned and retrieved a tall, golden papal-style hat from atop the dressing table, which she brought to him and placed atop his bewigged head. "Stand, São Januário," she told him. "Come see your holiness."

He blinked stupidly at her.

Her face darkened. "Come now!" She held out her hand. "You are guest of honor, most perfect Januário ever seen." She grabbed his hand and pulled him to the other side of the room, where an antique pier mirror tilted precariously against the wall.

He stepped toward it.

That's not me!

Indeed, the scruffy blond skateboarder had vanished. In his place stood the life-sized statue of some creepy old Catholic saint—with gray, sunken eyes and starved-to-death cheeks and bleeding lips and stiff black hair. He blinked, just to see if São Januário would blink in unison with him.

He did.

Ryan began to cry.

"You've got to tell me what's going on!" he babbled. "Come on, what's gonna happen to me?"

Rosa smiled. "That's good; the tears are good for the makeup," she said, and then began dabbing at his face with the rag in her hand. "Not too much, though, OK? Januário is martyr, but he is not the boo-hoo crybaby."

"Goddamn it, tell me!" he roared. At once the *menino* with the gun snapped to attention.

"*Shhh, shhh.*" She took his hand and led him back to the bench. "Sit down, São Januário. Please sit and calm."

"My name is *Ryan*," he stated, trailing her back to the bench.

She patted his hand. "You are the saint of our people," she began. "Tonight is your feast. The faithful are awaiting your appearance. You show yourself to them and they will come and ask for answered prayers. Your presence will make devotion. We pray, and then we have the *milagre de sangue.* This is the most beautiful night of the year."

"What's the *milagre de sangue?*"

"The blood miracle," she said. "One time each year, the dry blood of São Januário turns to wet, like fresh. It is the ancient *milagre.*"

She nodded to the men, and they left the room. Then she reached into the old purse once again and produced a small package of waxy black paper that had been folded origami style. She opened it, and Ryan saw that it contained white powder.

"Is that coke?" he asked, suddenly excited. He loved coke.

"It is better—we call it Devil's Breath. From Colombia. You'll like it." She fished a pristine medical mask from the purse and tied it on, picked up a shortened drinking straw, lifted the paper to Ryan's nose and pulled up the mask to expose her lips; then she closed her eyes and blew the powder forcefully into his face.

"*What the*"—he coughed violently—"*fuck?*"

At once a scalding heat and a tingling cold began in his sinuses, while a deathlike stiffness began overtaking his limbs. Moments later, he discovered that he could not move his hands or his feet.

He started slumping sideways.

Rosa caught him as he fell.

And then he realized that he was completely, utterly paralyzed—as if invisible ropes were binding his hands and feet.

The *meninos* entered the room, lifted him from the bench and carried him over to a bed in the corner, where they laid him. Then Rosa bent down to dab at his makeup. "São Januário," she whispered intimately, "your blood will give miracles tonight."

He heard some laughter and footsteps as the heavy door swung open, then saw, out of the corner of one eye, a carved golden coffin with glass sides being pushed into the room. He felt Rosa and the young men lift him from the bed, then heft him up and over into the mysterious container. Then they wheeled him out of the room, turned and pulled him along a tunnel to a freight elevator, which they boarded. This descended for some time before slowing to a stop. The doors slid open and they pushed him along a concrete walkway, which opened, finally, into the open air.

He made out, through his now blurred vision, clouds amidst the darkness. He heard people muttering in Portuguese—one giving orders while others shuffled about.

They loaded him into a van, which then proceeded down the road that had brought him up to the compound in the Mercedes just a short time before. After this they turned onto another road, which he could tell was very precipitous and snakelike by the way the van listed and swayed and the engine strained and the transmission shifted from low to high to low over and over. Finally the vehicle stopped, the cargo door was opened and his casket was unloaded.

Once again he saw the night sky and its shroud of fog.

And candlelight...or a big fire...they're gonna set me on fire!

His heart began to beat wildly as his mind became a hurricane of gore—if only he could just lift his hand or scream or rock himself out of this box—

As he was pushed toward the candlelit altar, he heard the growing murmur of a crowd, and he could even distinguish some words here and there; all around him was the hypnotic *zhuzhing* of people speaking Portuguese, and another crisper, more deliberate language that he did not recognize. But the murmur didn't sound like talking—the tone was too monotonous.

They're praying.

He decided to do a little praying of his own. But then he decided to count, because he figured that by the time he reached a thousand he would be either safe or dead.

One...two...three...four...five...

But what the faithful gathered this evening saw was their beloved, and peaceful, São Januário—named for the eleventh month of the old calendar—as he was carried in his gilded reliquary with its glass sides and open top; he who had again returned on his feast day to grace them with his miraculous blood. Holy São Januário, who, because of his great faith, had been submitted to the torture rack of Timotheus, had leapt from fires unscathed, then had been thrown, along with his deacons, to wild beasts—only to have those beasts cower in submission at their feet. Courageous São Januário, for whom the peasants had begged mercy, and for whom the peasants had won a quick beheading rather than the agonizing death of being dragged by galloping horses through the streets of Naples on that night so many hundreds of centuries ago. São Januário, whose blood still turns from red dust to life-saving *sangue* each year as the priest says those amazing Latin prayers and holds that sacred pair of vials before Christ on the cross—the Redeemer of Mankind.

Only this was Ryan McCauley, who'd decided to backpack through South America with his best friend, Kris (recently deceased), after graduating high school, instead of beginning their first semesters at college with the rest of their friends. Ryan McCauley, an almost skateboard champ and confirmed lover of blue-eyed chicks with big tits, whose greatest conflict in life—until this moment—had been the grief he'd received from his dad after "borrowing" his credit card and buying some chrome rims for his metallic blue '84 Trans Am. Ryan McCauley, who'd never spent a second in church, who didn't believe in the Redeemer of Mankind, and whose only aspirations were to be a business major and to own a skateboard shop and to attend spring break in Fort Lauderdale this coming year.

Ryan McCauley, who realized he was about to die.

At once, beautiful singing—from a boys' choir, in fact—rose up and filled the night air with silver caroled notes that were as pure and clear and ecstatic as they were restrained. Immediately the prayer mumbling ceased and the choir soared through its song—flowing and ebbing and rising, then falling, as they recounted the miracle of Creation's triumph over damnation, and Redemption's conquering of sin.

Silently, Ryan begged them not to stop. They wouldn't—*couldn't*—do anything to him while music this beautiful was being sung.

But they did finish their cantata, and after a few moments of silence someone began reciting an incantation. *"Lætámini in Dómino et exsultáte, justi,"* the authoritative baritone announced.

"Et gloriámini, omnes recti corde," the faithful responded.

"Istórum est enim, regnum cælórum, qui contempsérunt vitam mundi," he continued, *"et pervenérunt ad præmia regni, et lavérunt stolas suas in sánguine Agni. Deus, qui nos annua sanctórum Mártyrum tuórum Januárii et Sociórum*

ejus solemnitate lætíficas: concéde propítius; ut, quorum gaudémus meritis, accendámur exemplis. Per Dóminum."

As the incantation was ending, Ryan thought the voice familiar. But before he could determine where he'd heard it, the crowd responded with, *"Et gloriámini, omnes recti corde,"* once again.

And then he realized that he was having trouble breathing—it felt as if a concrete slab had been lowered onto his torso.

A rustling of fabric caught his ear and a face came into view: *Rosa*— but without the wig. He saw her makeup had been removed hastily, as evidence of it still polluted what might have once been a friendly face.

"Et gloriámini, omnes recti corde," the faithful stated again.

Rosa grinned and then leaned down to kiss one of his hands, both of which had been placed in the usual crossed-arms position favored by nearly all funeral homes since Egyptian times. And then she looked him in the eyes. "Do not worry, São Januário," she whispered with her stinking breath. "We do not cut off your head anymore, and this will not hurt any more than the needle from a good doctor. Then you will sleep, and when you wake you will see the face of God."

She straightened Ryan's right arm by his side, while two altar boys carefully lifted out and then removed the glass from the right side of the coffin—the side facing the crowd. And then Rosa's face disappeared and the boys' choir began singing again and he felt his cuffed sleeve being unbuttoned just before the vein in his arm was sliced open, from his wrist almost up to his elbow.

"Deus, qui nos annua sanctórum Mártyrum tuórum Januárii et Sociórum ejus solemnitate lætíficas: concéde propítius; ut, quorum gaudémus meritis, accendámur exemplis. Per Dóminum."

Darkness surrounded his field of vision.

One hundred seventy-seven, his brain screamed. *One hundred seventy- eight...one hundred seventy-nine...one hundred eighty...*and then he drifted off. But then something jarred him, and he realized that it was Rosa shaking his shoulder. "São Januário, look!" she told him. "The face of God. He welcomes you to come to home." And so with superhuman effort he did his best to focus his fuzzy vision for the very last time as the nighttime fog cleared and the gargantuan figure of Cristo Redentor—with his perfectly stern yet somehow forgiving gaze and widely outstretched arms—loomed hundreds of feet above him into the impossibly black, star-strewn sky.

"*Et gloriámini, omnes recti corde,*" the faithful droned. And then they watched their beloved São Januário once again give his miraculous *sangue* for them, as Ryan's strong young heart pumped all of his body's precious blood into an assemblage of the loveliest cut-crystal decanters ever created.

CHAPTER 4

The van's tires crunched the dead leaves in the gutter as he rolled to a stop. Arthur switched off the VW's ignition, cranked the wheel to the left and then rolled back to bump the curb before pulling on the emergency brake.

As he reached for the door handle, he glanced at the rearview mirror and caught the dread reflected in his gray eyes.

Just get it over with.

He grabbed his backpack and made his way up the front walk, and then opened the screen door and walked through it. "Hi, Mom. Hi, Dad," he called, trying his best to act as if he didn't hate every second under their roof.

"Hi, Artie," his mother sang out from the kitchen.

She's a good actor, too.

His father was in front of the TV watching a boxing match. Arthur went over and shook his hand. "How's it goin'?" he asked, glancing at the two glowering Hispanic guys, one in blue satin shorts and the other in gold, who circled each other with their fists guarding their jaws.

Blue-Shorts is hot.

"Pretty good," the man replied, never taking his eyes from the TV. Arthur dropped his backpack onto the floor; he wanted to go speak with his mother but sat down with his father instead.

They watched in silence as the fighters threw exhausted, haphazard jabs at each other.

His mom walked in drying her hands on her apron. "Come eat. I made you some spaghetti because we're having a roast, and I know you hate that. It's ready, so why don't you come sit at the table?"

"Sure," he replied as the salty tang of marinara caught his nose. He pushed up from the sofa and made his way to the dining room.

"How's school?" she asked as he took his place at the table and she slid a heaping plate in front of him.

"It's tough," he replied, screwing his fork into the pile of stringy noodles. "This semester's almost over, and I've got term papers due and then finals next week. And tuition's coming up for Cal State LA next month; I've gotta start going there 'cause I've taken all the classes I can at the community college."

His father cut into the bloody slab before him. "How's the sales?"

"I'm having an OK month," he told him. "But even a good month at Electronics Galore won't be enough for the university's tuition—and it's due by the tenth."

"Oh," said his mother. "Would you like some salad?"

Arthur reached out, and she handed him the Tupperware bowl filled with pale green lettuce and pink tomato slices.

The fight announcer droned in the background.

"Have you heard Gwen's news?" she asked.

"Nope," he answered flatly, shoveling salad onto his plate.

"She was accepted to UCLA."

He studied his plate. "That's great. How's she paying for it?"

"She got some scholarships," his mother answered. "And we're helping her. A little."

"She sure works hard," his father noted proudly. "I've never seen anyone so organized and who works as hard as her."

"Well, I work pretty hard," Arthur countered. "And I support myself."

"I supported myself *and* my parents when I was your age," his father boasted.

"But things cost more now," Arthur said. "My rent is seven hundred dollars. Do you know how hard it is to pay that when you're making what I make and paying for school—books and parking and tuition?"

"Maybe you should get a second job," his mother suggested as she picked up her dinner roll.

"What about that fairy roommate of yours?" his father asked. "He doesn't help out?"

"Frank." She glared at him.

"Peter moved in with his...*friend*, so now I'm paying all the rent until I can find someone else."

The older man chuckled, shaking his head. "Nice to have people you can depend on."

"You made the decision to move out," she reminded Arthur while pushing a knife full of margarine into her roll. "We told you if you did, we wouldn't help you with your school—and even still you *insisted* on doing that."

"I had to," Arthur said with his mouth full. "You kept giving me Bibles and *Playboy*s."

She sighed as she sliced her meat. "Someday you'll understand that we are the only people who truly care about you, and that's why we'll never accept this terrible decision you've made."

"It's not a *decision*, Mom. I was born this way." He put down his fork. "If I was born with no arms or legs, would you be shoving Bibles and *Sports Illustrated* at me, telling me if I just prayed hard enough Jesus would grow me some hands and feet?"

"No arms or legs is on the outside," she huffed. "You can't change the way your body was made, but surely you can change the way you think."

"There's a guy at work that used to have your problem," his father cut in. "And now he's got a wife and two kids. No desires *that way* at all."

Arthur laughed. "How 'bout if I go give him a little test?"

She made a face. "God doesn't make people that way, Artie; if he did, then mankind would've become extinct long ago. You're that way because you had the sort of relationship with your father that you had." She threw another glare at her husband. "Father O'Brien says this is your way of trying to get affection from men that you never got from him."

"So his perversion's my fault?" his father growled, glancing over at the television.

"It's nobody's *fault*," Arthur stated. "And it's not a *perversion*."

"Of course it is," she countered, her voice droopy with exasperation. "At first it was ours for not seeing it early enough to get you help—I admit that—but now it's yours for not accepting it. Didn't you read those booklets I sent you from the Catholic Medical Association? At least tell me you read those. They gave me such hope."

"Used 'em as toilet paper," Arthur mumbled as he reached for the green canister of Parmesan. "Did you know that they have a ridiculous long-term 'success rate,' and most of those priests, after teaching their 'Change Ministry' classes, are out trolling the skate parks for thirteen-year-old boys?"

"Can we not talk about this right now?" asked his father.

"We need to resolve this," his mother said.

"Not at the table, we don't," his father grumbled, and then took a swig of his Coors.

"It *is* resolved," Arthur stated imperiously. "I'm *gay*. Always have been, always will be. And the sooner this family accepts it, the better we'll all be."

"We'll never accept this about you," his mother told him. "Never."

"You just better never let Gwen find out about it," his father warned.

"Morgana's OK with it," Arthur said, and then shot him a look. "She said she's always known about me. And my relationship with Gwen has *nothing* to do with you."

The man shot him a threatening look. "Like I said, you better never let her find out about your *perversion*."

"She's old enough and smart enough that she's gonna start asking questions, Dad. And if she ever asks me, I'm not gonna lie."

"You'd better lie about it," his father threatened. "How's she gonna feel knowing her big brother's a fairy? Maybe she's gonna think she needs to be a slut, too."

"She'll just deal with it, like Morgana already did and you two should." He pushed his meal away. "You can't make me lie to her."

"You'd better lie!"

Arthur stared him down. "Or *what?*"

"If you ever tell your sister…you won't have to let AIDS finish you off, buster, 'cause I'll kill you!"

His mother stopped chewing.

"You did not just say that." Arthur's head was spinning from the man's vulgarity.

"You heard me," his father said, his voice low and vicious.

Arthur knew that, at this point, there were no rational synapses firing in the man's thick head. And he knew all too well when he'd start swinging, so he jumped up and headed for the living room, snatched his backpack from the floor, then made for the door. "I don't have to take this!" he shouted as the screen door slammed behind him. Then he trotted across the yard looking over his shoulder, hoping he wouldn't have to outrun the brute. *Again.*

But when he turned back he saw, through the dining room curtains, the silhouette of his father leaning back in his chair, while his mother sat across from him with her head in her hands.

I'm not even worth chasing.

He jogged to his van, started the engine and pulled away from the curb with as much force as the tiny engine could muster. As the distance grew between him and that horrible little house, he felt tears begin to build behind his eyes.

Two stop signs later, he was bawling.

Don't cry or I'll give you somethin' to cry about.

But he couldn't help it. He sobbed now as he drove, with his face screwed up like he'd sucked on a lemon and his mind playing his father's words over and over. And for his mother to just sit by! But then, no one knew his father's wrath as well as she.

He hated them both.

Because they made him hate himself.

As he motored down Pacific Coast Highway, some realizations bloomed:

I've got nothing to lose.

I've done what I could, but it'll never be good enough for them.

I've got nothing, really, to live for.

What's the point of going on?

He wiped his eyes and focused on his driving, and then realized that he was speeding and slowed down—not because he was afraid of getting pulled over, but because there was no one waiting at his crappy little apartment for him.

Just those off-white walls. And the stained carpet. And the stinking, worn-out furniture.

I'll always be alone.

And he believed, just as he'd been so efficiently trained to believe, that he deserved to be.

***

That night he lay in bed, feeling his heart pump its bitter sludge.

How would he do it?

How can I really, really fuck them up?

21

Then it came to him: He would take his porno magazines and tear out the pages, line some up on the dashboard of his van and tape the rest to the insides of the windows.

He would get behind the steering wheel, then strip off his clothes.

No seat belt—

He'd start from the top of the hill above their house. He'd floor the accelerator.

First gear—

Second gear—

Third—

And just as he shifted into fourth he'd steer directly into that old Chinese elm in their front yard—the one they made him prune every spring, when he'd climb up inside the branches and use a garden hose as a safety harness.

The explosion of metal and glass would be heard for blocks.

His parents would run outside and find his naked corpse squished between the driver's seat and the tree trunk—maybe his head would've exploded like a watermelon dropped from a rooftop—while photos of naked guys fucking and sucking and jacking and cumming fluttered down onto their perfectly manicured, guts-splattered lawn.

Some neighbors would gather, while some might only pull back their drapes.

And his mother would shriek while his father collapsed from a heart attack—or better yet, a massive stroke.

They'll be so, so, so fucking sorry.

And I'll be with Jonathan again.

CHAPTER 5

In the morning his outlook was no less morose, so he decided to skip school—after all, why should he sit through yet another mind-numbing political science class if he was going to kill himself?

I'll go for a drive instead.

After slipping on some jeans and his favorite sweatshirt—it was oversized and navy blue—he tied on his filthy Adidas, then went out to where he'd parked his van.

He headed north from his apartment in Culver City, fighting the morning's rush-hour swarm as he struggled up Pacific Coast Highway in his feebly powered steel box. Eventually, the traffic thinned as he neared his destination, with the road having narrowed from four to three lanes in each direction, and then finally down to two.

His turnoff loomed, so he pulled into the center meridian and stopped.

Finally, a break in the opposing traffic appeared. So he wheeled a U-turn, and then pulled up next to the wall of boulders the county had amassed to keep the winter's waves from obliterating the roadway. He pulled the hand brake tight, threw open the door and stepped out, slammed the door and then picked his way down to the shoreline. Once his feet hit the sand, he turned north toward the wealthy enclave atop the cliffs beyond Boulder Creek, which was the trickle of water that meandered down from the hillsides and served as Ballena Beach's unofficial *No Trespassing* sign.

He trudged for the better part of an hour before rounding a bend and seeing it: the familiar clay-tiled roofs of the Tyler compound. Then a few paces later he spotted the wooden gazebo perched atop the precipice, and the decrepit wooden staircase that zigzagged down through the dull, green cactus to the calendar-perfect beach below.

Looking up at it, barely two years later, he could hardly believe he'd ever been granted access to that castle. He gazed awestruck now as he craned his neck, while recalling the layouts of the expansive rooms inside, with names like *the sunroom* and *the conservatory* and *the rumpus room* and *the drawing room*. He was still able to visualize the stately sofas and prissy French antiques and gloomy paintings and shimmering crystal displayed in each color-coordinated vignette; he'd never before been exposed to that level of wealth and was certain he wouldn't be again, so he'd memorized each extravagant detail in between those sexual rumbles with his boy. And if he closed his eyes he could still feel the terrible silence of the rooms—a silence, he imagined, that might feel like being locked in a museum at night, all alone.

But he was never alone there.

He was always with *him*.

Jonathan Tyler. Equal parts valedictorian and rebel. Shipped to Ballena Beach after his father was killed in Vietnam and his mother overdosed on sleeping pills and Southern Comfort. Groomed by his controlling aunt, Katharine Tyler, and her creepy husband, Bill Mortson, to assume eventual control of the family's yacht-building and real-estate enterprises. The kid with the face of a dark angel and the body of a young Olympian, whose lust for expensive toys was rivaled only by his craving for Arthur's varsity-honed body.

Jonathan had charged all of that stuffy grandeur up there with an irreverent energy; his presence had been like a sudden thunderstorm on a stifling, stagnant summer night. And Arthur had been that storm's lightning rod—or so he'd considered himself at the time.

But that was before Tiffany—and the baby.

And the accident.

He trudged across the sand to Lay-Z-Boy Rock, so named by Jonathan for its prehistoric lounge-chair proportions, then sat and scanned the flat, gray horizon for some answers.

Did he really want to end it all? Yes…and no. But suicide was something he'd considered since his early teens, upon realizing his attraction to guys was heavier than any gravity girls possessed. But it wasn't just that—he really did struggle with long bouts of depression. He recalled those three black months at seventeen when he'd barely been able to rise each morning, but then somehow made it through his high school classes only to return home, sequester himself in his room until dinner—endured slumped before his plate, eating sullenly—and then do his evening chores before retiring to his waiting pile of homework.

After two months of this gloom-fest he'd actually set a date, which he wrote in his journal, along with the declaration:

Feb. 15, 1986
If I'm not happy in one month, I'm going to kill myself.

The acuity of that particular stretch of depression had to do with Jonathan, who'd become his best friend at Ballena Beach High even though Arthur was a senior and Jonathan was a sophomore. He had fallen completely for the boy, and his pining for him became the maraschino cherry in a suicidal cocktail mixed from his sexual despondency, his monstrous home life and his pervasive hopelessness.

And so one night, just a week before his "deadline," he and Jonathan had gone for a walk on this very beach. They'd sat in the sand, shoulder to shoulder, sharing how they hated school and their teachers and their lives at home. Then Arthur, in a moment of bravery that still amazed him even now, decided that if he had only a week to live, he might as well be honest with his buddy—at this point, he had absolutely nothing to lose.

Nothing. Just like now.

They'd been talking about girls, and Arthur had been doing his best to keep up with Jonathan's enthusiastic ruminations about some of the more popular females at school: the flag girls and the cheerleaders and some of the hot stoner chicks, et cetera.

"Krystal Loomis is beautiful, you know?" Jonathan remarked as his eyes tracked a low-swooping pelican. "I mean, she's not all fake looking like Stephanie Corran with that fried blonde hair, or Whitney Snyder—man, she wears too much makeup. She's naturally hot, I think. She looks twenty-five, huh?"

Arthur, in the meantime, had been scrutinizing some frothing water some distance out, wondering whether it was a whale disturbing the calm, or some dolphins. "So why don't you ask her out?" he asked, feigning encouragement.

Jonathan nodded but didn't say anything at first. "Yeah, maybe I will. But maybe you should instead," he suggested with a playful nudge to his shoulder. "You haven't gone out with anyone this year, huh?"

"I'm considering the priesthood."

"*What?*"

"Kidding." He shook his head, managing a weak chuckle. "Actually, Krystal's not really my...uh...type."

A barrage of waves, one pushing behind the last, encompassed the beach with sudden, *fumping* thunder.

"So what exactly *is* your type?" Jonathan nearly shouted.

Their eyes met and Arthur was struck again by Jonathan's beauty—those huge, flashing brown eyes with their impossibly long eyelashes, his ruler-straight nose, the trapezoidal planes of his cheeks, his pouty lips, the way the sea breeze tousled that hair down crazily over his eyebrows. *The cleft of his chin.*

Arthur looked away, appearing to wait for the waves to calm.

Finally, it was quiet again. "I guess my type is kind of changing," he muttered to the sand between his knees. *Please don't ask me anything more—I'm sick of lying and I want to kiss you so badly.*

"So, like, what?" Jonathan whispered. "Who keeps you up at night?"

Fear punched him in the gut, and he swallowed hard. To say what was in his heart was too dangerous—but then just yesterday he'd grabbed a chair and stepped up inside his parents' closet, where his dad kept his .30-30 Winchester with its dusty box of bullets, and he'd unzipped the weapon from its orange nylon case and looked down the shadowy barrel.

Try it on for size, a quiet voice had suggested, so he'd held the weapon in front of his mouth.

And now for the ultimate blow job, mocked that same voice as his lips closed around the hollow end, and the tang of burnished metal and spent gunpowder pinched his tongue.

"Artie?" came Jonathan's voice. "Hey, what's wrong?" He'd seen that his eyes were somewhere else, somewhere bad.

One squeeze and it'll all go away.

Arthur shook his head. The waves were too noisy again—he had to wait for them to get quieter; if he said anything now, he'd have to shout, and guys just do not shout about this. He looked up and saw that a big range of waves was heaving toward the beach, and then they fell onto the sand, and then more just kept coming. He shook his head and shook his head again, and held his knees, and his heart said, *Just tell him.*

If the waves get quiet, I will. Please, just make it quiet.

And as if Poseidon himself had heard his prayer, there was a long fizz, followed by sudden quiet.

Now or never, old buddy. "You," he managed at last. "You. You're who."

They sat together in silence, for how long Arthur could not tell.

It could've been ten seconds. It could've been an hour.

And then a burst of courage made him look over at his friend, and he saw that he was staring back at him in a sideways squint, with his head faced out to sea.

He looked away.

"Artie?"

A hand pressed his shoulder, and he flinched. He turned and their eyes locked. Fear gripped him again, but the memory of the gun in his mouth gave him strength. He closed his eyes. "You, Jonathan," he said again. "I have feelings for you. And I don't know what to do—they aren't, um, going away."

"Me, too," Jonathan told him at last. "For you, I mean. I just never said anything because I thought you'd...you know."

"Yeah, I know."

"Do you...feel this way about other guys, too?"

"Not really."

"Me, neither," he said. "We're just really close, you and me."

"Yeah."

"Yeah."

That night Arthur had his first thrilling kiss, when they embraced on the moonlit sand with the tide swirling around their ankles. And then, two nights later, after Katharine and Bill had gone out to a fund-raiser for Children's Hospital, they'd thrown open all the mansion's French doors and chased each other naked through the windswept rooms, and then fallen into Jonathan's immense, luxurious bed, where they kissed and coaxed and stroked each other and took each other's seed into their bodies. And if he thought that he was in love before, he discovered now how such a love, when reciprocated, can flourish into obsession.

Jonathan became his sun. And he, in turn, did his best to be Jonathan's planets, moons, asteroids and comets.

He was happy. His parents didn't depress him anymore. He started studying for tests again, and his GPA rose.

Arthur was about to graduate, so they talked about the future.

They made plans.

And then it ended. Mysteriously.

***

So here he was, years later, lying in the shadow of the Tyler compound.

Depressed—suicidal, actually—once again.

The bumps on Lay-Z-Boy Rock were starting to press uncomfortably into his back, so he slid off the boulder and made his way down to where the sliding waves turned the dry, beige sand a glistening cocoa brown. He looked up, scanning for some blue to signal that the gloom was burning off, but found none. He so wished it had been a prettier day— that perhaps a blinding white sun and some shimmering, cobalt water might have salvaged his spirits.

So he began padding back toward home, thinking—

What bounty might life offer to a young man like him? It was almost 1989, and the only fate that seemed certain was death by AIDS, just as his father had so viciously reminded him. So even if he didn't kill himself in a week, that horrible virus would most certainly accomplish the act he'd been contemplating—in slow motion. In fact, he could already be infected; there'd been that guy at the Frat House coffee bar last summer, and they'd been pretty quick to...

So suicide would just be getting a jump on the inevitable.

Suicide. Suicide. Suicide.

He was depressed, to be sure. But could he really, actually do *that*? Probably.

Because if he didn't, he'd have to face his fucking parents and work somewhere dull and somehow finish school and get some sort of career moving...but then he'd just wind up as a lonely, disease-ridden fag.

Annie, get your gun.

But something in him, some little morsel of his soul, still believed that happiness could be his, and he could, somehow, find someone to build a life with.

But not if you blow your head off.

His grandfather's words came back to him, when he'd explained that creatures have a craving to live—from all of humankind to the lowliest insect. To illustrate his point he'd found an ant on a wall, and tapped his finger behind the tiny creature.

It leapt into a microscopic gallop.

"It wants to live," he told him. "All creatures are the same."

OK. So maybe he wouldn't do it. *Yet.* But then where could he go, and what could he do that would pose as a life until he figured out what the hell his *real* life was going to be? He was already almost a month behind in his rent, with no prospects for a roommate; he'd even put an ad in the *Recycler* and had interviewed the few people who'd responded, but the thought of living with any of them was dismal, and none seemed interested in sharing his pitiful apartment. And tuition could never be scraped together in time and his phone was already shut off, and working at Electronics Galore sucked and his van was a piece of shit...

Where the hell could he go, a young man with a death wish who craved the company of men and had no family to speak of and no home of his own and few possessions and even fewer prospects for a happy, healthy future?

Yeah.

It wasn't the perfect solution, by a long shot. But it was something worth looking into.

Better, at least, than looking into the barrel of a rifle.

CHAPTER 6

He startled awake as the bus pulled into the parking lot of the Marine Corps Recruit Depot in San Diego, so he glanced down at his watch and saw, with some effort, that it was nearly four a.m. Then he heard the air brakes fart and saw the door swing open and a burley man wearing green pants, a khaki shirt and a funny round hat that looked too small for his big bald head jump into the bus.

"From now on the last word in your mouth is *yes, sir!*" he yelled at them. "Do you understand that?

"Yes, sir!" they all yelled in unison.

And Arthur thought, *But "yes, sir" is two words...*

"What is the last word in your mouth?" he screamed even louder.

"YES, SIR!" they all hollered back at him.

"Go stand on those yellow footprints," he ordered, throwing his arm out from his side in the direction of the parking lot, like a cop directing rush-hour traffic, "front to rear and left to right! *DO YOU UNDERSTAND THAT?*"

"YES, SIR!"

And so Arthur and the rest of the young men scrambled off the vehicle as if it were on fire, and took their places outside next to a rambling two-story redbrick building, and each placed his own feet atop a pair of jaunty yellow footprints arranged in long, precise rows in front and in back of one another.

"You'll do what you're told to do, how to do it, and when to do it without a question. Do you understand that?" the drill instructor demanded.

"Yes, sir!" Arthur nearly screamed along with the others as the thought *What've I gotten myself into?* raced through his brain.

And he would have this same thought countless times over the next twelve weeks.

And many more times over the next ten years.

***

For the ensuing thirty-six hours he, as well as the other recruits, was not allowed to sleep. And they were subjected to every sort of medical examination imaginable—DNA and blood samples, inoculations, teeth cleaning—as well as that famous identity-obliterating buzz cut, and the issuing of uniforms. And along each step there was no one to let him, or anyone else, know what was coming next—he knew only that the next step in the process would be tough, and he had to get through it, no matter how scared or confused he felt.

It was all too clear, by the end of the second day, that he had bought himself a purpose in life, and had paid for it with his free will.

By the beginning of the fourth day, the philosophy of what it means to be a Marine was starting to sink in: *I do not exist except for the role I play on this team.* It really was perfect for Arthur; he discovered that when he thought about what was happening, he was utterly remorseful for the decision he'd made, but when he shut off his brain and allowed himself to be nothing more or less than a "player" on this team, he excelled.

It was high school football again, but from now on the opposing team would be Death.

And Death always has the home field advantage.

So he decided to shut off his brain, or, more accurately, *his emotions,* permanently.

He learned how to hold a gun. How to load a gun. How to fire a gun.

He passed all of the strength tests and met the corps' stringent minimum fitness standards.

And he did his best to internalize the moral code that the drill instructors expected them to adhere to: A Marine never lies, he never cheats or compromises, and he never, never, never gives up.

Of course he had no problem with cheating or compromising, and he would certainly never give up—but he was afraid that lying was an irrefutable part of *this here deal.*

After all, he was *a homosexual.*

And a gay Marine was about as feasible as a straight makeup artist.

So he needed to make everyone believe that he was as much a man as they were.

He needed to *pass.*

For the rest of the first week, he went along with the routines for *forming*, or getting rid of bad habits. He did thousands of sit-ups and dips and back extensions; his muscles screamed during the hours of resistance training on the circuit course; and his hands were raw from traversing suspended metal bars and climbing rope ladders. But with the ensuing countless hours spent on the parade deck learning to march in perfectly perfect formation, the days seemed to go on forever.

At the same time, his very worn-out, very conflicted mind did its best to "form" around the ideals of *honor, courage* and *commitment*, as well as how best to demonstrate admirable ethical and moral behavior.

Even if he was *a homosexual*.

But there was only one event each day that he enjoyed: their hour of free time before bed each night, when they could read and write letters or square away gear.

And they could even socialize.

A *little*.

***

"Jeff Earl," the kid had said to him, and thrust out his hand.

Arthur shook it, trying not to notice how blue the young soldier's eyes were. "Art Blauefee," he replied. "Where're you from?"

"Tulare, up north a' Bakersfield. You?"

"LA." He didn't want to say Ballena Beach, as it might sound grandiose or poofy.

"What's it like there?" Jeff asked him, and then grabbed his shoe brush and began scrubbing away at one of his boots.

Arthur smiled. "Crowded mostly. And the traffic's a bitch. But the beach is nice."

"I never been to the beach until now," Jeff confessed. "That's why I wanted San Diego instead a' Parris Island—it's got a *real* California beach with *real* California girls." He leered at Arthur and Arthur did his best to mirror his expression and chuckle knowingly. "Why'd you join up?"

Arthur had been expecting this question, but he couldn't really come up with any answer other than the one he'd decided to use now. "Seemed like a good idea; nothing better to do," was what he said, but *It seemed like a better idea to blow someone else's head off instead of my own* was what he thought.

"Yeah, me, too," Jeff replied absently, his attention focused on his boots.

Arthur watched the muscles in his shoulders ripple as the black shine on the leather became more mirrorlike with each stroke. "You ready for 'Snapping In' tomorrow?"

Jeff laughed and looked up at Arthur. "*Shee-it,* I been shootin' since I was four. I betcha I got a better trigger squeeze than that old DI."

Arthur laughed. "I bet you do. That old drill instructor couldn't hit a garbage truck comin' at him through a one-way alley."

"Hee-hee." Jeff giggled as he looked up at Arthur. "Just don't better let Sergeant Riley hear you say that about hisself."

Arthur saw that when Jeff laughed his eyes sparkled, and his grin revealed flawless teeth.

Why does God torture me?

He looked away. "You get any letters yet?" Arthur asked him, and then bent to straighten the blankets on his bunk.

Jeff went back to brushing his boots. "Naw, ain't no one out there who's missed me. My ma don't even know I did this yet."

Arthur looked at him quizzically, his eyebrows raised high. "Are you serious? Nobody knows you enlisted?"

He shrugged. "Ain't no one who cares, anyhow." He picked up his finished boots, examined them one last time, and then slid them carefully under his bunk, as if they were glass slippers. "So you got any letters yet, then?"

Arthur shook his head. "Nope. Not yet."

"Not even from your girl?" Jeff asked, grinning slyly.

"No," Arthur replied absently, trying to think of what to say next. "She died. In a car accident a couple years back."

Jeff looked up, startled. "Jesus Christ, man. I'm sorry," he said, shaking his head. "So that's probably the *real* reason you're here?"

"Yeah, pretty much," Arthur replied, allowing his mask to slip just enough so that some true emotion actually registered on his face.

And based upon that half lie, Private Arthur Francis Blauefee made his first friend in the United States Marine Corps.

***

At chow time Arthur and Jeff sat next to each other and laughed or complained about the day's events while they ate. They even volunteered for the very dreaded laundry detail, as well as the sought-after mess detail, together. And when one had to rappel down a forty-five-foot wall, the other held the rope taut; and during pugil-stick jousting practice they smacked and slashed and jabbed and butt-stroked each other with their long, thickly padded sticks as hard as they could. They practiced their hand-to-hand combat on each other, and Jeff even showed Arthur some pointers on the best way to tear up a man's guts with a bayonet. And in a short time they became one of those mythic anomalies particular to the United States armed forces: "brothers in arms" who are neither brothers, nor spenders of time in each other's arms.

Much to the chagrin of Arthur, as he was developing quite an appreciation for Jeff's homespun, country-boy companionship. And he took pleasure in Jeff's simplicity—he reminded him of one of those Chevys from the 1950s, where you pop open the hood and you can see the air cleaner and the screws and the hoses and exactly where the oil's leaking or if your radiator hoses are about to explode. He was a piece of Americana—a good ol' boy who was actually a good guy. And likewise, he seemed to be gaining affection for Arthur—he actually listened to him and laughed at his wry observations and punched him playfully on the shoulder and almost became what Arthur thought a little brother would have been like.

Then one day everything changed.

The recruits were practicing their water maneuvers: One by one they jumped from a high dive into a frigid swimming pool while fully dressed and carrying a heavily stocked backpack, as well as a loaded rifle. Having grown up by the ocean, Arthur leapt off the diving board without a second thought, and then began paddling his way across the water toward the ladder on the opposite end of the pool. Jeff came after him—the picture of self-confidence—dropped from the diving board into the deep end of the pool and then proceeded to drown.

He hadn't disclosed to anyone that he didn't know how to swim.

By the time Arthur had wrapped his hands around the metal bars of the ladder, Jeff had already been down for almost a minute. Then, after he'd hefted his soaked frame and backpack (and rifle, which he'd managed somehow to keep dry), out of the pool, his new best buddy had been down for nearly two minutes.

He looked around for Jeff and couldn't see him, but then saw the dark form underwater and knew immediately what had happened.

He dropped his backpack and rifle and jumped in.

In six strokes he was at him; he grabbed him and then pulled him to the surface.

Their heads broke the waterline at the same moment.

Arthur gasped.

Jeff did not.

By this time, two other soldiers had jumped in and were swimming over to the pair. But Arthur wouldn't let them near. He pushed past them, dragging the lifeless hulk on his back over to the shallow end of the pool, where he pulled Jeff's pack off him and then pushed his body up onto the deck and pulled himself up and kneeled over him to begin performing emergency breathing on him.

Expertly.

With his right hand he pinched Jeff's nostrils shut and with his left he lifted his neck up and tilted back his head just far enough so that his own breath would go into his lungs and not down into his stomach, and then he locked his lips with Jeff's and pushed his breath into his mouth and then pulled his mouth away, but nothing came out, so he tried it again and their teeth clicked against each other's and Arthur's breath went into him and he pulled away, but still nothing happened, so he did the same thing a third time, and that was when Jeff regained consciousness, felt Arthur's mouth on his and then pushed him away with as much force as a straight man recovering from a near-fatal drowning might muster while having another man's open mouth actively engaged with his own.

"What the fuck?" Jeff managed to whisper, and then turned his head to gurgle up some water onto the concrete decking.

Arthur looked stunned, but he had to catch his breath before answering. "What…do you mean…'*What the fuck*'?" he said at last, his own chest heaving. "You…almost drowned!"

By this time a small crowd had gathered around them.

"Earl!" barked Sergeant Riley. Arthur's head snapped upward.

"Yes, sir!" Jeff managed to reply, weakly.

"When did you plan on informing the Marines that you can't swim?"

He tried a nervous smile, in between racking coughs. And then he glanced at the concerned soldiers looking down at him, and his eyes shifted from face to face.

Arthur could tell that he was trying to think of a plausible explanation for what had just happened but could not.

"Aw, he can swim OK," came a voice from the gathered recruits. "I think he was just tryin' to get a kiss from his best buddy."

Laughter stung Arthur's ears as Jeff pushed him away.

Arthur felt his face flash with heat. "You almost drowned, you dumbshit," he growled, and then pushed himself up from the wet concrete.

"Blauefee!" the sergeant called out.

Arthur turned around.

"You drop your rifle again and you're out of here," the man scolded. "What would happen if the enemy was in the bush and you did that?"

"It'll never happen again, *SIR*!" Arthur hollered back at him, and then hung his head as he made his way over to where his rifle and pack lay on the deck. And as he bent over to slip the soggy pack onto his back and to retrieve his abandoned weapon, he was surprised to discover that he had a lump in his throat and his eyes burned.

***

That evening at chow time they sat together as usual but ate in silence until finally Arthur couldn't stand it anymore. "The least you could say is 'thanks,'" he told Jeff, trying his best to not sound bitchy.

Jeff chewed his hamburger noiselessly, and then washed it down with some milk. "Uh, Artie," he began, not looking his way. "You're right. Thanks for helpin' me out. I was stupid not to tell anyone." And then he picked up his burger and took another bite.

"Then what's crawled up your ass?"

Jeff bit off another mouthful and began talking through his food. "I got restricted to quarters this weekend for what happened," he mumbled sourly. "It's graduation, and I was plannin' on going into San Ysidro with some of the guys after."

Some of the guys? What about me?

"Hey, Earl," Chad Rubin, a big redheaded potato of a man whom Arthur detested, asked Jeff, "what does your best buddy do for you when you're restricted to quarters?"

Jeff shrugged his shoulders and threw him a bored expression, and then popped the rest of his burger in his mouth.

"Goes into town and gets two blow jobs, then brings one back and gives it to ya."

Every man at the table howled and hooted except for Arthur and Jeff, who couldn't make eye contact with anyone.

"That's real funny, Rubin," Arthur told him finally, after the hubbub had died down. "But can you really afford to keep paying for more than one at a time?"

"Ooooh, he got you there, Rubin," one of the other guys cackled.

Jeff picked up his plate and then stood up from the table. "See y'all later," he announced dryly, and then made his way toward the cleanup station.

Rubin looked at Arthur. "Ain't ya gonna go after your girlfriend?"

"My girlfriend's dead, you fucker," Arthur snarled, and then picked up his plate to follow Jeff.

"That's what I hear," Rubin answered, but Arthur was already too far away to hear him, or the other guys, laughing.

***

Jeff was more than halfway to the barracks when Arthur caught up with him. "What the hell is goin' on?" he asked him as a camouflage-splattered Jeep sputtered by. "I don't get it. I probably saved your life—so wouldja mind filling me in?"

Jeff stopped walking, glanced at Arthur and looked away, then shoved his hands in his pockets. "I know about *it*, Artie."

Arthur's head felt woozy. "Know about *what*?"

Jeff looked around nervously. "About you being *that way*," he said in a near whisper, pulling his hands from his pockets and flipping his wrists like a fey Tyrannosaurus rex.

"How do you know, then?"

Jeff looked away, laughing. "*Everyone* knows, man! Rubin's got a buddy who went to school with you at that rich beach place; this dude said you'd joined up even though you're a fag, and your 'dead girlfriend' was really your faggot boyfriend who ran off the road somewhere. Sound familiar?"

Arthur was speechless, stunned. But it made sense—after all, his home really wasn't all that far from San Diego, and he'd disclosed to some of the other guys from LA, when pressed, that he was actually from Ballena Beach. "Yeah, that's what happened."

"So I'm sayin', *No way, man*, to everyone, and then this thing happens at the water maneuvers and it somehow puts a picture in their heads, and now everyone's calling me 'Earl the Girl,' like they did to me in junior high—like I'm your bitch or somethin'."

Arthur looked down. "Does Riley know?" he asked softly, envisioning his brief military career coming to an end.

"They haven't told him yet 'cause you did save another Marine's life; they're waitin' for the Crucible to see if you can pass what they got in store for you, and if you do, then no one's blowin' no whistle."

"I'll pass," Arthur told him, folding his arms across his chest. "You can bet your life on that."

"I wouldn't be so sure," Jeff said, shaking his head.

"Why not?"

"Because they're gonna make it rough on you."

"How rough?" Arthur asked, not wanting to know.

"You'll just have ta see." Jeff shrugged his shoulders, turned and began walking toward the barracks by himself.

CHAPTER 7

The aptly named "Crucible" is the culminating test for each Marine recruit. Near the end of the eleventh week of basic training, each platoon is broken down into teams of about a dozen members before embarking on fifty-four hours of nonstop duress. During this time the recruits are almost completely denied both food and sleep as they march forty miles with full packs on their backs, while simulating a resupply mission within enemy territory.

On the second night of this nightmare, they had been awakened at 0300 hours, after only four hours of sleep. It was unbearably cold in the damp night air, and Arthur couldn't remember when he'd ever been this uncomfortable; every muscle in his body was sore, his feet felt as if someone had beaten them with a baseball bat, his clothing was soaked through with equal parts sweat and rain, and his stomach was angry from days of deprivation. But the worst part was how his brain was spinning, almost to the point of rabid paranoia, with what events might be lying in wait for him during the coming hours.

Because Chad and his buddies had been "twisting the noose" since the moment they'd begun.

The first thing he'd noticed, on day one, was how heavy his pack was; after nearly three months of lugging a forty-pound hump on his back, he knew exactly, as did every living Marine, what forty pounds felt like.

But this wasn't forty—it felt more like fifty. So he resolved not to think about it and concentrated instead on the cadence of his strides.

And then after the first day of marching was complete, he'd pulled out two sizable loaves of granite from the bottom of his pack, which he placed strategically on either side of the flaps of his pup tent—to show that they'd come the distance with him.

Fuck you, said the rocks.

The next morning, after he'd trudged over a hill and dug a hole and squatted over it, he returned to find the damn things back inside his pack again.

But overloading his gear certainly couldn't be the most evil they might conjure; if he knew Rubin, something really twisted was waiting for him up the road.

He found out at the beginning of day two.

His boots didn't fit. They were at least one size too small. But he pulled the laces loose anyway, and then pushed his already swollen feet inside and tied the laces just the same. And when they all began to march, his toes jammed themselves up against the steel tips and the backs of his ankles began rubbing themselves raw and his ankles started turning in to compensate and he felt a brand-new pain streaking like wildfire from his big toe all the way up to his thighs, hips and ass.

So once again, he resolved to not think about it and instead concentrated on the cadence of his strides.

Then, there he was on the morning of day three, with a fifty-pound pack on his shoulders and boots on his feet that were probably better suited to a fourteen-year-old boy's, knowing that the combination of these two factors might even cause permanent damage to his feet or legs or shoulders or whatever, but he didn't care.

He had something to prove, and *nothing* was going to stop him.

So he began to embrace the pain as he trudged through the darkness of night along that mercilessly uneven dirt road. *I'm "forming"into a Marine*, he told himself when the pain got especially wicked, like when his ankle twisted for the ninth time as he stepped inside a dried-out rivulet that his eyes had been unable to pick out in the dark. *I'm "forming" into a Marine*, he told himself when he thought about how his father had so grossly berated and neglected him, and so he imagined the pain in his feet resulting from kicking the man in the side as he lay prostrate on the ground howling with pain (this made him smile). *I'm "forming" into a Marine*, he told himself when he remembered those stupid, monkey-faced motherfuckers referring to his beautiful Jonathan as his "dead faggot boyfriend." *I'm "forming" into a Marine*, he whispered as he saw himself placing the generous barrel of the Winchester in his mouth and closing his lips around the metal. So by the time they reached the site of the "battlefield"—when he couldn't feel his feet anymore and his body was ambulating completely without any known effort from his brain—Arthur looked to the heavens and saw the sky lightening with the coming dawn; then, moments later, as the formations slowed their steps and they assembled in front of Sergeant Riley, the only thought that accompanied each diminishing stride was *I'm a Marine…. I'm a Marine…. I'm a Marine…. I'm a Marine.*

The sergeant allowed them to catch their breaths and slug down some water from their canteens before calling "Attention." As Arthur snapped to, he saw that even though his knees were quaking, his head was held the highest of those around him, and he felt, for the first time, just a teeny bit proud of himself.

He fought a smile.

Riley cleared his throat. "Since a dead or wounded Marine," he brayed, "is never left on the field, one of you will be the designated casualty and will be rescued and carried through the infiltration course. You began this together and you'll finish it together, but just like on a real battlefield, you'll have only each other to depend on, so working together is the only thing that'll keep you alive. You'll break into your teams, perform a search and rescue, find your casualty and treat his wounds, then transport him back to base camp. Any questions?"

"*No, sir!*" the recruits sang out.

"The following soldiers are casualties: Campos, Blauefee and Jackson, you're to stay behind while the rest resume marching; then in ten minutes the troops'll about-face and come back to find them."

"*Yes, sir!*" they mustered as Arthur thought, *Now I can get off my feet.*

They all looked around and nodded at one another in weary agreement, and a few actually slapped each other on the back and murmured words of encouragement to those who were lucid enough to listen. Then the teams began marching in ragged formation down the road they'd just traveled up, while Arthur and Privates Campos and Jackson were separated and hidden away "behind enemy lines," where they would await rescue and evacuation.

Arthur decided to lie behind a crumbling outbuilding that, decades before, had been used as a smokehouse.

He curled his arm up under his head and decided that he might as well steal a few minutes of sleep.

Moments later he drifted off.

***

The scratchy woolen blanket thrown over his head jarred him awake. He tried to push it off, but then his arms were grabbed and restrained behind his back, while someone else had a hold of his legs and feet.

The blows were brutal and were intended to inflict as much damage as possible. At once he felt his face slammed and his kidneys punched and his stomach stomped and his legs kicked.

He couldn't see a thing.

And he couldn't fight back.

He tried curling himself into a ball—but the kicks to his spine and the backs of his knees caused his body to extend reflexively so that his front side became open to the assault.

"Get his nuts," he heard someone bark just before a blinding pain exploded between his legs and he folded back in two.

The body blows continued.

Time stopped. The pain became a dull rush. And then something in his brain clicked—like a charge of TNT that's been kissed by a spark.

He wrenched his right arm away from the determined hands that were gripping it and started swinging wildly. He made contact with soft flesh.

"Fuck!" someone cried out.

Then he pulled his left hand free, and as they tried grabbing for his arms they accidentally released his legs so he started pistoning his feet crazily and he felt his right foot hit bone and heard something crack.

Someone yelped.

Then he rolled over and tore the blanket off his head and started throwing punches and more kicks until he was up on his feet and crouched into the don't-you-even-think-of-fucking-with-me hand-to-hand combat posture.

And when he lunged at Rubin, the others—directed by Jeff— stepped back.

He jabbed with his left and crossed with his right, and the big man went down on his knees. "Throwin' me a blanket party, huh, you motherfucker?" Rubin flew backward and hit the ground hard. In an instant Arthur was on him, then straddling him, then pummeling his face.

Left.

Right.

Left.

Right.

In the gray daylight of morning he could see blood gushing from the man's nose.

Jab.

Cross.

Jab.

Cross.

Arthur's knuckles opened an angry red slice in the man's right cheek.

Then his hands went around Rubin's neck, and all of the hatred and sadness and frustration and misery and fear he'd been storing inside his heart zapped down his arms into his hands, where it made his fingers clench into vicelike pincers.

The man's face turned purple, the blood stopped running from his nose and his eyes bulged.

His mouth gaped and his tongue protruded, but no noise came forth.

He was screaming. *Silently.*

And Arthur thought, *None of them are helping him. They want me to do this.*

Still his hands squeezed harder, and those who could see it watched Arthur's face become a ferocious, snarling mask of itself. As Arthur shifted all of his body weight up and on top of him so he could press down harder, he thought, *I'm going to kill him unless I stop right now.*

He saw Rubin's eyes roll up in his head as his body went limp underneath him.

Arthur froze, and then released his grip.

"Jesus," he heard someone behind him whisper.

Rubin's limp head slumped to the side.

Everything was perfectly quiet.

And so Arthur kneeled over him.

And he began performing emergency breathing on him.

Expertly.

With his right hand he pinched Rubin's nostrils shut and with his left he lifted his neck up and tilted his head back just far enough so that his own breath would go into his lungs and not down into his stomach, and then he locked his lips with the other's and pushed his breath into his mouth, and then he pulled his mouth away, but nothing came out of the other's mouth. So he tried it again and their teeth clicked against each other's and Arthur's breath went into him and he pulled away, but still nothing happened, so he did the same thing a third time, and that was when Chad Rubin regained consciousness and Arthur pushed himself up and off him with as much force as any man who had just saved the life of someone he would actually have preferred to murder...*in self-defense or otherwise.*

"Is there some confusion about which one of you is the casualty, soldiers?" bellowed a gravelly voice from behind them.

Arthur jerked his head over and saw Sergeant Riley standing beyond their group, his arms akimbo.

They all, with the exception of Rubin, snapped to attention. "*No, sir!*" they answered in unison.

"No, sir," Rubin echoed hoarsely from the ground.

"Then, might I suggest that you gurney your wounded man and get him back to camp immediately; this delay is costing your team valuable time."

"*Yes, sir!*"

And with that, the recruits picked up their field gurney and brought it over to where Rubin was lying on the ground.

Riley began walking away but stopped, and then turned around to face the group. "And by the way, Blauefee, I'm impressed," he made a show of telling Arthur in front of the other recruits.

Arthur looked at him quizzically. "If I may ask, *sir*, how is that, *sir?*"

The man clamped a leathery hand onto Arthur's shoulder and shook him back and forth. "Saving two Marines' lives in a week, and you're not even out of boot camp," he told him, and then laughed. "You deserve that gurney trip back to the base more than anyone—oh, and Rubin," he barked while turning to glare at the prostrate figure on the ground, "you just make sure that his trip back is smooth, or there'll be hell to pay—and don't ever let your CO catch you sitting on your ass again!"

Chad Rubin struggled to stand before saluting his commanding officer. "Yes, *sir!*" he managed before the big man turned and marched away.

They'd started carrying Arthur to base camp, but he'd made them put him down, and then opted to walk the rest of the way instead, in spite of the damned boots on his feet. After all, it was clear to everyone who was the better—or rather, the best—man, and he saw no benefit in making the grueling trip back even worse.

Because they were, for better or worse, brothers in arms.

But then, as they neared the parade deck and Arthur climbed back onto the gurney to be carried home with his hands clasped behind his head, he decided to take one last verbal swing at his nemesis. "So how does it feel?" he asked him casually.

"How does *what* feel?" Rubin muttered back as they all strained to heft Arthur's dense musculature down the last stretch of road.

"I'm asking you how it feels"—he looked around and saw that all of the other guys' eyes were on him—"to have it be that the only reason you're still alive"—he thought he'd draw this one out for effect, so he paused—"is because the same *fag-got* that whipped your sorry ass…was gentleman enough to give you mouth-to-mouth."

Chad Rubin didn't reply, but the other men yowled and laughed.

Later that day, when back at the base camp the recruits were presented with their Eagle, Globe and Anchor pins, many of them wiped back tears. And it was easy to see why: Those who hadn't resorted to treachery along the way felt invincible in body and unassailable in character and fiercely loyal to both the Marine Corps and the United States of America.

But Arthur was not one of those who felt this way, because although he was now a "Marine"—albeit unofficially—the event held no joy for him. He was, instead, more frightened than he'd been even the night before the Crucible, with the knowledge of impending cruelty and possible attack.

Because it finally hit him that he would never feel safe with these men. And although he reasoned that no Marine on active duty ever felt "safe," it would always be different for him. Because for Arthur Francis Blauefee, regardless of how dizzying the rank he attained, the enemy would never be farther away than the next bunk.

***

Graduation went swimmingly at the end of the thirteenth week. Arthur, along with the other recruits, donned his blue pants and khaki shirt and beige belt and black shoes and precious white hat with its snappy patent leather visor. Then the platoons demonstrated their excellent marching skills before listening to some long-winded speeches.

After the formalities, Arthur watched from the corner of his eye as Jeff Earl first hugged his worn-out-looking mom and then shook hands with his hunky little brother, and Chad Rubin made a big show of French-kissing his soccer-ball-breasted, straw-haired girlfriend, and Sergeant Riley's bewigged wife sat bored and fiddling with her purse in the front row until being called upon to stand up—whereupon she flashed her shade-too-white false teeth while waving at the crowd appreciatively. Moments later the crowd dispersed and some of the Marines wept a little and everyone hollered with glee.

Arthur had tried his best to look appropriately proud and happy during the ceremony and the ensuing merrymaking, but it took effort. No one had come to see him graduate. When he'd asked them, which hadn't been easy, he'd been advised that his mother had the flu and his father's eyes were too fuzzy to make that long drive by himself and Gwen's morning sickness was in full swing and Morgana's boys had soccer games and her husband was gone that week on business and blah, blah, blah.

So that night, when he was back at the empty barracks lying on his bunk, Jonathan's handsome face—grinning devilishly, with dark eyes sparkling—seemed to swim comfortingly before him. *You would've come to see me*, he spoke to the apparition. *Kid or no kid, wife or no wife, you would have been here. And I know that wherever you are you're proud of me, because you know how hard everything is for me, just like you know I'll always love you.*

And that was the last time Arthur would contact his family for many years to come, just as it was almost the last time he ever danced with his jitterbugging self-pity.

Because now he was a Marine.

"Semper fi." Always faithful.

But to what or to whom, he wasn't yet sure.

And it would take him nearly twenty more years to find out.

CHAPTER 8

"Ihat time's your flight?" Danny asked from behind his
menu.

"I have to be back at Fort Myer by midnight; then we leave
around four in the morning, depending on orders," Arthur replied, and
then grabbed a roll from the basket on the table. He broke it in half,
dabbed part of it in the ramekin of olive oil nearby and popped it in his
mouth.

"Jesus. I don't know how you do it." He shook his head. "What are
you having?"

"Probably the chicken piccata. What about you?"

"You always get that. Why don't you try something else?"

"Because I like it. Want to split a salad?"

"Sure." Danny put down his menu and leveled his gaze at him.
"But if you've got to be back at midnight, then we won't have any time
together."

Arthur finished chewing his bread and then swallowed. "I know
this trip's been shorter this time, but that's how it goes. There's nothing
I can do about it."

"Except to leave."

"I can't and you know it. And I'm not going over all that again."

"You could retire early. Between your pension and what I make, we
could live pretty comfortably."

"And what would I do all day?" Arthur asked, eyebrows raised.

"I don't know. Have a second career. Do volunteer work. Go back
to school."

"The Marines is my career, and I'm not leaving until I have twenty
years. I'm only thirty-one, for God's sake. I'm only just now halfway
there."

"But you could get some kind of pension, right?"

"Are you saying I should throw in the towel?" Arthur asked. "I'd
lose most of what I've already put in."

"All the more reason to get out now," Danny said, and then put down his menu. "I mean, how much longer can you keep up with this? You always say how you're sick of the homophobia, the lies, of always looking over your shoulder. You should get out now before they find out."

"They aren't gonna find out." Arthur rolled his eyes. "If they haven't in eleven years, they sure as hell won't now. Anyway, can we please talk about something else?"

Danny sighed. "You're right. I'm sorry. It's just that I'd love for us to be together like other couples. Like David and Larry, or Lee and Andre. You know—a lovely house, two dogs, clever dinner parties...that golden boredom with each other that settles in after a while." He reached across the table to take Arthur's hand.

Arthur pulled it away. "You can't do that," he whispered, his eyes bugged out.

"Fuck you," Danny sneered. "I don't even know why I bother."

"Well, maybe you shouldn't, if it's so much goddamn trouble." They'd had this argument more times than he could remember, and it always ended in a stalemate. "Anyhow, here she comes."

"So what looks good, gentlemen?" asked the pretty waitress.

"How's the veal?" Danny asked.

Arthur shot him a *don't-you-dare* look, and Danny threw him back a *just-watch-me* smile.

"It's *fabulous*," she replied. "It's *everyone's* favorite."

"Why don't you just order the golden retriever stew?" Arthur suggested.

"Then, veal it is," Danny told the girl.

"You do and I won't eat at this table with you," Arthur warned him.

"Medium rare," he added.

"And for you?" she asked Arthur.

He looked from Danny to the waitress and back. "I'd like the chicken piccata, and another glass of Fumé blanc."

"And we'll split the Bellisima salad," Danny added.

"Thanks!" she piped, then turned and fled. They waited until she was out of earshot, then resumed their discussion.

"I'm serious, Arthur. You said yourself that sometimes they wait until the gay guys get close to retirement; then suddenly they uncover some 'new information' that triggers a dishonorable discharge. Then it's all for nothing…no retirement, no medical benefits, no cozy plot waiting for you at Arlington. You could put in nineteen-plus years and then 'Oops, we found these pictures of you on your knees in front of your attorney here.'"

"Look," Arthur began, "nine more years is gonna go by in a flash. And in the meantime we can still continue like we've done for the last six years." He smiled. "Has it really been so hard for you?"

Danny smiled wanly. "I guess not. I just…miss you so much sometimes. And I worry. A lot."

"But it's peacetime."

"I know. But what if something happens? I mean there was that whole thing on the USS *Cole* a while back. And there you are over in Germany, where anything could happen. I mean, it'd be different if you were here in the U.S."

"Things could happen here, you know," Arthur said, and then threw the last of his wine down his throat.

"What could possibly happen here in New York? Another bomb on Broadway?" He laughed. "There've been at least"—he counted slowly on his fingers—"four this year that I can remember."

"What could happen here is that you could get tired of me. And I would just get fat and lazy in six months if I didn't have the Marines kicking my ass." He eyed the waitress as she approached with his glass of wine, and their salads. "Anyhow, what's going on with that case you're working on?"

"I don't want to talk about work. I hate practicing law."

"And so you want *me* to quit my job? What would we live on then?"

"We'd live on *love*—and the proceeds from the sexual harassment suit I'll file against a certain soldier I know, as well as his beloved USMC. And then we could open our own little B and B up in Provincetown."

Arthur's smile vanished. "Don't even joke about things like that."

"I'm not joking. About the B and B."

"I know you're not, and that sounds *great*—when the time is right. I'm talking about your suing the Marines."

"Why not? Since they won't let us get married, I'm still allowed to testify against you, and then after I win there's no law to stop us from sharing the damages. I think it's all rather brilliant."

51

The waitress placed his wine on the table and a small plate of salad in front of each man. "Pepper?"

They nodded.

She twisted the grinder over each pile of lettuce, then vanished.

"You're crazy," Arthur told him, and then dug into his salad.

"Crazy about us," he said, his voice dropping suggestively. "So...whattaya say we flag down Missy and take the food back to the apartment?"

Arthur looked up at him. "What?"

"You don't want to be all pent up on that long flight to Germany with all those hot young Marines on board, do you?"

Arthur cocked an eyebrow. "So...what did you have in mind?"

"I just thought I should do my duty for God and my country. You know...maybe a hot shower followed by a hotter massage?" His fingers made like he was playing a piano in the air.

He grinned. "Well, when you put it that way—"

Danny grinned back at him. "Then it's a deal?"

As the waitress appeared with their entrees, Arthur withdrew his wallet and handed over his credit card. "Everything to go, if you don't mind," he told her, and raised his glass. "And a bottle of this nice Fumé blanc to go, too."

As she took the card from him, he felt Danny's shoeless foot rub his leg. The contact aroused him immediately.

Their eyes locked.

Arthur adjusted himself before standing. "Let's go. I'll sign the slip on the way out."

Danny folded his napkin on the table and pushed his chair back. "Let's walk," he suggested. "It still feels like summer tonight."

"It *is* summer. Fall doesn't start until the twenty-first."

"That's only next week."

"So we should enjoy tonight," he said as he signed the receipt. Then he took the plump white bags from the maître d'. "Because everything's going to feel very different when I get back next month."

***

The flight to Germany was uneventful, except for the presence of a couple of Marines who presented, to Arthur, very much like a couple. One was tall, dark and muscular, while the other was shorter, blond and wiry. They were typical soldiers; their talk, their practiced swaggers—everything about them said "men's men." But it was the intimacy between them that was the giveaway: the soft talk, the brevity of their sentences...as if few words were needed in public because so much had been shared privately. Arthur smiled while imagining the two sharing a bed, with their secret serving not only to sharpen their sex, but also to sweeten their time relaxing. He'd heard of couples like them hooking up in the military, and then spending their remaining civilian years growing fat and gray together, surrounded by a herd of silky terriers in a suburban ranch house. It was uncommon, but not as unusual as most people, especially the government, thought. After all, the military sated a hunger many men have for daring exploits and relentless fitness and exotic travel.

And the chance to be chummy with other men.

The pair brought to his mind those black-and-white World War II movies where the noble Allied soldiers were getting slaughtered by the enemy but then revived their exhausted courage to triumph, even under heavily uneven odds. Toward the end of each film, just before or after the heroes experienced the most thrilling of victories, a mortally wounded soldier—usually the youngest and the cutest—would be cradled in the arms of his usually gruff but now tearful buddy, who encouraged him, with their noses nearly touching, to "hang in there...everything's gonna be OK." After the pup whispers his final, fate-accepting phrase, his head drops to the side and his rag-doll body is engulfed by his comrade, whose hidden-from-the-camera, grief-stricken face says, *I loved this boy, and now my heart is broken.*

Scenarios such as this had pushed him to the recruitment center on that desperate morning more than a decade before. But after he'd enlisted, he kept scenes like those tucked away for good, because the thought of having to live through a moment like that was just too much to bear.

And things had gone well for him in the Marines, despite his rocky start at boot camp. He was well on his way to becoming a major by his mid-twenties and had earned the respect of the U.S. armed forces, as well as a small legion of men. But his personal life hadn't flourished as well as his career; he'd tried out a few relationships over the years, but nothing more than two months here or three weeks there. So he channeled his sexual energy into one-nighters or barroom encounters or sex-club jaunts, because his pewter eyes, calisthenics-hewn physique and "Semper fi" tattoos garnered him just about anyone who turned his head.

But no one he might cradle in his arms and cry over.

Until he met Danny.

He'd just been promoted to captain and had a four-day pass to spend, so he took a string of trains up from Fort Myer, then caught a cab from Grand Central Station down to Dick's Hangout in the meatpacking district of Manhattan.

The athletic build, Boy Scout's haircut and luminous blue eyes caught Arthur's attention immediately. But he learned very quickly that Danny's boyish appearance was the sheep's clothing for the Black Irish wolf lurking inside; he had a wit and a tongue and a temper that frustrated Arthur as much as it charmed him. Hence their frequently argumentative—but always passionate—relationship.

When he was on leave, Arthur lived at Danny's one-bedroom walk-up overlooking Franklin Park in Chelsea. And perhaps it was the size of the apartment, or the transient nature of their relationship, or Arthur's living in a military closet, or just the dynamic of two strong-headed men trying to make a go of it together that fueled the Sturm und Drang of their relationship. They argued too much, they both knew, but both were committed to each other, and the love that they felt for each other was real. And very, very strong.

Arthur missed Danny terribly when he was away, as Danny did him.

Besides Arthur, Danny's career was his other passion—in spite of his protestations to the contrary. He worked for a law firm in the World Trade Center in lower Manhattan that pursued corporate civil rights violations and did considerable pro bono work. He was only twenty-nine and was close to becoming a partner. They figured that in a couple of years, after Danny was promoted, they would buy a place in Brooklyn, get themselves a few silky terriers of their own and put some money away for their early-retirement B and B in P-Town. Fulfilling their dreams was still years away, but with each month's passing the vision that each had for their future together grew more focused, and a bit more tangible.

All they needed was to stay the course.

***

It was midafternoon when Arthur landed in Frankfurt. After grabbing his bags and reporting to his commander, he made his way to his quarters and unpacked.

He decided to ignore the stack of papers waiting for him and called Danny instead.

The phone rang. "Hey," said Danny.

"Hay is for horses."

"How was your flight?"

"Long. But otherwise uneventful."

"Thank God. What are you gonna do tonight?"

"Get settled. Take a nap, maybe. It's too early for dinner and too late for lunch, so I'll check my e-mail and get ready for tomorrow. What about you?"

"Oh, I don't know. There's some briefs I need to go over before tomorrow. We've got our big Tuesday meeting in the morning with the partners, and I'm determined to be overprepared, in case Steve the asshole tries to make me look like I'm not doing my job again."

"If he does, I feel sorry for him." Arthur laughed. "Are you having dinner with anyone tonight?"

"I called Margo but she hasn't called me back. So it'll probably be just me buried in my briefs."

"Better your briefs than someone else's."

Danny giggled. "That's something you don't have to worry about."

"Neither do you," Arthur murmured. "I better get going. I'll give you a call tomorrow."

"What time? I want to make sure I've got my cell on."

Arthur looked at his watch and did a quick calculation. "In the morning—I'll try to reach you about ten."

"OK. I'll talk to you then. Heedle-de-dee," he told him, which was their secret code, in case Uncle Sam was listening, for *I love you.*

"Heedle-de-dee. Big time."

Arthur hung up, shucked his clothes and took a hot shower, during which he decided to call down to the commissary and have some food brought up; it was too much to think of actually interacting with anyone this evening. He'd eat, do a little work and then go to bed early—maybe he'd even do a little fantasizing about that couple he'd seen on the plane.

He just knew he needed plenty of rest.

He had a lot on his plate for tomorrow.

***

He was at his desk the next afternoon when both his landline and cell phone rang. "Major Blauefee," he barked into the landline, figuring his cell would go to voice mail.

"I'm sorry, Major. You're needed at the command center right away," instructed the calm but urgent female voice. He recognized the speaker as the general's able secretary, Corporal Dorian.

"What's going on, Corporal?"

"There's been an attack. We're mobilizing."

"*What? Where?*"

"New York. The general will explain it all. He's waiting for you."

***

Because of Arthur's career, they had been unable to register as domestic partners, so he was not privy to information regarding the recovery of Danny's body. But eventually the sad proof was unearthed, and Danny's very polite family called him back to Connecticut for a small memorial service. As he stepped inside the white clapboard saltbox where his partner had learned to walk and fought with his brothers and did his homework and slept and ate and prayed, he looked at the simple bronze urn in the center of the simple wooden mantel, between the clustered snowy roses and the gaudily framed eight-by-ten photo, and thought, *Is that all there is?*

In the meantime, his dishonorable discharge had been processed at near record speed—for the military—after he'd requested a furlough to search for his missing partner (they hadn't *asked* him, but he'd *told* them because they were granting search furloughs only to immediate family members). Thus, he found himself unemployed and stripped of his benefits.

Then one grief-stricken morning, before leaving Danny's apartment for a job interview at a local Italian restaurant, he caught an article in the *Times* about some former gay and lesbian armed forces personnel who were flourishing at the FBI, as the bureau didn't have the same archaic, bigoted restrictions on sexual orientation as George W. Bush had for his own doomed troops. In fact, the article stated that the bureau preferred their queer agents to be "out," as their security clearances were only in question when they had something to hide, and this would make them more "vulnerable to blackmail."

A few weeks later he was notified that his application had been approved.

So, bravely he vacated Danny's flat and flew off to Quantico, Virginia, to undergo his eighteen-week training at their facility. There he did well: His background enabled him to speed through courses in hand-to-hand combat, as well as firearms, surveillance and cloaking. He dazzled the trainers with his gun toting in Hogan's Alley, the mock city that's peopled with pop-up plywood assassins, as well as ambling tourists and ladies pushing baby carriages. He also sailed through the exams on ethics and constitutional law and found that he was a natural interrogator—he excelled at playing both good and bad cop. With those successes, he'd been snapped up into a special investigations unit in Roanoke, with the promise of an eventual supervisory position.

At Roanoke he submerged himself in the cases he was assigned to: mostly mail fraud and Internet pirating and a few grisly crime scenes and an assortment of foreign nationals transporting goods illegally across international lines. Then one day, years later, after some big, scary computer had cross-referenced his own background information with new cases, they called him in to see whether he knew anything about Katharine Tyler and her allegedly crooked husband, Bill Mortson, back in his hometown of Ballena Beach. He'd told them everything he could remember, while glossing over the true nature of his relationship with Jonathan, and offered to go there on special assignment in a sting operation designed to snag Bill.

He even drew them a fairly accurate floor plan of the Tylers' house.

The case had been resolved to the satisfaction of nearly all, for he'd played the role of doting butler beautifully and had done a fine job of surveillance and reporting.

But one night, when he'd been happily undercover at a gay coffeehouse guarding Katharine's hunky nephew—Jonathan's son Jeremy—Bill had injected a drunk and passed-out Tiffany, Jeremy's diabetic mother, with an overdose of insulin.

She died.

That same night, while Arthur was still looking after the young Tyler, Jeremy's friend Darius borrowed his letterman's jacket to retrieve a cell phone from the car, and some thugs Bill had hired to pummel Jeremy into vegetablehood thought Darius was him and beat him viciously instead.

He almost died.

After that, since they believed Bill had fled to Brazil, Arthur was at the Tyler compound looking after Katharine when Bill materialized unexpectedly at the family's chalet on Lake Estrella and almost succeeded in killing both Jeremy and his lover, Carlo.

But Jeremy turned the tables on him.

And Bill died. *Finally.*

So he hadn't exactly earned gold stars when it came to protecting the Tylers. But in the process, he'd developed an intimate, yet platonic, relationship with Jeremy; they'd become rather like father and son: Upon his arrival at the mansion, he taught him how to throw a baseball and how to drive, and he called him "old buddy" like his own grandfather used to call Arthur, and tried to steer him around the pitfalls of being gay. Jeremy sought his advice on everything from boys to clothes to geometry, and how to negotiate Aunt Katharine's relentless, unending demands.

Arthur had learned to sit stoically during these exchanges, ignoring the fact that Jonathan had been his first love, and that *my, oh my,* the more Jeremy matured, the more he walked and talked and laughed and looked and even smelled just like his father.

So it was with considerable trepidation—mixed with glee—that he'd accepted Katharine's offer, after the case was closed, to stay on at the house as her assistant and the estate's overseer. Taking the position had meant leaving his post with the FBI, but the gamble seemed worth it: being paid to live in a seaside mansion while playing father to Jonathan's son fulfilled needs that, until then, he'd been blithely unaware of.

But now, as they were about to embark on some crazy business trip to Brazil—once Jeremy and Carlo returned from Hawaii—new concerns had arisen about those loose ends Bill had left that needed tying up, as well as Arthur's ability to stifle certain feelings that had arisen recently.

He rubbed the knot of tension in his neck and groaned.

Danny, if only you were here, none of this would be happening.

CHAPTER 9

The guy over there's Ramón; he's the owner," Ellie, their best girlfriend from back home, told them while pointing. "Actually—and you didn't hear it from me—his boyfriend, Jorge, actually owns the place, but he's in New York on business right now."

Jeremy looked across the patio, beyond the sparkling turquoise pool, to assess their handsome host, who was surrounded by a dozen gabbing and laughing young men. Their eyes met across the water, and both smiled. "He's cute," he whispered to Carlo.

"If you like those trashy Hispanical types," he replied.

Jeremy laughed. "I love 'em," he said and then pulled Carlo closer. "What's his boyfriend do?"

"He's someone high up with the NFL or KFC, or whatever," Ellie replied, sounding bored. "He's an absolute doll. But he's a lot—I mean *a lot*—older; like forty-five. I think Ramón changes his diapers."

"What's Ramón do?" Carlo asked.

"He used to 'model,'" she told them, making quote signs in the air, "but Jorge didn't like the clothes he wasn't wearing for the shoots, so now he's supposedly designing his own line of decorative pillows." She rolled her eyes. "But he's a sweetheart, and does make a very hot corporate wife—he's a big favorite with those Velvet Mafia girls when they go to LA—*if* you know what I mean. Come on, I'll introduce you."

They followed her around the pool, and as they approached, the small crowd parted for them, while the guys gave them the *twice*-over. "Hey, gorgeous," Ellie broke in, "this is Jeremy and Carlo, the most fabulous couple in Ballena Beach. And you can't have them. Unless you ask me."

Ramón held out his hand. "Glad you could come by."

They shook hands.

"This place is gorgeous," Carlo told him. "I can't believe you've got a view of Diamond Head *and* all of Waikiki. It must look incredible at night."

"Jorge bought it with his first lover about twenty years ago," he said, "but I got to redecorate it last year, thank God. I just wish it wasn't so far up the coast, because Kahala's a long drive from Hula Joe's after a few drinks. Speaking of, what're you boys having? We've got a full bar inside. Come on, Ellie. You're dry again."

The trio, arm in arm, followed the powerfully built young man as he steered them through gaggles of cruisy-eyed guests toward the lushly landscaped contemporary home. "When was this place built?" Jeremy asked as he stopped to admire the cascading fountains and ponds with their wriggling orange koi.

"I think it was in the 1960s, but Jorge remodeled it in the eighties," Ramón said as he stepped into the expansive living area adjacent to the deck, "so I just got to trash all that gross black lacquer and shitty dusty rose stuff when we redid everything." His arm swept out to the side. "Now everything's white granite and bamboo cabinets and limestone floors. Oh, and we had the pool redone with that little sitting wall around it so Joey, the dirty little bichon frise you'll probably trip over, won't keep falling into the water."

"I really like this," Jeremy said, taking in the sparse grandeur. "Our home is like a big old villa. It's scary."

"Oh, it is not *scary*," countered Ellie. "You should see it, Ramón. It's got a hundred perfect rooms and a mile of private beach."

"I'd like to see it, or you guys, the next time we're in LA." He stared at them and smiled, and Jeremy felt his crotch tingle. "So what do you guys drink?"

"Do you have any beer? Like a Corona?" Carlo asked.

Ramón laughed. "Carlo, your *huaraches* are showing, *mijo*. We've got mojitos or cocktails. And"—he went to the refrigerator under the bar and opened it—"we've still got some champagne left over from my birthday."

Jeremy's eyes sparkled. "I've never had champagne before. And happy birthday, by the way."

"It was last month, but we'll pretend it's today." He pulled from the fridge one of a dozen dark green bottles with simple bronze-colored labels, then grabbed four heavy crystal flutes from over the wet bar. "Jorge got me three cases of Dom for the party, but everyone guzzled the cheap vodka, instead. I think you'll like this." He popped the cork and filled each glass carefully. "To my new friends," he toasted.

"To new friends," the boys answered.

"To great booze," added Ellie as they clinked their glasses.

"Come on, I'll show you the rest of the house," Ramón said.

"While you do that," Ellie cut in, "I'm gonna take my camera and find the drunkest guys here and tell 'em my boyfriend's a big porn producer. I'll e-mail you the nasty pics when I get home." Then she was off, with a wag of her ass and a toss of her platinum locks.

"Jesus Christ, these men are hot," Carlo noted after being introduced to yet another cluster of Abercrombie clones. "Have you been doing genetic experiments?"

Ramón laughed. "It's Ellie—she's got some amazing tractor beam that sucks the pretty ones to her; then she drags 'em up here. Jorge says she's an old troll trapped in a bulimic cheerleader's body."

"She's like that back home, too," said Jeremy. "She's got a big collection."

"How'd you meet her?" Carlo asked.

"Jorge does business with her dad. He met her at a party and they hit it off, so she flew out last month for the weekend and she's been staying with us since. She's going back to LA the day after tomorrow 'cause she missed the first couple of weeks at USC and her parents are really, *really* pissed."

"I'm sure that being here with you," Carlo noted dryly, "she's been happier than a priest in a Jacuzzi full of altar boys."

Ramón cackled and threw his arm around Carlo. "It's good to finally have an *hermano* here, Carlito; it's lonely being the only *maricón* west of Catalina. Come on, let's see the master bedroom."

They followed him down a long hallway lined with dramatic black-and-white male nudes to a double door that opened into an immense room sparsely furnished with Danish modern pieces and ornamented with Japanese porcelains. Outside the west wall a Jacuzzi steamed even in the afternoon sunlight, and on the other side a trio of floor-to-ceiling glass doors opened onto a courtyard teeming with leafy palms and vermillion orchids and chartreuse ferns surrounding a trickling lava-rock fountain.

"This is what I want," Jeremy announced. "I'm sick of my aunt's creepy antiques—this place is *cool.*" He examined a wildly contemporary landscape of a tropical beach. "And this painting—I love it!"

"That's by Paul Blaine Henrie. Jorge collects him," said Ramón.

"Is this Hawaii?" Jeremy asked, moving in closer to examine the smeared riot of colors.

"I think it's Tahiti. He bought a bunch of his pieces from the guy's nephew right after he died. Now they're all worth a fortune."

Jeremy looked back at Carlo. "This is exactly the kind of place I want."

"Hey!" Ramón exclaimed as he sat on the bed. "You guys should come with us the day after tomorrow—we're going out to Molokai for the day, and our designer's coming." He patted the bed's silk coverlet, inviting them to sit. "You could talk to him about doing your place."

Carlo looked excitedly at Jeremy as they sat. "Can we?"

"But our flight's at eight a.m. tomorrow."

"Just call the airline and change it," Ramón suggested. "I do it all the time."

"Could you?" Carlo pleaded.

"I don't know..."

"Listen: There's about ten of us going on our yacht, and we're meeting up with some other guys from Black Point; they've got this fabulous eighty-one-foot Ferretti that makes Jorge's Cayman 38 look like a rowboat. We're having an all-day catered barbecue and the beach is totally private and it's just going to be all hunky, hot guys." He placed a hand on Jeremy's shoulder and squeezed. "Look, dude, if you two don't play, it's OK with everyone, but I *guarantee* you'll enjoy the show." He looked from Jeremy to Carlo and back. "So? You can use my phone to call the airline..." He pointed to the telephone atop the nightstand.

Since Jeremy had been sipping his champagne, everything in the room had taken on a honey-colored glow. He felt relaxed, so he closed his eyes and imagined the man-fest on the beach, with muscular guys laughing and sunning and eating and drinking and hugging, while out in the water two spectacular white yachts were moored just beyond the waves, waiting to take everyone back to their privileged, fabulous lives.

And then he remembered Arthur.

"Baby, no. My aunt needs us to come back."

"What's she need you for?" Ramón asked. "Is she in a wheelchair?"

"If only," Carlo muttered.

Jeremy shot him a look. "My family has this big real estate deal happening in Brazil, and we're going down at the end of the week to check it out—Carlo and me, and our friend Arthur."

"He's Jeremy's fairy godfather," Carlo added, "and he's this very hot ex-Marine. You'd love him—but not as much as Jeremy does."

Jeremy laughed and rubbed Carlo's knee. "But I love you more," he told him. "We'll come back, maybe over Christmas when it's summer down here. Yeah?"

"Hmmm." Ramón raised his eyebrows, nodding. "You should bring Arthur with you next time; there's always a couple of sons looking for a hot dad." He twirled his empty glass. "I need another drink, and it looks like you do, too. Be right back." He got up from the bed and disappeared down the hallway, and Jeremy collapsed back onto the bed.

He was feeling tipsy.

"I don't want to go," Carlo said, talking into his knees. "I don't. I really don't."

"Don't wanna go home or don't wanna go to Brazil or don't wanna go out on a yacht?" Jeremy asked, while scanning the rippling squiggles on the ceiling that were reflected up from the Jacuzzi outside.

Looks like glowing snakes.

"I don't feel like going home. I mean, we're finally here having this incredible trip—especially after all the crazy shit that happened this year with your family—and we're supposed to go windsurfing tomorrow and we could go to that incredible beach party the day after; we even talked about going to Maui." He downed the rest of his champagne. "What's the difference between leaving tomorrow and leaving on Monday or Tuesday? We're not even going to Brazil until Wednesday."

"Because there's stuff we need to do when we get home, and I don't want to fly in one day and go out the next. And I don't know how to change plane tickets—we could wind up in fucking Iraq." He was starting to feel defensive. "So I'll just leave it how it is. We'll go home tomorrow."

Carlo looked away, pouting.

"Look," Jeremy began. "Brazil's supposed to be amazing—kind of like this, with all the tropical stuff, but…weirder. Not American. And we'll be on a private island over there. Doesn't that sound just as cool?"

"No. It doesn't. Because we'll be with Arthur, so it's not going to be *our* vacation anymore. And I was really looking forward to us being together. *Alone.*"

"Yeah, I know." He nodded.

"And Brazil can be dangerous, Jeremy. My cousin Afonso lives in one of those favelas in Rio de Janeiro. Those are scary."

"What's a favela?"

"A Brazilian slum. Looks like…a tornado picked up a bunch of old houses and threw them on a landfill. Sideways."

"Huh?"

"You'll see." Carlo sighed and lay back on the bed. "I'm just surprised that you want to go there so badly. Why is that?"

"I just want to get it over with, you know, get Katharine off my back."

"That's the only reason?"

He shrugged. "Plus, it'll be an adventure—this whole huge resort place sounds incredible." He ran his hand up and down his torso, feeling his bumpy abs through his T-shirt.

The champagne was making him horny.

"I think it sounds crazy," Carlo said.

"Why?"

"Because anything your uncle Bill was involved in can't be good."

"That's why you think it's crazy?"

"Didn't you ever think that a place that says it has guaranteed security is an invitation for all the crazies out there to attack it, like they did to the Pentagon? And what do you, or any of us, know about building resorts anyway? It's like, we can look at the place and say, 'Yeah, that pool looks pretty and that hotel looks real big,' but what if they're doing a shitty construction job? How can we tell?"

"Katharine's sending over building inspectors after we come back. We're just gonna, like, look over the place and get to know this Dom Fabiano guy."

"I thought his name was El Gigante."

"I guess that's his nickname. Maybe he's really tall."

"What does your beloved Arthur say about all of this?"

He ignored the jab. "He says that everything in Brazil is about who you've paid off and who owes you favors. And because Bill invested a lot of our money over there before he died, they owe us some *big* favors." He glanced out the window and saw that some of the guests had dropped their trunks and were skinny-dipping.

He wanted more than anything to stop talking about this and to run out there, drop his shorts and leap in.

"But how can you make an island secure? What if someone traps you there? How do you run away?"

"I guess you need to make sure no one gets on it in the first place; it's kind of like...a castle with a big moat around it." He began rubbing himself through his floral-patterned board shorts, and his eyes closed with pleasure.

"Great. So now we're running off to a place with castles and moats...and giants. The next thing you're gonna say is there's this big ol' beanstalk." He looked to the ceiling, laughing sourly. "At least I can translate for you—although my Portuguese isn't great, I can still tell if they're gonna throw us off a cliff or feed us to the piranhas."

"Then it's a good thing you're going," Jeremy told him. *And I'm really glad Arthur's going.* He turned to his lover and smiled.

Carlo pursed his lips and kissed him.

"Hey, we don't leave for home until tomorrow morning, so why don't we go back to the hotel room...and I'll fuck you like a crazy man?" Jeremy grabbed Carlo's hand and placed it on his swollen groin.

Carlo grinned and began massaging him through the flimsy nylon. "I thought you wanted to go to Hula Joe's one more time," he said, and then licked the inside of his ear. "You said you wanted to see those go-go boys again."

"But I want to fuck you now, Carlito," he whispered. "We can go there after."

"Man, what'm I missing here?" Ramón announced as he walked in with another frosty bottle in his hand. "I'm glad I left you guys alone."

Carlo pulled his hand away and Jeremy sat up. "Sorry, dude."

"Sorry for what?" he asked. "Sorry for being cute and horny? Join the club."

Jeremy blushed. "It's just...we don't..."

"Don't worry. If you guys need a room, we've got 'em all over. And most've got locks on the doors."

"Actually, I think we're gonna leave," Carlo said.

"OK, but you're coming on Sunday, right? We're leaving from the old Gilligan's Island marina down by the Ilikai at nine a.m., and I just told the caterer to plan for two more."

Jeremy and Carlo looked at each other. "We've gotta get back home, *papi*," Carlo told him. "It's just the way it is."

Ramón smiled. "It's OK, dude. I just wish we'd met you earlier in the week."

"Us, too. Thanks for the party," said Jeremy as they pushed themselves up from the bed. "We've gotta go find Ellie and say bye. We'll get your e-mail from her, for Christmas. OK?"

***

The door of their suite had barely clicked shut before they shed their clothes and jumped onto the bed.

"My ass feels like a tour bus drove through it this morning, thanks to you." Carlo giggled. "But my hands feel strong enough to...milk a bull." He reached over to the nightstand and grabbed the small plastic bottle, and then dribbled its contents on Jeremy.

"Are you gonna give me what I love?" Jeremy asked, locking his hands behind his head.

"Don't talk...just think of Ramón getting plowed by all those guys on the beach." Carlo sat back on his heels and began massaging the slippery liquid over him. "I love how big it gets when I do this," he whispered. "It's like a magic wand."

"And I'm the wizard who gets to—ohhh," Jeremy moaned.

"Gets to do what?" Carlo asked him devilishly as he tightened his grip. "Grant wishes with it?" He began stroking him lightly, teasingly. "I love playing with my beautiful wizard," he whispered. "I love making him feel so good."

He saw that Jeremy's eyes were rolled back into his head and his breathing had quickened.

Then Jeremy's eyes popped open. "Mmm, oh, oh, oh, *oh!*" He held his breath and Carlo squeezed him. Then after he knew the moment had passed Carlo continued caressing him until he saw that there was no use holding him back.

His mouth on mine, his chest against mine, my cock, his cock—"Huh!" The first eruption hit Carlo on the forehead.

"Uh!" The second splattered his chin.

"Ho." The third landed on his chest.

"Mm," Jeremy murmured as the rest puddled onto his abs and Carlo's milking slowed.

"That's one wish," Carlo murmured as he watched the last drops ooze. Then he stretched himself alongside Jeremy.

And they kissed as Carlo's hand moved faster.

And Jeremy's fingers probed deeper and his tongue pushed farther into his mouth.

And he clenched his belly while he swam in love.

And his toes pointed at the wall.

And Carlo released one-two-three white strings onto his torso.

Then all was still.

"Wish number two fulfilled," Carlo panted, at last. "And I've only got one left."

"Why don't you just wish for three more wishes?" Jeremy whispered, grinning and waving his dick in the air. "I think there's still some magic left in it."

Carlo fell back onto his pillow. "Everyone knows that's illegal," he said, examining the ceiling. "Let's see. For my last wish, I'd like"—he put a finger to his chin—"yeah, I'm not telling you."

"Come on," he groaned.

"You know the rules. But I'll let you know when it comes true."

Within moments their breathing had calmed and Jeremy's eyes were drooping, so Carlo jumped up to retrieve a washcloth from the bathroom. After he'd wiped them both dry he collapsed back onto the sheets and let the tropical breezes dancing in through the open lanai doors spin them off to sleep.

***

Jeremy's cell phone woke them sometime later.

"Jeremy, dear?" Her voice beckoned from across the ocean.

"Hi, Aunt Katharine," he answered groggily. "How are you?"

"I'm doing wonderfully now, thanks to you," she said. "I'm so pleased to hear that you boys are going to Brazil with Arthur—although I must say I'm going to lose my mind here all by myself."

"We're only gonna be gone a few days. But maybe you can go to that spa you like in Palm Springs until we get back."

"That's a wonderful idea! I'll call them right away. When do you come home, then?"

"Our flight comes into LAX at about two; Arthur's picking us up."

"Wonderful. Maybe on the way home you can ask what's on his mind."

"What do you mean?"

"It's hard to say. It's just that...something's up with him. He's not being himself at all—just moons around the house, barely goes out except for groceries and errands."

"Maybe something happened with his mom."

"Perhaps...oh, and before I forget, the minute you get home there are some documents I've put together that I'd like you to study before you leave; they aren't terribly complicated—really just a series of thumbnails for things you should look for. And I have some exciting news about the resort."

"Uh-huh?"

"Our investment consortium has just partnered with a Canadian company that is on the verge of developing the world's first airline with guaranteed security."

"That sounds impossible," he told her flatly.

"I know it does, my dear. I was just as skeptical."

"How can they say something like that?"

"*Technology*," she told him, as if she had just coined the word herself. "They have technology that can practically read your mind. I'll fill you in on the details when you arrive. But just imagine: the world's only airline to provide guaranteed security whisking you off to the world's safest resort. The commercial possibilities are astounding!"

"It sounds great." Carlo had just awakened and was leaning over, nuzzling his neck. "So I'll see you tomorrow, sometime after, uh, four?"

"I am so looking forward to seeing you. I'll even have Arthur whip up some of that ghastly macaroni and cheese of which you're so fond." She laughed.

He laughed as well. "Thanks, Aunt Katharine. See you then. Love you."

"And I love you, Jeremy. Good-bye."

He switched off his phone.

And as his mouth joined Carlo's, he thought, *What's wrong with Arthur?*

CHAPTER 10

Nothing on the Internet or television held any interest for him, and he was almost caught up on his work, including everything on his list to get ready for their trip, so he decided to play hooky and walk along the beach, where the crashing waves usually lightened his black moods.

September's morning fog had cleared, and from his French doors the sky looked intoxicatingly azure, so he pulled on some cargo shorts and his extra-comfy T-shirt—the blue one with the cutoff sleeves and the Human Rights Campaign logo on it. Then after he laced up his running shoes, he turned to examine his reflection in the beveled mirror doors of the armoire in the corner.

He decided, after a studied glance, that he looked younger than his thirty-nine years, thanks to his morning regimen of three hundred crunches and two hundred push-ups, and his meditative late-afternoon jogs. But there was no denying that his physical self was changing; whereas millennia ago, the emperor Hadrian might have snatched up someone who looked as he did twenty years ago to model for statues of poor, doomed Antinous, he was now better suited to sculptures resembling Hadrian's *Lansdowne Herakles*.

Still pretty damn hot, just...older.

Since Katharine was at a meeting with her attorneys, he grabbed his keys and then trotted out the side doors, which he locked behind him. While crossing the property, he checked the water level in the drizzling Florentine fountain (it had developed a leak recently), noticed that the rose bushes needed cutting back, and began his descent on the newly installed steel stairs that zigzagged down to the hefty, spring-loaded security door.

His steps were heavy in the sand, so he began to jog. After moments of loping, he broke into a dead run—his legs sprinted and his arms pumped and he forced the air into his lungs, and his heart beat as if he were being chased by a flock of bat-winged Harpies—because he knew that if he punished his body, his adrenal glands would pour him a much-needed shot of antidepressant.

But as La-Z-Boy rock drew closer, he realized that even if he ran a marathon it wouldn't make a difference.

Because the voices that normally whispered his life's deficiencies were yelling lately, and he was no longer able to invent excuses with which to silence them.

He reached the rock and sat, elbows to knees, panting.

God, I'm sad.

He knew that part of his depression was due to Jeremy's absence, because since the boy's arrival at the compound a year ago they had been inseparable. The reason for this, at least in the beginning, was because he'd tried to be a good role model for him; for the more Arthur got to know him, the worse he felt about his having navigated the road to manhood by himself: learning how to shave without slicing open a zit, how to move your shoulders when you walk, how to butch it up with other guys and how to jack off quietly, so your mom doesn't hear you. And then, as the shroud covering Jeremy's heart fell away and he began revealing his longings and his fascinations and his frustrations and his dreams, Arthur found himself confronting something wholly unexpected:

Love.

So he'd been relieved when Carlo materialized, as the kid had a strong, level head and was as smitten with Jeremy as he was unapologetically queer. Arthur liked him, although he was sometimes abrasive, because you could always count on him to be authentic: He wore his heart on his sleeve, even after Jeremy did something to bloody his cuffs.

Thus, he learned to be content watching Jeremy bloom, from a few steps back.

But it wasn't always easy...

Such as when he appeared at Arthur's quarters sporting nothing but boxer shorts and his newly minted swimmer's build. He'd smiled blandly into those glittering dark eyes and dutifully handed over Jeremy's basket of folded laundry.

Then there was the night he was standing at the butcher block dicing onions, and his shoulders were killing him so he reached back to smooth the knot, completely unaware that Jeremy had padded up behind him until he felt strong hands squeeze the tension from his shoulders. He'd nearly cried because no one had done that for him in years, but when he felt the heat from the young man's body and smelled the chlorine and musk rising up from his skin, he'd pulled away with a polite "thanks."

The young man's scent lingered in his nostrils even after dinner was eaten.

Then, just before the boys left for Hawaii, Arthur was vacuuming upstairs when he heard splashing in the pool. He looked down and saw Jeremy practicing his backstroke, so he switched off the machine and watched, spellbound, as his strong arms windmilled and his torso twisted and his sculpted legs churned the water. But then he reasoned that maybe it wasn't Jeremy, exactly, that was making his heart beat faster…but rather the memory of another, much like him, who'd made his heart thunder years ago.

He leaned back on the rock, feeling the hot granite pushing into his shoulders and skull, as the sun beating down on his closed eyelids colored his world tomato orange.

***

"What's wrong?"

Jonathan's lips made a line. "I think she knows."

"What do you mean?"

"I'm not sure…I could be wrong."

"But why do you think—"

"My stuff—you know those *Mandate* magazines I keep in my bottom drawer, tucked inside those *Motor Trend*s? I came home last night and went for them and they were—I don't know—*different.*"

"Is that all?" Arthur laughed. "Maybe you just shoved 'em back wrong."

"No. She was in a real pissy mood this morning. Real cold, like Nancy Reagan. And she started grilling me about what girl I'm dating, and when I told her nobody, she wanted to know why."

"Shit." Arthur looked down at the sand. "That's why I don't keep any of that stuff in my place. If my dad ever found anything like that, he'd cut my balls off."

"She might not let us be together anymore," he muttered, "even as friends."

"Just because she might know about you doesn't mean she knows about *us.*"

71

He sighed. "You're right. I just figured that if she thought I was gay and you spend a lot of time here, she'd put it together. You know?"

"Yeah," he agreed, tracking the big white schooner in full sail slicing through the waves offshore. "And if she did, what would you do?"

"I don't know," he said. "I don't think I could be honest."

"Why not?"

"Because she wants me to be this *Kennedy*, or something." He got up from the rock and started trudging through the sand toward the edge of the water. "You know, yachts and royalty," he yelled, gesticulating wildly, "and a Ralph Lauren model–looking wife and politics and shit. I mean, she pretends like she's this lady who's really cool, with her fund-raising and all, but she's really just uptight...wants everything to be so fucking picture perfect, and me being a fag isn't something she's gonna brag about to her country club friends."

"Do you really think so?" Arthur got up and went over to him.

"You don't know her, Artie." Jonathan laughed. "She thinks gay guys are OK, as long as they're dyeing her hair or...dying of AIDS. She's like those parents who think they're all liberal and shit watching PBS, but then their daughter brings a black guy home and suddenly it's like, *The cultural differences are too great...*"

"Wow. I never took her for that kind of person. What about your uncle?"

"That fucker doesn't care about anything but our money. He can go fuck himself."

Arthur thought for a moment. "So are you going to wait until she says something to you? Or are you gonna come out?"

"No way, man. There's no way I'm sayin' anything to her. And if she asks me I'll deny it."

"But what about after high school? You can't hide it forever."

"After I get into college, maybe. Then when I turn twenty-one my trust'll be mine, so I won't have to worry about her, or asshole Bill."

"Is that what you're worried about?" Arthur laughed. "You think she'll take your money away if you're gay?"

Jonathan didn't answer, he just looked out to the horizon.

"Is that really it?" Arthur put a hand on his shoulder.

"I wish my parents hadn't died." Jonathan covered Arthur's hand with his own. "There'd be no way they'd treat me like this. They'd love me whether I was gay or not."

"Your aunt loves you. You know that."

"She loves what she wants me to be," he said. "She holds a lot over my head, you know. It's like she blackmails me all the time with *Be perfect, or else.*"

"It's pretty much up to you if you let her."

"But it's a lot of money, Artie. *A lot.* And she's paying for college; then she's putting me on the board of Tyler, Inc., when I finish school."

"How much is *a lot* of money?"

He crossed his arms. "I'm not allowed to tell anyone."

"It doesn't matter to me." Arthur wrapped his arms around Jonathan's waist. "I'd love you even if you were as poor as me."

***

Arthur made his way back through the sand toward the stairway, then fitted his key into the lock of the security door. Just as he crested the final stair's riser he saw her, in one of those dozen St. John suits she wore to meetings, as she exited the kitchen and looked around.

"Arthur?" she called out, waving.

He fixed a smile and quickened his step.

"May I bother you for a moment?" she asked as they drew closer together. "I've just come back from the attorneys', and I'd like to share our plan with you. May we talk in the conservatory?"

He held out his hand. "After you."

They walked together across the flagstone toward the glass-paned pavilion that hugged the west wing. Then he pulled open the door and followed her inside.

She folded herself down onto her padded toile chaise, while he lowered himself into a decrepit wicker chair that crickled loudly under him.

She slipped on her reading glasses and examined some papers. "Let me say that I very much appreciate your taking Jeremy down there. I would have been ill prepared to do so myself, and I cannot see this project going any further without your assistance. For that, I am in your debt."

He smiled. "Don't worry about it. I'm happy to go, and I haven't had a vacation since before Danny died, so I'm overdue. Thanks for paying my way."

"You're too modest," she told him. "In any case, I've just met with the attorneys, and they've drawn up papers for a spectacular lawsuit in the event that you suspect fraud of any sort."

He shifted forward in his seat, and the chair creaked ominously. "And what should I do if I see anything when we're there?"

"You'll cut short your trip; then we'll assemble a crew to travel there and conduct a predatory examination of their construction, as well as an audit of their books."

"But why don't you just send your henchmen there first, instead?"

She smiled. "Doing so would paint us as suspicious, and a bit paranoid."

"Why?"

She pulled off her glasses. "Since my late husband was Dom Fabiano's partner, he's been insistent about conducting business with only a member of our immediate family—"

"Which is extremely dangerous, considering the potential for kidnapping—"

She nodded and held up her hand. "I understand your caveat, Arthur. Believe me, I do. Just think of this little vacation as…a four-day mission of goodwill, and nothing more. Our international business relations speak highly of this man, and they assure me that the potential for return on our investment is *tremendous.*" She smiled, he thought a bit smugly. "And please understand that Jeremy is my only remaining blood, and I consider you to be a lifelong friend of ours, as well as his protector; if I thought either of you would be in harm's way I would never have agreed to send you two."

"Or Carlo," he added.

"Yes, of course," she agreed, nodding. "Nothing must happen to him, either."

He felt uneasy. Clearly she had no concept of the dangerous nature of the people they might encounter, or the political instability of the region. According to his research, if they returned home without incident it would be a small miracle. He would just have to throw his protective net around Jeremy and Carlo, and be hypervigilant. Only the knowledge that Dom Fabiano was gay made him believe they had a chance, as one seldom double-crossed a member of their sacred band.

Unless they double-crossed you first.

"I'll do my very best," he told her, then stood.

"I know you will." She shifted her attention back to her papers.

"Is there anything else you need?" he asked from the doorway.

She looked up. "Some tea? I'd love some tea."

"Comin' right up."

"Arthur?"

He stopped.

"I am doing the right thing, am I not?"

She looked worried, and it made him feel unsteady. "I'd die myself before I let anything happen to him or Carlo," he told her in his most reassuring voice. "You can count on that."

CHAPTER 11

T he location is *magnificent!*" she exclaimed as her eyes swept over the array of oversized glossy photographs displayed on the easels. Then she focused on the elaborate architectural model consuming the immense conference table in the center of the room. "And the resort—it looks simply amazing!"

Arthur had to agree; the pictures of the croissant-shaped island revealed a verdant paradise. The western side, where the triple resorts would stand, showed ivory-sand beaches and rocky hillsides with meandering streams and waterfalls, while the east end was covered with a dense rainforest. At the northern and southern tips the island curled toward its center to form a nearly symmetrical bay, in which guests would enjoy sailing and riding Jet Skis, water skiing or snorkeling, and in the center of the island a great rock rose up, like a huge potato set on end.

"Castle Mountain is where we're building the condominiums," Mr. Flores, the lead designer, told them. "They'll encircle the peak—like a crown. You can see it over here." He motioned to the miniature resort on the table and picked up a section laid off to the side that was the size of a chef's mold for a gelatin ring. This he placed onto the apex of the plaster hill.

It fit snugly, like a headband.

"What about the other side," Jeremy asked, "where the rainforest is?"

"The vegetation there is extremely dense, and much will be cleared for the bigger airport and the fuel tanks," Flores explained. "We need at least three thousand feet of runway to accommodate the blended-wing aircrafts that CanAire has ordered for its flights to the resort, because this newest design is the strongest and most fuel-efficient aircraft ever built. And the *safest.*"

"Can you tell us more about the differing theme of each resort?" Katharine asked.

"I was just getting to that. The most economical complex will be the Amazonia; it's modeled after the Hawaiian resorts of the 1960s, with vintage bamboo décor and pools like lagoons. It'll also have luaus and Polynesian shows, *palapa* roofs and staff dressed in tropical wear. The midrange resort, Espanha, will carry the flavor of fine hotels on the Mexican Riviera and the Costa Brava in Spain, with cobblestone streets and tiled-roof townhomes, and open-air restaurants with strolling vendors and trios. Our research indicates that these two themes are the most preferred by Western travelers."

"And what about the more sophisticated guest?" she asked.

"Our luxury-class resort will echo the amazing architecture of Brasilia, as we've been fortunate enough to secure, as head architect, one of Oscar Niemeyer's former apprentices. Brasiliana has the quiet sophistication of a classic midcentury utopia, and its lush setting will make it a favorite with jet-setters from around the world."

Arthur saw that Katharine was beaming.

"I love it," she declared. "It reminds me of the glory days of Disneyland, before they obliterated its charm."

"It does kind of remind me of Adventureland, New Orleans Square and Tomorrowland," Arthur added.

"Exactly," Mr. Flores agreed. "It's the same formula used by the hoteliers in Las Vegas, because different resort themes attract a wider range of visitors. Which leads us to the casinos—each resort will have three."

"Why three?" Arthur asked.

"Because gamblers are superstitious, and three is lucky. And if someone feels they are having bad luck at one casino, they'll have two more to try before their vacation ends."

"Something for everybody, and as safe as a bank vault," Katharine noted happily. "I cannot see it failing!"

"But how do you make an island safe?" Jeremy blurted. "I mean, couldn't anyone just drive up in a boat and blow everything up?"

Flores smiled. "That is a concern, young man, but think of the ocean surrounding the island as the ultimate buffer zone. And with the technology we have in place—above and underwater radar, motion sensors, infrared cameras, twenty-four-hour surveillance on all fronts— we could count the fish in the sea if we needed to. And we'll have our own security force, as well as a fleet of guard boats; it'll be small but extremely efficient...and very deadly if the need arises. We call this extremely comprehensive system the world's first *twenty-five-hour security*."

"But won't that freak people out, seeing guys with guns everywhere?" asked Jeremy.

"They won't be detected by the visitors. No one will even know when a guard is standing next to them."

Arthur smiled. Clearly, they had been studying the cloaking methodology of the FBI. But then a disturbing thought occurred to him. "If this resort is being billed as having 'guaranteed security,' won't that just serve as a challenge to every anti-American militia group and professional thief in the world?"

"Of course," Katharine agreed. "We understand that we're taunting a pack of hyenas with a very large slab of zebra."

"And you've prepared for an air attack, I hope?" Arthur asked.

"We've arranged with the Brazilian government to have a no-fly zone around the island, and we've partnered with the Força Aérea Brasileira—the Brazilian Air Force—and its new fleet of Northrop F-5EMs to handle that end of the security; there's no feasible way for even this very wealthy investment consortium to provide air patrols, especially over international waters."

"It sounds as though you've thought of everything," said Katharine. "Do you have the latest round of paperwork ready for us, with the changes we've discussed?"

"Not quite yet. We're still gathering documents and estimates for the additional building materials and contractors' bids, but we'll have it ready for you before your party leaves."

"That's good," she replied, "because I'd like as much time as possible to examine them."

"You should have them by the close of business tomorrow. And now, if you don't have any further questions, I have a videoconference with Dom Fabiano in a few minutes, so I need to gather my files."

She held out her hand. "Thank you, Mr. Flores, for doing such an excellent job. I must say that I am as pleased about your firm's designs as I am excited about this project moving forward."

He shook her hand, and then shook Arthur's and finally Jeremy's. "What you're doing here is providing something that's missing from today's world: absolute safety and security, combined with freedom, fun and luxury. The world will be clamoring to spend its money with you."

Jeremy and Arthur exchanged wide-eyed glances.

***

"I don't know," said Arthur as the elevator doors closed them in. "The first thing I learned in the bureau is there's no system that can't be hacked."

Jeremy nodded. "I think it sounds too good to be true."

"Nonsense," said Katharine as the elevator began descending. "I may be ignorant when it comes to some things, but this project looks to me as though we have a winner on our hands. It'll be...our own little Masada."

"What's a Masada?" Jeremy asked.

Arthur cringed. "It was an 'impenetrable' fortress on the top of a high mountain, where the Jews kept the Roman army at bay during, I think it was, the first Jewish-Roman war."

"So they—the Jews, I mean—won?" Jeremy asked, then reached for the handrail as the elevator's descent ended and the door dinged off-key.

"No, the Romans did," Arthur said, watching the twin doors slide apart.

"I'd forgotten about that," Katharine admitted. "But as I recall now, the Jews still triumphed...*by default.*"

Arthur humphed. "I guess you could say that."

"What do you mean?" Jeremy asked as they made their way across the lobby.

"The Jews killed themselves instead of becoming enslaved by the Romans," Arthur said, pushing open the glass door. "Actually, they killed one another, because suicide was against Jewish law."

"Yikes," said Jeremy.

"Well, our Masada will be different," Katharine suggested as she jingled her keys.

"How?" the men asked.

"Because this time, it'll be the Romans who are inside the fort."

CHAPTER 12

"What'm I supposed to pack?" Carlo asked, staring at his deflated suitcase on the floor. "I mean, the weather there is supposed to be incredibly humid, but then we're supposed to have some kind of business meetings, too."

"Take your funeral suit and those new black shoes," Carmen answered, pointing into his closet, "and then just take stuff you're comfortable in... shorts, T-shirts, *chanklas*. How long are you gonna be gone, again?"

"A few days, maybe a week at the most. Jeremy doesn't really know." He pulled a heap of clean laundry from the blue plastic basket on the chair beside his bed and began folding his clothes and stacking them in piles. "It all depends on how things go there, and whether or not Jeremy and Sergeant Arthur are happy with the progress."

"Have you seen any pictures of this place?"

"No. Jeremy says it looks a lot like Hawaii—but not as modern."

"Are you really gonna have time to look for Babalu?" she asked.

"God, I'd forgotten about his nickname." He laughed. "Where'd that come from?"

She shrugged. "Maybe he played the bongos, like in the *I Love Lucy* show. But that's what I remember him as—Babalu, not Afonso. Were you old enough to remember him visiting us?"

"No. Kind of. It's like I have this fuzzy picture in my head of him. All I remember is that he was really nice to me—he must've been in his twenties or something when they came here."

"That sounds about right." She nodded. "So now he'd be about forty or so, huh?"

"I guess."

"He might be hard to find, *mijo*. Should you even try to look for him?"

He stopped folding and looked at her. "When are any of us ever gonna be down there again? I feel bad about someone in our family being down there. He lives in one of those nasty favelas, and those are dangerous."

"Then you shouldn't go," she told him. "What's the point?"

"Because he's our cousin and he's gay and sick, so he probably needs help. It's not like they have Medi-Cal to help people like him." He picked up a pair of jeans, considered them, then put them aside. "I know you don't want me to try and find him, but just think: How'd you feel if we had a female cousin down there dying of breast cancer? Wouldn't you want to help?"

"You can't *catch* breast cancer," she said. "A long time ago, before my mom died, I overheard her telling my dad he's a *puto*."

"Well, maybe I'd be one, too, if I had to live there. The poor guy, I mean…if you're gay and poor, what kind of life is there for you down there?"

"Probably a better one than if you're gay and sick," she said. "It's not like twenty years ago when people didn't know as much about sexually transmitted diseases. He should've been more careful."

"You sound like Mom right now," he told her, then resumed his folding. "And you don't even know what he's sick with. You're assuming a lot."

"Do you even know what he looks like?"

"I'm bringing the only picture"—he bent over and dug into the pocket of his suitcase—"we have of him, but it's from a long time ago." He handed her a dog-eared photograph whose colors had faded into various shades of orange and green.

"He's *guapo*," she said. "Or at least he used to be." She turned the photo slightly, to catch the light better. "He looks a little like you."

Carlo leaned over to examine the picture. "I guess." He took it from her and tucked it back into his suitcase.

"So how do you think you're gonna help?"

"Any way we can. Do you like this with my suit?" he asked, holding up a black long-sleeve shirt.

She wrinkled her nose. "Too gangster-ish. Wear a white one—and don't forget a tie. So how're things with your man?"

He grinned. "Great."

"You guys had fun in Hawaii?"

"Oh, my God," he began, sitting down on the edge of the bed, "we had the best time—went to parties and bars and the beach and stayed in this gorgeous high-rise suite right on Waikiki. And the sex?" He rubbed his face. "My lips are still numb."

"Now who's the *puto*?" She laughed, then sat down next to him. "So how do you feel about having Arthur come along?"

"It's OK." He shrugged. "Actually, I feel safer—like having a big gay G.I. Joe around."

"Not jealous?"

"What should I be jealous about?" He pushed some folded shorts inside the bag.

"He's hot, Carlito, and I've seen the way he looks at Jeremy."

He shook his head. "He's *old*, Carmen. Old enough to be his dad—and they have this really cute father-son thing going; they totally adore each other that way. Arthur's probably the one thing I don't have to worry about on this trip."

"I don't know, *mijo*. If I were you, I'd watch that white boy. He's a beauty, and he's rich."

"Are you saying I should be worried about Arthur, or about other guys, too?"

She threw an arm around his shoulder. "I don't know what I'm talking about, baby brother." She kissed him on the cheek. "Any guy would be *so* lucky to be with you. I'm sure Jeremy knows that."

He leaned into her and put his hand on her knee. "Carmen, if he's gonna cheat on me, there's nothing I can do about it. He's a great guy and we love each other, but there's still gonna be some shit up the road for us, just like for everyone. You know?"

"I just don't want to see you hurt, Carlito." She held out her arms, and they hugged. "You've been through a whole lot."

He smiled. "I know. I don't want to get hurt, either. All I know is that when you love each other, you make it work."

"You're absolutely right, *mijo*." She squeezed his hands. "But still, I want you to be careful."

CHAPTER 13

Dinnertime was still about two hours away, and within the last hour, a bank of fog had begun swirling its smoky tendrils onshore, so he resigned himself to his exhaustion and decided to nap.

He'd just shucked most of his clothes, slid beneath the covers and hugged his pillow under his cheek when he heard a familiar rhythmic tapping on his door.

Jeremy.

"Just a minute." He swung his legs over the side of his bed, then wriggled into his jeans and pulled a sweatshirt over his T-shirt. Then he opened the door. "Hi."

"You busy?" he asked.

"Nope." He smiled in spite of his fatigue; he hadn't slept more than four hours each night for the past week. "Just gettin' some rest. What's up?"

"Should I come back?"

"It's OK. I can sleep on the plane tomorrow." He opened the door wider and threw a nod toward the veranda. "It's all cool and foggy right now—almost like fall. Wanna sit outside?"

"Sure." Jeremy made his way across the room toward the balcony, while Arthur threw his door open wider; he didn't want Katharine marching by and thinking he was up to anything unseemly with her darling nephew.

They each took a chair by the round table, whose glass top was now slick with mist. Arthur sat back, while Jeremy leaned forward, his eyes shifting nervously.

"Everything OK?" Arthur asked.

"Yeah, I guess so."

"So what's on your mind?"

Jeremy settled back into his chair. "It's Carlo," he said, grimacing. "We're having some troubles."

"Hmm. Like what?"

"It's like he wants different things than I do," Jeremy told him as he rubbed the crease between his eyebrows. "I mean, I still love him and everything, but he's starting to bug me. It's all about what he wants sometimes, and he doesn't really care about what I want. And he gets all bossy, like Katharine."

Arthur chuckled. "That's probably the biggest problem in any relationship, Jeremy. Finding, and then balancing, conflicting desires is an art that few couples ever master."

"I know, and we've talked about it, and it gets better—he does try. Really he does."

Arthur saw that Jeremy was shivering. "Sorry to interrupt, but you look cold. Want something to wear?"

He nodded.

He pulled off his sweatshirt and handed it over.

"But you'll be cold."

"I run hot. Don't worry."

He pulled on the sleeves, then pushed his head up through the opening. "It smells like you," he said, grinning.

"Sorry about that. So you were saying?"

"There's something more," he said, his knees jiggling.

"Would it make you feel better to tell me?" Arthur asked blithely, although he was dying to know.

"Think so."

"I'm all ears," he said, then waited for Jeremy to speak. But instead of continuing, the young man only looked out toward the ocean, and appeared to be assessing the pervasive gray gloom beyond the railing as if it were some complex math problem.

"It's other guys," he muttered finally.

"You're worried about your feelings for other guys?" Arthur laughed. "Baby, that's the most natural thing in the world. Everyone gets attracted to people other than who they're with. It's human nature."

"I know that," he said. "But it's more than that sometimes."

"How?"

"He's not as much of a guy as I'd like, and he complains a lot." He paused. "It's like he's more *bitch* than *butch*."

"Very clever." Arthur chuckled. "Just try to remember that everyone takes the bad with the good. Nobody gets to marry their ideal—it just doesn't exist."

"I know, I know. And that's what I've been trying to tell myself, even from the beginning."

"But then you got over that pretty quickly, if I remember."

Jeremy shoved his hands in his pockets and looked at him. "But then, it's like maybe I'm not as in love with him anymore."

"And why," he asked gently, "do you think that is?"

"It's like…he wants to spend all his time with me, and sometimes I want to do things with other guys, you know? And he doesn't really have any other friends, so now it's like I'm his whole life and I'm only eighteen and he's just too needy."

Their conversation paused while a white-and-red Coast Guard helicopter roared by, sounding like something out of a war movie.

"I'm really proud of you," Arthur said at last.

"Why?"

"Because a year ago you wouldn't have had any idea what you wanted, and now you're able to voice your dissatisfaction. You're taking a risk by being honest, and it's very healthy."

"But you're not listening to me."

"Of course I am. I've heard every word you've said. I've even heard what you *haven't* said."

"Then what do I do?"

"What do you think you should do?"

He shrugged. "Don't know."

"Have you tried talking to him about how you feel?"

"Yeah. But it didn't go so well." He smiled.

"What happened?"

"We got into a fight. And then we had *the gay sex.*"

Arthur laughed at their private joke. "And your *gay sex*, it still manages to captivate the two of you?"

"Oh, yeah."

"Such is the life of a horny teenager." He laughed. "Jeremy, what you're describing is the very fabric of human relationships. There's nothing unusual about the ebb and flow of your feelings for Carlo. In fact, I'd bet that his feelings probably do the same for you, on a different scale."

"But this is different, Arthur."

He sighed. "How?"

"Because there's someone"—he paused—"I have feelings for."

Arthur's stomach fluttered. He was used to seeing Jeremy with Carlo, but could he numb himself to the idea of Jeremy in yet another man's bed? And to announce this on the eve of their departure only faded further his already diminishing vision of a smooth trip. "Have you been seeing someone?"

"Nope...kind of." He shook his head. "Sort of."

"And this someone you are or aren't seeing...you have feelings for him?"

He nodded.

"And have you told this person?"

He looked up. "Kind of."

"Oh, baby." He reached over to take his hand. "What're you gonna do?"

"Don't know," he replied. "Maybe the feelings'll go away."

"They could, or they might not. But do you think this guy feels the same way about you? That could make all the difference."

"I'm pretty sure he does," Jeremy told him with a twinkle in his eyes. "But as long as I'm with Carlo, there's no way he's gonna let anything happen between us."

"He sounds like a good guy."

A grin lit up his face. "He's the best."

"Then I'd like to meet him sometime—that is, if things work out that way."

"You'll be the first, Arthur. If things work out."

"So how're you going to make it through this trip tomorrow?"

"I'm not sure...but I'll do whatever I need to because it's so important," he said as he stood to leave. "It's funny that when I'm with Carlo, even when he bugs me it's like he's all that matters. But then when I'm alone, sometimes I can't stop thinking about him, about this other guy."

"You sound confused, old buddy."

"I am confused, Arthur. You don't know how ripped up I feel."

CHAPTER 14

Katharine had considered chartering a jet for them, but when she learned how long the plane would be detained by Brazil's customs agents while the aircraft and its passengers and crew and contents were searched, she changed her mind. It was simpler, they all agreed, and in many ways safer to take a commercial flight—in first class, of course. So their flight to Rio de Janeiro on TAM Airlines was long but uneventful, with the exception of a nearly two-hour layover in Panama City, where they explored the small, old-fashioned terminal and marveled at the foreign look of the travelers, as well as the lush, green tangle of vegetation beyond the huge glass windows. Then all were herded back into the 757 for the final leg of their trip.

Finally, at a little after five o'clock in the evening, the plane landed.

They taxied for a bit before bumping to a stop; then the pilot, in his exotic accent, welcomed them to Rio before granting them permission to disembark.

"Get me off this thing!" Carlo announced, unbuckling his seat belt. Then he stood to retrieve his carry-on from the overhead.

"I'm sleepy," remarked Jeremy as he grabbed his own bag. "How long a ride do you think it'll be to the hotel?"

"No idea," Arthur answered, "but hopefully our car is already waiting for us. We'll just play it by ear." He felt the strap of his own bag bite into his shoulder. "But we need to get through customs first, and that's never quick."

After ducking through the plane's open door, they trudged up the long gangway toward the terminal.

They found the electronic information board, checked for their flight number and its corresponding baggage carousel, then followed the signs down the long, broad concourse toward the bustling baggage claim. There they squeezed in next to the revolving contraption amidst the wild variety of people, who chattered in their unintelligible tongues on their cell phones, or to one another.

Arthur, in the meantime, had slipped into Marine mode: Like some Department of Defense automaton, he assessed the mustachioed security guards—menacing in their camouflage and sunglasses—by their posture and the position of the rifles in their hands. Then he surveyed the exits, as well as the overall condition of the terminal structure, scanned for bland-faced pickpockets or anyone else who looked the least bit sinister, while his ears strained over the hubbub for any unusual noises.

Finally, they watched their succession of suitcases tumble down the baggage chute onto the groaning conveyor. They had barely grabbed the handles of their luggage and were wheeling them toward customs when they heard a voice booming, "Tylers? Tyler party? Tylers?"

The men turned to see a lanky, ebony-colored man dragging an empty metal cart behind him. "Tylers? Tyler party?"

Jeremy started to raise his hand but Arthur stopped him. "Wait until he gets closer."

The man had nearly passed by when Arthur caught his attention. "We're the Tylers," he said softly.

"Dom Fabiano sends me," he told them in a halting baritone. "I will take you to the hotel."

"We would appreciate that," Arthur answered. "Thank you."

"I am Flavius," he said as he began stacking their bags onto the cart. "The car is waiting through here." He pointed to a double-door exit, the front of which was blocked by a soldier.

"But we need to go through customs." Arthur pointed in the other direction, to the long counters and their lines of zombie-postured travelers inching along with their cargo.

Flavius laughed. "You come," he said, and then began pulling the loaded cart. "You follow me. Please."

They trailed the man toward the twin metal doors. As they approached, passports in hand, the soldier, instead of examining their documents or even acknowledging their presence, backed into the door's push bar and swung it wide.

Moments later they were blinking against the fading brutality of Brazil's evening sun.

"Jesus, it's hot!" Jeremy wiped his forehead with the back of his hand before fixing his aviator sunglasses back onto his face.

"When we get back to the hotel we can change into shorts," Carlo suggested as they followed Flavius across the parking lot to an idling white Denali.

"Which hotel, please?" Flavius asked as he pulled open the tailgate.

"The Copacabana Palace," said Arthur as he helped him with the bags.

After they were settled into the refrigerated interior of the vehicle, the silent driver—a broad-shouldered man with a sunburned bald head—pulled into traffic.

The hotel-lined, pothole-strafed avenue running alongside the ivory sands and sparkling waters of Ipanema Beach was jumbled up with vehicles of all sorts: big, dirty buses and Vespa scooters and blue Nissan taxis with yellow tops, and smoke-spewing dirt bikes and beat-up Ford pickups and old-style Volkswagen Beetles that fought each other for holes in the traffic; while shirtless boys with skin the color of dirty pennies threaded their way through the vehicles on their rickety bicycles, and work-weary Cariocas on the teeming serpentine mosaic walkway dodged street vendors and girls in bikinis and old people hobbling and fat-assed, or fat-bellied, American tourists.

Then they rounded a curve and he saw it: high above the city, overlooking Rio's half-moon bay. *He* stood on a towering, conical rock that looked as if it had been molded by God's hands specifically for the purpose, that gargantuan Savior of Mankind with his arms outstretched, as if being measured by Titans for yet another cross; his benevolent face gazing down onto the people and the hotels and apartments and favelas of Rio de Janeiro like a figure atop a wedding cake, ready to topple onto the champagne glasses.

Something about it gave him the shivers.

"Arthur, what *is* that?" Jeremy asked, pointing to the figure.

"It's called Christ the Redeemer, or Cristo Redentor."

"Oh, my God, it's huge!" exclaimed Carlo. "Why'd they build it?"

"I honestly don't know."

"Excuse me, sirs," Flavius cut in, "but Cristo means freedom to everyone in Rio—freedom from Portugal, like he is freedom from death to the rest of the world."

"Can we go up there?" Jeremy asked.

"We're only in Rio for one night, and we need to go out to the island tomorrow at noon, so I'm not sure." Arthur paused, thinking. "But I guess we could go afterward, before we head home."

"I want to see it up close," Jeremy said.

Arthur saw the excitement on his face. "Then we'll make a point of getting up there—that is, if Carlo wants to, also."

Carlo shrugged. "Sure, it looks cool. But I've gotta find my cousin first."

The car slowed as they pulled into the portico of the Copacabana Palace, and a small army of porters swarmed them. "This looks like the kind of place my aunt would pick," Jeremy noted sourly as his door was opened by a solemn man in a blue uniform with a matching visored cap.

Indeed, the hotel did reflect Katharine's luxurious, yet somewhat predictable, taste.

Instead of resembling the sort of tropical resort they all had been anticipating—*palapa* roofs and swaying palms and meandering lagoons with thrumming waterfalls and swim-up bars—this place looked more like a Manhattan co-op with whitewashed walls and rows of windows barred over with iron filigree. And it was even worse on the inside: glimmering chandeliers and thick, dark carpets and ominously carved antiques and people so stiff they looked like mannequins. The hotel was lovely—no one would dispute that—but it looked...boring. Like the Bushes and the Cheneys might stay there.

After they checked in at the desk, they were shown to their sprawling two-bedroom suite overlooking the beach.

"So what did you boys want to do tonight?" Arthur asked as he hung his suit bag in the closet.

"Can we go out somewhere?" Carlo asked, unzipping his case. "Maybe to a gay club or something? The boys here are supposed to be amazing."

"I could go for that," Jeremy agreed. "I looked online before we left, and there were a couple of clubs not too far from this place. I hear they can get pretty crazy."

Arthur shrugged. "I'm wiped out from the flight, but if you'll give me a chance to nap, I can probably muster the energy to be your faithful bodyguard tonight."

***

By early evening, they were showered and dressed and ready to have dinner at the hotel's restaurant, but the white tablecloths and multitudes of silverware at each place setting, not to mention the white-coated servers standing stiffly at attention, scared them off. Instead, they asked the concierge—a statuesque cocoa-skinned woman with green eyes who spoke English with an intoxicating accent—where to eat and play, and she gave them articulate instructions, as well as a knowing smile.

So they made their way from inside the vaultlike walls onto the teeming evening streets of Rio, where they ambled and looked and pointed and investigated amidst the chattering, chain-smoking locals.

There they happened upon one of the many Brazilian *churrascarias* that cater to tourists, and after succumbing to the friendly encouragement of the comely hawker out front, they enjoyed a meal of various barbecued meats, along with chubby empanadas and aromatic rice and strangely seasoned vegetables and sweet fried plantains.

Together they gabbed, they ate and they soaked up their exciting surroundings.

Jeremy's eyes never stopped sparkling.

Carlo was charmingly flippant.

Arthur laughed like he hadn't in years.

It was grand.

Then with one facet of their appetites thoroughly sated, they headed off down the crowded boulevard to quell their darker, more prurient hungers.

CHAPTER 15

They passed teeming sidewalk cafés and glaringly lit storefronts and haphazardly stocked clothing shops and towering hotels.

And then, just as Arthur expected, he noticed how the buildings started looking more disheveled with each block they walked, until they came to a section that looked downright ramshackle; and instead of people looking as if they had somewhere to go, he saw more and more people just standing around. *Watching them.*

"Wallets," Arthur warned under his breath, and then spotted, with relief, their destination across the street and up half a dozen buildings.

The Popsicle blue neon sign advertising Club Torneira looked as if it had been *hizzing* through Rio's steam-drenched evenings since the 1950s. And the peeling pink plaster of the facade, along with the sight of one of its windows boarded up, heightened Arthur's watchdog senses. But according to their concierge it was a favorite of gay men—she insisted the club offered an engaging cabaret show—so he took a deep breath and yanked the filthy door handle and ushered the boys inside, where a grim, baboon-shouldered bouncer took the appropriate *dinheiro* from them.

The place was filling up; he saw there were only two tall tables still available, so he placed a hand on each of the boys' shoulders and steered them quickly across the dance floor toward the table closest to the stage. Then once they had pulled themselves up onto their stools, he took a moment to appraise the crowd, assessing how rough it was, and to see if there were any potentially dangerous characters. And although he did see a number of men, and a few women, who made him wary, most everyone in the club looked like they were there for the same reason: to be entertained.

"Dude, I haven't seen cigarette smoke this thick since my mom was alive," Jeremy remarked as he waved his hand in front of his face.

"I thought some drag queen set her weave on fire backstage," answered Carlo with a fake cough.

Arthur saw the cocktail waiter approaching. "What do you want?" he yelled, because the sounds of people *hizzing* and *juzhing* in Portuguese had risen suddenly. "I'm buying!"

"Beers!" they proclaimed in unison.

Arthur squinted suspiciously from one to the other.

"It's not my first," Jeremy confessed.

"Mine, either," Carlo added.

"Three beers, please," he told the waiter, holding up three fingers. The man returned moments later with their order of Skol Beats. Arthur handed over the money, and then they all clanked their strangely shaped bottles together.

The house lights dimmed and the crowd hushed, and then some deafening music was cued.

Over the loudspeaker, a male voice pronounced a string of complicated-sounding words; then the crowd exploded with applause.

"What did they say?" Jeremy yelled to Carlo.

"Please welcome the internationally famous performer Rosa Caveira and her exquisite lover Paolo—or something like that."

Big, sappy orchestral music blared and crackled its way through a lengthy introduction, while a white shaft from the spotlight sliced through the darkness and cigarette smoke. Then the sparkling magenta curtain lifted to reveal a woman posed dramatically on a spray-painted gold metal stool.

"Eu não sou daqui," she sang in a breathy baritone,
Marinheiro só
Eu não tenho amor
Marinheiro só.

Her posture and mannerisms communicated an almost comical degree of sadness, as well as profound, utter exhaustion.

Eu sou da Bahia
Marinheiro só
De São Salvador.

She pushed herself off her stool and steadied herself, and Arthur thought that without the stool she probably would have toppled over—she looked that drunk. He also noticed that her scarlet-sequined dress hung on her as if she'd lost weight recently and no one had yet been able to alter the waist. But her long platinum wig and makeup were flawless, and her face appeared to be both ancient and ageless at the same time, no doubt a result of multiple visits to her plastic surgeon—or maybe she employed the old duct-tape-around-the-back-of-the-head-from-ear-to-ear-under-the-wig method of rolling back the many difficult years.

He thought this was what Mae West had looked like—*lying in state.*

And then a beautiful young man, not even half her age, dressed in a tight-fitting sailor's uniform appeared from the wings and stepped slowly toward her.

She turned to him melodramatically.

Marinheiro só
O marinheiro, marinheiro
Marinheiro só
Quem to ensinou a nadar.

The accompaniment became even more swollen, and during the interlude the boy circled her appraisingly—as if, hilariously, his eyes couldn't get enough of her. He then put two cigarettes in his mouth and lit them, and after the tips were both glowing he placed one in her mouth, while the other dangled thuggishly from his plump, rosy lips.

She drew on her cigarette, then blew out a waft of smoke through the lyrics:

Marinheiro só
Foi o tombo do navio
Marinheiro só
Foi o balanço do mar
Marinheiro só
Lá vem, lá vem.

The sailor caressed her cheek before snatching the cigarette, then stomped it out on the floor along with his own.

Marinheiro só
Ele vem faceiro.

The young sailor pulled his shirt over his head to unveil his muscle-stacked, sun-kissed torso—his abs buckling and unbuckling as he gyrated to the music, his nipples as big as sliced pepperonis.

Marinheiro só
Todo de branco

Then he pulled off his pants to reveal only a sequined G-string covering his manhood. The rest of his exquisite body, to the crowd's rowdy delight, was completely and beautifully naked—except for the combat boots that went up halfway to his knees, and the white sailor's cap that tilted rakishly atop his buzzed black hair.

Marinheiro só
Com seu bonezinho
Marinheiro só

Rosa rubbed his shoulders, then kneaded his round, perfect buttocks as he buried his head in her neck. She locked her thumbs into the G-string and pulled it down his body, teasingly, until it dropped easily onto the stage between his black-booted feet.

He kicked it to the wings.

The realization that he was now completely exposed sent a crazed cheer up from the crowd, and at once the music changed from the languid torch song she'd been caterwauling to a panicked, cheesy dance beat. Rosa then went from singing the words in Portuguese to lip-synching the lyrics (badly, Arthur noted) in English, while the boy rubbed himself on her, and one hand kneaded his ass while the other fiddled with the cock that was buried, at that moment, in her sequined folds.

I am not from here
Lonely sailor
I don't have love
I am from Bahia
From São Salvador.

Suddenly the young man spun around to wag himself at the crowd, and the audience released a barrage of whistles and howls and whoops, and Rosa held his backside against her body and tugged at his cock enticingly. Arthur looked over at Jeremy and Carlo and saw they were gaped-mouthed and their eyes were huge and blood blushed their cheeks and they were sitting ramrod straight.

Oh, sailor, sailor
Who taught me to swim?
Was it the sinking of the ship?
Was it the balancing of the ocean?

The sailor jumped from the stage and made his way from table to table as the dance beat spun, and he allowed everyone he encountered to grope him and tug him and knead his ass and kiss his beautiful crimson lips.

But when he arrived at Arthur's stool he climbed up onto his lap, then grabbed his hand and pressed it flat to his chest. And Arthur laughed in spite of himself, and squeezed the hard, hot, muscled flesh, and cradled his manhood before kissing the boy's neck. Next the young man did the same to Jeremy, while virtually ignoring Carlo, and Arthur saw Jeremy grasp the bobbing penis and pinch his nipples while the dancer rubbed the fabric atop Jeremy's crotch with both hands.

Finally the dancer jumped down and bounded up onto the stage, where Rosa, standing behind him, caressed his torso with one hand and jacked him with her other, and he threw back his head and bowed his legs and ejaculated onto the filthy stage.

Here he comes, here he comes
He is happily arriving
All in white, with his little cap.

The crowd roared, and Arthur glanced at the boys and saw that Jeremy's eyes were alight, but Carlo's smile had vanished.

At once he became self-conscious and regretted what had occurred; he knew better. He should have pushed the dancer away—politely, of course. *But why?*

Because each at the table knew the other was a rabid man-lover, but Arthur and Jeremy had never *displayed* any manifestation of their shared sexuality to the other; it felt now as if they had peeked into each other's bedrooms while the other was engaged.

The music finished and the curtain dropped and the three faced one another.

"I want another beer," Jeremy announced happily, but Carlo shook his head.

"I'm kinda tired," he told him. "I went to bed really late last night and didn't sleep on the plane. And I want to get an early start tomorrow so I can find my cousin—he's up in one of those big stinky favelas we went by."

"But there's another show right now," Jeremy argued. "You can't see stuff like this back home."

"Jeremy, we do have a big day tomorrow," Arthur countered, nodding at Carlo. "I think we should probably get back. But we shouldn't walk from here, and the later it gets, the harder it is to find a cab."

"All right," Jeremy said, his voice heavy with resignation. "I've seen more tonight anyway than I thought I ever would." Then he shot Arthur a leer.

***

The cab dropped them off under the portico of the hotel, and moments later they were breathing the fresh, refrigerated air of their suite. The young men wished Arthur good night, gave him a hug, and then rushed off to their quarters so that Jeremy, in accordance with Carlo's facetious demands, could sterilize his hands. Arthur, in turn, shut himself into his own room for the night, shucked his clothes and slid between the cool, freshly pressed sheets.

Moments later it became evident that the boys were playing, and the gentle moans coming through the walls, along with the last hour's contact with the stripper's sweating muscles, made him hard—so he flipped over and buried his face in the pillow.

He heard a rap on his door, so he pulled on his jeans.

Jeremy stood with only a towel around his lower half. "Sorry." He giggled.

"Not a problem. What do you need?" He tried to hold Jeremy's eyes with his own, so his gaze wouldn't drift down that perfect torso to the tube of flesh tenting the white towel wrapped around his waist.

"Do you have any lube?" he asked, shifting his stance into an alluring *contrapposto.*

"I think I have some in my shaving kit." He opened the door wider, and Jeremy followed him. "You need condoms, too?"

"Nah," he replied, while Arthur rummaged in the bathroom. "Carlo got tested, and he's the only guy I've ever been with."

"I'm not going to lecture you about safe sex," he said, while handing him the tiny bottle, "but you know there's more than just HIV that's transmissible, right?"

"Sure," he replied dully. "So what about you, Arthur? You always safe?" He shook the small plastic container suggestively back and forth.

"Of course," he lied, remembering how much Danny had loved to fuck him bareback. But then, they had been tested and were monogamous, as well. "But it's been so long that I can hardly remember."

"Well, I'll bet you get lucky on this trip."

"I doubt it," Arthur told him. "But if I do, I'll know where I can borrow some lube. Now, go play with your boyfriend—I'm sure he's got his ankles tucked sufficiently behind his ears by now."

"Thanks, Dad," Jeremy told him, then sauntered away.

He closed his door, dropped his pants and climbed back into bed.

Dad, the word echoed inside his head.

He flipped onto his stomach and wrapped his arms around the fluff of the hotel pillow, as Jeremy's nearly naked silhouette haunted him.

Did he really want to bed him? What would he do if the situation were to come his way? He knew he would never pursue him; his years in the Marines had trained him to do without, to deny his urges and to appraise quickly any crisis, then respond accordingly—with equal consideration given to both the short and the long run.

I'll never again allow myself to imagine making love with that boy.

Instead, he pictured Jeremy in bed with him. Spooning. The heat of his back against his chest. His velvet buttocks against his cock, and the backs of his legs welded to his knees. He'd rest his chin in the crook of his neck and throw his protective arms around his shoulders and sleep.

He smiled into his pillow; then his lips kissed cotton.

CHAPTER 16

"Mr. Tyler?"

"Mr. Blauefee...this is," he murmured drowsily into the phone.

"Your car, she awaits for you downstairs, please."

"Thank you," he replied, hung up, and then looked at his watch.

Shit! He'd forgotten to order a wake-up call.

Less than half an hour later they stepped from the lobby out into the oppressive morning heat of the hotel's portico, where they saw the barrel-chested, bald-headed driver from the day before, smoking and chatting into his cell phone as he leaned against the white Denali. The man's head jerked upward as they drew near; then he stamped out his cigarette and clipped shut his phone, while Arthur and Jeremy and Carlo, looking like out-of-uniform flight attendants, rolled their bags over to the idling vehicle. Moments later, with their luggage stored behind the seats and their armpits and faces moist even from that mild exertion, they strapped themselves into the backseat as the behemoth lurched away from the curb.

"Do you think we still have time to find Afonso?" Carlo asked Arthur. "The map I checked made it look like the favela Dona Marta is on our way to the airport."

"Why don't you ask your man?" Arthur suggested. "He's the tour director."

Jeremy shook his head, keeping his eyes focused out the window. "We're supposed to be at the airport by now," he said. "Sorry, but we got started too late."

Carlo's face reddened and his eyes narrowed. "But you promised me, Jeremy. You know how important this is to me—and it's not like we're taking a jetBlue flight. It's a *private plane*, so it'll leave when we get there."

"Oh, now you're going to keep a private jet waiting for us?" Jeremy asked with a sneer. "We'll find him when we get back. And *you* know how important this is to *me*."

"But Afonso's sick," Carlo pleaded. "What if something happens to him between now and then?"

"A few days won't matter. It's just gonna have to wait until we get back."

Carlo bit his lip and, with his arms crossed, looked out the window.

The driver snickered something under his breath in Portuguese.

"*Cale a boca e dirija*," Carlo told him crossly. And with that, none of the men made any more conversation for the remainder of their bumpy, frantic ride.

***

After being ushered through one of the airport's unmarked entrance gates, they rolled onto the tarmac toward the section that served as a parking lot for dozens of private aircraft. There the driver steered them down one row and up another, until hurtling finally toward a waiting Gulfstream III with its twin engines, like giant white lipstick tubes, sending heat shimmers above the outstretched, bent-tipped wings.

They stopped and unloaded; then, as they made their way toward the plane, the single clamshell door opened and extended tonguelike onto the tarmac. A slight, silver-haired man in a gray suit waved from inside the doorway, so Arthur raised his hand in reply.

After they'd pulled themselves and their bags up the stairs, the elegant man, who introduced himself as Mauricio, showed them to their seats—a narrow leather sofa paralleled by puffy leather loungers the color of marshmallows—where they sat down and snapped together their lap belts.

"This is so cool," Jeremy remarked as he ran his hands along a section of the glossy olive burl that ran the length of the plane's interior, and adjusted his chair's air-conditioning vents at his face. "I can't believe we're actually on a private plane."

"I thought I was about to get a cavity filled," Carlo noted sourly, pushing his lounger back into a reclining position. "I just hope the dentist washed his hands."

Jeremy snapped his head toward him. "Why do you have to say things like that all the time?"

Carlo raised an eyebrow. "You don't like me talking about dentists?"

Jeremy glowered. "You know what I'm talking about. Why can't you just appreciate where we are, instead of being so bitchy? It's not like you're ever going to do something like this for me."

"I'm just joking." Carlo's eyes rolled skyward and his lip curled. "What's wrong with you?"

"If you're pissed off at me, then just say it."

"OK." He leveled his gaze at him. "I'm pissed off at you. *Really* pissed off."

"About Afonso?"

"No, because I wanted the *pink* plane," he replied smartly. "Of course I'm pissed about Afonso! You promised me, Jeremy. You said that if I came along to help interpret, you'd help me find him. *Today.* Like we discussed."

"And we will, just not *today.*"

"Guys," Arthur broke in, and then did a head toss in the direction of Mauricio, who was sidling down the aisle toward them.

"You should've just gotten on this thing without me, so I could've found him," Carlo muttered.

"It's not too late for you to get off," Jeremy growled.

Mauricio drew up next to Arthur. "You have had breakfast, sirs?"

They all shook their heads.

"Omelets," he began, obliviously. "I buy them from Rio's best restaurant only an hour ago, sausage and cheese and almonds. And fresh bread. I will get them for you when we get into the air." He turned and marched off to double-check and shake and twist the handle of the exit door. After he was satisfied, apparently, that they weren't all going to be sucked out into a twenty-thousand-foot free fall, he disappeared into the galley as the whistling engines drew up an octave and the plane began speeding down the runway.

Carlo unbuckled his seat belt. "Is it too late to get off this fucking thing?"

"Shut up and sit down," Jeremy barked. "It's moving, in case you couldn't tell."

"Fuck you," Carlo replied. Then he buckled himself into his seat.

Moments later the nose of the aircraft tipped skyward. As they felt the landing gear tuck itself inside the belly of the plane, Arthur watched through his oval window as first some high-rise buildings, then the sand-ridged, cobalt bay of Rio de Janeiro tilted and shrank beneath them.

Because Jeremy and Carlo were still not speaking, he decided it was time to intervene. "Hey," he said, tapping on the glass, "they actually have cable cars going out to Sugarloaf. When we get back, you want to see that, too?"

Carlo looked over to peer through his window. "Yeah, sure. Maybe we'll get lucky and one of the cables'll snap."

"You're not making things better," Jeremy grumbled.

"Since we seem to be on such a *tight schedule*," Carlo began, shooting Jeremy a sneer, "I guess I'll just settle for seeing that King Kong Jesus statue. Do you know how you get up there?"

"I saw online that you can take these old red trams up to it," Arthur told him. "Or maybe they even let cabs go up there, too."

Just then, Mauricio appeared pushing a petite, chinkling cart laden with covered plates and pastries and coffee service. "Excuse me, sirs," he interrupted, "but if you want to see El Cristo, you must only ask Dom Fabiano. He can send you with the driver at night for a private tour; it is most amazing after sundown, then when everyone else has gone home."

Arthur was surprised. "They let private tours go up there?"

"For Dom Fabiano, they allow anything," he answered. "Look down there; El Cristo is already telling you to come back."

The three looked through their individual windows to see the enormous statue, glorious in the clear, full-day Brazilian sun, with its arms extended beseechingly.

"So what about this cousin of yours?" Arthur asked Carlo, while pouring himself some coffee. He'd decided, at this point, to ignore the fuming Jeremy.

Carlo grabbed a croissant and bit off half. "I only met him once, when I was a kid," he mumbled, then chewed and swallowed. "He was really nice to me, and he wasn't anything like my dad—I do remember that. He's gay, and he's sick, but I'm not sure with what. And I guess he'd be about your age now."

"And somehow, Carlo thinks we can help him," Jeremy added, cutting into his omelet.

"Help him with what?"

"Just give him some money so he can see a good doctor, if they have any down here," Carlo replied. "I don't have much money, but my wonderful boyfriend's *promised* me he'll do whatever he can."

Jeremy, looking completely exasperated, threw down his fork. "Look, I'm sorry. I promise the second we get back we can look for him…in three days, that's all I'm asking for. We'll be back in Rio in three days."

"*Really?*"

"I promise."

Carlo picked up his croissant, stuffed the remainder into his mouth, took his time chewing, and then swallowed. "Okay," he said with a satisfied smile.

"I think between the three of us we can find some way to help him," Arthur added. "We'll just take this adventure one step at a time." Then he pushed his recliner back and tried to enjoy the flight.

The jet was flying over open water, with the coast of Brazil now only a low strip of dirty emerald on the eastern horizon; there was no turbulence, and the strong, reassuring whine of the engines was soothing. Out his window he saw, even from their altitude, Curaçao blue waters so perfectly glasslike that even the ragged coral reefs—like submerged continents and archipelagos—were clearly defined against the ocean's sandy bottom. He even spotted an immense school of silvery fish under the plane's trajectory, as fluid and reflective as a billowing cloud of mercury beneath the surface, shifting and turning in on itself as some dolphins raced in. Then, far out toward the horizon, he noticed a loaf of clouds with billowy tops and flattened bottoms suspended low in the azure sky, their tips frosted vermillion.

It really was beautiful.

The plane banked gently and what appeared to be their destination drifted into view, looking like the oversized glossy photographs from the architect's conference room. As they drew nearer and the plane began its descent and the island grew bigger, Arthur began making out the details of the place: its crust of ivory sand and its broccoli-colored slopes, its shaggy, waving palm trees and its wrinkling, crescent bay. But the most startling feature of the island was the tremendous dung-colored monolith, like an immense granite breast that thrust up from the island's heart—as if from Yemanji herself.

The island, and its surrounding sapphire bath, was breathtaking and dazzling and unlike anything he'd ever seen before.

It was Hawai'i—as seen through the bewitched, doomed eyes of Captain Cook.

He tore his gaze from the window and saw that Jeremy was grinning at the glass, his dark eyes wide and his back ramrod straight.

"Oh, my God, Arthur, it's so beautiful!" he said. "Don't you think so, Carlo?"

Carlo nodded. "It's gorgeous, baby."

The plane banked more sharply, and they curved around to the other side of the island, where the resort emerged from the jungle. Arthur spotted the half-glassed skeleton of a modernist tower underneath a towering crane to the right, and next to that what appeared to be a meandering Spanish colonial town under construction, while at the farthest curve of the island a sprawling Tahitian village stood, with *palapa* roofs and an empty concrete lagoon rimmed with boulders. It looked exactly like the scale model from the architect's office, only halfway completed.

It's legitimate.

Arthur relaxed.

Mauricio's courteous voice suggested, over the intercom, that they prepare for landing.

The moment they belted themselves in, the plane dropped, then banked steeply as it began sinking toward the ground.

"It's prettier than I thought it would be," Jeremy announced, with his face pressed to the glass. "And it's so cool that we can come here whenever we want."

"With our kids!" Carlo added.

The aircraft leveled its turn and began its final descent.

Moments later, after the wheels barked on the tarmac, Arthur saw him through the window; standing next to a white Lincoln Navigator was one of the tallest men he had ever seen, with the tropical breeze throttling his immaculate white suit and the noontime sunlight glinting off his bald head.

El Gigante.

CHAPTER 17

Welcome, my friends, to Ihla Diabo," bellowed the man in a baritone that suggested the lowest tones from an upright bass. "You must be Jeremy."

"Great meeting you," he replied, while presenting his hand. "This is my family's adviser, Arthur Blauefee, and my partner, Carlo Martinez."

They stepped forward to shake hands, but he pulled them into a quick embrace, while kissing each man on the right, then the left cheek. "You Americans are so formal!" he told them, laughing. "Here in Brazil, we are all one family. You must be exhausted from your trip. I'm anxious to show you the progress we've made on our most fabulous resort, but only after I've seen to your comfort; we have the most delicious lunch waiting for you. Come!"

They followed him across the baked, shimmering blacktop to the Navigator, and had barely pulled the doors closed when he gunned the engine and began racing down the runway past the taxiing Gulfstream.

While the man blabbered at Jeremy in the front seat, Arthur watched the two-lane road as it cut through the jungle, then emerged as a black ribbon curling along the lovely waterfront—with waves like rolling mounds of turquoise glass that melted into the sand, or shattered themselves upon the massive, craggy boulders. But the feature that captivated him most, as it drew closer, was that immense rock sitting in the center of the island; clearly the same forces that left Corcovado and Sugarloaf thrusting skyward from Rio's bay had molded a similar anomaly here.

"Excuse me, Dom Fabiano, but how did that weird mountain form?" asked Carlo, as if he had read Arthur's mind.

"It is the heart of the mountain pushed up from Earth's belly millions of years ago," he answered as some low buildings with *palapa* roofs swung into view. "Her cloak of dirt has washed away, so only this magnificence of granite is left. But the old Yoruba say she is the work of the *orixás*, and I like this explanation. Don't you?"

"I'm sorry, but I don't know what an *orixá* is," Arthur confessed.

"They were the gods of the Yoruba, who were the unfortunate souls brought here as slaves from Africa; their presence can be felt all over Brazil, but is still especially strong on these islands."

"Is that the voodoo stuff," Carlo asked, "where they kill chickens and make zombies?"

The man laughed. "The chicken sacrifices are associated with Santeria, my friend. And although there is some Santeria here in Brazil, most is in Cuba—so I'm afraid you won't be finding many zombies here."

The Navigator slowed for an exit from the main road that curved to the left, between a pair of carved, life-sized figures that flanked the entrance to the first resort. "We found those old *orixá* statues"—he waved his finger back and forth at the windshield—"on the other side of the island; the one on the left with the pitchfork is Exu the Trickster, and he on the right is Ogum the Protector. They hate each other, so it is considered good luck to place them in pairs—they keep each other very busy."

The road continued through some heavy tropical growth to circle around the back of the resort, where the glass-walled, shaggy-roofed reception lobby came into view. "We didn't want any part of the beach view obscured by roads or vehicles, so the entrance to each resort is on the mountain side of the island," he explained. "And you'll notice there are no gates, except in the most exclusive part of Brasiliana. We want our guests to be free to explore the island, in the same way they might have visited different areas of the globe before this...*political uncertainty* changed everything."

As he pulled the Navigator underneath the portico, a pair of young, white-suited attendants rushed to greet them. "I am sorry we have no staff yet," the man apologized, "so I brought two from my own household."

The young men who approached were startlingly handsome twins, whose smiles were as dazzling as they were suggestive.

Likes 'em young, Arthur noted.

Upon disembarking, the group followed Fabiano through the empty lobby to a large poolside table artfully set with white linens, crystal glassware, ornate silver cutlery and plentiful orchids—both in vases and scattered around the table. They sat, and then a procession, by way of the young servants, of fruit, breads, salads and barbecued meats was brought to them, along with a pitcher of bloodred sangria with sliced oranges drifting inside.

In the meantime, Arthur looked around.

This resort looked to be about halfway finished, with the walls and roofs of the guest huts assembled, and the dozen-or-so-story hotel tower had most of its windows installed. The pool next to their table—with its infinity edge and soon-to-be-submerged boulders—was just now filling with water, but the landscape around the intricate man-made lagoon, with its canals and bridges and islandlike dining cabanas, was bare. In spite of this, he could see that everything appeared first-rate: the faux-organic design, the generous proportions, the gracious sightlines, the sturdy construction, the professional execution and especially the setting—it was breezy and sunny and captivating and peaceful.

Clearly the Tylers had another moneymaker on their hands, as long as the necessary details were attended to; the foremost of which, beyond aesthetics, was this eyebrow-raising claim of "guaranteed security."

"Where are the workers?" Jeremy asked, while digging into his berry-topped chicken salad. "I don't see anybody or hear anything."

"They've been given these days off, in consideration of your arrival," Dom Fabiano answered. Then he retrieved a crimson Dunhill cigarette pack from his breast pocket. "They've been working night and day for months, but my wish is to have you appreciate the tranquil mood of our island without the pounding and the drilling and the sawing of the construction workers and their *boom-boom-boom!*" He rubbed his temples for effect, then sparked the end of his cigarette with a golden lighter.

"Where do they live, while they're here?" Arthur asked, stabbing a fork into his own salad.

"In the tower," he answered. He pointed, and they all turned to look. "Many of the units are finished, and enough of the infrastructure has been completed so the island is livable; we are only still waiting for cell phone service, which was to have been installed weeks ago but has not." He sucked in a heavy drag and then blew out a white ghost of smoke. "You will be able to stay with us over the next week in Brasiliana, where we put the final touches on your apartment just this morning."

Carlo looked beseechingly at Jeremy. "We're going to stay here for a *week*?"

Fabiano laughed. "Of course! You must see the colors of the sunset, then hear the singing of the birds in the morning with the sunrise. You need to spend peaceful time here to 'unwind,' as you Americans say."

"But what about Afonso?"

Jeremy touched Carlo's hand. "It'll just have to wait."

"*But...you...promised*," he hissed.

"Excuse me," Fabiano cut in, "but is there anything I might help with?"

Carlo looked away. "We just had some *unimportant* plans, that's all."

Fabiano smiled. "Please, you've come such a long way. If there is anything I might do for you, I should be insulted if you did not ask."

"We're good, thanks," Jeremy answered, as Carlo sank fuming into his chair.

All except Carlo ate voraciously while going over the details of the resort; they discussed the conference centers—one large and one small—that would accommodate corporate meetings and special events; and the casinos, which were designed to rival the best of Las Vegas and Monte Carlo.

"Dom Fabiano," Arthur asked, "why is this venture privately financed?"

The man smirked. "Are you wondering why more of your American corporations are not here, with their infinite financial resources and sterile aesthetics?" He closed his eyes and nodded. "It's very simple: We have the funding of a private consortium to be free from your country's endless rules and heavy risks of litigation. And if we had waited for approval from any of the famous resort corporations, we would still be looking at an empty island, instead of what you see now." He leveled his gaze at Jeremy. "Mr. Mortson, your uncle was a brilliant businessman, in spite of what I understand to be significant deficiencies of character. His savvy reputation, as well as his sizable contribution, was the only factor that convinced some of the other investors to participate."

"So who are the other investors?" Arthur asked.

Dom Fabiano took a sip of his sangria, then drew heavily on his cigarette. "You may examine our prospectus for more detailed information whenever you wish. But I can tell you that we have two banking families from Italy, a sheik from Dubai...one man with large holdings in a British defense contracting company, and an old, very famous family from Mexico with experience in resort building and construction. And of course the Brazilian family, mine, who owns this beautiful island. But we needed the Tylers for their generous capital, as well as their ability to supply us with computer hardware and software; these are now as important as the beds and the pillows and the fluffy, fluffy towels in a five-star resort." He laughed but then began to cough deeply, as if his lungs were filled with mayonnaise. Then he cleared his throat. "When it is finished, this island will look still as if it was formed by the *orixá*'s hands, but it will be wired like your Pentagon: card-reader and hand-geometry technologies, long-range photoelectric detectors, cameras, monitors, activators, radar, night vision, motion sensors...everything to make our beloved guests *absolutely safe.*"

Arthur leaned back in his chair as Jeremy and Carlo did the same.

"Are we finished with business questions for now?" Dom Fabiano asked.

His three guests nodded.

"Then we must see you to your quarters. After you rest you will join me at my suite for cocktails and dinner; my residence is in the same complex as yours, but I will send one of my *meninos* to show you the way. And since you are now finished with your meal, we can see more of the resort on the way to your suites; I cannot wait for you to experience all that we offer."

***

They followed their wildly gesticulating host through the meandering paths and lush vegetation of Amazonia, then trudged onward to Espanha, where the winding cobblestone streets and the villas with peeling plaster, red-tiled roofs, wrought-iron window grates, and cheerful red geraniums emulated a sleepy Mediterranean fishing village. Finally, they rounded a curve at the end of Espanha's waterfront, passed through a pair of open gates, and found themselves gazing at the minimalist, midcentury grandeur of Brasiliana.

Arthur was spellbound.

It reminded him of the Brasilia he had learned about in sixth grade, when the public school social studies books touted it as the world's first master-planned city, a jet-age utopia designed to uplift and edify the unwashed masses. His fascination with the place stayed with him through the years, and it was still his dream to walk between those amazing concrete monoliths—the National Congress building with its twin towers and flip-flopped bowls, and the jet-turbine-inspired National Cathedral—of Brazil's fantastic inland capital.

But this was even better. More...*posh*.

Instead of the overscaled, imposing structures Niemeyer had designed, this part of the island, which extended along the most savage topography of the eastern beachfront, out to the superyacht-capable marina, looked intimate. *Yet luxurious.* And it had been designed with Brasilia's same ethos: horizontal, unadorned structures with white concrete walls interspersed with reflective plate glass, turquoise reflecting pools with mushrooming shafts of water, and sweeping colonnades that framed views, covered pathways, and bordered cliffs.

He looked at Jeremy and saw that he was grinning.

"Where's the line for Space Mountain?" Carlo asked dryly.

"I think it's cool," Jeremy replied. Then he turned to Fabiano. "How many times a year can we come here?"

Fabiano laughed as he pulled another Dunhill out of its pack. "This is no cheap time-share, my friend. You own a significant part of this paradise, so you and your companions are welcome here anytime you wish." He pushed the cigarette between his lips, then lit the end. "Now let us continue to your suites so that you might rest before dinner; we must all be at our best, so that we might come to know each other more intimately tonight."

CHAPTER 18

With one scan of the suite, Arthur determined that every detail had been executed in perfect taste: islands of fuzzy white shag floated atop eggshell terrazzo; ivory leather Barcelona chairs faced a simple, low-backed sectional; and a rectangular glass van der Rohe dining table, flanked by white leather Brno chairs, took center stage in front of the generous sliding doors. The lighting was restricted to simple halogen spots, with the exception of twin hanging cigar lamps in two of the corners, and each white wall served as a perfect backdrop for the exceptional reproductions of Franz Kline's black-and-white abstracts from the 1950s. The pairing of such stark, sleek quarters with the cerulean sky, turquoise bay and jagged, rocky coastline was stunning; it felt as international as it was classically chic—an environment suited perfectly to martini-fueled evenings filled with off-key samba, intense conversation and giddy laughter.

He loved it.

The boys had decided on the east bedroom because it overlooked the suite's infinity-edged pool, and Jeremy wanted to swim laps. So Arthur dropped his bag on the walnut credenza in the other bedroom, which lay, to his delight, at the gnarled base of the immense *orixá*'s rock.

Hot bath would be great.

He stepped into the bathroom, with its white marble floors—like huge slabs of petrified blue cheese—and floor-to-ceiling windows. He was ready for a relaxing bath, but after he had shed his clothes, he stood before the full-length mirror to examine his physique, and the sunlit nakedness that met his eyes unsettled him.

His eyes looked baggy and crow stepped, and more salt was visible now in his hair's usual quantity of pepper. He tried a smile, but this only revealed teeth that wanted bleaching. So he stood straighter and glowered at himself; then he clenched his stomach and saw that two cans of his usually visible six-pack had been swiped. Deflated, he reached over and turned on the shower, soaped his body and then rinsed off hastily.

After drying himself, he threw the towel on the floor, then flopped down onto the bed.

He was just tired; that was all. A good nap now and a solid night's sleep tonight would restore him to his usual self.

With the back of his head sinking into the pillow and the familiar, rhythmic *fah-boom* of the waves outside filling his head, he began to stop worrying about their safety. Instead, he pondered what this resort would mean for Jeremy in the long run; certainly, at eighteen, being involved in an international venture like this was a tremendous challenge. But after practically raising himself, he was more mature already than most adults Arthur had known; he was able to prioritize needs versus wants and dreams versus reality, and to make unemotional decisions—sometimes to the point of stoic blandness.

And he had so much going for him: He looked like a young Hollywood actor, he could be as charming as he was lovely to watch, and he had a lightning-quick, steady intellect. After he had received a proper education, Katharine's money would propel him to heights few in this world ever have the opportunity to gaze down from. He would, essentially, be Cristo on top of Corcovado—with the world worshipping at his feet.

There probably won't be room for me then, but that's OK.

The sea air caressing his naked flesh began to arouse him, so he flipped onto his front and buried his nose in the unfamiliar scent of the crisp pillowcase. He didn't feel like satisfying himself at the moment; he was just too tired. And he was afraid his conscience couldn't take the abuse another forbidden fantasy might invoke, especially under the circumstances of their present housing arrangement.

So he tried thinking of something else—his paltry bank account, improving his morning workout, how soon after they got back before he'd have to see his mother again—but his thoughts boomeranged right back to Jeremy.

The boy loved him; he knew that. And he loved him, too—more than anyone on this earth would ever know. And although he was now the American equivalent of pampered royalty, Arthur had noticed that ever since Bill's death, there had been...a change in Jeremy—in his demeanor, in his walk, even in the timbre of his voice. For young Jeremy Tyler had killed a man, his own uncle with his own hands, and it *showed* on him.

Not so much that anyone else might notice, but Arthur did—he'd seen that same look on some of the older Marines he'd known from the first Gulf War.

You could see it in their eyes.

A coldness.

That was the only way he could describe it.

Or maybe it was more of…*a distance,* as clear as the inch between God's and Adam's fingers on that amazing ceiling.

He wondered if Carlo felt it, as well.

Maybe he should ask him.

Nope, that was a little too personal.

He sighed. And then he wished he could…just *hold* him.

Protect him. Bring back that carefree high school boy he was just getting to know and to enjoy being around, instead of the ersatz prince Katharine was always putting though plan check.

So he decided to resurrect him; once they were through with this trip, they'd go home and lie around the pool together or play catch on the sand or go have coffee or maybe just sit and watch TV. He would make mac 'n' cheese, just like that first night when Jeremy came home from Fresno. And maybe he could finally show him *It's a Mad, Mad, Mad, Mad World*, his favorite movie of all time.

They'd laugh a lot, especially at Ethel Merman's braying.

And Dick Shawn's dancing.

And Jerry Lewis's goofy expression as he ran over Spencer Tracy's hat.

Just the two of them, laughing.

Once this was over.

My old buddy and me.

And with that thought in his head and a smile on his lips, Arthur drifted off—as the shadow from the mountain towering over his bedroom deepened and stretched.

CHAPTER 19

The afternoon breeze had recently announced the arrival of evening by its change from onshore to off, but there were no waves on the shoreline below; instead, the water slid smoothly onto the sand, and a pair of anchored boats bobbed lethargically in the bay, prows parallel, as if watching the sunset together.

Fabiano's compound was built into an immense, cantilevered ledge of granite that gave the impression that it defied gravity. And it was remarkable: a main house of generous, horizontal proportions flanked by reflecting pools and twin neo-Grecian colonnades that extended each side of the house like wings, and beyond that a patio that levitated dangerously over a sheer drop of perhaps a thousand feet or more to a grove of thrusting, jagged rocks. Arthur thought the environment to have been inspired by the lair of some James Bond villain, or taken from the pages of *Architectural Digest*, circa 1968. Either way, it was as dynamically picturesque as it was subtly disconcerting.

He sat at the round glass table opposite Jeremy, while Carlo faced Dom Fabiano. Their servers—that same pair of stunning twins from this morning, with skin the color of singed mahogany—attended to them. Arthur found them quite breathtaking in their unbuttoned white shirts and loose linen slacks and bare feet; up close now he noticed that each had iridescent green eyes that flashed mysteriously from a handsome, sun-bronzed face.

"Many Brazilians, because of the old Yoruban influence, still believe we are dominated by one of their *orixás*," Fabiano explained. "On these they blame their erratic behavior or poor decisions, instead of just their own laziness or stupidity."

"So are all of their gods supposed to be evil?" Jeremy asked before popping a forkful of barbecued meat into his mouth.

The big man laughed. "No, even Exu isn't all bad. But he does get blamed for everything from infidelity and murder to kidnappings and even drug overdoses. By the way, you must try the *bolinhos de bacalhau*," he suggested, then snapped his fingers at one of the young men, who trotted over to the buffet to retrieve the steaming bowl.

"What's that?" Jeremy whispered to Carlo.

"Just fish and potatoes," he replied. "My *avó* used to make it for us on Fridays during Lent. It's good." He snatched the ladle from the tureen and helped himself. "And could I please get some more *pao de oueijo?*" he asked one of the servers.

The other youth nodded, and padded over to retrieve from the buffet a basket stacked with cheese bread.

"What about that other god you mentioned?" asked Arthur as he took the ladle from Carlo. "I can't remember his name."

"And which *orixá* might that be?" Fabiano replied, cutting into his steak.

"I don't know." He raised his glass for another sip of the delicious sangria. "But you said something about him being the protector."

"Of course. You're referring to Ogum."

"Ogum." Arthur tried the pronunciation.

"He is also known as Ogun or Ogoun or Ogou. And as far as I'm concerned, as the god of protection, he is also the god of fools."

"Why?" asked Carlo, his mouth stuffed with bread.

Fabiano put down his fork and looked at him with a sanguine smile. "Because what is meant to happen is going to happen, my friends. It's that simple. You have no idea how many souls waste their time and precious resources praying to gods who simply do not exist, and then these same people"—he snickered—"are surprised when they burn alive in ramshackle buildings or have some street criminal put a bullet through their eye. It would make as much sense for me to pray to this fork for protection"—he grasped his eating utensil and held it in the air—"as it would for me to pray to Ogum."

"But what about Exu?" Arthur asked slyly. "He's supposed to provide strife to the Brazilians, and there sure seems to be a lot of that around."

"A valid point, my friend." He nodded while withdrawing his Dunhill pack from his breast pocket. "But then, what might be the point of praying to someone who only means to do you harm? Would you then be asking for mercy? If so, Exu would only laugh at you and torture you more."

Arthur shrugged. "I don't think I'd be praying to anyone for anything. I was raised Catholic, and the church angered me so much that I really don't believe in God or prayers anymore."

"Not any of it?" Fabiano asked.

He shrugged. "Nope, not any of it."

Fabiano's eyes narrowed. "So when your lover—I believe his name was Danny—died in the horror of that day in New York, you said not one prayer for him?"

Arthur shot him a fierce glare. "How do you know about that?"

Fabiano lit his cigarette, drew in his cheeks, then blew out his words in vaporous puffs. "Mr. Mortson told me the circumstances of your coming into his household; of course he knew nothing at the time of your working for the FBI, at least that he shared with me. But it was crass of me to have brought the matter into our dinner conversation in such a manner. Won't you please forgive me?" Without waiting for an answer, he snapped his fingers at the nearest boy. "The *moqueca de camarao* should be excellent; it is one of my chef's specialties," he announced brightly. "The mingling of shrimp and coconut, with the garlic and olive oil, makes a flavor that always surprises me—it is a specialty of Bahia."

Arthur was shaken, and he felt his appetite shrink as his anger grew. "How much do you know about all of us, Dom Fabiano?" he asked quietly, then sipped from his glass. "Or should I say, El Gigante?"

Fabiano narrowed his eyes. "So you know my little nickname?" He laughed. "I'm afraid it's followed me since I was a child, for my given name is Elegbara; but then my cruel father called me Elegante for my fastidious, and some would say feminine, ways." He turned to Jeremy. "But as I grew into a man, my considerable height...and enviable *size* resulted in this more primitive title, which I've come to embrace." He cocked an eyebrow salaciously and threw a suggestive glance at the young man. "As for you, my dear guests, I know little about your lives, except for what concerns my business." He pulled heavily on his cigarette again. "You might think me presumptuous to have gathered information about you, but I—like you—have learned to be suspicious of others, especially where great sums of my money are concerned." He nodded. "Wise men always examine their potential friends, just as we would be foolhardy not to scrutinize our enemies; this is the very foundation of the business of security, in which we are all engaged, like it or not. Because each person must be viewed as a potential threat, not to assume this posture, in these dangerous times, is pure foolishness. It would be like the four of us sitting here praying to Ogum to keep our guests safe," he chuckled, "instead of engaging the best security measures that technology has to offer, and our money has to buy." He turned his attention to Arthur. "Mortson also told me that you had a failed career as a soldier before being hired as the Tylers' housemaid."

Arthur laughed sourly before downing more of his sangria, which tasted better with each sip. "He told you that because he was too big of an idiot to figure out I was working for the FBI."

Fabiano ignored him and turned to Jeremy. "My dear young man, what I know about you is that your uncle murdered your father and was thought to have murdered your mother as well. And so you, in turn, killed him—in self-defense, of course. I also know that your mother had certain...issues, and that she raised you in abject poverty. But your lovely great aunt, Katharine Tyler, has rectified this."

Jeremy nodded. "Yeah, that's pretty much it."

"What about me?" Carlo asked, not wanting to be left out.

Fabiano reached over and touched him gently on the wrist. "All I know about you, my handsome young friend, is that you have suffered sadness in your life, but now you have the joy of loving your *amante* with all your heart."

"Who told you that?" Carlo asked him, smiling shyly.

He chuckled. "No one told me. It's what I see with my eyes." He turned to Jeremy again. "And you? Do you believe in prayers?"

"I don't think any of it matters, to be honest."

The big man grinned as he exhaled yet another smoky drag. "So then you are the pragmatist of your group," he said, and then paused in thought for a moment. "Please excuse the forward nature of this question, but would it be fair to assume that because you have *so* many wonderful possessions, and *so* much personal beauty as well as *so* much love from these men," he said as he reached over and squeezed Jeremy's hand, "that you have no need to ask the gods for anything? That you, unlike the rest of the mere mortals sitting at this table, have already received from heaven *everything* it has to offer?"

Jeremy shifted in his chair. "I guess you could say that, if you wanted." He shot Arthur an uncomfortable grin, and Arthur returned his glance so he might see the cold fury in his eyes.

"Please tell me how you find our little island so far," Fabiano told the group obliviously, signaling for more sangria to be poured. Then he glanced over at Arthur's plate and saw he'd hardly touched his meal. "By the way, if you do not care for the fish or the shrimp, we have the *frango ao vinho*—chicken with a red wine sauce."

"No thanks, I've had quite enough," Arthur replied curtly, leaning back in his chair.

"It's beautiful," Jeremy answered. "And it's a lot bigger than I'd pictured."

"And the resorts?" Fabiano asked after taking a dainty sip from his crystal glass.

Jeremy said nothing, so Arthur spoke up. "First-rate," he noted blandly.

The man nodded his huge head and grinned. "It pleases me to hear that. So many Americans think those monstrosities in Las Vegas are the pinnacle of luxury and taste, but most have no understanding of what a five-star resort should feel and look and even smell like. And this will be a five-star, when finished, although more on the intimate scale of Europe's finest boutique hotels."

"Clearly," Arthur muttered.

"And what about you, young man?" Fabiano asked Carlo. "Does this place agree with you?"

Carlo smiled, nodding. "I can't wait to come back when it's finished," he said. "Especially to the beaches. I love to lay out."

"Then you'll absolutely adore the beaches here. We will have two shorefront retreats on the other side of the island; one in the American style, with a buffet-style restaurant and private cabanas, and the other in the European style."

"What's the difference?" Jeremy asked.

"The European beaches, with their sidewalk cafés and simple umbrellas and lounges, allow nudity—where the young and the old are able to truly enjoy the sun side by side. Europeans are much less... judgmental about their bodies. So that's what we will offer here: a beach without judgment."

"How are people going to get there if they're on the other side of the island?" Arthur asked. "Are you gonna build another road and take 'em in buses?

"We will have vessels to ferry them, as well as private boats equipped with GPS; these will take you there via touch screen."

"All you'll have to do is set a nav system?" Jeremy asked, amazed.

"Yes. It will be as if each watercraft has its own invisible captain. You may go from port to port, or from beach to beach, or even around the island twenty times if it pleases you. We have contracted with a German company who makes such watercraft for tours on the Rhine. But enough about this; you will see the rest of the island tomorrow." He ground the butt of his cigarette into his dinner dish, just before one of the young men snatched it from the table. "Young Carlo, I understand your family is from Brazil?"

"Just on my mom's side. My dad's family is from California, way back when it was still part of Mexico," he replied proudly.

"And you know the Portuguese language?"

"*Eu entendo mais do que posso falar,*" Carlo told him

"Spoken like a perfect native!" Fabiano remarked with a clap of his hands. "So you must still have family here?"

"Only a cousin, at least that I know of."

"And where is he now?"

"In the favela Dona Marta. In Rio."

Fabiano grimaced. "I know of that place, but not very well. Please tell me you have asked him to come along to the island, as our guest."

He shook his head. "He's not well. So we're going to try and find him in the favela on our way home and see if we can help him. We've got an address, but we don't have any phone number."

He frowned. "No, no, no. You must not go there by yourselves; it is very dangerous. I will send you with some of my men; you will find him and bring him here for the remainder of your stay with us. For some rest…or is he in such ill health that he needs to be in a hospital?"

"Not that I know of. I think someone would've contacted my family if he was."

"You will go tomorrow," he announced.

Carlo exchanged puzzled glances with Jeremy.

"But we just got here," Jeremy protested.

"And we've still got so much to see here," Arthur added. "The hotels, the conference center and the theaters, and the other side of the island."

"Of course you need to finish your tour," Fabiano told the group. "So tomorrow morning, while we continue your inspection, with your permission I will send Carlo on our jet to Rio with two of my best men."

He turned to him. "If you choose to go, you could not be in better hands—these men are former guards to the president of Uruguay. They will assist you in finding your cousin, and after you locate him you will tell him you have a generous friend who offers him medical care, as well as possible employment here at our resort. Then you will both be back for dinner with us all."

Carlo's eyes bugged. "Really? Would that be OK with you, Jeremy?"

He nodded, shrugging. "Sure. Why not?" He turned to Arthur.

Of course Arthur preferred that they all stay together, for a myriad of reasons—not the least of which was Carlo's safety. Then he realized it might be the timeliest solution to the young man's mission, and voicing his own dissent might paint himself as ungrateful or unduly paranoid—or both. "I think it's a reasonable proposal, as long as you can guarantee Carlo's safety," he replied, "or should I say a little prayer to Ogum instead?"

Fabiano ignored him again, and sat back and clapped his hands instead. "Wonderful. I'll have the jet readied after breakfast. Now, what else should I tell you about myself?"

"I know! Why don't you tell us about your family and the source of their wealth?" Arthur asked innocently.

Fabiano peered at him. "I see that I am not the only man who has been collecting information."

Arthur smiled. "Doesn't it make you just the least bit uneasy," he began, "to make even more profit from land that was paid for with innocent blood?"

"Since I am now in the business of *saving* blood instead of spilling it, Mr. Blauefee, I see nothing wrong with cultivating my, or should I say Mr. *Tyler's* and my, investments."

"What's going on, Arthur?" Jeremy asked, wide-eyed.

"Should I tell him or would you like to?" Arthur asked casually.

The big man paused. "I'm afraid it's not a history of which I am proud, but it is a true one," he said finally, grasping his hands together atop the table. "My family was involved with the slave trade from the Congo to Brazil. We used this island, and its deep harbor out there"—he pointed and they all looked—"as a port until slavery was outlawed in the nineteenth century—and even after that, illegally. And with our money, my ancestors bought land for growing sugar and coffee beans, then used many of the slaves they brought in to work on the hillsides and the docks and in the warehouses."

"Jesus," said Jeremy. "Your family actually sold people?"

"And many died or were killed by his family in the process," Arthur added brightly. Then he drained the last of his sangria and toasted his host with his empty glass.

Fabiano glared furiously at him; then his face glossed over. "But we have been completely removed from that sordid business for over four generations. Now we only grow the finest coffee beans in the world, on almost a million acres throughout Brazil. And we sell to countries on all seven continents."

"A *million acres?*" Carlo asked. "Who works there now?"

"Young men, young women, old men, old women. Anyone who wishes to escape the poverty of the favelas or the countryside, or who needs an honest job after being released from prison. But this means we must have a very strong method of managing the workers; some years ago they attempted to form a union and we had to deal with them forcefully. It was very ugly. And now, with technology, we use fewer people each year, so the workers are more appreciative of the opportunities we provide. No one speaks of unions anymore."

"So where we sit right now, this was all a complex used for human trafficking," Arthur stated.

Fabiano nodded. "Yes, this very lookout point was the site of an armory, with cannons and a massive gunpowder magazine. And where the conference center stands was formerly a jail. There is even a cemetery on the island—I went there only once as a boy but have not been since; although I do not believe in the *orixás*, I do believe in ghosts, especially since my family is responsible for making many of them." He took a swig of his sangria, then signaled one of the boys for more. "I am not proud of what we did, but because it was nothing under my control, neither am I ashamed."

Jeremy nodded. "I know what you mean."

Fabiano looked at him. "How so?"

"My uncle Bill was involved with drug and gun trafficking, software pirating and of course even murder, and my mother—"

"Your mother couldn't help herself," Carlo cut in.

Jeremy smiled sideways at him. "You're right. She couldn't help herself. But she did make some pretty bad decisions."

"Who has not made some bad decisions?" Fabiano asked jovially. "The bad decisions make the wise man determined to make better ones. No?"

"That depends on—" Arthur began.

"For example, in my family," Fabiano interrupted, "we became involved with the church here in Brazil, in order to help those who could not help themselves. We even paid for much of Cristo, because the church could not raise enough money to fund the statue." His eyes opened wide; his eyelids peeled back. "Can you imagine Rio de Janeiro without Cristo, who reminds the people every day about freedom from the Portuguese, and gives hope to everyone in both the penthouses and favelas that God is great?"

"But what do the people who worship the *orixás* think about Cristo?" Jeremy asked.

"People in Brazil, like the rest of the world, give consideration only to whichever god best meets their needs," he stated.

"What's that supposed to mean?" asked Arthur.

"It is human nature to seek out whichever god will best heal your wounds...will most fully quench your desires, and will help you live your dreams while you walk during the day—then help you sleep peacefully at night. And because Brazil is as troubled as it is complex, many here have, for centuries, worshipped faithfully two most completely different religions at the same time."

"People really do that?" Jeremy asked.

Fabiano laughed heartily, while looking slowly from Arthur to Jeremy, and then to Carlo. "If we can do this with our lovers, then why not with our gods?"

CHAPTER 20

His first awareness was that day had broken.

His second was that he felt hungover.

He squinted over at his watch on the nightstand and saw it was still very early. So, knowing the boys were still asleep, he pulled on his shorts, slid his feet into his sandals and went out onto the lanai to watch the sun rise over the bay, and to have the fresh morning air soothe his aching head.

Dawn's light was gentle on the awakening island, making it look candlelit; there were no shadows to be seen, and the steel gray water was flat and glassy. Arthur pulled a chair from the café set by the railing and sat, knowing he had at least a couple of hours to kill before breakfast, and wishing he had a huge cup of coffee in front of him, and a pair of ibuprofens dissolving in his belly.

A bagel would be nice, too.

Then the memory of their dinner conversation hit him, and he winced.

He'd said too much. And he'd been more than a little antagonistic, but who could blame him? That blowhard came from a long line of slave smugglers who'd graduated to exploiters, albeit legal ones, of the poor. He hadn't even planned to tell Jeremy about this, and wasn't going to bring it up, until Fabiano taunted him with that reference to Danny before carrying on in that grossly flirtatious manner with Jeremy.

He'd asked for it. But why?

Why would that man intentionally jab his stick into Arthur's cage?

Maybe he was just an asshole. People with money get like that. *A big case of the mee-mees*; that's what Danny used to call it when someone went on and on about himself—or treated "mere mortals" dismissively in social situations.

Or maybe he had some ulterior motive....

Perhaps it was just that sangria, which tasted like red wine and Kool-Aid and oranges and rum and caused them both to say things they shouldn't.

Loudmouth soup.

But neither Jeremy nor Carlo had seemed inebriated.

They'd just had less to drink.

To the contrary, he'd had too much because he felt nervous and stressed and his appetite had vanished and he hadn't eaten enough; thus, the booze had tarnished his usually sterling judgment.

So what now? Should he go for a walk and do some snooping on his own—maybe run into the big jerk and feign a sincere apology? Or should he stay back and wait for the boys to wake?

He decided on the latter, so he tiptoed into the suite and found an unopened bottle of water in the fridge, which he brought back outside to drink.

He settled down into the chair again, cracked the seal on the plastic cap and guzzled half the bottle down, then watched the streaks of tangerine glowing under the horizon's bank of clouds transform, almost imperceptibly, into smears of cheery fuchsia.

Red sky at night, sailors' delight.

The breeze on his skin was cool still, but he supposed it wouldn't be for long; that rising sun would soon microwave all this delicious moisture in the air into a tropical frenzy.

Red sky at morning, sailors take warning.

He flexed his shoulders up toward his ears and heard his joints crack. Then while gulping another swig of water, he spilled some onto his chest.

As he brushed the puddle from between his pecs, he noticed something new: five—he counted them again—*five* gray chest hairs.

"Shit," he muttered, plucking the wildest out between pinched fingers. Then he did the same four more times, until none remained.

Gray hair on his head was one thing, *hot* even, but on his body it was another. Because gray chest hair was for middle-aged—*and old*—men.

Was this proof he was entering middle age?

What is middle age?

Was it a sum of years that signaled being halfway along some stairway up to heaven or down to hell? Or was it signaled by a retreating hairline and an expanding belly and deepening forehead creases and doubling chins? He figured that at best, entering middle age meant he was now beginning the process of fading, like a photograph fades in the sun: hair pales, skin washes out, muscles lose their fabulous ridges, and one becomes less distinguishable from the waddling masses. But physical deterioration aside, what made this thought unthinkable was that he had no partner with whom to weather this degradation. And he owned no appreciating real estate, he knew his family wouldn't miss him if he simply evaporated tomorrow, and he didn't have a real job anymore—having been granted his *cocksucker's discharge*, as the Marines so cleverly refer to it, then turning his back on the FBI once the Tyler case was closed.

What intention, if any, did his life have?

He was basically a nanny. For an eighteen-year-old kid.

No. He wasn't going to have this debate with himself.

Not now.

He had more pressing matters at hand than his existential hysteria— such as the safety of his two young charges. And he wasn't a *nanny*; in essence he was a bodyguard for a wealthy scion, as well as an assistant to one of the most powerful women on the West Coast.

As for feeling old, well, it was just too soon for that.

I'm not pushing forty; I'm pulling thirty.

And he had another ten years to enjoy before turning fifty.

Now, fifty *was* middle-aged.

He decided to put the issue out of his mind, and to concentrate on the day's coming events—which begged the question: How comfortable did he feel having Carlo go on some scavenger hunt without known protection? He should have asked him last night after dinner, but his wobbly head combined with his jet lag made him sleepy, so he'd wished the boys good night, then shuffled off to his room, instead.

He'd ask him this morning. And if they all didn't feel completely comfortable with his leaving, they would go together—or stay here and do it at the trip's end, as planned.

But then a thought grabbed him.

A feeling. *A pang of desire.*

They could have some alone time.

Jeremy and me.

They hadn't had any in weeks because of Jeremy's vacation. And Carlo's demands on Jeremy's free time before that. And Katharine's demands on Arthur.

And the fact that Arthur had been, consciously or not, avoiding him. *Ever since they'd gotten back from Hawaii.*

Because there'd been that conversation when he'd called Jeremy at their hotel to say Katharine needed them to go to Brazil, and he should cut short his fabulous summer vacation with Carlo.

Their conversation should have ended with that announcement. In fact, it was really over when he'd almost accidentally muttered what was in his heart.

He'd told Jeremy he missed him. More than he thought he would.

Jeremy had said he missed him, too. More than he thought he would, too.

And after they'd hung up, he'd fallen back on his bed and realized his heart was thumping and he was light-headed and thirsty and his skin felt flushed and all of a sudden he couldn't wait for him to come home.

I'm in love with him.

That thought sent him tailspinning into one of his worst depressions since his teens, as his demons awakened from their hibernation, cleared their throats and began their discordant chorus: *You're stupid. He's a kid. You've got nothing in common. You can't build a life with someone young enough to be your son. You're too old. He'd leave you. You're practically a child molester. He can't possibly find you attractive. He only wants a dad. Katharine would kill you. People will laugh. You're already looking older. You should find someone your own age. You have nothing to offer him. He'll break your heart. Everyone you love dies...*

Then he'd gone to meet them at the airport.

Their eyes had met.

And Jeremy's face had transmitted a feeling of such love, of such openness.

But Carlo's eyes had looked...cold; to Arthur it had been like seeing two houses, and in one the drapes were open so you could look inside, but the other had windows, and yes the lights were on inside, but the drapes were shut. Tight.

Carlo knows. He's smart.

On the drive home in Jeremy's Range Rover, with its wide center armrest, their forearms had brushed each other—but neither had moved his away. And for the rest of the trip home Arthur had rested his arm there, steering the whole way with his left hand, and at one point he had even pressed his arm deliberately against Jeremy's, and Jeremy, Arthur thought, had pressed his purposefully back.

After they'd dropped off Carlo, they rode home in silence because there was so much he wanted to say but he was afraid his tone would give away the intensity he felt, and Jeremy had made no move toward conversation, but they had kept pressing their arms together and Arthur had wanted to grasp his hand and thread his fingers through his own and bring his hand to his mouth and kiss it, *so, so gently.*

And then kiss his mouth. *Not so gently.*

Instead, they had driven north along Pacific Coast Highway toward Ballena Beach in silence, until they'd reached the Tyler compound; and as the huge iron gates motored open Jeremy had said, finally, "It's really good to see you."

Arthur had almost cried because he wanted to say, *I love you so much,* but couldn't, so he had said, "It's really good to see you, too. I'm glad you got home safely."

But for the rest of the week, as they had prepared for the trip to Brazil, Arthur had transformed back into "the good soldier."

Vapid eyes. Bland smile. Calm voice. Ramrod posture. *Do you need me to wash anything for you for the trip?*

Then every night, after silencing those voices with a glass or two of the Tyler wine cellar's very, very good chardonnay, he would strip off his clothes and lie in bed and spoon his pillow...imagining that instead of polyester batting, his arms were filled with *his* muscle and *his* perfectly warm skin.

And they wouldn't even have to have sex.

He just wanted to hold him. To be held by him. To fall asleep hearing his breathing, to awaken and see his mouth agape; to know he'd shared a bed with one of God's most perfect creations—this young prince with the face of an angel and the body of a warrior and the heart of a lion

It will never be.

"What are you thinkin' about?"

"Oh!" He looked up to see a shirtless, bleary-eyed Jeremy grinning down at him, then stifling a yawn as he extended his arms into a semaphored stretch. "Nothing really. Just what we have to do today," he lied. "Listen," he began, with his eyebrows scrunched together, as if no other thought had been firing his brain's synapses, "I think we should go with Carlo. I'm not sure I feel comfortable letting him go without us."

Jeremy's smile straightened into a line. "Why? Don't we have a lot of work to do today?" He sat down in the opposite chair, and Arthur saw him glance at his bare chest.

He sat up straighter. *Glad I spotted those hairs.*

"Half a day or so won't make a difference. And it'll be safer if we're all together."

"Are you *still* worried about Fabiano?" Jeremy laughed. "What's the deal? I mean, the guy's kind of an asshole, but he seems safe and all to me. What are you still worried about?"

"Rule number one for bodyguards: Never lose sight of who you're protecting."

"But you're protecting *me*, Mr. Secret Agent," he reminded Arthur. "If Carlo is OK with it, then we should be, too. Remember"—he poked him on the *Semper Fi* tattoo on his biceps and cocked an eyebrow—"I'm the one with all the money."

"And all of the modesty, apparently." Arthur rolled his eyes playfully. "Still, it might be best if we all go together. But we're going to have to insist on it with Fabiano; something tells me he wants to separate us."

"Well, maybe he does."

Arthur peered at Jeremy suspiciously. "What do you mean by that?"

"Maybe...he can tell that we need some time together—some father-son time. You know, playing catch, building model airplanes, talking about girls and football and stuff."

Arthur laughed. "I'm sure he's not that well versed in the intricacies of our relationship."

"Well, we could use some," he said softly, then locked his gaze with Arthur's.

Arthur's crotch tingled.

"Could use some what?" Carlo asked, emerging from the open sliding door.

"Use some...relaxation time," Jeremy suggested. "Like after you come back, we could all maybe go down to the European Beach and go swimming. *Without judgment.*"

The boys laughed and Arthur smiled. "You two can do whatever you want. But a lot depends on whether or not you can even find Afonso, and if he wants, or is even able, to come back here."

"So you're cool with Carlo going by himself?" Jeremy asked, eyebrows raised.

Arthur looked from one to the other, knowing exactly what his answer should be. "Sure," he lied.

***

After a breakfast of scrambled eggs, tangy grapefruit, some weird breed of ham and a tall pot of very strong coffee from Fabiano's own plantation, they washed up. Then they were driven in their host's Navigator, by one of the silent waiters, down to the airstrip, where Jeremy and Arthur watched from the tarmac as Carlo, in his best impersonation of a spoiled celebrity, stepped first up the stairs, then through the clamshell doors of the gleaming white Gulfstream, with his bodyguards in tow. Finally, with a deafening whine from engines that looked too small to generate such a din, the craft sped down the runway before tilting its nose effortlessly into the azure Brazilian sky.

Money begets such privilege, Arthur noted silently as the aircraft shrank quickly into a rocket-propelled speck. *And somehow, I've become a part of this.*

So for Arthur and Jeremy, the rest of the morning was filled with tours, guided by a much friendlier Dom Fabiano, of cavernous shells built to house elegant dining rooms and casinos, of cement-lined pits on their way to becoming a water park, of a high residential tower built for generous suites, of tile-roofed villas for privacy-seeking honeymooners, and of acres bulldozed to make way for a championship golf course. While above it all, hugging the big, bald granite bowling pin known as Giant's Peak, hung the elaborate structural beginnings of what were to become some of the safest, most exclusive properties for sale in the world: the resort equivalent of time-share bomb shelters.

Arthur and Jeremy oohed and aahed and asked questions and pointed and nodded with studied enthusiasm.

And throughout the entire tour, Arthur couldn't stop thinking about Jeremy.

And their upcoming time that afternoon.

Together.

CHAPTER 21

The driver, whose name Carlo learned was Braulio, wheeled the white Denali left from São Clemente, then started the climb up Barão de Macaúbas to Francisco de Moura, where he made another left. Then he took the vehicle straight up a quickly tapering street, and pulled into the last parking spot available.

"Up there somewhere," the man told him in Portuguese.

"But where's the street with this address?" Carlo protested, holding out a slip of paper.

"Ask around. No signs." The driver switched on the radio, lit a cigarette and settled back in his seat, while the second bodyguard, whose name was still a mystery, did the same.

So I'm on my own, he realized. *Then, fuck you.*

Being as angry now as he was determined to find his cousin, he looked around, trying to get his bearings. Then, with the old photograph tucked inside his back pocket, he found himself entering the favela Dona Marta, on the outskirts of Botafogo, which looked, actually, like a decent neighborhood. While scanning his surroundings he spotted Cristo facing the favela high on the hill directly across from where he stood, only a couple of miles away.

That's not such a bad view. Unless you're Cristo.

He started on his way up.

But whatever semblance of order there was at the street level gave way quickly to the most confusing urban chaos he'd ever seen. The concrete stairs at the base of the climb were supplanted by nothing more than flimsy boards barely nailed together, and beyond that the path transformed into nothing more than packed dirt. The walls and roofs of the houses, if you could call them houses, were constructed from plywood and cardboard and sheets of corrugated tin or fiberglass nailed together higgledy-piggledy. The smell was terrific: sewage and food cooking and exhaust and dogs and chickens and God knew what else, and the noise made as much an assault on his ears as the surroundings made on his eyes:

traffic from below jumbled with rap music from above and kids squealing and babies crying and some guys arguing and televisions blaring—all in such a frenzy that after a moment he was able to diminish the din as one big drone.

He'd never been in a place this filthy, this beat-up, or this unsafe before, so he did his best to ignore the fear that was building within him with each step upward.

He heard some crazed laughter. Then two ragged boys, about twelve or thirteen, rounded the corner. One was dark, almost African looking, and the other was tawny skinned with kinky blond hair and watery blue eyes. Both wore cutoff shorts and filthy T-shirts; neither wore shoes, and their feet were blackened with grime, up to the ankles. Each clenched a brown paper bag in his fist.

"*Gostaria?*" The darker boy asked him. He held the bag toward Carlo, still keeping it closed. "*Vinte reais.*"

"No, *obrigado*," Carlo replied. "What is that?"

He opened it to reveal a plastic bottle inside. "*Cola de sapato.*"

Shoemaker's glue. The drug of choice for poor kids in Brazil. "No, no. *Obrigado.*" He said, noticing that the boy with the blue eyes looked stoned out of his mind. How was he going to make it down all those stairs?

"*Cocaina?*" the boy asked, hopefully.

Carlo shook his head.

The blond smiled, raised his eyebrows and rubbed his crotch. "*Sim, sim?*"

"No!" Carlo waved his hands in the air. "*Estou procurando por Afonso Peres. Sabe onde posso encontra-lo?*"

The pair burst into laughter, then continued their descent, so Carlo continued upward. Then he glanced down and saw, with relief, Braulio and the other bodyguard leaning against the car.

They waved up at him and he waved back.

Pendejos, his father would have called them.

He spotted an ancient woman sitting behind an open curtain; she was crocheting something from yellow and green yarn. "*Com licenca, Nana,*" he called out to her, "*estou procurando por Afonso Peres. Sabe onde posso encontra-lo?*"

She eyed him suspiciously, then reached forward and snatched the tattered drapes together.

He looked around for someone else but saw no one, and was wondering what to do when a teenage girl in a denim skirt and red bandana halter top emerged from a doorway and began picking her way down toward him.

He shot her his friendliest smile. "Excuse me, but I'm looking for Afonso Perez," he asked her in his best Portuguese. "Please, do you know Afonso Perez?"

Her eyes quickly examined him. "I know no one by that name."

As she sidled past him, he had an idea. "Babalu. Do you know Babalu Perez?" He pulled the photograph from his pocket and held it up. "He is my cousin."

She turned. "Babalu?" She smiled, and he saw she was beautiful. "He is my friend. You are his cousin?"

"From California. Los Angeles. I'm trying to find him. Please, I am Carlos."

She held out her hand, and he placed the photo into her palm. "So that was young Babalu?" She giggled before handing the picture back. "I am Xuxulu." She pointed up to the left, at a door painted bright yellow. "Babalu is there. A pleasure meeting you." Then she continued her descent.

"*Obrigado!*" he yelled to her back.

He leapt up the remaining stairs, then stood before the door and knocked. "Babalu?" he called out. "Babalu Perez, please?"

No answer.

"Babalu Perez?" He knocked again. "Babalu?"

"*Entré,*" answered a meek voice.

He pushed open the door.

He was surprised to see a comparatively tidy room with a cleanly swept floor, one chair and a small bed in the corner. And sitting in the other corner of the room, smoking a cigarette and watching a game show on his tiny color TV, was the man who might be his cousin.

"What is it you need?" the man asked in English, with a voice that could not be described as male or female.

"Are you...were you Afonso Perez?"

"Who are you?" the man asked suspiciously.

"I'm Carlos Martinez, your cousin from the United States. My mother, Eva, was your mother's sister. I've come a long way to find you."

The man abandoned his cigarette on the side table, then pushed himself up, with the help of a cane, from the chair. He approached him, squinting. Then he smiled, and Carlo saw there was still handsomeness underneath the evidence of many difficult years.

"No one has called me Afonso in some time," he said. "Please call me Babalu; it is my only name now."

"I go by Carlo now, too. I wanted to be different from my father."

The man looked him up and down. "You are very handsome. And *muito forte*," he added, puffing out his scrawny chest.

"Thanks. My sister Carmen said we look alike."

The man laughed. "I might have looked like you many, many years ago. Now no one would say such a compliment to me. Please sit." He motioned to the chair. "May I offer you some drink? I have white wine, but only some popcorn if you are hungry."

"No, thanks," Carlo replied as he went over to the chair and sat. Babalu, in turn, perched himself on the side of his bed, still clutching his cane. "So tell me, why do you come so far to find me?"

"First, I have some sad news. My mother has died."

Shock registered on his face. "I am so sorry, Carlitos. She was my mother's favorite sister." He withdrew another cigarette from his pack, then lit it. "Of what cause did she die, if I may ask?"

"She had cancer of the...womb."

He sighed. "Of this my poor mother also died. It is sad that what gives so much life to you and me can rob the givers of theirs. It does not make sense."

"I'm sorry your mother has passed away also. I remember her as a kind woman, who laughed a lot. Especially with my mother."

He smiled. "They are together, once again," he said, pointing skyward. "Perhaps they are sharing a joke even now?"

Carlo nodded, on the verge of sudden tears because of the picture in his head. "How long ago?"

Babalu looked at the ceiling. "Three years, this November. And your mother?"

"It was a year ago this past June."

"And how is your father? He must be very lonely without her."

Carlo's face darkened, and he shrugged. "He's OK, I guess."

"He was not the nicest man, if I recall my mother's stories."

"He hates my being gay. But I don't care."

"So you are like me, then?"

"I guess." He looked at the broken-down man in the hovel that was his home, and felt sorry for him. "Yes. I'm like you. We're very much alike in that way."

"I hope not so alike," he stated ominously, then sucked on his cigarette.

"Why not?" Carlo asked, already knowing the answer.

Babalu laughed bitterly. "You cannot tell by looking at me? Or by the smell of death in the room?"

"I was told you weren't well. That's one of the reasons I'm here."

"You are kind to come, but I am not yet ready to die. You must be here for some other reason; this is a long way from your home."

"My *amante* brought me down here on business, and I wanted to find out if there was anything I could do for you while I'm here—like to give you money. For a doctor."

"There is not much that can be done for me," his cousin said. "I have not been well in so long that I cannot remember what it feels like to feel good. So this is what I am used to."

"Then maybe I can offer you something else."

He raised his eyebrows, and Carlo saw they were painted on. "Please do not play with my hopes. I'm afraid I do not have much patience, so if you have something to make my life better, will you please tell me?"

"I might have an opportunity for you. But it would depend on your health, and what you're able to do."

His eyes narrowed. "Tell me what you know; then I will be the judge."

"I know someone, a friend. I told him about you, and he has offered to give you a job. Some work, if you can do it."

"Do not tell me it has to do with drugs."

Carlo laughed. "No, no drugs. Or anything else illegal. It has to do with a resort we're building—beautiful hotels and pools and casinos. On an island about an hour's flight north of Rio."

"To work at an American hotel?" A smile opened his cousin's face. "That is something I have always wanted to do; the people are so elegant, and the food is perfect. When I was young I visited clients in the Copacabana Palace many times. Is it like that? When will the resort be finished?"

Carlo felt excited—this was what he'd come here for. "That's funny, because we're staying at the Palace, or we stayed there when we got into Rio. So that's something you'd be interested in?"

Babalu stood, and began hobbling back and forth in the tiny room. "To think I will have a beautiful place to work again, and then I can have an apartment, maybe down near Ipanema." He turned to Carlo. "When can I meet this friend of yours? I will need some new clothes to see him. Do you,"—he hesitated—"think you could give me money for some new clothes? I would not like for him to see me like this. I will pay you back. Please tell me you did not tell him I am sick. He won't hire me if I am sick, not in a fine hotel."

He held up his hands. "He already knows, Babalu. He made the offer knowing you're not well."

He shook his head. "Who can this saint be?" he asked. "What is his name?"

"His name is Elegbara. Dom Elegbara Fabi—" Carlo started to say.

"Fabiano?" Babalu interrupted.

They locked eyes.

Then they both said, "El Gigante," in unison.

Babalu laughed bitterly. Then he coughed. And coughed.

Then he sat. "How do you know this man?" he whispered suspiciously.

"It's a long story."

He paused. "What is more important is what you do with him now. Your business."

"My lover has investments with him. Real estate. Hotels, like I told you. We came to Brazil to meet with him and to inspect the hotels he is building."

"Your *amante*; he is an old man?"

"No, *primo*, he is young like me."

"And he is already rich?"

"His family is very rich."

"And he is an honest man?"

"Why do you ask?"

Babalu looked away, then began speaking in a low voice. "This man you speak of; he is…very bad."

"How bad?"

"You need to leave, my cousin. Go home. Take your lover and get out of here."

"But his work isn't finished yet."

"Do you love this rich boy?"

Carlo managed a smile. "Very, very much."

"If you love him, you must protect him; the less you know the better it will be for you, because you still need to smile into Fabiano's face. Just find a way to go home today or tonight if you can. You cannot know how much danger you are in."

"But I came here to help you," Carlo insisted, trying to calm his rising panic. "And I want to, still. What can I do to help you?"

Babalu smiled. Then he pushed himself up from the bed, and made his way to Carlo. "There is little left for me in this life," he said. "And what life gave me I already used; you can see the proof of it in these bruises on my hands and by how I walk. Time for me is growing short."

"I guess I can see that." Carlo tried to look away from him—his breath stank.

"You...you have much to live for." He put his hands on his shoulders. "This world belongs to you. You live in America. You have youth...and most importantly health. You have the rich boy's love. Take him away from here and—"

There came a knock on the door. "Dom Martinez," a man's voice called.

They exchanged glances.

"Si?" Carlo stepped to the door and opened it, while Babalu turned to face the wall.

Braulio was standing outside. "We must leave, please," he announced in Portuguese. "The weather is getting bad for flying." He pointed to the sky.

Carlo surveyed the looming clouds and decided they looked bad. "Just a minute." He closed the door and turned to Babalu. "Don't worry about me, *primo*. And I'll be back to help you. But here, take this." He pressed the money he'd brought for him into his hand. "This isn't much, but take it anyway."

Babalu threw his arms around him. "The gods arranged for us to meet today. They are watching over you, even now."

"I'll come back with more money if I can."

"You were so kind to come find me. I'll pray that we see each other again." He kissed his cheeks, then whispered, "Please...if you can, remember this saying of my mother's: 'If you dance with Exu, he'll make you think the full moon is the sun,'" he recited slowly, squeezing Carlo's hands, "'but moonlight cannot warm you—no matter how white the sands beneath you, or how black the shadows behind you.'"

CHAPTER 22

Y ou're gonna need a hat," Arthur told Jeremy as they were heading out the door. "It's gonna be unbelievably hot today."

Jeremy stopped to glance out the window. "But it's cloudy."

"Doesn't matter. You can get some of the worst sunburns on days like this."

Jeremy shrugged. "I didn't bring one."

"Use mine." Arthur took the straw hat off his own head and pushed it onto Jeremy's. "Now you look like some dorky farmer kid from Kansas," he said, smiling.

"Then what're y'all gonna wear then there now?" Jeremy drawled.

He laughed. "Where'd you learn to talk like that?"

"Fresno, remember? The first dude I was ever hot for talked like that; he lived on a farm out in Clovis. Total hick, but could've been an Abercrombie model. Anyways, here. I'm OK." He started to give the hat back, but Arthur stopped him.

"I'll be fine," he said, going over to his luggage and grabbing an old blue bandana from his stash, "as long as you don't mind being seen with a pirate."

"Does that mean I get ta see y'all's booty?" Jeremy giggled.

"If you mean my sunblock and towels, then sure," Arthur told him with a playful punch on his shoulder. "Let's go." And as he tied on the bandana, they walked out the door and began their shoulder-to-shoulder descent toward the waterfront.

Earlier, after their morning's tour concluded, Dom Fabiano offered them one of the island's powerboats for a trip to the future European Beach on the other side of the island. So after a quick stop at the catering kitchen for some barbecued chicken and flatbread, cheese and grapes, and sodas and bottled water, they made their way across Brasiliana to the unfinished marina, where they threw their backpacks into a red-and-white twenty-four-foot Sundancer. Then, with the ropes from the moorings coiled neatly aboard, they headed out, with Arthur at the helm doing his best to maneuver the big boat, and Jeremy laid back and grinning on the seat next to him, his heels perched on the dash.

Once out of the harbor, the graceful watercraft cut through the waves beautifully, after rising up on plane with only a gentle nudging of its throttle; the familiar drone of the big V-8 burbling through the wet pipes at the stern excited Arthur—it reminded him of being a kid at the lake where his family went camping every year, where he'd spent afternoons on the shore hugging his knees watching the ski boats he'd never ride in roar by, in all their orange or red or blue metal–flaked glory.

With the wind in his face, the steering wheel in his left hand, and the throttle lever in his right, he tried to relax, for he was as delighted as he was nervous to be alone with Jeremy—even if it was only for a few hours.

Fabiano had instructed them to travel counterclockwise around the island at medium throttle for about ten or fifteen minutes; then, after they passed a sizable jetty of rocks, there would be an inlet where the approach was deep enough for them to beach the boat easily, or to anchor fairly close to shore, and swim or wade in.

But he was anxious to get there. So he pushed the throttle all the way forward.

"Whoa!" Jeremy exclaimed, as instantly, the engine's drone went from growl to bellow and the prow rose up and at once they were tearing through the wind and slicing through the whitecaps, and a delicious, cooling sea spray curled up around the hull and misted his face and sunglasses. "Look!" he yelled, pointing off the starboard with one hand and holding the straw hat on his head with the other. "Dolphins, Arthur! They're running with us!" He stood and grabbed the windscreen's edge. "*Woo-hooooo!*"

Arthur turned and saw the glorious creatures as they breached, then dove, and breached, then dove. "*Woo-hooo!*" he howled along with Jeremy, feeling for a moment like that hot dad from the old TV show *Flipper*— with Sandy, his adonic son, by his side. Then he looked up and saw that the clouds overhead were cleared almost to the horizon and the sky was now a Crayola blue and the coastline to the port side was pristine and savage, and his body felt tight and young and energized, and he puffed out his chest and breathed in deeply and squared his jaw and grinned at Jeremy, and Jeremy stepped sideways over to him and put his arm around his waist, and Arthur put his arm around Jeremy's shoulder and hugged him to his side and thought, *I have to remember this perfect, perfect moment.*

Ten or so minutes later, after passing a fair-sized peninsula of scattered boulders, they spotted it: a tilting semicircular stage of sand nestled inside a grand amphitheater of verdant hills.

And not a soul in sight.

Arthur nosed in and slowed toward a flat patch of sand, and moments later, as if he'd been doing this his whole life, he cut the throttle at the perfect moment and trimmed the propulsion system upward.

The sand made a lovely sound against the fiberglass hull, like dry hands skimming together.

They stopped.

"Nice job, skipper!" Jeremy laughed as he whirled his backpack as far as he could out onto the sand and hopped over the side into knee-high water. Arthur threw him one of the tie-downs, which he caught; then he trudged up through the sand to knot it clumsily around the closest palm tree.

Moments later Arthur dropped into the water and waded toward where Jeremy was already setting up camp on the beach.

"I wanna be in the sun, if it's OK with you," Jeremy announced upon Arthur's approach.

"Sure. If I get too hot, I can find some shade. Wherever you want is fine."

"That boat is great!" Jeremy exclaimed. "We could get one, you know? Keep it at the marina in town—I didn't even know you knew how to drive one."

"Neither did I," Arthur told him, peeling off his shirt. He tried not to watch Jeremy do the same; instead he turned to scan the water, which was the precise Technicolor hue of those swimming pools in movies from the 1960s.

Doris Day blue, someone once called it—only this was a blue so blue it almost burned your eyes.

They stretched out their big white towels side by side.

Arthur wore his modest board shorts; they were generously cut, and patterned with huge vermillion hibiscus flowers. But he saw now that Jeremy had forgone modesty, as he slipped off his cargo shorts to reveal a skimpy black square-cut Speedo that accentuated provocatively the bulges and curves of his glorious body's lower half.

"This place is so great, huh?" Jeremy asked, pumping sunblock from a brown plastic bottle onto his legs, then rubbing it in.

"It's unbelievable. I didn't know there were still any places like this."

"You know what it kind of reminds me of?"

"Hmm?"

"Do you remember that dream I had a long time ago, where my dad and I were walking along this deserted beach at night, and one second I'm a kid and then the next second I'm full grown, like I am now?"

Arthur furrowed his brows. "Was that the 'Father's Star' dream?"

"Yeah! So you remember!" He lay down, and slipped on his sunglasses. "Remember what he said to me?"

"Something about making a wish on a star?"

"Remember what else?"

Arthur shook his head.

"He said that to be a 'real man,' I had to be courageous, honest and selfish. And I thought that was the weirdest thing, because it didn't seem right to be thinking about myself only, you know? Like you learn that being selfish is bad, even back in kindergarten."

"So what do you think about it now?" he asked, holding out his hand for the sunblock.

Jeremy handed it over. "Actually, I was kind of wondering what you think about it."

Arthur pumped the oil onto his forearms, then his chest, stomach and legs. "To be like that really wasn't how I was raised, so I still spend my life only doing what I think is the right thing, I guess." He began rubbing the sunblock into his skin.

Jeremy laughed. "I didn't ask you what you always do; I asked what you *think* about going after the things you need to be happy. About being 'selfish.'"

Arthur stopped rubbing and stared at the younger man. "Why do you ask?"

"Because I think you're kind of afraid or something to go after things you want in life…like right now you'd probably want me to put this stuff on your back, but you won't ask me because you don't want to bother me— you'd rather get a horrible sunburn, or wear a shirt all day than ask."

Arthur blushed. "That's ridiculous."

"You did it with the hat this morning."

"You needed one, and I had my handy bandana, which I always take with me when I go into hot climates. Old trick left over from the Marines."

"But it's *your* hat," he protested. "You always do stuff like that for me."

"It's because that's what I'm supposed to do. Look out for you."

"But then who looks out for Arthur?"

He paused. "I look out for both of us, or rather the three of us—at least on this trip." He grimaced. "I sure hope Carlo's OK."

Jeremy laughed. "Sure he's OK. People don't fuck with him; he's too..."

"Sassy?"

"Yeah. *Sassy.*" Jeremy chuckled. "Plus he's smart. He'll be fine. Now, what about the sunblock? Are you gonna ask me to put some on you? But I won't do it unless you ask me *real nice-like.*" He tugged down the brim of the straw hat over his eyes in classic "howdy" fashion.

Arthur rolled his eyes. "OK, Jeremy. Will you *please* put some of that on my back?"

"Only if you'll put it on mine after."

"Deal." He turned facedown on his towel.

An instant later, he felt the cold spray on his shoulder, and then shivered as it was spritzed down his spine. But then the coolness gave way quickly to the warmth of Jeremy's hand as it traced circles up and down his back. And surprisingly, Arthur felt no erotic thrill from this experience; if anything, he was both preoccupied and deeply unsettled by Jeremy's uncanny appraisal of him.

"My turn," Jeremy announced, and moments later Arthur had returned the favor.

That was easy enough.

"So," Jeremy began as he slipped the hat back on, "if there's one thing in your life that you're missing, that you could change just by going after it and being *selfish*, what would that be?"

Arthur laughed. "I'd get myself one of those pretty new Jaguars. Black. Convertible. Chrome rims."

"I'm not kidding."

"Neither am I," he replied. "Why are you asking me these things?"

Jeremy sat up and pulled off his sunglasses. "Because sometimes you seem kind of...sad. And even though you think you hide it pretty good, I can still see it in you."

"You really can?" Arthur asked, suddenly disarmed.

"And it makes *me* sad. And so I...want to do something nice for you but I just don't know what you need."

Arthur shook his head. "You're just used to looking after adults, Jeremy, because of what your mom put you through. It's a reflex for you to see someone you care for that's in pain and to try and fix them. I think it's called *codependency*."

"So you admit it. You are in pain."

Arthur closed his eyes, then drew in a breath and let it out slowly through his nose. "Maybe. But everyone is at one time or another. It's part of life, and sometimes it gets more painful the older you get."

Jeremy reached over and touched Arthur's arm. "So why is it wrong if I want to make someone happy? Just 'cause my mom was all fucked up doesn't mean everything I do is because she damaged me. I mean, from what you've told me it sounds like your parents were all fucked up, too, and you came out all right."

Did I?

"Look, old buddy, I'm fine. And I'm touched right here," he put his hand flat over his heart, "that you want to 'fix my sadness' or make me think about changing my life. But please, *please* don't worry about me. You've got enough to think about these days." He was growing more uncomfortable with where the conversation was heading, so he decided to change the subject. "Which reminds me, how are things going with you and Carlo?"

He shrugged. "Good, I guess."

"I'm glad to hear it. So what's gonna happen with that other guy you told me about before we left—when we were out on my patio?"

"Don't know," Jeremy answered curtly. "But I'll figure it out."

"What about Katharine? Is she still riding you as much as before?"

He lay back and folded his hands behind his head. "Naw, not really. Can we not talk about her right now, Arthur?"

Arthur nodded, also laying back. "Absolutely. To tell you the truth, I really don't feel like talking about her right now, either." What else could he ask him? "How 'bout college? Are you looking forward to that?"

"You never answered my question."

Arthur sighed. "Which one?"

Jeremy sat up and glared at him. "You *know* which question."

"OK, OK." He chuckled. Then he looked skyward, as if divining a reasonable answer from the seagulls orbiting haphazardly overhead. "If there was one thing I could stand to be more selfish about, it would be... probably finding a partner. Someone to build a life with, even at my age."

"Thought so. So how *do* you find someone? *Even at your age?*" He laughed.

"That's the problem, Jeremy. I already did."

He looked down. "Sometimes I forget about that, you know? And after what you went through with Danny, I don't blame you for not trying to find someone now." He reached into his backpack and pulled out a soda. "Want one?"

"Sure. Do you want one of those chicken sandwich-y things?"

"I think they called it a *sanduíche*." Jeremy laughed as he handed over a can. "See, I'm learning Portuguese."

Arthur chuckled, but then his face grew serious. "I guess I just don't know how to look for someone," he said as he withdrew their lunches from his bag and cracked open his soda. "That's the funny thing, you know? Because when I was younger, guys always came sniffing after me. But now that I'm older, it's harder—plus, I'm pickier, I guess." He handed over one of the stuffed flatbreads.

"About what?" Jeremy asked, then took a bite.

Arthur thought for a moment. "I guess about...settling. Because when you've really fallen in love with someone and built a life with them, it just seems like too much at some point to start all over."

"But why? I think that'd be the fun part."

"You're right. And some of it is really fun. It's just that I'm going to be forty soon. And in a few years, I'll be the same age my parents were when my sister Morgana got married.... I mean, some guys my age are already grandfathers, and here I have nothing."

"Why would you say that? You have a lot," Jeremy told him, though he knew the man had very little to his name.

"I've got my health, which is so important. But other than that, it doesn't seem like I have very much, to be honest. Now, you, you hunky rich kid, *you* have a lot."

Jeremy looked out toward the water. "Not really, Arthur. Sometimes I think it *looks* like I do, but I really don't—no parents, except Katharine, who drives me crazy, and not a whole lot of friends; and I do have Carlo, but sometimes I don't think he's 'the one.'"

"That's totally normal at your age. I'd be worried if you thought any differently."

"But I don't feel my age. Never have. I've always felt like I was ninety or something. I mean, I feel so old and worn-out inside that I'm surprised sometimes when I look in the mirror and see a young guy." He popped the last bite of his sandwich into his mouth, then downed the rest of his soda.

"I remember that feeling, too, when I was in my teens; I wonder if all gay guys feel that way, because there's so much more we have to go through."

"Maybe," he said, looking wistfully out to sea. "Jesus Christ, it's getting hot." He wiped the mustache of sweat from his upper lip.

"See what I told you? Do you want to move into the shade?"

He threw Arthur a sideways grin, his dark eyes sparkling. "With all that water out there, are you crazy?" He pulled off the straw hat and tossed his head toward the bay. "Come on, old buddy." He jumped up and held out his hand. "I wanna go swimming! And I need to work off this lunch—otherwise I won't have any guys sniffing after me."

Arthur took his hand, pushed himself up and followed Jeremy toward the water.

As he watched him jog across the sand, he was once again amazed by his grace and youthful perfection: his flawless skin and the taut shift of his ass, the impossible narrowness of his waist, and the glossy sheen of his buzz-cut, minky hair…hair that looked as impervious to the impending gray as a spring leaf is oblivious to the coming crimson.

In a splash he disappeared from the horizon and was visible only as a telltale wake of water. Arthur stood at the water's edge, then decided to go in.

He tossed his bandana onto the sand, held his breath and dove.

The water was almost as warm as the air, and required no acclimation.

Mmmm.

He swam a few meters before allowing his head to break the surface.

Jeremy was bobbing some feet in front of him wearing a grin on his face, and his Speedo around his neck. "No judgment, right, Dad?" he exclaimed with a leer.

"I don't know, Son," Arthur answered brightly, trying to echo Jeremy's insouciance.

"The water's great, huh?" Jeremy asked. Then he drew some water in his mouth and spit it in a perfect stream at Arthur's face.

"Hey!" Arthur giggled as he splashed him back.

"See what they teach us in swim team?" he hollered. "We do it in the showers. I can hit the guy over four spigots, no problem."

"How proud your coach must be of your capabilities," Arthur yelled back.

"So where's your European spirit?" Jeremy teased, then pulled the Speedo up over his head and turned to hurl it toward the beach.

"Firmly around my waist, where it belongs."

"Hey, come on. No one's looking..."

"So now you're no one?" Arthur laughed. "Earlier you told me you were the one with all the money—"

"And you said I was the one with all the modesty, so I guess you were wrong. Anyway, what's money good for if you can't have fun?" He ducked his head, and in ten strokes he was an arm's length from Arthur.

"Let's go in. You know I'm not that great a swimmer," Arthur suggested calmly, even though he was not calm—his heart was beating fast, and he hoped he'd been able to disguise the shakiness in his voice.

He turned and began swimming toward shore.

Suddenly, Jeremy's arms were locked around his neck and his chest was up against his shoulders and his knees clenched the tops of his hips. "Piggyback, sir?" came the breathy whisper in his ear. "I don't think I'm a very good swimmer, either."

Jeremy's naked, on my back, with his arms around me.

He felt two hands slip down from around his neck and rub his chest.

His eyes drooped with pleasure. He felt himself harden.

He managed to dog-paddle them closer to shore. But as his feet hit the sandy bottom and he started to rise out of the water, Jeremy's considerable heft began to droop on his back from the lessened buoyancy; and instead of letting go, Jeremy shortened the clutch around his neck and shifted forward, and Arthur felt that unmistakable ridge of hot flesh as it pushed into the small of his back.

So he instructed him, in the gentlest voice he could muster, to please let go.

Jeremy climbed off him.

Then he took Arthur's hand and intertwined his fingers with his own.

Arthur could only look down and close his eyes, because he was afraid that if he turned to him, he couldn't help but proceed with what was sure to become one of the biggest mistakes of his life.

"Hey," came Jeremy's whisper.

His hand made contact with flesh. Jeremy's chest. He could feel his heartbeat.

He opened his eyes.

It was his chin he saw first, and how his beard stubble filled the cleft in it, and next the rosy pout of his lips. Then his eyes lifted to Jeremy's and saw neither mirth nor mischief in them, but seriousness…intensity… perhaps even fear—made evident by his lidless gaze, as well as the gentle crease between his lowered eyebrows.

"Hey," Arthur said back to him. His other hand lifted from his side and went to his shoulder as he turned to face him. "Baby, this'll change everything."

Jeremy's mouth formed the words *I know,* but no sound came out. Then he closed his eyes and nodded, and Arthur couldn't help glancing down to see that he was, in fact, magnificently erect; his shaft with its shiny, lip-colored dome strained enticingly up out of the water.

Jeremy's hands reached down and released the ties on Arthur's board shorts.

They drifted in slow motion through the water down to the sand.

Arthur pulled his love to him and mashed his nakedness against him, and his arms encircled his shoulders while Jeremy's arms bearhugged his waist. "Ohhh," he moaned into his ear as they held each other chest to chest, and cemented themselves together as one writhing beast from knees to clavicles. Their cheeks met, and as Jeremy's mouth inched its way along Arthur's cheek, he heard him breathing in a manner he'd never heard: His exhalations were unsteady, jagged, lacking rhythm— like someone recovering from a crying jag.

Their mouths locked together.

With their tongues twisting and thrusting like wrestling pythons, their hands grasped and smoothed and hugged and jacked and cupped and rubbed and kneaded crazily.

"*I love you.*" The phrase drifted in whispers about their ears, seemingly alchemized out of the sunlight and the foam fizzing about them, with neither aware of who was the speaker or who was the recipient.

"*I love you.*"

Together they made each other spill their seed; then they hunched in a slickened embrace as their breathing calmed and Yemanji's waves swirled around them, jealous over the pearlescent potion that dripped like sweat from between their bodies.

Jeremy's mouth left Arthur's and began nuzzling his neck, and Arthur pulled close his naked back and opened his eyes, looking out to the horizon.

Red sky at morning...

Then Jeremy sighed and Arthur forgot about the impending storm.

Because that sigh, it sounded so...contented. Full. *Safe.* As if every God-filled cell in Jeremy's body knew that he belonged in his arms; it was like the sigh of a child just tucked into bed, of a mother with her sleeping baby in her arms, of a father gazing at his soldier-son as he watched some old reruns from the sofa he used to jump up and down upon.

I love you.

Arthur sighed back.

CHAPTER 23

As they returned to their towels, the winds kicked up, and moments later they were shivering as a disapproving blanket of clouds slid in, blocking the sun. So they gathered up their possessions hastily, then scampered back through the water into the Sundancer just as the first sprinkles dotted its windscreen.

After a full-throttle reverse and a tipsy U-turn, they were headed out to sea.

You should've known better than to go there alone with him.

How could you let that happen?

They didn't talk. Arthur was just too stressed, and a bit frightened; he knew nothing about operating the vessel's complicated navigation equipment, and hoped he wouldn't have to try. So he pushed the throttle all the way forward once again, and hoped they could outrun the belly of the squall.

That was a big mistake.

But navigating the craft before a blustering headwind proved more of a challenge than he'd imagined. For one thing, the tank had been less than half full when they'd left the marina, and now, with the engine straining against the gale, the V-8 devoured its fuel greedily. And the waves buffeting the craft necessitated his overcorrecting their wagging trajectory; it felt as if there were another boat tied to their stern, dragging them off course. But by and by the marina swung into view, and they managed to pull alongside the dock just as the downpour broke.

What're you gonna do now?

"Are you OK?" Jeremy asked as he threw down the bumpers and Arthur wheeled the helm back and forth, trying to get as far inside their berth as he could without careening into it.

"Yeah!" he barked over the bray of the engine as he threw it into reverse. "I'm just glad we got back OK!"

You fucked up. Big-time.

Jeremy waited until the boat was close enough to hop onto the dock, then jumped. Arthur threw him the ropes, and he tied them as best he could just as a big wave rolled in and squished the boat up against its dangling bumpers. Then, with the craft securely in place, Arthur cut the engine, tossed their belongings to Jeremy and jumped onto the dock.

You should've stopped it while you could.

You could've, you know.

While squinting against the rain Jeremy smiled sheepishly, and Arthur did his best to smile back. "Come on," he told him, and slapped him on the shoulder.

They jogged by the unfinished waterfront up to their suite.

Something really bad is gonna happen now.

Moments later they were standing with water pooling at their feet inside the suite, with the sliding doors shut securely against the relentless deluge.

"God, the weather here sure turns fast," Jeremy remarked as he peeled off his wet shirt.

"It's like that in the tropics. But it'll go away as quickly as it came."

"Do you think they'll be flying in this?"

"I hope not." He shivered from his own sopping T-shirt and shorts. "Do you want to take a shower first or should I?"

Jeremy looked at him beseechingly. Then he got the message. "You go."

"Sure?"

He nodded.

"I'll be quick. And then we can talk, OK?"

Jeremy blinked silently.

"I think you'll agree that we need to talk. All right?"

He folded his arms across his chest and nodded. "OK."

Arthur closed himself into the bathroom and cranked on the water. Then, after dropping his clothes into a soggy pile on the floor, he stepped under the scalding spray and moaned—the heat went into his bones.

The water drenched his head. He lathered himself quickly, then rinsed.

There's only one thing to do now.

He twisted off the water, toweled dry and slipped on jeans and a black T-shirt.

"Your turn," he said after returning to the living room.

Jeremy padded into the bathroom.

A downpour drummed the glass, so he went to the windows and saw that the usually placid reflecting pools were fuzzy from the downpour, and the white concrete pavilions beyond were glossy and slick.

How long would the storm last? Was Carlo's plane even now circling the island, or had they had the sense to stay in Rio until the storm passed? Had he been able to find Afonso? What if he returned with the man—how would this new presence affect their increasingly strange group dynamic? And how the hell could he face Carlo without allowing his expression to show what had just happened?

And how would he deal with Jeremy?

He felt like he had in boot camp when he'd fallen asleep, and those fuckers, led by Rubin, had thrown him that "blanket party"; he was even now just as bewildered: It was like waking up again with a tarp over his head, legs and arms, waiting for the inevitable blows to begin.

He tucked in his T-shirt and sat back waiting for Jeremy so he could clear up this whole thing.

I'm a moon, he thought. *That big planet in space in front of me is love, and I'm made of the same material as it is, but I'm apart—left out for some reason—and yet here I spin dutifully. Everyone else is a part of that planet—that big human experience I'm somehow excluded from: children loving parents and parents loving children, couples growing old together, buddies getting together to watch a game, and talking about their pregnant wives. And it sucks, because love is what I'm all about. I'm a moon.*

His mind drifted back to that moment in the water. And even though his usually implacable conscience was split now with fear and regret, there was still part of him that felt giddy. Joyful. Hopeful.

Jeremy emerged from the bath wearing low-rise sweats that hung well beneath his adonis belt, and no shirt.

"Will you please stop torturing me and put some more clothes on?" Arthur pleaded. "Or better yet, why don't you wear one of those ugly, giant bathrobes that're hanging in the closet, along with my sunglasses."

Jeremy cracked a smile. "Am I that hard for you to resist?"

"You've got no idea, my love. So now that the cat's out of the bag, I think we should have a serious talk. But hurry, because your real lover might walk in the door any second."

He returned wearing an oversized sweatshirt.

"Much better." Arthur motioned for him to sit.

They faced each other, their arms crossed and eyes shifting, with Jeremy in one of the white Barcelona chairs and Arthur on the long part of the sectional. It occurred to Arthur that to the casual observer, of which there were none at the moment, they might have looked like a father questioning his teenage son about his errant credit card usage, or where the new dent in the Chevy Tahoe originated. And in some sensible, parallel universe—of which there was also none—perhaps this very scene was being played out in exactly that way.

But not here.

Their universe had never been sensible.

"What happened today can never happen again," Arthur announced, finally.

"I *knew* you'd act this way." Jeremy rolled his eyes and huffed. "Why're you making this into such a big deal?"

"Because it *is* a big deal. Changing our relationship into *that* just isn't right."

Jeremy shot him a challenging glare. "But it sure seemed to me that that's what we both wanted. Yeah?"

"Look, what people want and what they should do are usually very different things. I love our relationship just the way it is. And I think you do, too."

"I'm in love with you, and I'm sick of acting like I'm not—and I think you are, too."

"You're not in love with me. You're just confused."

"Don't tell me how I'm feeling."

Arthur looked away, then focused back on Jeremy. "Then can I ask how long you've been feeling this way?"

"I don't know," he mumbled. "It seems like forever."

Arthur felt bewildered again. *Blanket party.* "What should I do?"

Time passed, but Jeremy made no effort to indicate he'd heard him. "Jeremy?"

His eyes lifted to him finally, and Arthur saw fear in them. "Isn't it obvious? You told me—no, you *showed* me today that you're in love with me. And I've felt it for so long from you, and I know you've felt it from me. I knew...I *knew* it when you called me in Hawai'i; it was what

I'd been waiting for. But up until then...you don't know what I've been through."

Arthur's stomach tightened as he saw tears well up in Jeremy's eyes. "I don't want to hurt you any more than you've been—"

"But you want this!" he shouted. "I know you do!"

Arthur shook his head. "If there is one thing I can tell you for certain, it's that you don't know what I want...mostly because *I* don't know what I want."

"I do about *this*."

Arthur needed to be firm. "Of course I love you," he replied flatly. "But not that way. I just got carried away at the beach because it'd been so long and we were having such a great time. I took advantage of you, and for that I'm sorry. You're like a son to me, and I don't want that to ever change."

"*Bullshit!*" Jeremy laughed. "Would you do what we did with your 'son'? You're just saying that because you're trying to convince yourself. And you're trying to convince me."

"But, Jeremy, that's what our relationship is based on: your need for a father and my need for a son."

Jeremy's face reddened. "I only had one father, and he's dead—and so, by the way, is my mom. And since I've lived my life without a dad, I sure as shit don't need one now. I'm beyond that, Arthur. Waaaaay beyond that. What I need is someone I can count on to love me and not to screw me over, and someone I can love back. Who the fuck else is out there for me that I can count on as much as you?"

"What about Carlo?" Arthur asked, sounding more judgmental than he'd intended. "Or had you forgotten about him?"

"Carlo is just...Carlo. I told you back at home that there were problems, and I was interested in somebody else; I just needed to find out that you felt the same way about me first before I figured out what to do about him."

"Yeah?" he asked. "So then what happened to this other guy—the one you told me about? Exactly how many guys are you in love with, currently?"

Jeremy stood up indignantly. "Don't ever say things like that to me, Arthur. If you'd thought about it for two seconds, you would've known that *you* were the one I was talking about."

"*What?*"

Jeremy shook his head, and then began speaking slowly, as if he were addressing the stupidest man on earth. "Remember when I told you that I'd sort of been seeing someone that I had feelings for, and I'd kind of told him how I felt, and that you would be the first one to meet him when the time came, and that as long as I was with Carlo he wouldn't let anything happen between us and that he was *the best?*"

Arthur nodded dumbly.

"Make sense now, *Mr. FBI Agent?*"

Arthur got up from the sofa and made his way to the window. "OK. I get it now," he said, speaking to the glass. "Carlo or no Carlo, I'm just trying to imagine us as partners, as equals. It's just that our age difference...it's *huge.*"

"Will you stop with that shit?" Jeremy yelled. "I don't care!"

Arthur turned to him. "I can see that you don't care, and I'm flattered; really I am. But it's not the numbers, my love. It's *developmental*, or whatever you want to call it. You have so much you need to experience in this life: college and grad school and making friends and losing friends and finding your own way...finding what it is that you want out of life, and building a life with someone who's going through the same things you are, or at least walking with you down that same path."

Jeremy began pacing. "You must be thinking that you're talking to someone who's had a normal life, but that's not me; I guess you already forgot that whatever *developmental* experience I was supposed to have got thrown away when my uncle killed my father, or when my mom drank herself to sleep every night, or when my aunt tried to make me into the resurrection of her *dear, dear nephew.*" He laughed bitterly. "The truth is this: You're the only person in my whole life—on this whole planet— who's ever seen me for who I am, and has ever loved me for *me*—but not because now I'm some cute rich kid. And because you think you're *too old* or that *it's wrong*, you're gonna keep us both from being together and loving each other?"

He went to him, and Arthur turned away, but Jeremy wrapped his arms around his waist anyway and put his chin on the back of his shoulder. "From that first night when I got to Ballena Beach, I saw something in your eyes that I'd never seen before in my whole life."

And I saw something in your eyes, only I had seen it before.

Jeremy's hands smoothed the hard muscles of Arthur's stomach.

Arthur felt himself becoming aroused. "Don't do that. Please."

Jeremy began untucking the shirt from Arthur's pants, and his mouth gently kissed the back of his neck. "I love you," he whispered, and then nuzzled his earlobe. "So, so, so much."

Arthur squeezed shut his eyes. How could he tell him that sometimes, when he imagined them making love, it was Jonathan he saw himself with? And his body perfume—that haunting mix of chlorine and water and simmering testosterone—he'd savored it on the boy's father, and even from the beginning had found himself inhaling next to Jeremy, just to get a reminiscent whiff.

Now here he was. Being held by him. Feeling the rise and fall of his chest against his back, and the swell in his pants pressed against his ass. *I love you so much* was the only thought his brain could stammer, just as it was the lone thrum of his soul.

Should he turn and kiss him and take him here, right now, or even be taken by him, with the threat of Carlo walking in the door any moment?

"We'd better sit down." He turned and their eyes met. "There's something I need to tell you."

CHAPTER 24

When I was almost eighteen, I fell in love for the first time. With a boy; he was younger than me—sixteen—but in some ways he was much more mature than I was, or at least I thought so at the time. He was beautiful, and smart, and proudly gay. He turned my world upside down. I don't know if I've ever loved anyone as much as I loved him; maybe in some ways I didn't even feel as strongly for Danny as I did for him. And since then I've spent most of my adult life looking for someone who could make me feel the way he did…someone I could feel as passionately about, and up until now I haven't. I've come close, but there's something unforgettable about your first love, as you know."

"What does this have to do with us?" Jeremy asked impatiently.

"Just wait," Arthur said. "This boy, this wonderful creature and I spent nights making love on the beach, and we did everything else together; we really were inseparable. We loved each other; I know we both did—we were both each other's firsts…you know, we'd been virgins up 'til then. We talked about the future, made plans for college and even after that. Our friends knew we were together, even some of the guys on the Ballena Beach High football team knew. I was graduating that year, so we decided I would get a head start on getting us established, as crazy as that sounds. Everything was set, and we were going to make a go of it."

Jeremy's eyes belied his polite boredom. "So?"

"Oldest story in the book," Arthur said with a sigh. "He broke my heart. I found out through friends that he'd been fooling around with this other kid from our high school, some hot Latin kid named Jaime. Sound familiar?"

Jeremy nodded absently and folded his arms across his chest. "I know the type."

"So I confronted him, and he admitted what was going on, and we broke up, and then he and Jaime continued their relationship.

"Then something happened between them. I never found out what it was, but they broke up suddenly, and my ex-boyfriend, this proud gay kid, well, he started dating a *girl*. And he wound up marrying her after getting her pregnant, if you can believe it."

Jeremy laughed. "I guess that's what they did back then, huh? I mean, that kind of sounds like what happened with my dad."

"It's exactly what happened"—he locked eyes with him—"with your dad."

Jeremy's smile froze. "Huh?"

"Jonathan was my first love. *My first lover.* He's one of the reasons I joined the Marines in the first place; I just couldn't stand the thought of carrying on with our life plans without him. Plus, I was really, really depressed."

Jeremy paced from the chair to the windows and back again. "So the Marines turned into the FBI…and Katharine starts investigating Bill…and the FBI assigns you to our house?" His eyes were wide. "That's just too fuckin' weird."

"Not really. When the case came up against Bill, they asked me if I wanted the job because my file said I was from Ballena Beach, and they thought this would be an asset to the case. But later they found out that Jonathan and I had been involved, so they disciplined me for not disclosing that to them in the first place."

"Does Aunt Katharine know? About you and him?"

"Not that I know of. I don't even know if she ever knew about Jonathan being gay."

Jeremy chuckled. "Oh, she knew all right."

Arthur's brows scrunched. "How do you know?"

"Well, she told me his name was *Jamie*, not Jaime. She caught them together, in the house. *Having the gay sex.* And she made him go to therapy to get 'fixed,' and I figured he was so embarrassed by the whole thing that he started screwing my mom to prove to Katharine that he *was* all fixed up."

"And she got pregnant."

"*With me.*"

"How convenient. So that's what happened with Jonathan and Jaime…." His voice trailed off. "And that explains Jonathan's big turnaround; it was creepy to see him all of a sudden being Mr. Hetero Jock, especially after…"

"After what?"

Arthur smiled. "After I *knew what he liked*. And I'll leave it at that."

"Hmmm. Well, my aunt can be pretty convincing, as you know."

Arthur got up from the chair and made his way back to the windows. "If she had caught them, I can see why Jonathan would have done exactly what he did. He was scared of her and of being cut off from the money, and he really didn't have anyone else he could count on, except for me. But I wasn't enough."

"You guys were real young."

"Yes, we were," Arthur agreed, staring straight at him. "Just like you are now, we were very, very young."

"So back when I came to Ballena Beach you told me you knew my dad, and I remember you saying something like you knew him, 'but not the way I wanted to.'"

"I lied. No one knew him as well as I did. And I'm glad you know that now."

"I kinda wish I didn't."

Arthur nodded. "But can you see now why I had to tell you?"

"Yeah. I see. Is that why you're so freaked out about us *having the gay sex*?"

"Do you think?" Arthur laughed. "It's bizarre on so many levels.... I mean, that in so many ways—as you know—you're so much like him. Like his twin. And that's great, especially since you really have become your own man, since you've found yourself and your own identity. But what really gets me is...that if...how can I say this, if Jonathan and I had stayed together, maybe we would have had a child, and that child, in some bizarre way, should've been you."

"That doesn't make any sense."

"I know it doesn't. It's not rational. But if you think about it, I guess I'm speaking more in a cosmic sense. I was Jonathan's lover. Lovers stay together and have kids. You're Jonathan's kid. See what I mean?"

"I guess...but I'm not yours."

"You're right. But then, here I am put on this earth to protect you from Bill and teach you how to throw a baseball and help you be a proud gay man. I mean, for the past year I really have been sort of like a father to you. You even gave me that Father's Day paperweight you made in school."

Jeremy smiled, remembering. "Yeah. You were. But even from the beginning, I felt like, something more than that for you."

"Like what? Or maybe I shouldn't ask."

Jeremy shoved his hands deep into the pockets of his sweats. "I remember the first time I saw you, I thought, 'Jesus, he's hot.' And...this is confession time, right?" He paused, but Arthur said nothing, so he continued. "Sometimes, it wouldn't be just guys from the swim team I thought about in bed at night. You know?" He raised his eyebrows.

"I know." He visualized a dollhouse-like cutaway of the Tyler house, with Arthur pleasuring himself downstairs thinking about Jeremy upstairs while Jeremy was upstairs pleasuring himself thinking about Arthur downstairs.

It was sort of French-comedy material, in a way.

"And that first time you held me, remember? We were in your room?"

"Of course I remember. We were talking about Jonathan and Danny being out there somewhere, together even."

"And you put your arms around me, and hugged me."

"And at first you didn't hug me back."

"I couldn't." He looked down. "I was scared of you."

"*Scared of me?* Why on earth would you've been scared of me?"

"Because you're a man. *A real man.* Powerful, and experienced." Jeremy looked up at the ceiling, trying to find the words to express what was in his heart. "And even though I know you love me, I think you forget who I am. And that's scary."

"That's impossible."

Jeremy laughed. "Think for a second where I was a year ago, and what my life was like until my mom went into rehab."

He pondered the question. "OK?"

"Don't you get it?" His jaw clenched and he glared at him.

Arthur sighed. "I guess I don't."

"You see me as Jonathan almost as much as Katharine does. But I'm not. Underneath all of this, I'm just that fucked-up, ass-poor kid who grew up in that shitty apartment in Fresno with a drunk mom. And what pisses me off is that everyone forgets that who I really am isn't what you see. I'm what you *don't* see. I"—he fought sudden tears—"I want you to love me and I want to love you, because I've never had anyone *ever* who put me first, except you. So much that you make me feel teeny sometimes."

"What do you mean, 'teeny'?"

Jeremy made his way over to him. "You make me feel like I could"—he reached out and took his hand—"be safe. Forever. That you could protect me and bring out the best in me. Like you did already."

Arthur reached down and took his other hand, and they stood face-to-face.

"When you held me that night, it was like a wall came tearing down, a wall I didn't even know was there before. It was the beginning of...*me*; it was when I started *feeling* things that people—normal people—are supposed to feel. And I felt right then that we belonged together, that we fit together like...like socks fit feet. Perfectly, you know?"

"I felt it, too," Arthur said.

He slipped his hands around Arthur's waist. "I still feel it," he murmured, pulling their bodies together. "I feel it every day."

Arthur resisted, with every rational synapse in his brain screaming *no!* But when he felt the heat and smelled the scent from Jeremy's body, his head spun crazily with desire. In an instant their contact became too much for him to refuse, and Jeremy clenched him harder, and raised his mouth to his and pressed their lips together, and Arthur hugged him fiercely and wrenched his mouth open with his own. Their tongues mashed and twisted, and Jeremy shoved his body tighter against Arthur's and slipped his hands up inside his T-shirt. And as their kisses became deeper and more furious, Arthur heard him whimper.

He breathed him in.

Seawater...skin...my Jeremy...

He broke his mouth away and pressed their cheeks together so hard that Jeremy thought his skin would tear from the scrape of the man's stubble. "You have no idea how much I love you," Arthur's tortured voiced managed, at last. "Or how scared I am."

"But what are you—," Jeremy started to ask, but stopped.

He heard footsteps running up the front stairs.

CHAPTER 25

They pulled away from each other, wide-eyed.

Arthur pointed to the bathroom, and Jeremy trotted on tiptoe into it and pressed the door shut. Once inside, he turned on the sink faucet full blast.

Arthur, glad that his T-shirt was already untucked, adjusted his aching erection before making his way to the entrance. *Don't look guilty.* He rubbed his face, then reached down to slide open the door. "Thank God," he said to Carlo, meaning it. "You made it back safely." With one glance at the young man's face, he could see he was worried. *Could he possibly know what just happened?* "Did you find Afonso?"

"Hey, Arthur," Carlo said, stepping inside. "Where's Jeremy?"

"In the bathroom." He threw a nod toward the closed door. "I guess lunch didn't agree with him."

"Neither did my visit to that favela," he replied, making his way toward the sofa sectional. "I did find Afonso, but it took me a while because now he goes by the name 'Babalu.'"

Arthur chuckled. "Babalu? Like Lucy and Ricky?"

Carlo shook his head as he began unlacing his soggy shoes. "It's an old family nickname I'd almost forgotten about. But once I found him we had a nice little chat and he gave me some very interesting information. We all need to talk. *Now.*"

"I'm sure he'll be out in a second." Arthur made his way to the kitchenette. "Want something to drink?"

"Naw. Sure. Yeah, that'd be great." He looked around the room, trying to regain his bearings. "Hey, how much do you know about Fabiano?"

"Just what that friend of mine from the bureau told me: family was in the slave trade, some shady union squelching, stuff like that." *Was that what this was about?* "But I guess like any good businessman, he's a shark—and he's probably done some things he doesn't want us to know about. By the way, how's your cousin's health? Is he doing OK?"

"He isn't doing so great," Carlo told him. "But not as bad as I thought. It's hard to tell; I'm still not really sure what's wrong with him. Didn't want to ask."

The bathroom door opened and Jeremy emerged, smiling brightly. "Hey, baby," he said, and went over to Carlo and kissed him. "How'd it go?"

"Not so good. But I did find him."

"What happened? God, is he really sick?"

He shook his head. "I was just telling Arthur he's doing better than I thought." He lowered his voice to a whisper. "It's what he said, or *didn't* say, about our host that freaked me out." He looked at the men and saw identical expressions of concern.

"What?" Arthur asked as he handed him the glass of water.

"He said we need to leave—the three of us. Right away. That it's really dangerous here." He looked from one to the other. "But he wouldn't give me anything specific; just as I was gonna beg him to tell me, those two gorillas came up to his shack and said we had to leave 'cause of the weather. And they were right, because the flight back was really bumpy."

"And you don't have any idea what he meant?" Arthur asked.

Carlo shrugged, then finished his water.

"Then we need to go back and find out," Jeremy suggested, "then come back here."

Carlo shook his head. "No. He said to *leave*."

"We can't just *leave*," Jeremy countered. "There's too much going on here, and too much I still need to do. Aunt Katharine would kill me if I cut the trip short without finding out what I needed to."

"Who gives a shit about Aunt Katharine?" Carlo snapped. "Babalu said *get out*. So that's what we need to do."

"How reliable do you think he is?" Arthur asked.

"If you mean do I think he was telling me the truth, absolutely."

"What, exactly, did he say? Tell me as much as you can remember."

"He said something like, 'The less you know, the better it'll be for you, because you still need to smile into Fabiano's face,' and we should 'just find a way to go home today or tonight if you can; you don't know how much danger you're in.' He even knew that he goes by the name El Gigante, and said he was a very bad man."

"Shit," said Jeremy.

"We need to find out what it was he was going to tell you," Arthur stated. "And if it's that bad, we're on the next flight home."

"Then I'll go back there," Carlo offered. "Tomorrow, if I can get that plane to take me over there again. I'll just"—he looked up at the ceiling—"throw some aspirins in a little bag and tell them it's some kind of AIDS drug, and that I need to get it to him right away. Then I'll smile all pretty in his big ol' pumpkin face."

Jeremy glanced at Arthur, then back at Carlo. "We'll go with you."

Arthur nodded. "Yeah. We'll go together; it was stupid for us to separate even just once. In the meantime, I think we've seen enough here to report our findings to Katharine. And if there's anything more we can find out from Babalu, we'll add that, too."

"If we're all leaving suddenly," Jeremy asked, "then what'll we tell Fabiano?"

"We can tell him"—Carlo squinted—"someone at home is really sick, like my dad, so we need to go."

"But none of the cell phones work here," Jeremy reminded. "How would you know if someone was sick back home?"

"Because I just got back from Rio, dummy, and got my voice mail there." Carlo smiled brightly while pulling his phone from his pocket. "Which I did, by the way, and he is really sick. Food poisoning from some old *chorizo*."

"And we'll tell him we're so happy with what we've seen, we're recommending that Katharine throw him even more support."

"Yeah," agreed Jeremy.

Carlo stood. "Then let's get out of here. First thing tomorrow."

CHAPTER 26

Was that her cell phone ringing in the kitchen? She thought she'd heard it earlier, but when she checked it there was no voice mail, and no evidence of a missed call. So she left the phone on the granite countertop and went back into the conservatory, where she continued poring over the revised trust papers her attorneys had sent over that morning.

Settlors, trustees, deeds, appointers, beneficiaries, tax liabilities. She was sick to death of this language, of this unending legalese. But it was necessary that she scrutinize every line; Bill's embezzling from her had demonstrated clearly that she could no longer sit on the sidelines and just expect her corporation and investments to flourish.

She heard a noise, and cocked her head. *Yep, that's it.* But who could be calling? *God, please let it not be about Jeremy.*

She jumped up from her seat and marched quickly across the room, through the long dining room and into the kitchen, and was just reaching for the phone when it stopped ringing.

She picked it up and looked for the missed-call icon.

Nothing.

They'll call back.

She clutched the phone in her hand and made her way back to the conservatory. She had just folded herself down onto the old wicker chaise when it rang again.

"Katharine Tyler," she announced.

"Mrs. Tyler," the man's friendly baritone announced, "this is Special Agent Carl Singer. I work for the Federal Bureau of Investigation."

"Are you the one who's been calling?"

"Yes, we've been trying to reach you."

"Then please, Agent Singer, you should know that it's good manners to leave a voice mail. Now, what might I do for you?"

"We've obtained some information that concerns your corporation, and we'd like you to come down to our office immediately."

"I'm rather engaged at the moment," she told him flatly. "But I'll be happy to give you the number of the law firm that handles these matters."

"It's urgent. It concerns your venture in the Brazilian resort."

She felt her face flush. "Has something happened to my nephew?"

"Nothing we are aware of, Mrs. Tyler." He paused. "It's of a sensitive nature, and the bureau would prefer that we convey this information to you in person."

She huffed. "Could you please tell me what this is regarding?"

"I'm sorry, but I'm not permitted. Do you remember where our office is located?"

"How could I forget?" she answered dryly. "At what time?"

"As soon as possible. And I'm sorry to inconvenience you with such short notice."

She looked at her watch. "I can be there within the hour. Should I ask for you?"

"Yes, please. My office is on the fourteenth floor; we'll be waiting for you."

"Should I take anything with me?"

"That won't be necessary."

"Then I'll see you soon, Agent Singer."

"Thank you, Mrs. Tyler. Oh, and one more thing."

"Yes?"

"For future reference, you should know that the bureau doesn't leave voice mails concerning matters of this nature."

CHAPTER 27

Some urgent business with his bankers had necessitated Dom Fabiano taking the jet into Rio de Janeiro that morning, so he was glad to oblige the trio with their request to visit Carlo's cousin again, and then leave for home. So Carlo, Jeremy and Arthur, in their best impersonations of double agents, sat opposite the big man, making small talk during the quick flight back from the island, telling him how excited they were about the resort, and how Jeremy would recommend his family's continued participation in the venture, and might even pledge more support in case it was needed.

Fabiano seemed satisfied with their response but appeared more glum than he had on the island. In any case, as the plane began its descent into Rio's airport, Arthur figured they were home free.

That is, after they paid their last visit to Babalu.

Fabiano insisted on calling a car for them; Arthur wanted badly to refuse his help, but to have done so would have appeared suspicious. So this time it was a black Denali that wove its way through the narrow streets leading up to the favela.

After it pulled curbside, the three let themselves out of the backseat and began making their way up the crazy stairs toward Babalu's, as the bodyguards below leaned against the SUV, smoking their cigarettes.

Arthur looked up to see the morning haze beginning to clear, while across the hills Cristo vanished and reappeared through the floating shroud of clouds. He considered the statue for a moment, and concluded that although Flavius said the statue represents "freedom from Portugal's imperialism," it now seemed the perfect metaphor for oppression, considering how those rosary-clutching, genuflecting Portuguese had been some of the most rabid pope worshippers of all time. Thus Cristo seemed an assurance that the Brazilians would never throw off the church's imperialism; because if *imperialism* meant having foreigners dictate your life, how much more insidious to have their religion imposed upon your mind and soul, even into their supposed afterlife?

Up and up they climbed, while the people they encountered looked at them as if they had just stepped out of a flying saucer. Up beyond this shack and that wall and another pile of garbage they followed Carlo, until he slowed his climb, made a left and came to a yellow door.

He knocked.

No answer came, so he knocked again.

He tried twisting the doorknob, but it was locked. So they went around to the window and peered inside.

Babalu's bed and belongings were untouched.

Had he just left for the morning? When would he be back?

"Ela não está aqui," an old woman's voice rasped from behind them.

Carlo turned. *"Sabe onde ele foi, Nana?"*

She shook her bandana-wrapped head and held up two fingers. *"Dois homens. Ele saiu com dois homens."*

Carlo's stomach flipped. *"Eles estavam armados?"* he whispered to her.

Her eyes widened; then she held up her hands in the universal I-don't-know gesture.

"Fuck!" Carlo exclaimed. "She said he left with two big men!"

Carlo and Jeremy looked at each other; then the younger men looked at Arthur. "We need to get out of here," he told them.

"With those gorillas?" Jeremy asked. "Do we trust them?"

"We don't have a choice right now," he said. "In twenty minutes we'll be back at the airport, and we should be safe there until we can catch a flight—any flight—out of here." He looked at Jeremy and saw he was breathing hard. "Carlo, you lead the way down. And for God's sake, don't look like anything's wrong. When we get into the car, make sure Jeremy's in the middle."

"Why?" Jeremy asked, sounding panicked.

"Because, young man, you are the proverbial chicken who lays the golden eggs," Arthur joked, trying to alleviate the tension.

"And we don't want any big bad giant stealing you," Carlo added.

They picked their way back down the hillside, and when they approached the vehicle Braulio and his sidekick threw their cigarettes in the gutter.

Carlo went around to one side and got in, while Jeremy entered the car on the other, followed by Arthur.

Carlo fixed a casual smile on his face as they buckled themselves into the backseat. "He went out for breakfast," he told the men in Portuguese. "So I guess we'll just go to the airport now."

"*Si, si*," the men acknowledged. And with that, Braulio pulled and pushed the gearshift into drive, then back into reverse, over and over as the huge vehicle made a five-point turn in the narrow street, then snaked its way back down the hill.

Minutes later they were lurching along with the rest of Rio's crazed morning traffic.

But what happened next took everyone by surprise.

CHAPTER 28

They were sitting at a stoplight perhaps only ten minutes from the airport—Arthur was counting the minutes since they left Babalu's favela—when the Denali was rear-ended. *Hard.*

"Shit!" Carlo exclaimed, after his head snapped backward from the impact.

"What the fuck was that?" asked Jeremy, looking around.

Arthur knew exactly what had happened.

Braulio put the car in park and reached for the door handle. *"No! Go, go, go!"* Arthur barked at him, but he was already halfway out the door.

As was the other.

The vehicle was swarmed by five men in ski masks holding Uzis, and the bodyguards had their hands in the air.

"Jesus, Jesus, Jesus," Arthur muttered.

I've got to protect him—I'll do anything—I should've known—

The soldier in him came to life as the rear glass windows were shattered.

"Maos pra cima!" a man's voice screamed.

"They said get our hands in the air," Carlo hissed.

"Jeremy, don't move!" Arthur instructed. "Keep your head down. *Now!"* Arthur pushed his head down and covered his body with his own. He heard Carlo cry out, and looked up in time to see a man's arm reach inside the door and open it, then yank him out as Arthur reached for his arm but missed.

"Senao bou atirar!" the voice commanded.

"They'll kill us if we don't do what they say!" Carlo yelled from the street.

Arthur heard the *TATATATATAT!* of the Uzi being discharged in the air; then the smoking barrel was shoved through the window into Jeremy's back. *"Ow!"* he cried, as the familiar smell of spent gunpowder filled the interior.

"Baby, they've got us," Arthur told him. His training told him to surrender. "Just do what I do. They'll take us together. All they want is money."

Arthur's hands went in the air, and he slowly made his way out of the vehicle. He looked back to see Jeremy copy his movements, and the look on the boy's face any other time would have made him cry.

They threw Arthur onto the street next to Carlo, with booted feet holding them down, as well as a gun barrel pressed into the backs of their skulls.

Then moments later he heard some of the most sickening sounds he'd ever heard—sounds he would file in his memory right next to the phone ringing that day in Germany—the screech of wheels spinning and an engine gunning, and the unsteady sobs of Carlo lying next to him.

CHAPTER 29

Their hands were bound and their mouths gagged and their pockets emptied of their wallets, passports and cell phones before they were pushed into a van, then blindfolded, and driven through the city somewhere up into the hills; Arthur detected their locale from the vehicle's shifting from low to high, and its listing from side to side. During this excursion, the only way he could tell Carlo was OK was by tapping his foot with his own, upon which Carlo would tap him back.

He'd learned about kidnappings during his stint with the FBI, and knew that in most cases they either ended with death—if the ransom amount was refused—or quickly with release, if the demand was paid. But he figured Katharine would be forthcoming with the needed money, considering the purported bounty in the Tyler coffers. The only complication might be if their capture had been politically motivated; then the State Department would refuse to become involved, due to their zero-tolerance policy on negotiating with kidnappers of political targets.

The thought made him dizzy.

Until he considered the money.

This has to be about the money.

Finally, the van stopped and he heard the squeal of metal hinges as a door was moved aside. They continued a short distance, then stopped again, and the engine was switched off. He heard men chattering in Portuguese, then the rolling open of the vehicle's cargo doors. He felt hands grab at his biceps and push down his head as he was pulled from his seat.

"Take those blindfolds off them at once!" he heard Dom Fabiano's voice shriek. "And cut those ropes. Are you stupid?"

At once the blindfold was slipped from his head and he could see again; they were inside some sort of large garage or warehouse with hewn stone walls.

The air inside was cool and damp.

We're inside a mountain.

They cut the ropes binding his hands, and the gag from his mouth was untied. He looked over and saw Carlo was being cut loose, as well.

Where's Jeremy?

"My poor friends!" Fabiano exclaimed, rushing down a flight of stairs.

Arthur stepped toward him. "What the fuck is going on?" he growled. "What did you do to Jeremy?"

Fabiano held up his hands. "What the *fuck* is going on is I have paid for your release!" he stated indignantly. "But if you'd like I can deliver you back to the monsters who were responsible for your capture."

What's going on? He looked at the man's face and saw he was telling the truth. "Thank you," he said, rubbing his wrists. "But please, tell us where Jeremy is."

"You were captured and ransomed by a militant group. Kidnappings like this have been taking place for the past decade; some wealthy Brazilians have even resorted to travel by helicopter to evade this phenomenon."

"But where's Jeremy?"

"We are working toward his release. We don't know where he is, but we have been assured he is safe. *For the time being.*"

"Does Katharine Tyler know about this?" Carlo asked, hugging his shoulders.

He looked like he was about to faint, so Arthur threw a steadying arm around his shoulders.

"Of course. She is the one who caused this."

"That can't be," said Arthur.

"Come with me. There is so much I need to tell you. But first, you should have a drink and some food; you have been through a terrible, terrible ordeal today. I can explain everything while you rest and eat. Please, come."

And with that, Arthur and Carlo followed him up the stairs, and into the bowels of the mountain.

CHAPTER 30

They passed through an old, unused catering kitchen into a long hallway that stank of mold, then pulled themselves up yet another long flight of stairs to a door that opened onto the grand foyer of Fabiano's once elegant modernist mansion.

Arthur noticed, with a quick scan, the neglected state of the extravagant materials: the limestone walls were dirty and had even drawn algae in places, the terrazzo floor was a map of bulges and cracks, and the mahogany-paneled walls were faded and sun bleached. Even the simple chandelier bowls overhead were missing strings of crystals.

They continued at a fast clip through the entrance hall, then through the sparsely furnished salon, then stepped outside into the viewing garden, where the teeming beachside city lay below, and Cristo peered down from just the next hilltop.

Carlo and Arthur took their places in chairs around a glass table, while hot coffee and pastries were served.

"This is a very sensitive situation," Fabiano said after sipping from his cup, "that could have been avoided. But there is still an easy remedy."

"Could you please tell us what's going on?" Arthur asked.

He looked from Arthur to Carlo and back. "To be brief, Katharine Tyler has withdrawn all funding and support for this project. She attained a court order to withdraw millions of her dollars from the consortium's escrow account."

"*What?*" they asked.

"As a result, one of the members of our consortium, with apparent ties to…a militant group, organized this kidnapping in an attempt to recover their money."

"But you said she took *her* money out," Carlo blurted. "Why would some group be trying to get *their* money back by kidnapping us and Jeremy?"

"And why would she have taken her money out in the first place?" asked Arthur.

"It's complicated," Fabiano stated, withdrawing his cigarettes from his shirt pocket. "The order came directly from your government's State Department, with her name and signature, as well as those of her attorneys, on the papers. If you'll recall, Carlo, when you asked to come find your cousin again, I mentioned some urgent business I had with my bankers in Rio. This was that very issue. Of course I did what I could to remedy the situation, but I had no idea that any of you were in danger; even I am wholly surprised by this terrible turn of events." He pushed a cigarette between his lips and lit it with his gold lighter.

"But I don't understand why they would've made her do this," Arthur said. "We didn't give her any reason to pull out; in fact, we haven't even had any contact with her since we got here."

"It wasn't you, dear friends. It was your government." The man sucked heavily on his cigarette, then pushed his huge frame up from the chair and began pacing back and forth, emitting smoke with each word spoken. "The world has become a difficult place to do business, a place that becomes more complex each year. Simply put, your government alleges that since the Tyler family is part of the consortium where one of the members has alleged ties with this militant group, then the Tylers have been, de facto, funding anti-American activities throughout the world—especially in the Middle East and Southeast Asia."

"But I'm certain that Katharine didn't know anything about this, so how can they hold her responsible for contributing to some militant group?"

"Clearly they are strong-arming her," Fabiano replied. "And I'm certain they threatened her with very serious charges had she not withdrawn her support, immediately."

"But why would they kidnap Jeremy?" Carlo asked.

"As I said, this is also complicated," Fabiano said, blowing out another drag, "but since this group of investors, which I assure you appeared to be completely legitimate, has been exposed for what they are and their funds have been seized, they are attempting to recoup, by force, that which they will most certainly lose—not only from the loss of their initial capital, which is frozen now and will most certainly be tied up in litigation for years, but also from what they imagine they should lose in the long run after being excluded from our wonderful resort."

"That's just crazy," Arthur said, shaking his head. "But I understand why the State Department would have reacted that way. Now the only thing that matters is getting him back."

Fabiano dipped his eyelids and nodded. "The group holding him has been in contact with me, and they assure me that he is fine, and is being cared for appropriately. But they have given us, as well as Mrs. Tyler and your government, a very short time frame for payment."

"So what's the deadline?" Carlo asked, not realizing his choice of words.

"Tomorrow. At nine p.m."

"And if Katharine can't get it together by then, what'll they do?"

Instead of answering, Fabiano shook his head.

"What have the police said about this?" asked Arthur. "I assume you've contacted them and they're working on their end?"

He laughed. "Involving the corrupt Brazilian police would be foolish. They would only complicate the situation. Remember, this is an international issue—not some little traffic accident."

Arthur thought for a moment. "So do you know how much they're demanding?"

"The amount has not been disclosed to me. At this point, I am simply the mediator: cash for a life, all or nothing. I'm sorry to be so blunt."

"I need to call Katharine, and my phone's gone. Carlo, do you have yours?"

He shook his head. "They took mine, too."

"Is there one I can use?" he asked Fabiano.

"Of course. In my office. Please." He stood and motioned for them to follow, and they made their way back through the house into his office. Arthur sat behind his desk and dialed first the international code, then her number.

It rang once. "Yes?" Katharine's panicked voice asked.

"It's Arthur."

"Oh, thank God it's you. Are you all right? I've been trying to reach you about this fiasco."

"Carlo and I are fine."

"Have you heard anything about Jeremy?"

"We're working on it. Fabiano's mediating. They've given us a deadline of tomorrow at nine p.m."

"*Nine p.m.?* Then they've moved it up from midnight!" she cried. "You cannot believe this mess our government has us in! And if you can believe it, they have some pompous jackass telling me that because this is the work of a militia group that's an 'organization of interest' and an 'enemy of the United States,' they are refusing to negotiate with them on our behalf, because 'negotiating with these groups only encourages more kidnappings'! You should hear the doublespeak from these idiots at the State Department; you'd think I was only trying to get my car registered at the DMV!"

"I was afraid of that." Arthur's skin crawled, and he shivered. "But why would some anti-American 'organization of interest' want to throw money into some resort with security that was guaranteed to keep their kind out?"

They both answered his question. "Money laundering."

"Remember, Arthur," she continued, "remember what I said that day down at the architect's office about 'our own little Masada'?"

It took him a moment, but her words came back to him. "You said this time it would be the Romans who were inside the fort."

"What was I *thinking*?" she said, beginning to cry. "I should've known that anything Bill was involved with would be supremely corrupt. And to think that my money, Jeremy's and my money, has been going to pay for such *atrocities!* And then to negotiate with these...*these beasts for his very life!* I can't stand it, Arthur; I just cannot stand it!"

He had to think quickly to calm her. "But you don't have to negotiate with them. Fabiano's doing the mediating. You just need to get him the money, and he can do the rest."

"Hah! That sounds easy. *Have they told you how much they want?*"

"No. He said it was inconsequential; an all-or-nothing situation."

"*One...hundred...million...euro,*" she told him, her voice quivering. "At today's exchange rate, do you know how much money that is?" she cried. "Do they think I keep that kind of money in my purse? Who the hell do they think they're dealing with? *And where the hell am I going to get nearly one hundred fifty million dollars by tomorrow evening?*"

"Who's your liaison at the bureau?"

"Some man named Singer; he seems nice enough, but I don't know how effectual he is. Do you know of him?"

"No. But it doesn't matter. What did he tell you? When are they sending down their liaison team?"

"They are not. Sending one down, that is."

"*Why not?*"

"Because apparently in Brazil, kidnappings are almost as commonplace as instances of shoplifting. And considering his statistics—now let me read them for you." She shuffled around through the papers atop her desk. "Here it is...'there are nearly ninety kidnappings of Americans each day on foreign soil, and eighty-eight percent of these end favorably, so long as the ransom is paid.' So he's telling me to just pay the money and hope they drop off Jeremy alive somewhere before they toodle away with nearly everything I own!"

"So they're not going to do anything," he muttered.

"Apparently not. And to make matters worse, after I spoke with the Brazilian police, I learned that they are so overwhelmed with this 'kidnapping craze' that even they have to make certain this is not a 'virtual kidnapping,' whatever the devil that is, before they send even one man out on the case!"

"I remember those from the bureau," he told her. "That's when they get someone's name, then call their family saying they've been kidnapped when they really haven't; they'll even play a recording of someone screaming so the family runs to the bank and gets the money." He thought for a moment. "But there was nothing 'virtual' about this; I was in the car when it was rear-ended and they fired their Uzi into the air. I'm sure the police know this by now."

"No one seems to know anything, Arthur. And can you believe one of these idiots suggested I should be 'grateful' that the kidnappers contacted me, because sometimes people are abducted and that's the end? No ransom, no grainy videotape, just a corpse? Grateful, indeed!"

"So what're you gonna do?"

"Agent Singer told me—off the record—that I should make them an offer based on however much cash I can scrape together, and there's a Swiss foundation that can make us a loan if I put up Tyler, Inc., as collateral. They help victims' relatives, for a substantial fee of course, to come up with the difference in situations like this; we'll just have to make a good-faith offer and hope these monsters accept it. So I'm working with Singer, that Swiss company and those idiots from the State Department. *But no one is doing anything! Nothing is getting done!*"

"Katharine, the only thing you can do at this point is to send as much money down here as you can, right away. And I'll do whatever I can, too."

"Thank you Arthur," she muttered. "But please don't let anything happen to him; I don't know what I'd do, how I'll live if Jeremy—"

"I'm *not* going to let anything happen to him."

"I...know," she managed between sudden sobs, "you...won't."

He looked up and saw the impatience in Fabiano's eyes. "I've gotta go. I'll call you when I know anything." Then he hung up.

"What did she tell you?" he asked.

He looked from Fabiano to Carlo and back. "Our government won't help us negotiate with the militant group because they are an 'anti-American organization of interest,' and Jeremy qualifies as some sort of political hostage."

"I was hoping they would not go that route," Fabiano said gravely.

"So what happens next?" Carlo murmured, clutching his stomach.

Fabiano leveled his gaze at them both. "We wait for the money. And we pray."

So Arthur and Carlo began that arduous process of waiting under duress, where minutes stretch interminably, and nothing possesses the mind but one's worst fears interwoven with arching hope.

But Carlo and Arthur and Katharine were not the only ones suffering this anguish.

For in a locked room just one floor down, awaited Jeremy.

CHAPTER 31

W here am I?" Jeremy demanded, thinking the bald creature opposite him looked familiar somehow. "What are you gonna do with me? *Who the fuck are you?*"

"Shhh! *Menino!* This is the good part," Rosa told him, then turned her attention to the *novela* blasting from the tiny TV next to her. "Hector is to discover his *novia* is his dead wife's daughter's sister." She sucked in a heavy drag from her unfiltered cigarette, blew out a gray cloud, then pinched some stray tobacco flakes from her tongue. *"Que escándalo!"* she exclaimed, fanning herself dramatically with her free hand. Then she opened her purse and pulled out a tiny brown vial, from which she snorted some white powder.

It hit him: *Marinheiro só.* "You're the one from the club—with the sailor!"

She peered at him coyly. "So you seen my act? You like me singing?" Then she looked him up and down dismissively. "No, you like the boy with the big pee-pee." She giggled, her hands held up and spaced wide. "I make him happy," she announced. "These"—she pointed to her stained teeth—"they come out." Then she mimed some sloppy fellatio.

Jeremy wanted nothing more than to spring up and kick her in those false teeth, but the handcuffs and shackles binding his limbs precluded that possibility. "What's going on? How long'm I gonna be here?"

"Depends on the money," she replied casually, shrugging her bony shoulders. "If money doesn't come, then tomorrow night we take you to church."

"What church?"

"You'll see," she told him, lifting the vial for another bump. Then she squinted at him. "You are so handsome and *macho*. I did not think you are faggot."

"Is that supposed to be a compliment?" he snapped. "I can't even tell if you're fucking male or female."

She shrugged and stuck out her bottom lip dismissively. "I just say what I think," she said, then pressed the little bottle to her nose again and sniffed. "You need to be nice to Rosa. She can make your days happy." The creature smiled at him and arched her painted eyebrows coquettishly. Then her features became a snarling mask. "Or not so happy. You decide."

***

He was grateful for the television, because it kept Rosa's attention from him, and helped to speed the crawl of time; at one point the device's nonsensical drone helped him drift into a fitful nap—but he could only skim the surface of sleep, because of the devilish contraptions on his hands and feet.

And during this ordeal the only thing that kept his hope blooming was the belief that Arthur and Carlo and Aunt Katharine were out there somewhere working feverishly on this situation; because if he allowed himself to dwell on the facts that his freedom was stolen, his lovers might also be imprisoned or even dead, his only blood family was a hemisphere away, and he'd spoken to no one but a crazy drag queen, he would simply go berserk.

This feels like being buried alive.

But he'd been through hard times before, and knew that mental gymnastics could make tolerating the anguish easier. So instead of being chased by his fears, he imagined his rescue: Arthur and Carlo would break down the door, and he'd be picked up and carried over Arthur's strong shoulder to the safety of a waiting car. Then after the handcuffs and shackles were cut off, they'd fly back to Ballena Beach, and by this time tomorrow he'd be lounging by the pool, or strolling along the beach, or cuddling with his new lover in bed.

Instead of being taken to their "church."

He could almost feel Arthur's body heat, could nearly smell his skin. But because he became so entrenched in his fantasy, and because there were no windows to watch the sunlight dim, he was unaware that afternoon was slipping into evening.

Then evening fell to night.

And as he nodded into an uneasy slumber on the tiny bed in that cavelike room, midnight passed and more precious minutes trickled away, like blood pulsing from a slashed vein.

While upstairs, as well as thousands of miles away, neither Arthur nor Carlo nor Katharine slept.

They were all too sick with worry.

CHAPTER 32

They waited. And waited some more. Arthur encouraged Carlo to sleep, but he refused; both men's adrenaline was the equivalent of jet fuel for their metabolisms. So they paced. They sat. Then one paced while the other sat.

"You should really try to get some rest," Arthur told Carlo again. Something was eating at him, and he needed to concentrate in order to figure out what it was.

"I can't. You try." He folded his arms over his chest and looked out the windows at the glimmering lights of Rio below. "I just can't believe I could've been so stupid."

"What do you mean?" Arthur asked. "Stupid about what?"

"I shouldn't even tell you this, because for one thing it doesn't matter, and for the other it just shows how fucking stupid I am."

"What does?"

He sighed. "When we were in Hawaii, Jeremy and I were messing around and he asked if I had three wishes, what would they be, so one of them...was I wished that...that you weren't coming along on this trip." His eyes began to well up. "Can you believe that? Instead of wishing for good health or a safe trip or a cure for fucking cancer, I wished you wouldn't be here. And now look what's happened—it's like God's teaching me a lesson for being greedy, or for taking everything for granted. Can you imagine if I was going through all this down here by myself? What would I have done? What would I do?"

Arthur went to him and hugged him. "None of us knew this was going to happen. And you can't think that just because you wanted to have Jeremy to yourself that somehow God is punishing you—that's so Catholic, by the way." He reached up and smoothed his hair. "See, now, here I am feeling this is all my fault, and I need to fix it somehow, but I can't think of how."

"How's this all your fault?" Carlo rolled his eyes. "The way I see it, this is Katharine's deal. She's the one who made us come down here;

Jeremy told me you said it was too dangerous, and *woops!* here we are." He paused, thinking. "Anyhow, it's probably my fault, because if I hadn't tried to see Babalu again we'd have just gone to the fucking airport and we'd all be home right now, downloading our pictures."

"I'm just sick of sitting...of being here," Arthur said. "Standing around like this goes against everything I've ever been trained to do."

Something's not right.

"So what do you think we should be doing right now?" Carlo asked.

"Searching the city. Working with the bureau back home. Following leads. Anything but just *sitting* here."

"So let's go," Carlo suggested.

Arthur shook his head. "I don't think the time's right. But I'm still wondering about what Babalu said about this guy being so dangerous. I mean, what if this whole thing is a setup? What if he's in on it all and we're all going to be killed once they get what they want?"

Carlo saw the fear in Arthur's eyes, and it frightened him. "You can't think that way."

Arthur laughed. "I *have* to think that way!" He began pacing the length of the room again. "Assuming Babalu's right, let's suppose Fabiano's a horrible guy and is in on this. So what's to prevent him from walking in the door right now and blowing us away? They'd never find us, or Jeremy!"

"So if that's a possibility, then shouldn't we get out of here, like three hours ago?"

"But what if Fabiano really is trying to help? Then we run the risk of pissing him off, or of not being here in case he needs us." Arthur folded his arms over his chest. "But something isn't right, and I can't put my finger on it."

"Is it that he didn't call the police?"

"Uh-uh." Arthur shook his head. "The police here are supposed to be even more corrupt than the drug lords." He bit his lip. "It's something else. Something that I"—he scrunched his eyes shut—"Oh Jesus, why didn't I see it before?"

"See what?"

"He didn't pay for our return! How could he have, when we came straight over here?"

"What do you mean?"

"Carlo, if someone besides Fabiano had kidnapped us, we would've gone somewhere else first, before coming over here. Some time would've gone by. They would've had to exchange some money. Right?"

"Maybe. But what if Fabiano just made a deal with them over the phone?"

Arthur laughed. "No one accepts a promise of ransom over the phone. It's always cash first, then you get your groceries." He began pacing more quickly now. "This whole thing is a setup."

Carlo nodded and raised his eyebrows.

"And we need to get out of here. *Now*."

Carlo's eyes bugged. "Now?"

He nodded.

"How?"

"We'll find a way. A hole in the fence, a guard who's asleep. You just follow my lead and we'll get out of here and find Jeremy."

"Jesus, Arthur. I don't know..."

"*Trust* me on this one; I don't know why I didn't see it before. Getting out of here is Jeremy's only chance. And ours probably, too."

"OK, then. But before we go"—he hesitated—"I need to ask you something. It's kind of important."

Arthur closed his eyes and cracked his neck. He'd felt this coming. "Carlo?"

Carlo looked at him expectantly.

"Does this have anything to do with what we're about to do, or with Jeremy's—or our—safety, in any way?"

Carlo shook his head slowly.

"Then let's have it wait until later." He tried out a smile. "OK?"

He smiled sadly back at him. "I get it."

"Then let's do this." Arthur held out his hand and Carlo grasped it. "Come on!"

CHAPTER 33

Arthur's training had taught him that people reach their deepest sleep after 2 a.m., and since it was nearly that hour they began to prepare.

They were in a room on the third floor, so they pulled the sheets off the bed and tied the ends together; they would use this cliché—yet effective—means to rappel to the ground, then pick their way around the property until they found a way out.

There were a total of four big sheets on the beds, which would do the trick beautifully if Arthur tied them right, so they gathered objects from around the room and did the old summer-camp trick of humping up forms under the remaining covers, so it looked like the pair were slumbering peacefully.

Arthur suggested they communicate with only hand signs and arm movements, and if any danger was evident, a quick snap of the fingers, or a tap on the back, would be sufficient warning.

They slid open the glass door.

While tying the sheet around the sturdiest metal pole that made up the lanai railing, Arthur was relieved to discover that his hands still remembered how to make knots. But he wasn't as confident about his arms' ability to handle his body weight the way they had twenty years ago, when he'd rappelled effortlessly down similar heights while training for the Crucible.

He decided to go first, so if his knots didn't hold he would be the one injured, and also because he wanted to hold the sheets tight for Carlo.

He straddled the rail, grabbed the sheet-rope tightly between his hands, and began easing his way down. Moments later he made the short jump to the ground. Next he pulled the makeshift rope securely while Carlo followed his descent; Arthur grabbed Carlo's hips when he came within reach, and set him gently onto the dirt.

Carlo grinned at him—they were on their way!

Arthur took the lead and almost immediately found a path leading down through the underbrush away from the compound; he figured it would be best to circle around on the path toward the entrance gate in a wide arc, then parallel the wall's path down away from the armed guard's kiosk while keeping an eye toward the road. Once they reached the corner of the property closest to the road, they scaled the tall iron fence—whose spikes, they discovered, were bent toward the street only to keep people out—then dropped down onto the road.

Moments later they were jogging downhill toward the heart of town.

But where could they go? The Brazilian police might even be tied to Fabiano, so their help was questionable; they could try to find the American consulate, but at this hour it was doubtful they could find anyone to help, especially since the State Department was already "handling" the case back home. And how could they explain escaping from a safe locale, and refusing the protection of someone who'd allegedly paid for their own release, and was already in negotiations for Jeremy's?

There was only one thing to do: go back to the favela on the slim chance that Babalu was home, and see if he knew anyone who might help.

But Rio is a big city. A very big city. And they had no map; they had no money. But they did have their recollection of a ramshackle favela somewhere along the Rua São Clemente, directly under Cristo's holy stare, where his dying cousin might or might not be sleeping.

With the statue as their beacon, they walked down from the posh hillside. The suburb gave way quickly to high-rise condos, and those transitioned into lower-rise apartments, and these dissolved into stores and markets and bars shoved between ragged hotels.

"How much farther do you think it is?" Arthur asked as they passed a park.

"I'm...not sure. But some of this is looking familiar. I kind of remember that café over there"—he pointed—"but I really wasn't paying that much attention when we drove over here. I think if we can just get across from the statue, then cut up into the hillside, by then maybe we can find someone to ask."

So they walked, they looked, and Carlo did his best to follow the laser-guided beacon he imagined was shooting out of Cristo's eyes at Babalu's shack. And he did his best not to think about where Jeremy was at that very moment.

Arthur looked at the sky and figured it was after three o'clock; they had been walking for more than an hour down São Clemente, and had less than two to go before it got light. "We need to go faster," he said, and Carlo's pace quickened to match his own.

"Wait!" Carlo exclaimed. "This place, the Praça Corumbá. And this street, the Barão de Macaúbas—I think we're supposed to turn up here! Yeah, look at Cristo! He's right there!"

Arthur saw that, indeed, the giant statue appeared directly opposite to their position, facing the little enclave where they were headed.

Carlo grabbed his arm. "Come on! I know this is it."

Moments later, they entered the favela.

They were stepping quickly now, almost running as they negotiated the now familiar stairs and pathways up to Babalu's. But what would they find? Would he be there? What would they do if he were not?

And there it was. The yellow door.

But there was no light visible through the tiny window.

Carlo leapt up to the stoop and knocked.

CHAPTER 34

There was no answer.

He knocked again. *"Babalu!"* he nearly shouted, doing his best to whisper. *"Babalu! It's me, Carlo!"* He knocked one last time.

A light brightened behind the drapes, and the men shared an excited glance.

The door opened and they found themselves looking at a burly young man who clearly had just awoken. "What is it?" he asked, rubbing his shoulders. "What do you want?"

Carlo took a step backward, and Arthur put a hand on his shoulder. "Babalu, my cousin. Is he here?"

"He is sleeping. You are the cousin from California?"

Carlo nodded. "We've got a big problem." He held his hands up wide. "We need his help."

"He is not well," he said. "The doctor today gave him stronger medicine, and it makes him sleep too much."

"May we please come inside?" Arthur asked. "I'm sorry, but it's an emergency."

"Let them in," said a faint voice from the back of the room.

The young man opened the door wider, and they entered.

Babalu switched on the lamp next to the tiny bed where he lay. Then, looking perplexed, his eyes went from Carlo to Arthur and back again. "You told me your lover was young," he said.

"Arthur's just our friend. Jeremy, my lover, was kidnapped, and we don't know where he is. We need your help—we have no one else to help us."

Babalu winced as he struggled to sit upright. "He," he said, while nodding toward the young man, "is my son, Ernesto." The three men shook hands, while Arthur and Carlo exchanged quick, puzzled glances. "When did this happen with your lover?"

"Yesterday, on our way over here to see you, before we left for the airport. A car rear-ended us and they took him out of the car with guns."

Babalu's eyes narrowed. "Tell me what you know. *Everything*. Then I'll tell you what to do."

So they relayed the events that had transpired, from the moments after the kidnapping to Fabiano's explanation to Arthur's conversation with Katharine to their decision to escape.

When they were finished, Babalu looked at them with eyes that communicated utter exhaustion. "There is something I must tell you, and I hope I am mistaken."

The men looked at him expectantly.

"Today is nineteenth *de Setembro*, yes?"

They nodded.

"You were right to escape—this sounds like his work. He, your Jeremy, is most likely up at El Gigante's villa, as there are many rooms there underground; it was built upon the ancient site of the Morro do Castelo. There are very many places for bad things to happen without anyone ever hearing, without anyone ever knowing."

"Are you saying Jeremy was up there at the same time we were?" Arthur asked.

"I am not sure, but that is a possibility. It is not unheard of to kidnap someone, then to act as mediator, as this makes you the very rich hero." He paused. "I know that place, that villa, very well. We have to get your Jeremy, quickly. *Ernesto!*"

"*Si, Papa.*"

"You will drive us there; I remember how to reach the back road that climbs to his home; it will be safer than going up the front. We will get as close as we can, then I will tell these men where to find him in that miserable place. But we have very little time."

CHAPTER 35

The mood driving back across town in Ernesto's tiny Fiat was quietly tense; both Arthur and Carlo were as exhausted as they were exasperated, because even if Babalu knew exactly where to find Jeremy, which neither Carlo nor Arthur believed he did, he had neither the will nor the health to lead their charge. So the search and rescue would be coordinated via Babalu's and Ernesto's cell phones, one of which would be loaned to Arthur.

But they were missing the one important element needed to pull this rescue off: *guns*.

Their "plan" was far-fetched, at best, and everyone in that vehicle knew it.

In spite of these bad odds, Arthur did his best to feel confident. He dropped into soldier mode, the way a driver throws the transmission into low when approaching a steep hill. His heart was beating, his armpits were moist and his synapses were firing at three times their normal rate. Every organ in his torso, every muscle in his body and every part of his brain was focused on the single task at hand: rescuing Jeremy.

And nothing would stop him.

"Turn here!" Babalu exclaimed suddenly, upon recognizing a curlicued iron fence that began at the base of São Clemente and then swooped up the hill. "This is the way!"

But as soon as the car began its ascent, all hope vanished.

El Gigante's compound, and the entire top of the hill, was lit up brighter than Cristo.

Clearly, their absences had been discovered.

"Shit!" Carlo exclaimed. "How're we gonna sneak in there now?"

Ernesto slowed the Fiat and pulled over.

"You cannot go there," Babalu told them. "We will go back to my home, and we will think of something."

"What about the American consulate?" Carlo suggested.

Arthur shook his head. "They aren't going to investigate Fabiano, because right now he's the only one who's supposedly working on our side. But we can go there after we save Jeremy—that'll be the safest place until we can get on a plane."

Ernesto snapped the gearshift into first, then made a U-turn and continued back down the hill. As they drove back to the favela Dona Marta, Arthur looked over at Carlo and saw he was dozing, finally. "So, Babalu," he said quietly, leaning forward in his seat, "what's happening today, on the nineteenth, that's so important?"

"I'll explain when we get home," Babalu answered, his voice barely a whisper. "Now my heart is so heavy, and my body is too weak. Whatever we think to do, we must do it well. Too much bad can happen, for all of you. As for me"—he chuckled—"I do not care, for my time is almost over, so I will do whatever I can for my *primo*." He looked back at Carlo's head bobbing at an angle against the tiny headrest. "This boy, he was my mother's sister's favorite child. And I will not allow him to have a shattered heart for the rest of his life; even after I have turned to dust, I will still do for him what I am able."

CHAPTER 36

Once inside the man's dwelling, they began brainstorming.
"Babalu, please," Arthur asked, "what's going to happen to
Jeremy today? Why is the nineteenth so important?"

"You were in school in America in the 1960s, yes?" he asked.

Arthur shook his head. "I didn't really start school until the early seventies."

"And were you not taught that Brasilia was to be the utopia of Latin America—the buildings, the government, the roads, all engineered with the idea of 'freedom,' and hard work making life better, as it is in America?"

"That's one of the reasons I wanted to come down here, to see all of that."

"It was all lies," Babalu announced with authority. "So much about Brazil is lies. You will not find this in the history books, but the lie of Brasilia was financed by the American government and its tobacco companies. Brazil was to be the land that died in your civil war, where the wages were so close to slavery, and the roads would carry your big American cars and trucks, and tourists would swarm our beaches and support your puppet politicians."

Arthur had never heard this before; in fact, Brasilia's American presence had vanished quietly from American life by the time he graduated junior high. "So what happened?"

"Your big war in Asia, in Vietnam. Your money and attention went there, and it starved Brasilia. And without the money, many promises were broken to our people, so our presidents broke many promises to your presidents. So today there is nothing to see in the capital but half-empty buildings and brown grass."

"So that's what happened," Arthur muttered. "But what does this have to do with Jeremy?"

"This is to show you my beloved Brazil is built upon lies, old and new. Do you know how Rio de Janeiro came to be known by that? It's very name?"

They shook their heads.

"The story taught in schools declares that on January first, 1502, this city was claimed by the Portuguese explorer Gaspar de Lemos, and he named it the 'River of January.' Are we to believe he was so blind that the bay looked like a river? *Ha!*"

Carlo and Arthur nodded politely, wondering if he would ever get to the point.

"But this bay is not to be mistaken for a river; any child can see that. This is Guanabara Bay, with Sugarloaf and Corcovado overlooking it.

"Of course," Arthur agreed quickly. "But what about Jeremy?"

"It does not have to do with Jeremy, my friend. It has to do with God."

"Then what does God have to do with Jeremy?" Arthur asked impatiently.

"This city," Babalu continued, now whispering, "was named after a very powerful saint—the saint of Naples, Italy. San Gennaro—Janeiro—January—Januário, it is the same word in Italy as in Portugal as in America. The truth is, de Lemos did not discover this city; the man who discovered it was Dias de Solis, the Portuguese sailor. But Dias de Solis, although Portuguese, was sailing in service for Spain, and he landed here years before de Lemos on São Januário's feast day, September nineteenth."

"Today," said Carlo.

"Yes. De Solis was so grateful at landing here after so long at sea, and because he was the only Portuguese on a Spanish ship with sailors who were ready to murder him for his poor navigations, he thought his arrival on the nineteenth was a miracle. So he convinced his Spanish captain to name the bay, and what would be the city, after São Januário."

"Who was São Januário?" Arthur asked.

"He was a priest who visited Christians in jail, who was beheaded by the Romans after wild beasts would not devour him. The Italians love him especially, but the Spanish and Portuguese also revere him."

"And Jeremy?" Carlo asked.

"I am getting to that." Babalu held up his hand. "But first you need to learn the entire story, so we know what to do. So where was I?"

"The Spanish?" Arthur grumbled.

"The king of Portugal became angry that a traitor named this rich place. So after the Portuguese gained control from Spain, he changed the story, saying *his* people landed here on January first. But even the locals still call the old Morro do Castelo as São Januário's Hill." He nodded knowingly. "They know after who this city is named."

"And this is the actual hill where Fabiano's house is?" Arthur asked.

"The very place. It is a very ancient fortress"

"What about the *rio*, or the river," asked Carlo.

"The Portuguese thought us so stupid that we should believe the bay was named as a river, but this would be like...naming the mountains as the valleys," he laughed. "The *rio* is his blood; it means "the blood of São Januário," where his dried blood becomes fresh every year like the River of Life in the Bible. This happens in Naples every September nineteenth, and also here when the old people, the ones who remember this, they come from the plantations and mountains and faraway towns to witness the miracle—just as they do in Naples."

"The saint's dried blood actually becomes wet again?" asked Arthur.

"In a manner of speaking. It is very important for the peasants to see the *milagre de sangue*, the miracle of the blood. Because in years when the blood stays dry, there have been horrible things: disease, earthquakes, no rain, famine, children dying. So the wealthy men of the city make certain the blood always becomes fresh each year. It keeps the poor people happy and not worried about such misfortunes.

"Each year a statue of São Januário is brought in a procession up to Cristo, and the people come from everywhere to witness the miracle where blood flows like the *rio* from him. After this, they go home knowing this will be a good year, with no horrible things for their children or for Brazil, and they work happily but very hard on the plantations and factories."

"And does real blood really flow from this statue?" Carlo asked. "Or is it fake blood?"

"It is real blood, *mi primo*. It flows...because it is no statue, but the blood from a real man each year, poisoned with plants that make him almost dead and perfectly still—like a statue."

"No!" they exclaimed.

He shrugged. "I do not think El Gigante would sacrifice such an important man as your Jeremy, because usually he gets a boy from the gutters who no one will miss. But he has him captive, and you said the rich aunt is having trouble with the money and your government does not care, and the Feast of São Januário is tonight."

The men looked at each other.

Arthur stood. "What should we do?"

"Your only chance is to attend mass tonight up at the chapel Nossa Senhora Aparecida under Cristo, and to find some way to save him, in front of people who will not allow this to happen to a real man."

"But what if the people stop us from stopping Fabiano?" asked Carlo.

"El Gigante is very rich and very bad, but he is afraid of what the poor people can do to him; he witnessed them kill his father during a demonstration of the unions—he was stoned to death—and he is afraid ever since they will kill him also. But then others say that Fabiano orchestrated his father's murder himself, as he was a very cruel old man, and was very rich. El Gigante had much to gain from his father's death, just as he has gained his father's taste for cruelty." He thought for a moment. "But there is someone who is not afraid of anything or anyone. His accomplice in this, she calls herself Rosa Caveira. She is pure evil."

"What does she do?"

"I'm not certain what she still does, although my blood runs cold at the thought of what tasks she was talented for when we were young. But for the ceremony she is the priest, and she makes the drugs and gives them to the victim, and she paints him like a statue and prepares his look of holy presence, and then..."

"Then what?" Arthur asked.

He sighed. "Then she slices the wrists and lets the young man bleed to death while the faithful watch the Rio de Januário spill into the holy crystal vials."

"How do you know all of this?" asked Carlo.

"Rosa and I...we were once friends, many years ago. We spent many, many nights in El Gigante's home, and have seen many horrible—and wonderful—things happen there. Such a place of sophistication and beauty it was, at one time; parties, banquets, balls, international people of the jet set whose names you have heard and faces the world knew very well. But El Gigante, he has strange tastes for passions, and he loves to see innocent people suffer. *Miserably.*"

"You two were friends?" Arthur asked. "You and Rosa?"

"We worked together...for his guests' pleasure," he whispered, with a head toss toward Ernesto. "That is how I became a father of my two strong sons, of who I am so proud."

"You have two sons?" Carlo asked.

"The other will stay with me tomorrow night," he replied. "But working for Fabiano is also how I became so very ill. And I do not forget this, not any day that I still breathe. That man," Babalu said, pointing at the wall in the direction of the compound, "he gave me two lives, but he took one away: *my own*. I will not have him take away another from this family." He looked at Carlo and smiled. "Your Jeremy, he is one of my family now, too."

CHAPTER 37

Jeremy, having suffered through an extremely fatiguing day, had drifted off just after midnight, in spite of Rosa's blaring TV and its seemingly nonsensical Portuguese blathering. But he dozed miserably, and each time he shifted in his sleep, his shackles and handcuffs woke him with wicked pinchings and a halting of his normally languid movements.

But the worst part was how his spirits had fallen; he couldn't remember feeling this low or hopeless or despondent since his move from Fresno to Ballena Beach. *It was all too good to be true*, he thought as he heard Rosa light yet another cigarette, and the television's flickering bled through his clenched eyelids. *Arthur, Carlo, the house, Aunt Katharine, my Range Rover, my future. Not even a year it's been…not even a year. I guess none of it was ever really meant for me.*

Sometime later, he dreamt he was back in Fresno, and Tiffany, his mother, was lying on the sofa, drunk and passed out. *'Mom, come on. Get up.'* He shook her shoulders, but she wouldn't revive. *'Mom, wake up!'* But still there was no response. He began stomping around the apartment in a panic, imagining they were supposed to be somewhere or do something very important or flee some imminent danger, but he couldn't remember any of the details. *'Mom! Mom!'* There were voices outside their door. Men's voices that were shouting. *'Mom! We need to leave! Get up! Come on, now, get up!'*

As the door burst open, he woke with a startled yelp—as did Rosa—and tried to raise his hands in front of his face, but the cuffs bit into his skin mercilessly.

Three men with guns swarmed the tiny room; two grabbed Rosa while the other pointed his revolver at her.

"Don't shoot me!" Jeremy yelled.

"Cai fora, macacada!" Rosa shouted at them, and spat on the floor.

"Cale a boca, puta velha!" one of them shouted back, and she was shoved out of the room with her hands in the air and the gun pressed to her temple.

Jeremy craned his neck hopefully, his heart bursting with relief and hope.

Arthur? Carlo?

"Jeremy!" Dom Fabiano announced. "My poor friend!"

The towering shadow darkened the doorway.

He bent down and unlocked Jeremy's feet, then hands. "Are you all right? Did they hurt you? Thank God you are all right!"

"Oh, thank you!" Jeremy leaned back on the bed, rubbing his sore wrists and ankles. Then he stood up unsteadily, and Fabiano pulled him into a hug.

"We were all so worried about you. Everyone has been very sick with worry."

He returned the man's embrace, then pulled away. "Where's Arthur? Where's Carlo?" he asked. "Are they OK? Has my aunt called you? What's going on?"

"What is important is that you are fine, my young friend. I'll tell you everything in a moment, but now we have to get you someplace absolutely safe." He placed an arm around his shoulders and began leading him toward the door. "Please, come with me. Your terrible ordeal is almost over."

Together they left the room and went down a narrow corridor, where they passed a seething Rosa as she was being questioned, gun to her side, by some officious-looking men. Then they descended some stone steps and passed through another long, dimly lit hallway that emptied into an old, unused kitchen.

"Where are we going?" Jeremy asked as they sidled between counters and cabinets and sinks that hadn't been used in ages.

"To my home," Fabiano said. "It is the only place I know where you will be safe. My staff is already waiting for you." He pushed a final door open, and they went through it. "They have prepared a lovely meal, as well as a very comfortable room especially for your recovery, before your trip back home to America."

The dark garage they entered was empty, except for a windowless cargo van whose motor cranked suddenly to life. They made their way down some steps; then Jeremy stepped through the rear doors of the vehicle and sat on the bench seat, while the big man sat next to him.

Then a huge, old wooden door swung wide, and Jeremy squinted as the van drove through the opening into the blinding morning glare.

"What did they do to you?" Fabiano asked as they swung out onto an access alley and began winding their way down the serpentine road.

"It was only that Rosa man-lady-thing with me. She just watched TV all night and chain-smoked until I fell asleep." He tried to watch the scenery as they descended the hill, but from the backseat not much was visible except for the metal ribs inside the van. "Where are Arthur and Carlo?"

"They are with the authorities, where they are learning how to transfer the money to the criminals safely. Then they will take the ransom to a meeting place for the exchange. I am acting as the guarantor of the transaction—they have guaranteed your safety because I have guaranteed their money."

"But is that safe for them?" Jeremy asked, scared suddenly that his lovers would be dealing with those gun-wielding criminals. But then he knew how capable Arthur was, with his military background and all.

"Kidnappers usually demand a person of the family to deliver the ransom, because a police officer might recognize the kidnappers, or run off with the money. But do not worry, my friend. The money is already with some trusted authorities, and they are just now learning of the location and the protocol for the exchange."

"That's great!" Jeremy began to relax. "So where're we going now? To meet them?"

"Not yet—they are still being advised. But in the meantime, we will have a lovely afternoon together, and then your gentlemen will meet us up at my villa after the exchange. And tomorrow, you will all be on the first plane back to the USA."

He grabbed Fabiano's hand. "Thank you so much for everything," he told him. "I didn't know what was gonna happen; I mean, in a situation like that you just get some crazy ideas about everything that could go wrong. You know?"

"I do know." Fabiano nodded, smiling benignly. "Now, sit back and forget your troubles, for we will be at my compound shortly."

And while imagining his impending joyful reunion with his lovers, filled with tender kisses and bone-crushing hugs, Jeremy was so preoccupied that he failed to notice the van was now traveling up the front side of a mountain whose back they had descended, just moments before.

CHAPTER 38

As he followed Fabiano from the portico up the wide front steps of the home, he ascertained that the modernist property was spectacular, or had been at one time. Having been built in the same style, scale and splendor as the buildings of Brasilia, its monolithic concrete walls were imprinted with a random geometric relief, and the colonnades outlining the perimeter of the mountaintop property soared over the now empty reflecting pools—like an elevated roadway built over once shimmering canals. Neglect showed on every surface; even the once graceful rows of eucalyptus tilted upward the edges of the walkways, and forests of philodendron crowded their root-bulged concrete planters. When new, he guessed the estate would have rivaled even his aunt's imposing cliff-top compound back home. But now the broken-tiled reflecting pools, fissure-laced walls and dirt-streaked plate-glass windows told him the man's priorities, as well as his money, lay elsewhere.

They made their way up a short flight of terrazzo stairs into the grand main hall, where one of Fabiano's staff nodded politely as he passed, and another, upon laying eyes on him, made the sign of the cross.

Jeremy felt like a celebrity.

He was handed off to a strongly built manservant, who led him to his own quarters. Then the young man directed him into an immense bathroom veneered in white marble, where a steaming bubble bath awaited him in a sunken tub overlooking Rio, and its glorious sunlit splendor.

"*Por favor,*" the servant instructed, while motioning to the snowy bubbles. So he pulled off his T-shirt and dropped his pants and boxers into a heap on the floor, then descended the steps into the tub, where he slid his exhausted, aching frame into the gardenia-scented bubbles.

Once submerged to his chin, he closed his eyes and sighed.

The young man vanished, but reappeared moments later with a tray laden with food and drink, which he placed on the floor beside the tub.

Jeremy was ravenous. So, he grabbed a fork and started stabbing at the assortment of pastries, eggs, potatoes and fried tomatoes topped with crème fraîche. He also poured himself a cup of coffee, but then decided against drinking it, as he was more interested in sleeping than in feeling perky.

He'd nearly finished his breakfast when the door to his quarters squeaked open, and he heard heavy footfalls approaching.

Fabiano's silhouette towered over him.

"How is your breakfast?" he asked. "Is it to your liking?"

He nodded enthusiastically, his mouth jammed full with hot buttered croissant. "It's great...thank you."

"And the bath, not too hot or cold?"

"Great, yeah."

"And this boy, is he to your liking?" he asked, as he eased his huge frame down onto a nearby marble bench.

"He's been real nice. Thanks for him, too."

A sly smile spread upon Fabio's face. "*Tire a roupa,*" he rattled to the boy. "*Faz o que ele quer.*"

The boy lowered his eyes and took off his shirt, revealing a very smooth, very brown and very muscular torso.

"He is beautiful, yes?"

Jeremy looked up, then away. "Yeah, he's pretty hot."

"*Qual e o seu problema?*" Fabiano asked, and the boy, very obediently, slid off his pants. He then stood naked in front of Jeremy, fiddling with himself in an obvious attempt to achieve an erection, while grinning lasciviously. "*Vire-se,*" Fabiano ordered, and the boy turned around and bent over, displaying his perfectly molded buttocks.

"Hey, no," Jeremy said, waving his hands in the air, although he felt himself becoming aroused. "Really, that's OK."

Where do I know him from?

Fabiano frowned. "If he is not to your liking, I can get for you something different. Do you want older or younger? Darker or lighter? More African or European?" He paused, waiting for an answer that did not come. "My wish is for you," he continued finally, "my young friend, to relax and enjoy yourself, and to feel released. You are my very special guest today, and you have been through hell."

Jeremy blinked at him, trying to think of what to say without offending the man who had just saved his life. "I'm not like that," he said at last.

"You say you do not like beautiful boys?" Fabiano asked, laughing.

"I like...*men*. I mean, I like my man, Carlo. He's *meu amor*. I don't want to play with anyone else." He was suddenly very aware that he was naked, and the bubbles were starting to disintegrate—while his clothes were across the room.

The man chuckled. "But what about Dom Arthur? You like to play with him, too."

His eyes shifted. "No, I..."

"But we saw you. On the beach. On the security cameras. You and Dom Arthur, you—" And he began masturbating the air with his fist, laughing. "You've forgotten that our wonderful island is wired like a big computer. We even have a video of your encounter, should you like to view it tonight by yourself."

Jeremy felt himself blush.

"Oh, I see," he said, condescendingly. "Your Carlo, he does not yet know about you and Arthur." He slapped his knees. "Do not worry. I won't say a thing; you've all been through so much, and a broken heart for someone so young might never be repaired."

"Thanks for not saying anything."

He shrugged. "It is none of my business anyway. You are all grown men," he said, and then made his hand into a fist, which he held up. "And you, Jeremy, my friend, you are *very* well grown." He stood and turned to leave. "Please, after you've rested and dressed, come out to the patio, where we can finish our business before your stay here is over." Then he turned to leave, and smacked the manservant hard on the ass as the boy was bent over and pulling up his pants.

The slap left a scarlet imprint of El Gigante's hand.

Then the boy, tray in hand, trotted out behind him.

After languishing—nervously—for a few more minutes in the steaming water, Jeremy dried himself and slipped on a bathrobe; then after making certain the door to his room was locked, he dropped his robe and slid naked between the covers.

His mind was racing, turning, twisting, stalling. He hugged his pillow and squeezed shut his eyes.

He loved Carlo—of this there was no question; he was almost as important in making him into a proud gay man as Arthur had been. But there was something missing in their relationship, and he hadn't the experience or the words to understand it—he only knew he often became annoyed with him, and at other times was flat-out bored. And even though this was the first "relationship" of his life, he knew it wasn't a good sign to feel these emotions after only six months. But at least their sex was still hot—he loved the feeling of Carlo's hot skin, and of their hungry kisses and sweaty, sticky love sessions.

But Carlo was girly sometimes, and he complained a lot. And it seemed as though anytime Jeremy tried to bring up anything that bugged him about their relationship, Carlo got completely defensive and sulked, or tried to shut him up.

But Arthur...Arthur thrilled him. The width of his shoulders, the musk of his skin; the armor of his chest, and the dolphin gray of his eyes. He loved his broad grin...his deep baritone...those friendly crow's-feet and the sparkling silver flecks in his hair. But he'd never before told anyone how he felt; his attraction to Arthur had been his little secret, just as a year ago his attraction to men had been just as closely guarded.

Maybe it had to do with how much like a father Arthur had been to him, because he certainly felt that, like a good father, Arthur would never leave or hurt him, and would always treat him with complete and utter consideration.

So he would do the same. He'd buy Arthur things: a new car—like that black Jaguar convertible he'd recently pointed out as they waited at a stoplight, and then mentioned again two days ago at the beach. And he'd buy a boat like the red and white one they took to the cove; they'd take it to Catalina for the day—maybe a week—then maybe cruise down to San Diego or up to Santa Barbara. Maybe they'd move out of Katharine's stuffy mansion and buy a place of their own...a place like the one from that party in Hawai'i...down the beach in Malibu, where the young celebrities partied. They'd get a dog and have friends over, and every night they'd fall asleep together in their beach house with the waves crashing outside and the fireplace flickering and their legs entwined knowing they had all the love and money that anyone would ever need.

We'll live happily ever after.

It was what he wanted—now that he knew Arthur felt the same way about him.

And as he began to nod off, a single question drifted up into his consciousness, like a road sign materializing through a shroud of fog:

How'm I gonna break up with Carlo?

CHAPTER 39

W*hat do you mean it's not acceptable?*" Katharine screamed into the phone. "I understand it is not what's been demanded, but it is still a *huge* sum of money! Even you should understand there are limits to what an individual can do without any aid from their godforsaken government!"

"Of *course* I understand. I am only the negotiator, *as you will recall.*"

She caught her breath, remembering their calls were being recorded. "I know that," she stated flatly.

Fabiano was silent for a moment. "We're doing the best we can," he told her at last. "We've tried to assure them that this is as much as you are capable of raising, especially in light of their unreasonable deadline, but they are holding fast to their request; I'm afraid that because they had access to some of your financial records, they are...aware of the Tyler family's worth."

"But that's tied up in real estate, futures, and other long-term investments. It would take months to liquidate the amount *they're* demanding, especially in this economy!"

"I understand, Senhora Tyler, really I do." He raised the cigarette to his lips and sucked on it. "And I suppose I am somewhat to blame for this, having disclosed the quantity of your financial assets to such an unseemly group. But it was my duty as the head of the consortium to familiarize each member with the others' worth as investors."

"Well, you certainly didn't familiarize me with the brand of evil I'd be dealing with, now, did you?"

"I did not know, Senhora Tyler. No one but they themselves knew about their evildoings—and for my ignorance I heartily apologize. But I've heard of other groups of this sort accepting a *slightly* lower amount, after some careful consideration. In the meantime, we will have to wait for you to raise more money, and then I will continue to negotiate, as we discussed."

"Wait? *Wait?*" She was now officially ranting. "We only have"—she glanced at her gold Cartier and did some quick math to allow for the time difference—"nine or so more hours until they are going to…to *kill* him!" Her brain scrambled for questions that, perhaps, this monster could answer. "And when was the last time you had any contact from Arthur and Carlo? Where the devil are they?"

"I'm sorry, but I do not know; they appear to have refused my offer to reunite them with Jeremy, perhaps out of some irrational fear that they might be held accountable for your, shall we say, *failure* to produce the required ransom."

"Isn't there someone else that can help me?" she demanded. "Isn't there someone else with whom I can reason?"

"As you very well know, I am the only one in charge. And you just need to let me do my best—*perhaps after you do yours.*"

She tapped her pen on her yellow legal pad. "What"—she searched for words, hoping if she phrased her question correctly the answer would be more optimistic—"are the chances, in a situation like this. I mean, what happens when…when there's not…I mean—"

He cut her off. "Every situation is different. What I understand is that even if every demand is met, the holding group still has the option of doing *whatever* they wish. Then again, sometimes the hostage just winds up on a road somewhere walking aimlessly, and gets picked up by someone driving home from work. But in this case that possibility is very, very, *very* unlikely."

"That's a terrific comfort, thank you."

"What about that Swiss foundation you mentioned? The one whom your government suggested you contact for assistance?"

"They've only offered me a paltry sum, based on the fact that Tyler, Inc., had a change of management in the past year, due to my husband's death; a more sizable loan to me, as I've been told, would carry with it too high a risk."

He paused. "In the meantime, then, I suggest you ask your wealthy American friends to help you generate an offer much closer to that of the requested amount. You do have friends, don't you, Senhora Tyler?"

"Of course I do," she spat.

"Then I suggest you start making some very important phone calls. And in the meantime, I'll let you know if we make progress on Jeremy's release, or if I receive any word from Arthur or Carlo." He took a drag from his cigarette and blew it out noisily.

She closed her eyes and nodded, rubbing her left temple with her free hand. "Yes, Dom Fabiano. And thank you *so much* for everything. I'll *never* forget what you've done."

After hanging up, she stood and went over to the French doors, where she could see the waves break upon the sand below. "Where is Arthur?" she whispered to the silent room. "Please, God, if anything has happened to him, then there's just no hoping—"

No! She would not allow herself this indulgence of maudlin thinking! There had to be something she hadn't thought of...someone whom she could count on in a situation like this.

She paced to her desk and back to the doors again. Then she returned to her desk. Tirelessly, she had exhausted every reasonable resource: the State Department; Homeland Security; the FBI; that useless foundation in Switzerland; the American consulate and the Brazilian police—all had given her the same answer: *Give them as much money as you can possibly find, and hope for the best.*

How could this all have gone so wrong? This wasn't the way it was supposed to happen. Wasn't there someone who could help her? *Anyone?*

Then she realized that there was no one left because she'd sent her dear, strong little army away to ensure her money, but now she realized her dear money wasn't nearly strong enough to ensure her little army.

"Our own little Masada," she heard herself say.

She collapsed onto her perfect French Empire fainting couch— recently upholstered in crimson Chinese silk with the most darling hand-embroidered gold bumblebees—and began to pray.

CHAPTER 40

J eremy woke from his nap, stretched his arms over his head, swung his feet over the side of the bed and stood. Then he saw that instead of his own clothes, which were probably off being laundered after his ordeal, the only garment awaiting him was a floor-length white linen robe. He pulled it over his head and let it fall to his feet. As he moved around the room, he was amazed by how comfortable it felt—he enjoyed the feeling of being naked under the pristine, flowing garment.

He looked out the windows and saw that it was already early afternoon. *Good.* He'd slept away some of the time before being reunited with Arthur and Carlo. But now he had to go find Fabiano, which was something he wasn't looking forward to after their conversation in the bathroom.

A deep rumble met his ears, and as he looked up to see a passenger jet arc through the cloud-dappled sky, he thought, *We'll all be on one of those headed home soon.*

He smiled.

He found Fabiano relaxing in a chair on the expansive concrete deck outside, seated at the end of a long glass table, with the remains of what looked like an incinerated steak on a plate in front of him, as well as an untouched salad, a plate of melon, half a pitcher of lemonade and an overflowing ashtray. He was chattering into his cell phone.

He snapped shut the device upon Jeremy's approach. "The view from here is magnificent, no?" he asked cheerfully, motioning for him to sit.

Jeremy's eyes panned the scenery. "You're up really high here," he said. "You can see the bay, and Sugarloaf's cable cars and Cristo, all from this point."

"This is the very site of the first Portuguese fortification. My grandfather had it taken down in the 1920s after it fell into such a state of disrepair it could not be saved. Some still call this area Castle Rock, but others remember it as São Januário's Hill."

"Why all the different names?" Jeremy asked as a plate of steak and salad was put before him.

"It all depends on whom you wish to believe in," Fabiano replied, lighting a fresh cigarette. "The wealthy, or the saints." He lifted his glass in a toast, and Jeremy did the same. "But I believe in both, my friend," he said, and clinked their glasses together. "And I suspect you do, too."

Jeremy smiled and drank his lemonade. "So when are we going to meet them?"

"I am only now just waiting for the telephone call, to let me know the exchange has been made and they are headed here," he said. "We should be hearing any minute."

Jeremy's stomach was queasy again, so he didn't have the appetite for the bloody slab in front of him. "Has anyone made any plane reservations for tomorrow?" he asked. "I mean, did Arthur or my aunt make any that you know about? I should call her and find out."

Fabiano smiled reassuringly. "I've been told that everything is in place." He interlaced his fingers and nodded. "As I said, I am only waiting—"

His cell phone rang. He reached for it. "*Si*," he said.

Jeremy searched his face for clues that everything was all right.

Instead, he saw the man's face redden. Then he pushed himself up and marched away from the table.

He didn't know whether he should follow him.

What's going on?

He heard him rattling off something in Portuguese. Instructions, probably.

Then he was yelling.

Not good.

Jeremy stood. Then his feet, apparently of their own volition, began making their way over to the man.

Fabiano held up his hand: *Stop.*

Jeremy stopped.

Fabiano yelled some more.

And in between his rantings he heard him say, *No, no, no.*

Oh, God.

Fabiano snapped the phone shut.

Then he looked at Jeremy and shook his head. His mouth hung open, and the top of his bald head was sweating.

He pointed at the table. "Please. Sit down."

Jeremy stumbled to his chair and sat.

Fabiano did not sit. Instead he paced back and forth, then stopped finally and faced him. "I have some bad news, my friend," he said as he dug his cigarette pack out of his pocket.

Jeremy's heart pounded. He didn't respond. He couldn't even breathe.

"Your lovers, Arthur and Carlo," he began.

"What?" Jeremy demanded. He was trembling. *"Tell me what happened!"*

He padded softly to him and laid a hand on his shoulder. "The exchange, it did not go well." He shook his head. "Your aunt, she did not have the amount promised. She deceived them, and when the package was opened they became very, very angry."

"No! She wouldn't do that!" He clenched the arms of the chair.

"Jeremy, my friend. I'm so very sorry. Your aunt, I do not know what she was thinking to lie to me, to them, to all of us. So now...I am afraid they are dead. Your Arthur and your Carlo are dead, and they are coming even now to take you back. It is over for you, as well."

Jeremy felt his head rock back and forth and was faintly aware that his breathing had ceased. Then he blinked at his host, gasped, blinked some more, then vomited his breakfast onto the table and down the front of his lovely white robe. Darkness began swarming his vision from the outside in—crowding his spectacular view of Guanabara and Sugarloaf and Cristo, until utter sorrow defeated his eyes.

He fainted.

Fabiano looked up to the second-story window beyond and waved at Rosa, who held up her cell phone and waved back at him. Then the two handsome young servers from the island appeared with a wheelchair, hoisted Jeremy into it, and wheeled his slumped-over, vomit-splattered form into the house. They pushed him into an elevator that descended into the belly of the hill; down to the labyrinth of cells and passages that made up the ancient Morro do Castelo—also known as São Januário's Hill—from which he had been released only hours before.

CHAPTER 41

"We need guns," Arthur announced. "Or at least one. We should be able to find some around here. Right?"

"You cannot take one up there," Babalu told him. "The security at a religious event like this is better than at your airports, especially with El Gigante's paranoia getting worse each year."

"Do they have metal detectors?" Carlo asked.

He nodded. "You must remember what you told me about Fabiano and his security measures on that island; you should be certain that he has installed, under orders from the government, at least those same measures around Cristo, especially now that the holy statue is one of the Wonders of the Modern World."

"Then what do we do?"

"We go there now, and make our way through the crowd toward the front, and we wait for the opportunity to save your Jeremy."

"But he'll recognize us, immediately," Arthur said. "Especially if he's part of the mass. If we want to get up to the front, we'll need some sort of disguises—as stupid as that sounds."

Babalu shook his head. "No, it does not sound stupid. But we have a good chance, as they will not expect you to be there; I am one of the only people outside Fabiano's circle who still knows what he does for São Januário, and they don't know that you know me." He paused in thought. "There is one part of the ceremony where the people come up to donate *dinheiro*, and to pick up the glass vials with the fresh blood inside; they give the church more to actually receive a vial that is still warm."

"So we'll have to approach them at that moment," Arthur added, "with our money in hand, and overtake them and save Jeremy...and we'll have to act quickly, because he could bleed out. *Or worse.*"

"What's worse than that?" Carlo asked.

"Permanent brain damage from not having enough blood oxygen."

"Jesus. Then what would we do?"

"We'll just have to get to him right after the incisions are made."

"So we'll have to be one of the first groups of people up front."

"But not the first," Babalu added, "because we don't want to give them the chance to look at us for too long."

Arthur and Carlo nodded at each other.

"There are hundreds, maybe thousands of people there already," he told them, glancing at his watch. "I'm sorry, but I should have mentioned that they begin their pilgrimages well in advance. We will have a very difficult time being near the front."

"We'll just have to, that's all…but what kind of disguises can we use? They'll spot me a mile away!" Arthur exclaimed.

"We could go in drag," Carlo suggested.

Babalu shook his head. "Maybe you and I should do drag, but not him. He would look terrible."

Arthur thought for a moment, trying to picture what sort of crowd would be gathered so they could blend in. Then it hit him. "We need to look old," he said. "Old people are harmless, and there should be many of them there, trying to get 'healed.'"

Babalu's eyes brightened. "Yes! We can get a wheelchair, and hide a gun inside the seat, because it wouldn't make any difference to the metal detector."

"I had some training on how to look elderly, and I think we can pull everything together here."

"But what about me?" Carlo asked. "Do you think you can really make me look old?"

Babalu and Arthur looked at each other and smiled. "You," Babalu began, "you can go as a young girl. We will be a husband and wife from the country, and you will be our daughter, pushing me in the wheelchair."

Each looked to the others. Then they stood.

***

Babalu drew up a list for Ernesto, and moments later he was out scouring the favela for accessories and props.

Within the hour, they were gazing with wonder at one another's transformations.

For Carlo they found a tight black T-shirt that read *Yo Baby Yo*, and they made substantial breasts for him out of socks stuffed with uncooked rice. Over the T-shirt he wore a knee-length jumper of sorts, and from a drag performer nearby they borrowed some white espadrilles that were the right size, and had just enough slope so he could run fast, if the need arose. In addition, the generous man had been so gracious as to contribute his best weave—a blond-streaked brown wig that looked as if it was lifted from Jennifer Lopez's very dressing room.

Babalu was much less flamboyant, having slipped on the traditional shapeless black garb of a Brazilian widow, the stomach of which he stuffed with towels; and he was able to retrieve a jet-black wig from his own stash, which he topped with an opaque veil.

As for Arthur, they decided he would pose as her son rather than her husband, as his skin still looked too wrinkle free, and he had no discernible double chin. So he slipped on some huge pants, which he padded with rolled-up towels and belted to keep in place, then stuffed his belly with a sizable throw pillow. Finally, he donned a simple straw hat.

Babalu and Carlo looked at him and frowned. He still looked like Arthur.

"He needs glasses," Ernesto suggested, taking a moment away from another game show. "Use some of your old glasses, Papa, without the glass."

Babalu went over to where the hot plate served as his kitchen, and retrieved a pair of reading glasses. "I use these when I cook," he told Arthur. "You could probably use them now even with the glass in them, at your age."

Arthur smiled thinly at him and put them on, then looked down at his hands. To his chagrin they worked perfectly; they actually improved his vision—close up.

"He still needs something else," Carlo suggested. "Your face—it's still yours."

Then Arthur remembered a trick that a more experienced agent had shown him once. "I need some strips of cloth," he announced. "Any kind of cloth."

Ernesto leapt up and retrieved an old, but clean, pillow case. Arthur took it, then ripped two thin strips from it; these he rolled into balls the size of apricots, which he shoved into his mouth against his upper molars on each side.

He looked up at the men and they smiled. "No more Dom Arthur," Babalu said.

Their only other task was to find a wheelchair, but in the hills of a favela, Ernesto discovered there were none to be had. So they decided Babalu would have to use his cane instead, as it was just as convincing for an elderly person, especially the way he walked.

But it did not allow them to hide a firearm inside.

They still needed some sort of weapon. What could they use?

There was nothing Arthur could think of that a metal detector couldn't discover. So he decided he would save Jeremy with the only weapons he had:

My hands.

He would gladly fight to the death.

For without Jeremy, there was really no point in living.

CHAPTER 42

Ernesto gave the trio, for protection, three sets of his very best rosary beads—not the cheap, plastic kind, but the much-sought-after variety carved from brazilwood and strung with stainless-steel links—then dropped them off at the bottom of Corcovado, where they stood nervously in the security line with the other pilgrims.

After the trio was wanded and scrutinized by the guards, they took their seats on one of the old red trams, which lurched and groaned and squeaked its way up the long, steep railway. Finally, after disembarking, they rode the escalator up to the top platform, where they stood beneath Cristo's placid gaze.

The long, narrow platform was already crowded along the sides, as the center was roped off for the procession, so they pushed their way to the front as far as they could, then continued inching forward after they could walk no farther. When they got almost to the front they stopped, leaned against the balustrade and waited—with two of them praying quietly, and clicking their beads like veteran nuns—because the mass would not begin for another hour or so, just after sunset.

In the meantime, across the hills in a chamber deep within Morro do Castelo, Jeremy's disguise was being readied.

As was he.

***

He had revived from his fainting/throwing-up spell quite quickly, and, after finding himself back within his all-too-familiar cell, he was as angry as he was despondent.

Did Fabiano actually turn me back over to the kidnappers? Why didn't he protect me? Why didn't Katharine pay the ransom? Doesn't anyone give a shit about me?

He pounded his fists on the door. He yelled obscenities.

But no one seemed to hear.

Then he got sick to his stomach again—after realizing he'd been worried only about himself, while he should have been just as concerned about Arthur and Carlo as, clearly, they'd been about him.

And now it was too late.

So he searched every inch of the room for a way out, because he decided that with both Arthur and Carlo gone, there was no point in playing it safe anymore.

He was out for blood, even if it meant spilling his own.

So he continued pounding his fists on the door. He screamed threats.

Then, after he'd continued his tirade for the better part of an hour, he heard a key scrape in the lock.

The door was shoved open.

By Rosa.

With Dom Fabiano behind her.

They wore identical smug expressions.

"What are *you* doing here?" he asked Rosa. "Didn't they arrest you?"

She smirked. "*Si*, they arrest me, and then take me for a beautiful lunch like they did for you"—she sniffed the air—"but from how you smell I think you did not care for yours."

Fabiano pushed his way in front of her. "We're short on time. You need to get him ready. Get started."

"So you're in on this together?" Jeremy asked as he looked unbelievingly at one, then the other. "What are you gonna do to me, you big fat faggot motherfucker?"

Fabiano backhanded Jeremy hard across the face.

The force sent him to the floor.

"You don't ask questions, you little bitch." El Gigante laughed. "You, you are *nothing*. Your wicked aunt doesn't care enough about you to send the money, so now you have no Arthur and Carlo, you have no freedom, and in a few hours you will have no life!"

"You killed them!" he screamed. "They did nothing to you!"

"We gave her some very realistic deadlines, but after the first six hours passed and she didn't pay, *bang!* I killed your Carlo, and then the next six hours passed and *bang!* I killed your Arthur. You should know that Senhora Tyler told me it was too much for her to pay, that all of that money from her bank would ruin her. So *bang!* in their heads." He mimed the crime with his thumb cocked over his extended forefinger. "I have some funny pictures to show you in case you don't believe me," he lied. "They died crying and begging for their lives; even your big stupid Arthur died like a coward faggot!" He bent down and slapped Jeremy again, and threw him on his front and clenched his hands so Rosa could snap the handcuffs back on.

"You'll die, you fucking monster!" Jeremy screamed into the floor. Then he began pistoning his legs.

The big man kicked him hard, and Jeremy screamed in pain, thinking his femur had snapped. "Silence!" the man bellowed. "I'll rip you apart if you are not quiet!"

Jeremy stopped struggling and Rosa slipped the shackles back on his ankles. "Just kill me; just fucking kill me!" he begged, realizing that the two loves of his life were gone, just like his mother and father before. "I don't care! *Just fucking kill me!*"

The big man bent down and put his mouth an inch from his captive's ear. "You Americans have no talent for suffering." He chuckled, and Rosa echoed his cackle with her own creepy, falsetto version. "If I wanted to, I could draw out your death for days or weeks; I could drive you to such a state of terror that you would pull out your intestines or saw off your feet rather than face another second of my tortures. But tonight you are lucky…tonight we need São Januário to give his *river of life* to the faithful, to the sick, to the nearly dead." Fabiano threw his arms into the air. "How many people can die a saint?" he shrieked. "And here, you have done nothing to deserve it! You, with so much money and privilege; you, who do nothing good for the world except to be a cocksucker for old men, you who live off the money of others and do nothing but offer your young body to perverts; you who do nothing but complain about wishing to die. You are nothing, Dom Tyler, and such nothing like you does not deserve to live." He looked at his watch, then turned to Rosa as he pulled Jeremy to his feet, then shoved him down into the chair. "We have little time before the procession. Everything is ready, yes?"

"Bring me my case," she told him. "It is out in the hall."

He sneered at her. "You get it yourself, *puta velha.*"

She huffed, and went to retrieve it.

Moments later she returned with a tattered makeup case, which she placed on the floor and opened. Then she reached inside and produced a small package of waxy black paper that was folded over. This she unfolded and placed on the table next to the bed; Jeremy saw that the inside contained white powder. He also saw, out of the corner of his eye, Fabiano step backward out of the room.

"Is that coke?" he asked, suddenly afraid. His mother had loved coke, and he dreaded the sight of it.

"This is better—from Colombia." She fished a dirty medical mask from the case and tied it around her face, picked up a shortened drinking straw, lifted the paper to Jeremy's nose, then pulled up the mask to expose her lips and closed her eyes and blew the powder forcefully into his face.

"*Jesus*"—he coughed violently—"*Christ!*"

At once a scalding heat and tingling coldness began in his sinuses, and the next moment he felt that same sensation in his hands and feet as a dead stiffness started overtaking his limbs. He began to slump sideways.

She caught him as he fell.

His veins were burning as though injected with ignited gasoline, he couldn't feel his feet or his hands, and the area of his leg where he'd just been brutally kicked no longer hurt. But when he tried to move his arms, he realized those felt dead, too; and his torso and limbs felt as if he'd just been plunged into a tank of scalding tar or freezing water—it burned as much as it froze. Then his eyesight began to blur, as if Vaseline had been rubbed onto his corneas.

And although he was completely and utterly paralyzed, his mind was working brilliantly. He saw the silhouette of Fabiano disappear into the hall, then reappear with the same young manservant from this morning, as they dragged an armchair into the room, then rolled in what looked like some sort of glass-sided coffin, edged with gold. Then they all lifted him from the floor and sat him in the chair, and strapped him into it so he was sitting up straight.

Rosa bent down and took out her makeup kit and went to work. "Such a handsome São Januário you will be," she cooed as she smoothed his face with chalky white foundation. "We haven't had one so handsome as you in such a long time."

She began humming a cheerful tune.

CHAPTER 43

Night was coming. And as the sun inched down toward the mountains, Arthur's anxiety rose.

Could they really pull this off? There were thousands of people here who would witness their holy disruption. What if the supplicants rose up against them? How could they, completely unarmed, interrupt the ceremony and rescue Jeremy before someone—either Fabiano's security detail or otherwise—was able to stop them?

"It's getting really crowded," Carlo told Arthur after someone bumped into him and he nearly lost his balance because of the tilty espadrilles on his feet. "If we're gonna make it to the front, we'd better do it now."

"Let me go first," Babalu suggested, his face a mask of determination behind his willowy black veil. "People will not refuse an old woman— except, of course, for other old women." So they pushed their way deeper into the crush, with the elderly Brazilian widow in the lead.

They sidled through the mass of broken-down people; people barely able to stand, people missing limbs, people bent over sideways from a life of cruel labor, people filthy, people sad. The entire scenario reminded Arthur of a Hollywood reenactment of the good folks at a leper colony, awaiting the arrival of Jesus.

Finally, they were within throwing distance of the carved wooden altar, which had been set up against Cristo's black granite base, along with an assemblage of white roses and towering brass candlesticks and a cluster of spooky saint statues adorned with high, pope-ish hats and black-as-coal faces. To the right of the altar, the three dozen or so members of the boys' choir fidgeted restlessly in their matching red robes, while to the left sat some of the more important citizens of the city; the murmuring men were dressed in expensive black suits, while their women sported shimmery dresses, vampiric makeup and baubles wrought from gold and diamonds.

"The choir," Babalu whispered, nudging them. "There's some room off to the side." So they made a final push and wedged themselves between the ziggurat of boys and the rest of the crowd.

Arthur took a moment to look around and assess any possible opponents, then decided that with the exception of the chain-smoking gentility seated up front, the people looked pretty harmless; these noisily chattering folks, he gathered, were probably from the country: tall, prune-faced men and squat, bandana-headed women with pendulous breasts, immense hips and strangely bow-legged calves.

Just after the sun slipped below the western mountains and the sky's smears of red and orange faded to gray, he noticed a pair of altar boys approaching with long sticks that were lit at the end; these they used to ignite, one by one, each of the standing candles. Then the conductor appeared—a short bald man in a badly fitting suit—so the choir snapped to angelic attention. The man raised his stubby arms, and at once Arthur heard the most beautiful note of song—it was as pure and as steady as the ringing of a silver bell. That sound, along with the candlelight and the descending darkness and the immense face of Cristo overhead, made him shudder.

Suddenly the crowd turned away from the altar, and everyone ceased their *zuzhhing* and bouncy muttering, so the only sounds audible were the singing choir, an occasional cough and the soft clicking of rosary beads between dry, desperate fingers.

It was starting.

He looked down toward the end of the crowd and saw embroidered silk standards bobbing and weaving toward them, as well as even more candles held aloft by a dozen or so pairs of altar boys in tandem. Bringing up the rear towered Dom Fabiano, his gold-trimmed monsignor's hat poking above the destitute crowd like the spire of a cathedral over a slum.

Arthur stood on tiptoe looking for Jeremy but couldn't make out anything yet, as the procession was still too far away.

The choir finished their first song, then launched into another quieter, more funereal hymn. The holy parade was drawing closer now, perhaps only a few meters or so away, as the candles and torches flickered about them in the hilltop breeze, and the choir's dirge built into a disconcerting crescendo of minor chords layered atop major.

"Can you see him?" Carlo whispered.

Suddenly Arthur gasped.

That can't be him!

Carlo's fake nails dug into his arm.

For inside the rolling glass reliquary, with its fanciful gilded corners and thick glass sides, lay the statue of a saint—a saint garbed in a luxurious white silk cassock festooned with swirly gold braid; a saint with hands and face as white as the silk covering him…a saint with lips painted cherry red and cheeks gauntly hollowed, who lay staring at heaven from unblinking eyes rimmed in black.

"That can't be him," Carlo protested. "There's got to be a real statue!"

And Arthur hoped it was. But then he recognized the cleft in his chin and the flair of his nostrils. "No, baby. That's him," he mumbled, the wads of fabric stuffed into his cheeks distorting his words, but not disguising his despair.

After the procession stopped, six of the suited, wealthy men lifted the reliquary up onto the altar. It was then that Arthur noticed the rows of what looked like empty perfume bottles sitting on a table below.

All watched as Fabiano stepped up to the microphone and held his hands in the air. "*Lætámini in Dómino et exsultáte, justi*," he announced.

"*Et gloriámini, omnes recti corde*," the crowd responded.

"*Istórum est enim, regnum cælórum, qui contempsérunt vitam mundi, et pervenérunt ad præmia regni, et lavérunt stolas suas in sánguine Agni. Deus, qui nos annua sanctórum Mártyrum tuórum Januárii et Sociórum ejus solemnitate lætíficas: concéde propítius; ut, quorum gaudémus meritis, accendámur exemplis. Per Dóminum.*"

"When do we do it?" Carlo asked, shifting from foot to foot.

"We'll know," Arthur whispered. "Just follow my lead—we'll wait until the line starts to form, then we'll push our way to the front. We also need to find Rosa, but I don't see her."

"Oh, she's there," Babalu told them. "Right there." He pointed to a bald priest standing to the right of Fabiano.

"That's *Rosa*?" Carlo asked.

"I'd know that evil whore anywhere. Very soon he will start preparing the rite."

"*Lætámini in Dómino et exsultáte, justi*," Fabiano recited again.

"*Et gloriámini, omnes recti corde*," the crowd answered.

They watched as some old metal lanterns were waved about, spewing wafts of noxious incense; then a bell was rung and the priests behind the altar started lining up behind the reliquary.

"They're getting ready," Babalu whispered. Sure enough, the three men looked around and saw the crowd starting to amble, as a herd, toward the altar. "Follow me," he said.

Carlo sashayed convincingly in front of Arthur, with his head bent reverently and his rosary beads clicking expertly in his hand. Then with Babalu in the lead, they took their places in line about a dozen or so people back. From their position they watched in tense anticipation as Rosa leaned down to kiss Jeremy's hands, and then pushed up the sleeve of his right arm, while two altar boys carefully lifted up and then removed the glass panel from the right side of the coffin—the side facing the crowd. The choir's voices swelled again and Rosa placed a golden sluice under the bared white arm, then picked up a golden scalpel from a plate on the altar and slashed Jeremy's veins.

"*Deus, qui nos annua sanctorum,*" Fabiano roared. "*Mártyrum tuórum Januárii et Sociórum ejus solemnitate lætíficas: concéde propítius; ut, quorum gaudémus meritis, accendámur exemplis! Per Dóminum!*"

The crowd gasped delightedly and the trio watched in horror as Jeremy's ruby-colored blood began streaming down the sluice into the first crystal decanter; Arthur's heart was nearly beating out of his chest, but he grabbed Carlo's arm and reminded him, through his teeth, "*Not yet. Not yet. Not yet.*"

"Only Ogum can save him now," Babalu muttered.

And up on that altar Jeremy was crying but not crying because he couldn't, and his eyes were seared with pain from not blinking and he just wanted this to end so he could die and not have to think about Arthur and Carlo having been shot in the head, and he felt bad about leaving Aunt Katharine but maybe there was a heaven and he'd see his mom and dad again, and he could tell his dad that he'd fallen in love with Arthur just like he had, and he'd tell him what a great guy he still was, and…he was getting sleepy now, he thought…he was…tired. Just tired. And it wouldn't…be so long now…his dad…*Arthur*…

The first decanter had been filled, so now a second empty one replaced it. Then the hot, scarlet contents of the first was gently, delicately, reverently tipped by Rosa into a golden funnel, which emptied into one of the perfume bottles, and then the second bottle after that, and then another, and another.

They were creeping their way toward the front of the line, where Fabiano, looking as stoic as he was arrogant, handed each of the faithful their tiny glass vial—after, that is, they dropped their donation into the receptacle by his side. Arthur checked himself to make certain that, although his body was a tightly wound spring, his posture was bent and his stomach pillows were in place, as were the rags stuck into his cheeks; the closer they drew the greater the risk became of discovery.

Now Babalu was third in line to receive his vial, with Arthur and Carlo shoulder to shoulder behind him. Arthur had to make sure both of Fabiano's hands were occupied before making his move; he was pretty certain he was carrying a gun somewhere under that billowing, holy robe.

Babalu, money in hand, stepped up to receive his gift.

He dropped his donation in with the others.

He opened his hand and the vial of Jeremy's blood was placed into it.

"*Gracias,* Padre," he announced, using the signal they had agreed upon.

A switch in Arthur's brain clicked.

He let loose a war cry and flew in swinging.

CHAPTER 44

He landed a strong right uppercut on Fabiano's chin, and the man stumbled backward. There was a great wail of confusion from the crowd, and Arthur knew he had to work quickly; otherwise, some of the men in attendance would launch a counterattack and obliterate him—throw him over the edge, maybe. He jabbed with his left and crossed with his right, and the big man went down on his knees. He performed a quick left roundhouse kick and felt his foot make contact with the side of the man's head.

Something cracked and Fabiano fell backward in a heap.

"Jesu Cristo!" someone screamed.

Then Arthur was on him, then straddling him, then pummeling his face.

Left.

Right.

Left.

Right.

In the flickering of the torchlight, he saw blood gushing from the man's nose.

Jab.

Cross.

Jab.

Cross.

Arthur's knuckles opened an angry red slice in the man's cheek.

Then his hands went around Fabiano's neck, and all of the fear and grief and frustration and misery he'd been storing inside zoomed down his arms and into his hands, where it made his fingers clench into vicelike pincers.

Fabiano's face turned purple, blood stopped running from his cheek and his eyes bulged.

"Arthur!" he heard Carlo yell. "She's got a gun!"

He looked up to see Rosa raising a revolver in his direction; in an instant he knew he had no cover and this was it—she had a clear shot at him.

In slow motion, he saw one of her eyes squeeze shut.

Then her head jerked back and her eyes startled open and her hands went to fight whatever it was that had her by the neck.

The crowd erupted into a roar.

Suddenly Rosa's face flushed purple and her mouth gaped and her tongue protruded.

She was screaming. But no sound came out.

Then she dropped the gun and slumped to the ground and Arthur saw that Babalu was standing behind him strangling him...with something that dug into his neck so deeply he could barely make it out.

The rosary beads!

He looked up for an instant to see that Jeremy's limp arm was streaming blood onto the pavement now as it dangled from the reliquary, and in that horrifying moment he was thrown to the side and Fabiano was on top of him, his hands around his neck, his face a ferocious, snarling mask. And as the demon shifted all of his body weight up and on top of him, Arthur realized, *He's going to kill me. This is it.*

His eyes rolled up into his head as darkness overtook his vision.

His lungs fought valiantly for air.

His body went limp.

POW! POW!

The bullets tore through Fabiano's right temple, and his hands fell away just as a scarlet geyser exploded out of the left side his head.

He collapsed halfway onto Arthur.

The shock of the man falling on him made him open his eyes one last time. He saw Carlo standing with his legs splayed and elbows locked, and the revolver gripped between steady hands.

Arthur's head slumped to the side.

He heard perfect silence.

Jeremy, are you here with me?

In a flash Carlo, still holding the gun in one hand, reached down and pulled the two soggy strips from inside Arthur's slack mouth; these he knotted together, then used as a tourniquet around Jeremy's bicep.

Then he yanked the tangled weave off his head, shoved El Gigante's body off Arthur, bent down and began performing emergency breathing on him.

Expertly.

While Babalu chattered into the microphone, in frenetic Portuguese, explaining to the terrified crowd exactly what had just happened.

CHAPTER 45

The first sensation he became aware of was the siren wailing—not like those in the United States, but in that singsong *EEE-AAH-EEE-AAH* of European rescue vehicles. He looked around the van as it bumped along and saw there was no one riding in back with him. So he panicked, thinking maybe this was another of Fabiano's tricks.

A gunshot. Yes, there'd been a gunshot. Who was hit? *Was I hit?* He patted down his body, doing a quick inventory of limbs and trunk. *Must've been someone else.*

But who?

Was Carlo safe? What about Babalu? He couldn't even begin to think about Jeremy; last he remembered was he was bleeding...to death.

Did we do it? Is he safe? Where is everyone? Will anyone be there when I get to the hospital?

He closed his eyes and drifted off.

He was awakened by the slowing of the ambulance, and the flood of lights from the hospital through the back windows of the van.

They bumped to a stop. Then the back doors flew open, and his gurney was unloaded.

Carlo stood over him. "Are you OK?" he asked, his eyes moony with concern.

"My—" He tried to speak, but his throat was filled with razors. Instead he pointed at his neck and shook his head.

"He strangled you," Carlo told him. "Fabiano."

"Jeremy?" Arthur managed, ready to hear the worst.

Carlo's eyes shifted away, then back. "He's in the ER. They don't know yet."

Arthur closed his eyes and sighed. At least he was alive—and in a safe place.

"Fab—" he began.

"Dead." Carlo smiled slyly.

Arthur's eyes widened.

"I killed him," he announced proudly. "With that fucking Rosa's fucking gun."

Arthur grinned, and Carlo rubbed his chest affectionately. "Ya did it, big guy. You saved Jeremy's life."

Arthur shook his head. "You." He pointed at him. "Babalu?"

"He's OK, too. He's talking to the police right now, and with someone from the American consulate."

***

After he was admitted, he was shuttled to a draped cubicle, where he was finally allowed to stand on his own. He really wanted to check on Jeremy, but first he needed to be evaluated by a doctor.

The attending physician, after checking his vital signs and peering down his throat, determined that he was in satisfactory condition, so he pulled on his clothes and followed the arrows down to the ICU, where he found Carlo seated on the edge of a chair, and a doctor standing over Jeremy while scribbling notes into a folder.

But what met his eyes horrified him.

"You had to intubate him?" he asked, upon seeing the tube down Jeremy's throat and hearing the rhythmic *fwick-pssh...fwick-pssh* of the machine filling, then deflating his lungs.

The doctor nodded. "Scopolamine," he told him. "Or *burundanga*, some call it. It is a strong paralytic that without assistance can stop the breathing in an hour or so. Without this machine, he could not breathe on his own."

"What about brain damage?"

"It is too soon to know. But his blood-oxygen level was not yet critical when he came in, so we believe he will recover."

"Completely?" Arthur smoothed the sheet over Jeremy's robotically inflating and deflating torso.

"We must hope so," he replied. "He is young and strong. I have seen worse." He pointed to a second chair in the room. "You should sit and pray, like your friend does. God does wonders, especially in hospitals."

"Thank you," Arthur told the physician. Then he bent over Jeremy's head, with the greasy white makeup still thick on his face, and kissed him on the forehead. "You're gonna be just fine," he whispered, caressing his cheek. "We need you too much." He looked over at Carlo. "I do, Carlo does, Katharine does. We all need you." He kissed him again.

He made his way over to the chair, where he sat with a grunt. The exhaustion was starting to hit him, and he was on the verge of tears. And it was going to be a long night—waiting and dozing and waking and waiting and dozing until morning. But he was already starting to feel relieved. And even hopeful.

About what, he wasn't quite sure.

He felt a hand smooth his back. "Are you OK?" Carlo asked him gently.

"Yeah, but I'm sorry to tell you that I've gotten my voice back—although I'm sounding a bit like Suzanne Pleshette."

"Who?"

"Never mind. How're you?"

Carlo blew the air out from trumpet-player cheeks. "I'm all right, I guess. I've never killed someone before, and I guess I should feel…different, but I don't—probably because there are lots of people I've wanted to kill but never had the chance to." He chuckled. "Have you ever?"

"Thank God, no." He shook his head.

"That's funny, you know? I mean, here Jeremy killed his uncle and now I killed Fabiano, and Babalu almost killed Rosa and would have if the beads hadn't snapped; but here you're this Marine and FBI guy and you haven't ever killed anyone."

"I guess I'm a crappy soldier."

"No, you're not. None of us could've pulled this off without you, and you know it."

Arthur tried to smile. "I guess we all did what we had to do."

"And we're all OK now…at least I hope so," Carlo said, gazing at Jeremy. "I don't know what I'd do without him; I would've rather died up there myself than him. You know?"

"I know *exactly* how you feel."

Carlo looked at him, opened his mouth, and then snapped it shut. Their eyes locked, then Arthur looked away.

"You love him, too, don't you?"

Arthur smiled innocently at him. "Of course I do. Who doesn't?"

"How much?"

He didn't answer.

"Arthur, how *much* do you love him?"

Arthur rolled his eyes. "Do you really want to have this conversation *now*?"

"Hey, we're all here together. What could possibly be a better time?" Carlo asked sarcastically.

"I don't think it's the time, or the place."

"You wouldn't talk to me about this yesterday because it 'didn't have to do with Jeremy's safety,' so I let it go. But he's safe now. And when he wakes up I need to know how I'm gonna deal with things."

"Please don't insist on discussing this." Arthur slumped back in his chair, talking to the ceiling. "Tomorrow, OK? We can talk about this tomorrow."

"Jeremy told me that he's in love with you. Actually, he's been for a while."

Arthur's head snapped forward. *"He what?"*

"But you already knew that. He told me he was going to tell you, and see how you reacted." He crossed his arms over his chest. "Did he?"

Arthur waited for a moment, then nodded.

"So what did you tell him?"

He searched for the right words. "I told him if we slept together it would change everything."

"So didja fuck?" he asked.

"No."

"Didja...*mess around?"* Carlo asked, raising an eyebrow playfully.

Arthur was not feeling playful. "Yes, we messed around."

He smiled. "He's got a huge cock, huh?"

"Please don't do this. It was a mistake, and I'm sorry—it only happened once. He loves you at least as much as he loves me."

"No. He loves you more." Carlo shoved his hands deep into his pockets. "Look, Jeremy's got this whole 'daddy complex,' and I'm a lot of things, but a 'daddy' isn't one of 'em. You guys are lucky you found each other, you know? Square peg, square hole."

"I'm not taking him away from you."

"You're absolutely right about that; you're not taking him away from me because I'm giving him to you. *He's yours."* He swept his arm out to the side, like a game-show hostess.

"No. When he wakes up you two should talk it over, see where you want things to go. I'll stay out of the picture until you two figure it out, OK?" He put a hand on the younger man's shoulder. "Deal?"

"Look, that's really noble and all…" Carlo paused, "But what you don't know about me is I can't stand to be second choice, you know? Like there was this guy I was boyfriends with, before Jeremy, and I just didn't feel like being with him anymore. But I didn't have anyone else around who was interested in me, so I stuck with him and wound up kind of treating him bad so he'd just go away, and that was mean." He looked over at the prone figure in the hospital bed. "And if Jeremy ever did that to me, I don't think I could…take it—I mean my self-esteem wouldn't survive my having to be so *desperate*. So this way, I get to be the one in charge, and you guys get each other. *Win-win*."

"But—" Arthur began to protest.

"Are you in love with him?" he asked insistently.

He bit his lip and shrugged. "Yeah," he said finally, with a slow blink.

"Done deal," Carlo announced. *"Believe* me, it's better this way. I just wanted to make sure you feel the same way about him because"—he started fighting back sudden tears—"because I can't…*stand* the thought of Jeremy loving someone who doesn't love him back the same way, you know?"

Arthur put his arm around him. "I know," he told him softly. "I know."

"I just love him too much, Arthur." He went over to Jeremy and ran his fingers through the velvet of his buzz cut, then began to cry. "I just do."

CHAPTER 46

Around sunrise he was awakened by the sound of Jeremy thrashing around in bed; the doctor had told him to notify the staff immediately if this should happen, as he didn't want his patient fighting the ventilator. So he left the room while the staff performed the uncomfortable task of pulling the tube out of his throat and cleaning him up, and then waited until the room was clear before stepping in again.

Jeremy was lying in bed with his eyes closed, and was looking much more like himself without the makeup on his face (Carlo and he, the first chance they got, had wiped his skin clean), or the tube and its apparatus taped over his mouth, even though an IV machine still creaked reliably next to his bedside.

Arthur stepped lightly along the linoleum, in case he was asleep, and sat down quietly in the chair next to him.

His eyes lingered over the face of his beloved, who looked—for the very first time that he could recall—tired. While doing so, he saw his cheeks were wet with tears, probably from his eyes being stuck in that terrified gaze for so long.

But then he heard him moan—a moan of pure anguish.

Is he awake, or dreaming?

Then his features pinched tight as he began to cry.

This is no dream.

"Hey, what's wrong, old buddy?" he asked, stroking his arm. "What hurts?"

Jeremy's eyes burst open as he snapped his head toward him. "Arthur?" he gasped. "Arthur!"

He reached over and placed his palm on his forehead. "Right here."

"Oh, oh, oh, oh! Where's Carlo?" His eyes darted frantically around the room.

Carlo began stirring from his position on the room's benchlike couch, where he'd been sleeping all balled up since midnight, even through the nightshift's intermittent parade. "Yeah, I'm here," he mumbled while sitting up, rubbing his eyes.

Jeremy's face contorted into a mask of terrible grief, as his eyes shifted from Arthur to Carlo and back. "I thought you were dead."

Carlo stroked his chest while Arthur raised his unfettered hand to his lips and kissed it; and Jeremy's body deflated, as if tension were leaking from him like air from a punctured raft. "Did you dream we were dead?" Arthur asked.

He began sobbing, looking from man to man. "He said—" He tried to speak, but coughed from the effort, because his throat was scratched from the intubation. "He said that—" He coughed again. "That Aunt Katharine said it was too much money and she wouldn't pay it, and then first he killed"—he looked up at Carlo and more tears spilled down his cheeks—"you, and then six hours later you. I thought I'd never see you again!"

"Oh, my God," Arthur said. "That has to be the cruelest thing he could've done."

"So what happened? Where did you go after I got kidnapped?"

"We were up at Fabiano's villa until we left there to find you," Arthur explained. "And we didn't have any idea you were up there at the same time we were, until Babalu told us that's probably where he was keeping you."

"But I wasn't at his house. I was in some cell underground."

"That's right under his home," Arthur said, "built into the mountain right underneath it."

"Then Babalu said you'd probably be up at that ceremony, where they'd bleed you to death," Carlo added, "and sure enough there you were. So when the time was right Arthur jumped Fabiano and smashed his face in."

"You did?"

"I did my best, but he's a lot bigger than me, so I needed help."

"What's the last thing you remember?" Carlo asked.

"It's all kind of fuzzy, because something was wrong with my eyes."

"Do you remember when Babalu strangled Rosa with his rosary beads?"

Jeremy shook his head. "Uh-uh."

"Well, right after that happened, I grabbed Rosa's gun and shot Fabiano in the head," Carlo stated proudly, "killing him instantly."

"You killed El Gigante?"

"He saved my life," Arthur stated. "Fabiano was strangling me; another few seconds and he would've crushed my windpipe. Then after Carlo shot him he gave me mouth-to-mouth, and he even made a tourniquet on your arm so you wouldn't bleed to death."

"But how'd you know how to shoot a gun?"

"I grew up on a ranch, silly," Carlo replied, smiling for the first time in days. "I could shoot the tassels off a throw pillow."

"You should've seen him with that gun, wearing that wig; the whole scene was right out of *Charlie's Angels*. Your boyfriend's quite the big hero, Jeremy, saving all three of our lives at the same time. I'm in awe."

Carlo shook his head, waving his hands dismissively. "*Anyhow*, so now that we're all OK and the bad guy's gone forever, how're you feeling?"

"I guess I'm all right." Jeremy closed his eyes. "I just still can't believe this all happened."

"I talked to Katharine just before midnight," said Arthur. "She wanted to come down here but I told her not to, because we'd be on the first plane home."

"When can we leave?" Jeremy asked. "Can we go today, like maybe this afternoon?"

"The doctors need to make sure you're healthy enough to travel." Arthur rubbed the top of his head. "They're not sure about those things they cut your arm with, so they need to watch out for infection, and make sure your blood pressure is back up to normal, and your other vital signs are stable. But you know that as soon as we can, we'll be out of here. And the police have to ask you some questions, too."

"I forgot about Rosa doing that to me; can you believe it?" he reached over and touched his thickly bandaged forearm. "I'm just so glad you guys are OK," he said at last, looking up at them. "I couldn't see myself living without you," he told Carlo, and then Arthur. "When he said you were dead, I wanted to die—I *really* did."

"We're all safe now," Carlo said. "We'll get out of here, go home, and then everything's gonna go right back to normal." He glanced at Arthur, but Arthur looked away.

"What about Babalu? Where's he? I wanted to meet him."

"He's actually downstairs in another room," Carlo answered.

"Oh, God, I hope he wasn't hurt!"

"He's having some tests run, you know, to see if there's anything they can do...to help him."

"I told the hospital," Arthur cut in, "that we'd pay for anything he needed; I didn't think there'd be a problem."

Jeremy smiled. "That's what you came here for anyway, huh, Carlo?"

"I just hope it's not too late for him, you know?"

Arthur shook his head. "Sometimes when you think you're out of time, you're about to get some more."

"I sure hope so for him," Jeremy said.

"Me, too," added Carlo.

"Yeah." Arthur smiled. "He sure deserves it."

"I love you guys so much," Jeremy said, then took a deep breath.

"We love you, too," Arthur murmured.

"More than you know," Carlo echoed, then caught Arthur's eyes with his own.

CHAPTER 47

They flew from Rio to Miami, where they met their connection to Los Angeles. Then five hours later they were home.

Of course she was waiting for them at LAX, curbside in her pearl white Bentley Continental, with an escort of four motorcycle cops, which she had somehow wrangled.

Upon seeing the men dragging their bags through the doors, she hopped out of her car and descended upon them, arms wide and resplendent in cream-and-black Chanel. "You're really here!" she exclaimed, as she embraced Jeremy with such enthusiasm that a large Asian family actually stopped to stare. She made her way to Arthur next, then Carlo, kissing each on both cheeks. "What brave, brave men are here, standing before me!" she exclaimed, looking from one to the other. "I knew you'd get through that terrible ordeal—I never doubted any of you for a second." Ignoring the diaperlike bandage on Jeremy's arm, she grabbed his hand and pulled him toward the curb. "Come, let's take you all home. Carlo, your sister is waiting at our place; I told her to make herself comfortable by the pool, because it's such a gorgeous day by the beach. My, but she is a beautiful girl! Your mother must have been quite extraordinary."

Jeremy climbed in the front, while Arthur and Carlo belted themselves into the back, and moments later they were speeding in their own motorcade along the curvy exit route headed toward Century Boulevard. "They're only funeral cops, you know." Katharine giggled as one of them signaled for her to slow down. "I just couldn't think of anything else that might make your return feel quite as special—and besides, there've been these pesky reporters outside our place for days now."

They took the 405 freeway north to the 10 west, then motored up Pacific Coast Highway all the way to Ballena Beach. Finally, Katharine made a left into the driveway, where they waited as the rent-a-cops shooed away the paparazzi; and after the gates of the Tyler compound motored open, then swung shut behind them, they were safely home.

Arthur snapped into his good-butler mode the minute the car stopped: helping Jeremy out of the car, looking after Katharine, and exhibiting businesslike courtesy to Carlo; he rolled their luggage to the laundry room and was even separating colors and whites before taking the time to use the restroom.

Katharine had arranged for a small homecoming party for the group, having invited the boys' friends Ellie and her girlfriend Reed, in addition to Carmen. She had done her very best to decorate the place, with sprays of fresh flowers scattered about, while the lavish catering had been provided by the best Mexican restaurant in town. And with the sound system set to Jeremy's favorite satellite channel, and the Florentine fountain splashing and the sun brilliant overhead and the waves thundering on the sand and boats in full sail skittering along the blue expanse beyond the cliffs, it was a blissful afternoon, in perfect Katharine Tyler fashion.

"EeeeEEEEeeeEE!" the three girls squealed as they got up from their chaises and ran to meet the boys. Then after bear hugs and sincere kisses were exchanged, Jeremy excused Carlo and himself to his quarters to shower and change. Arthur wished to do the same—but stayed instead to help serve and engage the guests, and then after the boys returned he would sneak off for a tune-up.

"So did Carlo really kill that horrible man?" Ellie asked as they made their way over to the long glass dining table. "I still can't believe all this crazy drama happened to you guys."

"I'm sure he'd prefer to give you his account of what happened, but yep, he did," Arthur said as he pulled out chairs for her and for Reed. "And none of us can believe it all, either."

"Is Jeremy really OK?" Reed asked as he sat next to them. "That bandage looks totally scary, and Katharine said they gave him drugs that almost killed him."

"Oh, he's fine, I think," Arthur said, grabbing a Corona from the ice bucket in the center of the table. "At least physically. But we all had a really close call down there. It's a picture that's gonna take a few decades to fade in all of our heads."

"Why did they do that to him?" Carmen asked.

Arthur sat back in his chair and popped the cap off his beer. "The main thing was the money, of course. When our government found out who was involved, and made Katharine pull out of the project, Fabiano staged the kidnapping but pretended someone else was behind it, then made himself the 'mediator' for the ransom between 'them' and Katharine. And it would've worked except that she couldn't come up with that much money on such short notice."

"She couldn't?" Ellie asked. "That's weird."

"I'm sure she could've if they'd given her more time to liquidate some assets, but it was a lot of money. *A lot.* And a really short ransom period—I don't think it was even forty-eight hours." He thought for a moment. "I guess even rich folks wind up feeling poor, sometimes."

"But what about all of that anti-American stuff we heard about?" Reed asked. "Why would they be involved in something like that resort, especially one that's supposed to have perfect security to keep them out?"

"Because," Katharine broke in as she approached the table with a glass of wine in her hand, "they needed a guaranteed investment, something that everyone would want to throw money at—and of course no militia group would blow up their fattest cash cow, so of course its security was 'guaranteed.'" She pulled out a chair and sat. "We've found out more, since all of this transpired, by the way." She took a long sip, then shook her head as she swallowed it. "Our sources theorize that their long-range plan was to bilk the consortium for additional money once the enterprise was open, while showing less of a profit after the first gangbuster years. And then"—she took another sip—"they would begin to show bigger and bigger losses, which would need additional investor support to keep the island 'afloat,' so to speak. And if that didn't work, our sources believe they may have even planned to hold the entire island, and all of its inhabitants, hostage."

"That's crazy!" Reed exclaimed.

"But it's also brilliant, young lady. The world has changed over the past decade, and people are justifiably frightened, especially when certain American entities have done their very best to fuel, and then to capitalize on, people's fears." She looked at each of them at the table as she spoke, as if starring in her own infomercial. "'Fear' has become the 'damnation' of the new millennium, with a growing number of people and groups advertising their specific—and costly—remedies for 'salvation.' And I am ashamed to say that my late husband had us involved with such a loathsome group."

"But we're not anymore," Arthur said. "And thank God we got out of that situation alive."

"So my little brother was the big hero, right?" asked Carmen, sounding awestruck. "Even his dad is so proud of him."

"If it weren't for him, we'd all be dead right now. We were only seconds, like maybe *three* seconds, from being—"

Katharine pushed her chair back noisily and stood up from the table. "Does anyone want anything more to drink?" she asked cheerfully. "I'm going into the house."

Ellie held up her glass. "Could I have just a teeny bit of that white wine?"

Katherine smiled slyly. "One glass, young lady. And not a word to your mother; she'd have me arrested. Anyone else?"

"I'll have some, too," Reed said.

"I'm good," Arthur stated, lifting up his Corona.

"Very well." And with that, Katharine shoved her chair back under the table and began marching toward the house.

They heard some laughing, and turned to see Jeremy and Carlo, with their arms around Carmen's boyfriend Darius, as they descended the stairs toward the seated group.

"So where's your gorgeous boy toy been hiding all this time?" Ellie asked Carmen.

"He had to find someone to cover his shift at the restaurant," she answered, as Jeremy and Carlo pulled out chairs next to each other and sat, while Darius made his way over to Carmen, then kissed her lightly on the lips. "Hey, baby," she said.

They spent the next few hours talking about the ordeal and relaxing while catching up on everyone's summer, and Arthur busied himself with playing host, while hiding how much he needed to just relax and recuperate. Katharine, he noticed, was making herself uncharacteristically scarce, as well as unusually helpful. She hardly sat down, and seemed to flee when someone made any reference to the gory specifics of their nightmare.

But he had more important things on his mind than Katharine Tyler, as he was scrutinizing the body language of Jeremy and Carlo, and trying to divine exactly what the hell was going on—because for a couple who was allegedly on the verge of breaking up, they sure looked chummy. In fact, they looked like newlyweds: knowing glances, hands intertwined, soft words exchanged, simultaneous giggling.

Hadn't Carlo told him yet?

No. He needed to relax. It was still really soon.

He would speak with Jeremy tonight to find out what was going on.

But sitting here at the table with them was becoming more and more unsettling; it was clear there were two groups present: *the kids and the oldsters.*

And clearly, he and his beloved were in opposing groups.

He decided it was his turn to go inside and freshen up, as the second beer had hit him hard, and he was zonked as it was from all the air travel. And if anyone blamed him for not reappearing, then *fuck 'em*—because he was just too exhausted, too shell-shocked and too heartsick to care.

"Will you please excuse me?" he asked everyone and no one in particular, then pushed his chair away from the table. "I think I need to lie down for a bit."

A chorus of *sures* and *of courses* and *we'll be heres* ensued, so without making eye contact with Jeremy or Carlo, Arthur made his way back up to the house, through the kitchen and into his quarters, where he started the shower and found that, as his clothes dropped into a pile on the marble floor, he was on the verge of a colossal depression.

***

He was awakened by tapping on his door.

His eyelids pushed themselves open and he saw it was already past twilight; he'd been asleep, apparently, for hours.

"Come in," he said, not caring that he'd slipped into bed naked after his shower, as he was far beyond worrying about such trivia anymore. After all, it was probably just Jeremy, because when Katharine wanted anything from him she always used the intercom.

He had just pushed himself upright against his pillows and gathered the sheets around his waist when the door swung open, and there he stood, grinning at him like a fool. Jeremy squeezed the door shut behind him, then dashed over and threw his arms around him.

Arthur returned his hug vigorously, feeling Jeremy's mouth smooching along his jaw toward his mouth.

Their lips touched, and he heard himself whimper. He wrenched his body up on top of Jeremy, his naked skin now fully exposed to the evening breeze coursing in through the open windows, while Jeremy's tongue twisted and licked the inside of his mouth and his body slid up to mirror his position: knees to knees and chest to chest and lips to lips. He drew a full breath of him through his nostrils and became dizzy with desire; the smell of him, the taste of him, and the dense heat of his body, even through his clothes, made him swoon.

"I was so worried about you," Arthur managed to whisper at last. "I was so afraid, during everything, that we'd never get a chance to be here together—and that's what kept me going."

"Me, too. But I knew, somehow."

"So did I."

"Where's Katharine?"

"The fifth glass of wine knocked her off her pumps." Jeremy chuckled. "I just put her to bed upstairs; she was snoring like an old bear when I closed her door."

"She drank *five* glasses of wine?" Arthur asked. "How do you know it was five?"

"Growing up with my mom, I counted 'em as a reflex."

"Boy, she still must be freaked out about everything."

"That makes four of us."

Arthur reached up and ran his finger inside the cleft on Jeremy's chin. "Did...Carlo and you talk?"

Jeremy grinned at him. "We worked it out; we both knew it was coming. But it's OK. He understands."

"He's amazing, even besides the fact that he saved our lives."

"Yeah." Jeremy smiled sideways. "We're still gonna be each other's family, though. Really good friends, you know?"

"I'm glad, 'cause I'd really miss him." Arthur grinned and kissed Jeremy again. "God, I love holding you."

"And I love"—he nuzzled Arthur's neck—"you."

Jeremy peeled off his T-shirt, and Arthur took in his sculpture-perfect torso. "How did you ever get so beautiful?" he asked, tracing a finger under his rigid pectorals, then sliding it down his buckling abs to the follow the crease of his adonis belt.

"The same way you got so fuckin' sexy," Jeremy growled, grinning. Then Arthur collapsed on top of him, so both could feel the other's rigid sex pressed up against his own.

But Arthur wanted to take this moment slowly; this was something he'd fantasized about for some time. "Wait," he said.

"I can't," Jeremy whispered as his hand massaged him.

Suddenly nearing the crest of his pleasure, Arthur clamped his hand down on Jeremy's. "Patience, my love," he told him, while guiding both arms around his neck.

They kissed and held each other and kissed some more; then Jeremy pulled Arthur's hands to the buttons of his jeans. And as each one lower was popped, the men's breathing quickened proportionately.

Finally, Arthur slipped his thumbs inside the waistband and slid Jeremy's pants down off him—while purposefully squeezing shut his eyelids, as if savoring the moments before lifting the lid from a box he knew contained a treasured gift.

Then he allowed his eyes to drift open.

Even in the diminished light, the naked, uncompromised male beauty that met his eyes called up his basest lust. But what seized him, as his mind and soul and psyche scrambled to make sense of the vision before him—beyond the bashful smile and flashing brown eyes and lyrical musculature and burgeoned, begging manhood—was the purity of emotion he felt.

Love. Without doubt. Without hesitation. Without confusion.

Love, clear as knowing green will always be green and will *never* be confused with red.

Love so absolute that he, Arthur, ceased to exist in his own mind.

Jeremy reached out and pulled him close, awakening him from his ecstatic void; and Arthur, now delirious with desire, felt the fullness of his own hot skin pressed gently against his lover's.

Their arms encircled each other and they clenched each other, and their mouths locked and twisted within the other's and their thrusting shafts dribbled with anticipation against their taut, concave bellies and moist, hairy thighs. "Ahhh," Arthur moaned, as he felt himself brim with tears that were not tears, but rather the inhaled gasping of his soul that sometimes erupted during pieces by Handel or Copeland, whose fiercely beautiful passages transposed into song moments like these.

Their hands smoothed each other, teased each other, grasped each other while they took turns biting each other's lips and nuzzling each other's necks.

Then Arthur's tongue began teasing a haphazard trail, as his mouth descended Jeremy's heaving torso.

"You do that and I'm gonna come," he whispered.

"Uh-uh," Arthur replied, knowing he could very fully control his lover's pleasure. But he paused momentarily with his ear to Jeremy's stomach anyway, so he might hear the faint creaking of Jeremy's bowels, and the urgent rush of air filling and leaving and filling his lungs.

His mouth watered.

With his own rigid member insistent against Jeremy's shin, he kissed the drooling plum. Then his lips parted and his tongue extended as he relaxed the back of his throat to receive his lover's eucharist.

"Ohhh…," Jeremy moaned as he felt the slick heat of Arthur's mouth sheathe his shaft. And with his own hand he encouraged the back of Arthur's nodding head as he suckled him gently, and his teasing fingers massaged his naked thighs.

Jeremy's hips began pistoning faster, and his back began to arch.

Arthur's mouth surrendered its prize, and he stretched himself fully alongside him and kissed him, with one arm under him and the other rubbing the sweating, rigid contours of his flesh.

"Do you?" Jeremy's voice managed, with the faint taste of himself on his lips.

Arthur shook his head, then nodded gently, while their eyes met in the dark without benefit of sight. "You."

They shifted positions.

Then they prepared themselves.

One raised his legs high, while the other climbed onto his knees and nudged himself at his opening, while running his hands up and down the backs of his thighs. "Tell me if it hurts," he said, "or if I'm going too fast." And the other put both hands on his shoulders and strained up off the bed to meet his mouth, while the splendid sword slid slowly inside, then stopped.

"My love," Arthur said, as they began undulating as one.

Slowly. Gently.

He pushed himself all the way in, then pulled himself nearly all the way out.

Gently. Slowly.

He halved himself, pulling his ankles toward his shoulders. Then he began teasing himself, as the other man held his calves and began to thrust madly.

Arthur lost himself in the pleasure, as the sensation and the realization of what was happening brought him to the edge. *We're fucking,* came the thought like a Times Square ticker across what little remained of his conscious mind. *Jeremy and I are fucking we're fucking Jeremy and I are fucking we're fucking...*

They rocked together and their mouths found each other and they moaned through their kisses and gasped through their moans, and his thrusts became pounding became thrashing and he felt himself being carried toward that line which signifies there's no holding back—that what's coming has all of the unstoppable inertia of a boulder tumbling down a steep mountainside.

"I'm coming, Arthur, I'm coming!"

He emptied himself inside him while the other striped his torso.

He collapsed upon his chest while they were still conjoined.

They hugged each other and kissed, while glued together by their pent-up love.

It took them a moment for their breathing to slow.

"When did you know?" Jeremy murmured, finally.

"After you left for Hawaii. I ached. What about you?"

Jeremy giggled as he released him, then snuggled into the crook of Arthur's arm. "It was right after you gave me the baseball glove and the cap. Remember?"

"You cried. Which hardly seems like someone in love."

"I cried because I felt so much for you and I was so confused," he whispered, with their noses almost touching. "I mean, here you were this ultimate nice guy, running around doing everything for me and teaching me how to drive and all, and then you give me this Christmas present like you're my dad and I'm feeling totally guilty because...I guess because I'd already started having feelings for you and wanted you to be more than my dad, but didn't know how to tell you. You know?"

"I think so."

"It's like you were giving me this perfect gift, but it was, uh, the wrong color."

"So is it the right color now?" Arthur asked.

Jeremy grinned and climbed on top of him, and Arthur saw that he was hard again. "It's my favorite color now, old buddy."

Arthur threw his arm around him and held him, and then flipped him onto his side to spoon him, with his chest to his back, his spent cock against his taut, velvety buttocks, and his knees against the backs of his legs.

He kissed his shoulders; then his hands reached around his back to smooth his hairless chest and run his hand along the ridges of his abdomen. "I love you so much," he murmured, as his hand began to caress him. "You've got no idea what I went through when I thought I'd lost you."

Jeremy closed his eyes and drew Arthur's arms tighter around him. "I know," he said as his eyes drifted closed, and he pushed his ass up tight against him.

"When should we tell Katharine?" Arthur asked.

But no reply met his ears.

So he held the snoring boy in his arms, while smoothing the wrinkled bandage covering his wrist.

CHAPTER 48

His eyes scanned the list of agents' phone extensions as they scrolled up on his computer screen.
Rodriguez, M.
Roswell, B.
Samuels, H.
Shipston, K.
And then he spotted it: *Singer, C.*

He flipped open the brand-new cell phone Katharine had presented to him—as she had to Jeremy and Carlo as well—at the party yesterday, and pressed the numbers.

"You've reached the voice mail for Special Agent Carl Singer with the Federal Bureau of Investigation. Please leave your name, telephone number and the nature of your call, and I'll get back to you at my very next opportunity. Thank you."

He waited for the tone. "Hello, Agent Singer, this is Art Blaufee, formerly of the FBI. You helped us out with that mess down in Brazil with the Tyler family; I was down there with Jeremy Tyler when he was kidnapped, and just wanted to say thanks for whatever you did." He thought for a moment. "No need to call me back. I just wanted to say that everything's good now, and we're all recovering, safe and sound at home. Thanks again—you did a great job."

He ended the call and slipped the phone inside his jacket; he had to run by the market and pick up some things for an impromptu trip Jeremy wanted to take up to the chalet at Lake Estrella—that is, after they had their discussion with Katharine.

Which he was dreading.

***

He was about to load the final bag of groceries into the back of Jeremy's Rover when he felt his phone vibrate in his pocket. He flipped it open and looked at where the number should have shown on the tiny screen, but it read only NO INFO.

"Hello?"

"Is this Art Blauefee?"

"Speaking." He hefted the bag over the tailgate and slammed shut the hatch.

"This is Carl Singer, returning your call."

"Oh," he said, making his way to the driver's-side door. "Thanks for calling me back. But you didn't have to."

"Yeah, I know. But I was curious about how everything was resolved. I heard the official version, of course, but something didn't smell quite right. And since the State Department follows up on these foreign affairs, I wasn't privy to all the details."

"What did you hear?" Arthur asked as he hefted himself up into the big vehicle.

"That everything was textbook. Hostage returned. End of story."

Arthur laughed. "Nothing could be further from the truth." He twisted the key in the ignition, and the engine roared to life. "She couldn't come up with the money in time—Katharine Tyler, that is—so Fabiano and his crew were actually in the process of serving Jeremy up as a human sacrifice when we rescued him." He buckled himself in.

"Really." Singer paused. "Well, I guess everything turned out OK, and that's what matters. So what happened to Mr. Fabiano?"

"One of our party—and I wish it'd been me—killed him. Shot him in the head during the rescue scuffle."

"Christ. It sounds like you guys barely made it out of there."

"Pretty much."

"So can I ask you something, off the record?"

"Shoot. Off the record." He began backing out of the parking space.

"What did Mrs. Tyler tell you about the negotiations? She's a piece of work, by the way."

He chuckled. "I know it." He double-checked his mirrors. "She said just what I said earlier, that it was too much money and she couldn't liquidate her assets in time."

"Did she tell you how much they were asking for?"

"One hundred million euro," Arthur said as he slipped the transmission into drive and began weaving his way through the crowded parking lot.

Singer laughed. "Try a fraction of that. Ten million."

"*What?* She could've paid that."

"That's what I thought. Then when I made the mistake of telling her that we usually start negotiations with an offer of ten to twenty percent, she wanted to give them even less."

Arthur felt suddenly as if he'd been punched in the stomach. He slammed on the brakes and a car in back of him honked. "Are you telling me that she only made an offer of one to two million euros, on her nephew's life? On all of our lives, in fact?"

"It's still a lot of money, man. But from what I understand, the lady's loaded. It was weird that she was trying to cheap out. Especially since she had that K and R policy."

"What's that?" His foot pressed the gas, and he began moving again.

"That's right, you've been out of the business. That's kidnap and ransom insurance, and it's the newest thing for corporations to take out on their executives who travel overseas—especially to South America."

"She never told me she had that. How do those work?"

"The insurance company does all the work. Negotiations, transfers, everything."

"So why didn't she use their services?"

"Says she tried, but the kidnappers would only deal with her directly. And I confirmed this before we handed the case over to State—they would only deal with her."

"That smells fishy."

"Bingo."

He paused. "Are you sure about all of this?"

"I've got the transcripts from our phone calls; I could e-mail 'em to you if you wanted. Off the record, of course."

"No," Arthur replied. "That's OK." He waited for an opening in the traffic and then eased out onto the boulevard. "But if I need anything else, can I call you?"

"Anything for a former bureau man," Singer said. "Just let me know."

"I appreciate the info, Carl."

"Anytime. Take care." They ended the call.

He drove back to the compound in an angry daze.

She lied to me.

She lied to us.

CHAPTER 49

A bsolutely not!" Katharine bellowed. "The thought of you two being together is disgusting, incestuous, reprehensible!"

"Yeah, I'd forgotten he's my dead dad," Jeremy agreed sarcastically.

"You know what I mean, young man. And as for you"—she stared down her nose at Arthur—"I should have known that as a lonely homosexual, you would have eyes for him, for this...*child*."

"Now, wait a minute," Arthur cut in. "He's no *child*, Katharine. He's legally a man, and he's old enough to make decisions about who he wants to be with."

"Oh, forgive me, you're correct as usual," she snipped. "What I should have said, Mr. Blauefee, is that *compared to you*, he is a child. He's young enough to be *your* child. You're a middle-aged man. Have you no shame?"

Her words stung him. "Jeremy, let's forget this. She's not gonna budge." He stood up to leave.

"No! I'm not gonna give up that easily, Arthur. And you shouldn't, either."

"But she's not my family; she's just my employer. She has no motivation whatsoever to see my point of view."

"No," Jeremy countered. "You *are* our family. She counted on you to save me from Bill, and then she sent you down to Brazil to risk your own life, which you did. And you saved my life." He turned to her. "You *owe* him that much, that you should at least listen to us, Aunt Katharine. *Wouldn't that be the proper thing to do?*"

Arthur saw that she was fuming, and her skin was almost the same color as her henna-enhanced hair.

She ignored Jeremy and addressed Arthur, instead. "I have come to expect faulty reasoning from the young men in my family, Mr. Blauefee, especially as it pertains to their bad taste in 'romance.' In fact, my beloved Jonathan was rather an expert in that field, as you will recall. But I have no reason to stomach it from someone in my employ; the fact that I have compensated you quite adequately for your time, and the danger you were exposed to as a result, has, I believe, absolved me from any responsibility in that regard." She looked from Arthur to Jeremy and back again. "My decision about this matter has been made, and it is intractable; you will have no further contact with my nephew from this day forward, and I shall obtain a court order if need be." Then she turned on her heels to leave.

"Why are you acting this way?" Jeremy screamed at the back of her head.

She stopped, turned around slowly and smiled at Arthur. "Have you not told him?" she asked, her voice deadly sweet.

Arthur stared her down. "I've been very, very honest with him. About everything."

"So you've told him that you taught my Jonathan your perverted ways, and that you were the one who ruined his father's self-esteem so completely that the only woman he thought he deserved was a gutter slut?"

"Don't call my mom a slut," Jeremy warned.

"And you"—she blinked wildly at her nephew—"are you not absolutely repulsed by the idea that *he*...and *your father*...? Am I the only sane person left standing in this room?"

"Did Jonathan tell you I 'perverted' him?" Arthur asked. "Because it happened very, *very* differently from what you just said."

"His therapist," she snapped. "She told me everything you did to him, and you should thank me for the rest of your natural life that I ignored her advice and didn't have you carted off to prison for child molestation, or statutory rape. After all, you were the adult, as I so clearly recall, and he was still a child of sixteen. And now look at you," she said, her voice low and gravelly, "once again polluting my family's waters, ruining yet another generation of Tyler men." She shot a grimace at her nephew. "Be careful of this one, my dear, and be grateful you won't be having sons anytime soon—because he'd probably be screwing them behind your back, as well."

With that, she turned to storm off.

"Then why did you keep me here?" Arthur asked, but she kept walking. "If you knew all of this, *why?*"

"I had my reasons," she shot back without turning. "Have your bags packed and be out of here by seven tonight. You're fired."

And she was gone.

"I can't believe she just did that, after everything you've done for us, especially for her," said Jeremy with a shaking voice. "I'll go talk to her."

Arthur was filled with cold fury. "No. You stay here."

"What're you gonna do?"

"She can fire me, but she can't shut me up," he said, and then went to find her.

The entrance to her office was closed, but he could see the bar of light under the door. He twisted the lever and opened it without knocking.

She looked up over her tortoise-shell reading glasses, from where she sat at her desk. "Get out of here," she ordered, then went back to the pile of papers spread out before her.

"The real reason you want me out of here is because you don't want me to tell him," he said.

She smiled, tapping the desktop with the gold pen in her hand. "You're going to leave now because, once again, you've betrayed my trust, and you can be sure that if I find out you did *anything* to him before midnight on the eve of his eighteenth birthday, you'll be sitting in jail by this time tomorrow. Other than that, I've no idea what you're referring to. Now, get out before I call the police." She picked up her phone.

"Ten million euros, Katharine? Isn't he worth that much? Why didn't you just pay it? What were you thinking?"

She blinked up at him for a moment, and then placed the phone slowly back down on her desk. "It's still a tremendous sum of money—more, I can guarantee, than you'll ever see in your lifetime." She looked away from him. "Even I couldn't raise it in time."

"That's ridiculous."

"No, it is not." She looked at him squarely. "Does he know any of this?"

"Not yet," he replied. "I just found out today."

"And you won't tell him."

"Why shouldn't I?"

"Because the truth would crush him."

"Then tell *me* the truth. What the hell happened?" He looked at her and crossed his arms over his chest. "Why didn't you just pay the money and get us out of there?"

She shook her head sadly. "You've no idea what I've been through. What mayhem I've wrought, trying to make this all work out."

"Try me."

"Then sit," she said, motioning abruptly to one of the high-back leather wing chairs flanking the front of her desk. "None of this was supposed to happen this way."

"What're you talking about?"

She sighed. "As you well know, since Bill's death I have been doing my very, very best to run Tyler, Inc. And although I've had some good advice from my board, some of the investments we've been involved with have been hurt, tremendously, by the shift in the economy. Especially with respect to our stocks, as well as our real estate holdings."

"Sure. But I'm sure you've diversified appropriately."

She smiled. "Certainly we have. But like every corporation, we've had some ups and downs. And as a result, I've thrown a good portion of our personal worth into some new endeavors, much of which went into that godforsaken resort."

"So let me guess," Arthur broke in. "Some of your other investments started failing, and you needed to get your cash out of the resort, so you had the government do it for you."

She laughed. "Good guess, but even I couldn't have orchestrated that whole 'organization of interest' mess. I'm afraid my ulterior motives were much less creative."

"How so?"

"You gave me the idea, yourself," she told him. "You told me that kidnappings were common in Brazil, so, as a prudent businesswoman, I had kidnapping insurance taken out on Jeremy."

"So I've been told."

"You knew about this as well?" she asked, looking genuinely surprised.

"I have my sources." Then his eyes grew huge as a terrible thought occurred to him. *"Don't tell me you and Fabiano were in on this together!"*

She closed her eyes. "It all went so terribly wrong. He double-crossed me—and I know I'm sounding like some old spy movie right now, but that's exactly what happened. He was to stage a kidnapping, keep Jeremy and you and Carlo safe but separated at his home, and then act as the mediator with 'the kidnappers.' Then instead of delivering the ransom to someone else, we were to split it—hence the exorbitant amount requested. It was all his idea, if that matters…which I suppose it does not; he suggested this plan when I tried to back out of the business."

"So why did you only offer to give him two million?"

"Because that's all I had available in the conversion of my liquid assets; the policy insists on a deductible, just like some cheap HMO. They require ten percent, plus fees. I thought maybe I could pay him the two million and forgo the insurance policy, because I was afraid they would find out somehow and I'd be indicted on charges of fraud."

"But why would an insurance company offer to cover Jeremy in the first place, without some sort of tangible protection for him, overseas? To not do that would be too risky."

"He had protection." She smiled slyly. "*You.* I offered, and they allowed, your credentials as a former Marine and FBI agent."

The realization that she had used him to further her escapade flared his anger, but he decided to let it go…for the moment. "So why did Fabiano do what he did? Why didn't he just go along with the original plan?"

She got up from behind her desk and began pacing, with her arms folded over her breasts. "He wouldn't believe that we were—that we are—cash poor, so he upped the ransom to far beyond what even the policy paid…. I suppose he remembered how flush we were when Bill was alive; then, when the government came in with their 'anti-American' findings, he thought it was just an orchestration of mine to pull out my money, instead of what it was: plain, old-fashioned bad luck."

Or bad karma. "So Fabiano was the only one who knew about this?"

"As far as I know. But now you know. And I suppose after my saying what I have about you and Jeremy, you might consider going to the authorities with this information. But you will not."

He smiled, leaning forward in the big chair. "And why won't I?"

"Because if I suffer repercussions from this, no one suffers more than Jeremy. And you wouldn't like that, now, would you?"

"Of course not," he said, feeling relieved that he finally had some ammunition against her. "And I'm sure that since I know everything now, you'll want to, as they say, 'keep your friends close and your enemies closer.'"

She stopped pacing and raised her eyebrows. "Are you my enemy now, Mr. Blauefee?" she asked coyly.

"No, Katharine, of course not. I'm just disappointed that you went off like that in front of Jeremy, telling me I'm fired and calling his mother a gutter slut."

"Well, she was one, and you are. Fired I mean."

"Do you really want to do that to me?" He laughed.

"You've given me no choice, considering your violation of my nephew," she told him. "I never suspected you would seduce him, right under my nose—not to mention under poor Carlo's nose, for goodness sake." The look on her face suggested sheer disgust. "But since you've done this, I'm going to do you a favor and suggest you take a look at yourself, a *good* look, so you might see what I see."

"And what's that?" he asked, not caring. He sat back in the chair and crossed one leg over the other.

She cocked her head sideways at him and pulled off her reading glasses. "I see...someone who's been a failure in everything he's done—a failure as a soldier, as an FBI agent, as a son, from what I understand, and more tragically, as a man. And I must ask you: is it too difficult for you to find someone of your own ilk, or better yet, someone who might challenge you to become your better self?" He only looked at her blankly, so she continued. "No, you'll never do this because, developmentally, you're stunted—you're as immature as a tantrum-throwing brat."

"You've got no right to speak to me this way," he warned, "unless you're gonna give me equal time about what I think of you."

"No right?" She laughed, then got up and began walking in a slow circle around him. "You prey on boys because you think you can bamboozle someone like poor, gullible Jeremy into believing you actually have something to offer him. But what is it, exactly, that you possess? While he is the picture of nobility and youthful promise, you're an unemployed, forty-year-old houseboy! Why, he's so out of your league, you're not even playing the same sport!" She cackled. "What could you possibly offer him, except for an aging, puffed-up body and some occasional bad advice?"

"That's not fair, Katharine. I've done a lot for him, and for you. I would give my life for him!"

"Oh, so now you're the big noble man willing to give his life for his 'lover'?" She laughed. "Taking the bullet is the easy part, in my book; strangers do that for each other all the time in liquor store robberies. The real test of a man"—she pointed her finger at him—"is how far you'll tax yourself, push yourself and stretch yourself to please your lover, and to provide for him while always doing *what's in his very best interest.*"

"You know I'd do anything for Jeremy, whether he was my lover or not. Any of the things you just mentioned I'll do."

"Is that *really* the case, Mr. Blauefee?"

"Of course!"

"Good. Because I intended to ask you what your plans were with him, after dropping that bomb on me today. Did I hear something about the two of you running off to my mountain chalet to frolic in the woods?"

"Jeremy wanted to go there," Arthur stated defensively. "And what does that have to do with what I'd do for him?"

"Of course you've missed my point, which is, exactly *how long did you plan to live off my money?*"

She paused, waiting for an answer, but he did not reply.

"Just as I thought. You'd never given gainful employment a moment's thought, so long as you could languish here by the sea, while occasionally running to the dry cleaner for us and vacuuming our carpets. Well, let me tell you that a real man would never, *ever* stand around on someone else's dime. And I'd sooner give everything I own to a dozen drunken hobos than to allow someone like you to deplete what's mine, or to take away from Jeremy anything that's coming to him. You're an *embarrassment* of a man, *Mr. Blauefee*. And someday you'll thank me for what I'm doing now, as will poor Jeremy. Now, pack your paltry belongings and get out of my sight."

He looked down at the floor, feeling like an idiot; she was right, and he knew it.

"You love him very much, don't you?" she asked him in the most condescending tone he'd ever heard. "And he thinks he loves you, as well."

"That's what he tells me," he muttered bitterly.

"Then I want you to listen very, very carefully to what I am about to say, because I'm going to make it very, *very* easy for you to do the right thing." She was almost whispering now, as she clutched the corners of her desk. "*If you do not leave here tonight with the promise you will end this illicit relationship, never to see or speak with him again, I will strip from him everything he has. I will disinherit him; I will revoke his trust. I will cast him from this house, seize that monstrous Range Rover he's so proud of, drain his college fund, and empty his savings and personal checking accounts. And when he returns to that gutter from whence he came, it'll be all your fault.*"

He felt the blood drain from his face as he looked up at her. "You wouldn't do that to him."

"It would *kill* me to do so. Believe me, it would *kill* me. But as I see it, this is the only way to be rid of you." She shook her head. "And you'll *never* tell another soul on this earth that I was responsible for what happened to him in Brazil, because you love him too much to have him find out I nearly killed him, for money's sake. It would *crush* him, *destroy* him, *obliterate* him—more, I dare say, than it'll hurt his foolish pride when he discovers you've run off." She placed her hands on her hips and raised herself up to her usual Victorian posture. "After all, we know how fickle teenage boys are when it comes to 'love.' Why, just yesterday, he was out there poolside holding hands with poor, jilted Carlo."

Arthur's eyes shifted from side to side as he tried to make sense of it all. "Katharine, you can't do this. Somehow, and it won't be from me, but he'll find out what you're doing—what you've done. And he'll *never* forgive you."

"Oh, but I can do this, and I am doing this," she stated calmly. "This is a matter of life and death for me; I've never forgiven you for your role in Jonathan's demise, but I was willing to look the other way, so long as you washed our dirty dishes and served as our 'protector' and adhered to what I considered to be rather obvious rules of propriety." She narrowed her eyes at him. "You've overstepped your bounds gravely this time, Mr. Blauefee, so you've given me no choice. You will vanish, disappear—and in the spring, Jeremy will be off to school, where I'm certain he will meet a charming individual *his own age* and build a real life with him—*or her.*" She strode across the room, opened the door and held it wide. "I suggest you do the same," she suggested brightly. "And unless you are completely, absolutely lacking in common sense and integrity, you'll do the correct thing for once and leave us be."

He pushed himself up out of the chair and made his way to the doorway, where he stalled momentarily. "What...should I say to him?"

"I'll keep him sequestered while you pack. And you'll say nothing, but you may...send him an e-mail, which you will cc to me. One more, only. But you'll reveal absolutely nothing of what we've discussed, and you will do your absolute best to consider his feelings, and to give him peace about this very correct decision of yours to leave his life. Is this understood?"

He nodded, then quietly turned to leave. "This'll kill me, Katharine."

"Better you than I."

CHAPTER 50

"Mom?"

"Hi, Artie. What's wrong?"

Numbly, he looked around his quarters for the last time, at his bags packed on the bed and the ocean roiling outside his window. "Nothing. Everything. I mean...I'll tell you when I see you. But I'm OK. I just need a place to stay for a couple days."

"Where are you?"

"Down the beach. Can I, uh, come stay with you?"

She sighed. "Of course...I've got some stuff piled in your room, so it'll take me a while to clean off the bed."

"Don't, Mom. I'll do it when I get there." He couldn't believe he was going *back there*, after all these years, after all he'd been through; but he wanted at least to say goodbye to her. "I just wanted to make sure it was OK without just showing up."

"I have a doctor's appointment this afternoon, so I might not be home when you get here."

"Is the key still there?"

"Where it's always been."

"Thanks, Mom."

"It's all right. I'll see you in a little bit."

He ended the call and grabbed his bags, fished his keys out of his pocket, pulled off the trio that belonged to the Tylers, opened the door to his quarters and looked out.

Neither Jeremy nor Katharine was around. *Good.* He needed to make this quick.

After leaving their house keys on the counter, he stole out through the kitchen door, hoping and not hoping to see him, then decided it was better not to; he needed to ensure a break, and anything lingering would only serve to depress him further.

After backing his old Taurus out of the stall, he headed up the cobblestone drive toward the gates, which he opened with his clicker.

After he passed through the gates, he stopped, got out of the car and slipped the device inside their bomb shelter–like mailbox. Then he belted himself back in, drove down to Zumirez Road, and waited for traffic to clear before making a slow left into the opposite lanes.

As the Taurus wheezed lethargically up to speed, he realized he didn't care about going slower than the rushing traffic. He also didn't care about seeing his mother. And he didn't care about finding a job or looking for an apartment or getting older or being lonely. He just didn't care about anything.

He made his way up Pacific Coast Highway toward County Line, then turned right on Sea Crest and made his way halfway up the hill. After pulling underneath the ancient Chinese elm in front of the house, he cranked the wheel into the curb, set the parking brake, grabbed his bag, then lurched up the driveway of the tiny, Spanish-style house. He approached the few steps leading to the front entrance, but instead went around to the side of the house where the key was hidden—under an especially ugly black flower pot with yellow roses silk-screened onto it. Then he went back to the front and let himself in.

If he was depressed before, just being in the old living room made him despondent. There were too many memories here, and few of them were good. The place even still stank faintly of cigarettes, as if the remains of his father residing in the urn on the mantel had just snuffed out another one.

Ashes to ashes. Now, that would be a fitting slogan for Marlboro...

As he made his way to his old bedroom, right off the dining room, he spent a few moments looking around the house to see what had changed.

Nothing.

So he went back into the living room and sat on the old sofa, where he saw a framed photo of the family at his sister Morgana's wedding, back in '89.

Almost everyone was still alive then, including two of his grandparents. And most everyone was healthy—even his father, who posed, grinning, with a telling cigarette in his hand.

Time doesn't pass here...it just gets more constipated.

He went back into his room, took the boxes and old clothes off his bed and flopped down, face-first.

E-mail to Jeremy.

He got back up, unlatched his laptop case and pulled out his sickly Compaq. After it finished grinding through its lengthy start-up, he began his final communication:

To: Tylerboi@ballena-beach.com
Cc: KTYLER1@ballena-beach.com
Re: Us

Dear Jeremy,
It is with the saddest and heaviest of hearts that I write this to you. Katharine is right. We don't belong together. But I want you to know that it's nothing you've done, and knowing you has been one of the great joys, if not the greatest joy, of my life. I've known love before, but nothing like how I've felt for you. You are one of the most dynamic, gifted, sweet and generous people I've ever met. But you have a path to take in this life, and it's very, very different from mine.
I understand that this is probably very hard for you to understand, just as it's really hard for me to write this, and it's taken some really tough words from Katharine to make me understand it all. But it's for the best in the long run—I'm absolutely, positively certain of this. If we had tried to make this work, I'd be stealing from you everything you're meant to experience, and this would be wrong, because you have so much ground to make up, having lived through what you have.
I crossed a line with you that I wish I hadn't, but then as the old saying goes, you can't un-ring a bell. So this is my gift to you—a new bell. One that you can ring yourself, as stupid as that sounds.
I will never forget each and every minute we had together, and the joy I felt every time I saw your face, or heard your voice call my name. I will always remember you, and your amazing transformation from awkward boy to splendid man. I like to think that I had a little something to do with that. But however I helped you, please remember me only for those things.
So go out there and find yourself a partner—maybe even consider resuming your relationship with wonderful, brave, loving Carlo. But whoever it is, please carry with you the knowledge that I will always love you with all of my heart, and I will try my best to learn to live with the regret I feel for having destroyed our beautiful, innocent, perfect relationship.
I'm just so glad that I was there for you when you needed me to be there, as your protector, and as your friend.

You cannot know how hard this is for me to say, but I do not want
you to look for me. We need to cut this off, like surgery, so we can
both heal.
Please know that I will miss you terribly, just as I miss you now.
Please take care of yourself.
You will always be my one 'old buddy'.
Love, Arthur

He was amazed, upon finishing, that somehow his fingers knew
exactly which keys to press. After he composed the message, he read it
over five times, and changed only a word here or there with each pass.
Then he held his breath and pressed SEND. Once that was accomplished,
he opened his e-mail's TOOLS tab, then the MAIL tab, clicked on the
REMOVE ACCOUNT prompt and pressed YES.

It was finished.

He curled himself into a ball on his old bed, and began dancing
with his regrets.

The creak of the back door swinging open, as well as the familiar
clops of his mother's footfall on the kitchen linoleum, startled him out of
his misery. "Artie?"

"Yeah, Mom," he called back, rubbing his eyes and sitting up. He
swung his feet to the floor and stood. Surprisingly, he felt hungry. Then
he remembered he'd eaten only a bowl of oatmeal early this morning.

He went out to greet her, hid the shock of seeing how old she looked
and gave her a peck on the cheek. "Hi."

"Are you hungry?" She set the little white pharmacy bag, along with
her purse, on the counter next to the bread box.

"A little. But I don't want you to go to any trouble."

"You're still my son. Sit down and I'll fix you a sandwich. Is tuna
salad OK?" She went over to the sink and washed her hands.

"Sure." He sat at the old Formica breakfast table but avoided the
chair that used to be his assigned seat. "How are you?"

"Surviving," she said, unscrewing the lid from a jar of Miracle Whip.
"My hip is killing me, and I haven't slept one night through in three
years." She dug out a white glob with her knife and smeared it on two
slices of wheat bread. "Why are you here? What happened?"

How could he possibly tell her what had happened? "I quit my
job."

"*You quit the FBI?*" She glared at him with the knife poised in midair.

"I haven't worked for them for six months, Mom. I told you."

She furrowed her brows. "Then what've you been doing?"

"I've been working for some rich people down on the cliff, the Tylers. I was overseeing their estate, working as their chef, and being the bodyguard for the young man of the family, Jeremy's his name—he's Jonathan's son. I don't know if you remember my friend Jonathan."

She squared a look at him. "Oh, I remember *your friend* Jonathan," she replied dryly.

He ignored the look and the intonation. "Anyway, we just got back from Brazil." *Where I had sex with him and he got kidnapped and we were almost killed.*

"Oh, that's nice." She spread a heap of tuna salad between the two slices of bread, then squished the sandwich down and sliced it in half diagonally. "So then what happened? Why did you quit?"

"It just wasn't working out, I guess. I needed a change. Something more challenging."

"And so you quit—just like that?" She snapped her fingers, then slid the plate in front of him, with a frosty glass of ice water.

"Yep. Just like that." He snapped his fingers back at her. *But louder.*

She pulled out a chair and sat next to him. "People in my day never just 'quit' a job without something better lined up. I'm surprised at you."

He shrugged. He was immune to her disapproval. "How's Morgana?"

"She's all right, I suppose. I just see her working herself to death over those kids and her job. She never seems to get a break."

"What about Gwen?"

Her face brightened. "She's expecting again, didn't I tell you?"

"No. Boy or girl?" He took a bite of his sandwich and winced; the pickle relish she always mixed with the Miracle Whip gave the fish a nasty, sweet flavor.

Bleh.

"They don't know yet. So how long do you think it'll be before you find another job?"

"I'll start looking first thing tomorrow."

"Why not today?" She glared at him.

"Because I'm wiped out. But don't worry, I won't be asking to move in here," he said, knowing he'd rather give himself liposuction with a chain saw.

"Where will you look?"

"The paper, I guess. Do you have one?"

She heaved herself up from the table. "Yesterday's. I'll get it."

"Thanks." He took another bite, and washed it down with his water.

She went over to the coffee table, rustled through a pile sitting atop it and withdrew the newspaper. "Did you get fired?" she asked, handing it over.

"No, Mom. I said I *quit.*"

"You know your father went through that whole period in the late seventies when he just couldn't seem to hold a job." She sat back down.

He nodded, remembering the string of company cars that appeared and disappeared, with the transition from LTD to Malibu to Fury to Granada signaling each episode of his father's job hopping. "What was that all about? I remember all that."

She sighed. "He just wouldn't work. He'd get a job and say everything was going to be different; then after a couple months he'd find any excuse to stay home, or go into work late, or come home for a three-hour lunch, or…whatever. Of course his sales were horrible and he'd used up his three-month draw against the commission and they'd fire him." She looked away, as if watching an invisible black-and-white television from across the room. Then she focused back on him. "You know, you'd make a good salesman," she suggested brightly.

"You guys were fighting all the time," he told her. Then he took another bite of his sandwich. "Especially after you had to go back to work."

"That job at the junior high was a godsend, because we would've probably lost the house otherwise. But I hated it. I used to think being there was like working on a ship that hit an iceberg on its first day out, and was sinking slowly ever since."

"I remember you saying that when I was a kid. Did you make it up?"

"The principal—he was an alcoholic—he used to say that." She fiddled with the ancient cut-crystal salt and pepper shakers before her. "I was going to have the perfect marriage," she said wistfully, wiping the crusted salt from the top of the shaker. "I thought about leaving him and taking you three, at least back then."

"I always wished you would've, when I was a kid."

"That's so sad, Artie. I never wanted it to rub off on you."

"But it was so obvious. You would argue about anything; then he'd yell and you'd cry and we'd just be sitting in the back of that headache-blue Granada getting nauseous. Fun times."

"What's 'headache-blue'?"

"It's that pale metallic blue; Morgana came up with that because we always got headaches in the backseat with his smoking and your fighting."

"I think he was depressed," she told him.

"Well, who wasn't, in this house?" He laughed. "He bullied us, Mom. *All of us.* And even though he's been dead for three years, we're still bullied by him."

She shook her head. "You shouldn't speak of him that way. He loved you."

"He did not, and you know it. He hated me and I hated him. We never had anything in common...except for our mutual loathing."

"You're right there, about not having anything in common. He used to say that if he hadn't known me so well, he would've sworn you were someone else's son."

"I wish I had been."

"No, you don't." Her eyes met his. "You got a lot of good things from him: your strength, your intelligence and your looks. You look just like him, you know, more and more with each passing year."

"Don't remind me." He finished his sandwich, then got up to take his plate to the sink. "I'm gonna go out for a bit. I think there's an Internet café close by where I can get some coffee and check the classifieds." He washed his plate in the sink, then placed it atop the drying rack. He waited for her to say something, but she didn't, so he turned to her and saw she was staring at him and fiddling with a yellow paper napkin. "Mom?"

"One thing I never told you," she said quickly. "Before you go."

He stopped. "Yeah?"

She stared at him, and Arthur wondered if she'd forgotten what she was saying. "What?" he asked softly. "What didn't you tell me?"

"His father," she said, then pulled her lips in together, like an old woman without her false teeth in place. Finally her mouth opened and she breathed in. "He was terrible to them."

"Rotten tree, sour apples."

"Yes." She raised her eyebrows. "I suppose that's true. But you need to know something."

He put one hand on his hip and glared at her.

She paused, to make certain he was listening. "He made your father shoot his own dog."

He leaned back against the counter. "Did it have rabies or something? Was its name Old Yeller?"

"His father was sick, Artie." She stood and began clearing the table. "When he was eight or nine—it was during the Depression—your father's dog—he named it Spot, if you can believe it—caught one of the chickens and killed it. And your grandfather…"

"*No.*"

"He told him his dog was his responsibility, and his dog had cost the family money, so he made him take his rifle out to the yard and—"

"Oh, my God." The tragic incident flashed in his head. "Why didn't you ever tell me that before?"

"Because I didn't want to upset you. And I don't want to now. It's just that he"—she looked away, her crow's-feet pinched—"he tried to be a better father than his own father was. And I think—I *know*—that he was."

"*How*, I mean besides not making us murder our guinea pigs and lizards?"

"When they were kids, if your father or his brothers did anything wrong, their mother would lock them up in the woodshed for the rest of the day until their father came home. Then he would beat them. *Mercilessly.*"

"And?"

"Your father stopped at one point with you kids. After he knocked out Morgana's front teeth."

"What a great guy." He laughed. "Good for him."

"No, Artie, I'm serious. After that he never hit any of you kids again. He saw that he was becoming like him and stopped. And we agreed that I'd handle the discipline from then on."

He shook his head. "You're forgetting the 'playing rough'—and he *did* hit us after that; and even if he toned it down, we always knew what he was capable of."

"What's 'playing rough'?"

He couldn't believe she didn't remember. "He'd grab me and throw me down and push me onto the bed, and when I'd try to run away, he'd grab me and throw me down again and tackle me and bend my arms back and not let me go, and you'd be yelling, 'Frank, you're hurting him, Frank, stop it, you're hurting him,' and I'd be crying and he'd be laughing and sometimes I couldn't breathe—I'd get an asthma attack and couldn't breathe. *Remember now?*"

"Now I remember." She smiled sadly. "I'd forgotten about that until now. You must have been terrified."

"Yep. I was." He paused for a moment. "But you know what amazes me?"

Her eyebrows rose expectantly.

"When I was probably four or five, when you'd fight, I was so afraid he was going to hurt you that I remember standing in front of you, waving my arms and telling him, 'Don't hit her, don't hit her.'"

"Dear God," she whispered. "*You remember that?*"

"How could I forget?"

"You were so brave to stand up to him," she said softly. "I used to cry about that at night."

"So did I," he told her. "I'm sorry he treated you that way. You deserved so much more."

"So did you kids," she replied, fingering the wattle under her chin. "All this talk's exhausted me, so I need to lie down for a while," she told him, getting up. "And then if you want to, later we can go into town for dinner."

He nodded and smiled thinly. "OK."

"Artie?"

He stopped and looked back at her.

"He did love you."

He huffed. "Did he ever tell you he did?"

"Not in so many words."

"It's OK." He smiled. "Some men are just not meant to be dads. I'll see you later."

"You need to forgive him."

He stopped in midstep. "He's been dead for more than three years. What good would it do to forgive him now?"

"He never forgave his father, and I can see his same anger in you." Her eyes bored holes in him. "I'm afraid you're going to make the same mistakes he made."

He laughed. "That's never gonna happen, and you know it."

"I'm not talking about being a bully, or hitting your nonexistent kids. I'm just hoping that...you don't let your anger stop you from finding real happiness, or even someone to love."

His head was about to rocket off his neck. "I have found love! Jonathan, who turned straight; Danny, who was killed, and now Jeremy—"

"You're in love with his son?" Her eyes bulged, then shrank. "Oh, Artie." She restrained herself from shaking her head disapprovingly. What could she say? "I just want you to be happy. That's everything. And I think...I *know* that forgiving him is part of what you need to find happiness."

"Do *you* forgive him?" he asked.

She looked down, then lifted her eyes slowly to meet his. "I do. I have. And you need to remember that no one lived with his wrath as much as I did. But...something changed in him when he was sick; you wouldn't come around much then, so maybe you didn't see it. He became gentle...even appreciative sometimes. It's like the cancer gave him peace; maybe because his father made him believe that's what he deserved: a miserable ending. So when it came to him, he was finally able to accept his...*destiny*."

"That's absolutely sick."

"It is what it was. But the fact is, he could never forgive what his father did to him, so he let it destroy him—he smoked and drank too much, and his anger ate him up from the inside out. And I don't want the same thing happening to you."

"Never gonna happen," he stated convincingly.

"Good." She smiled. "One more thing."

"Uh-huh?"

"He used to wait for you."

He cocked his head sideways and stared at her. "What do you mean?"

"When he was sick. He would ask me when you were coming to visit him. And I would lie."

He closed his eyes and shook his head. "Don't tell me that. Please, not now."

"He did. And I'm not saying this to you to make you feel guilty; I'm only hoping that it'll be...healing somehow. To know he needed you."

He felt his anger grow. "Why are you telling me this? Why are you trying to make me feel so guilty? He was an asshole, Mom. The only thing he cared about was work and making us all quiet and invisible!"

She clutched the back of the chair with one hand, rubbing her thigh nervously with the other. "But I'm not trying to make you feel guilty, Artie. I only want you to know that he appreciated you, as his son. And I know he was sorry for the way things turned out."

His fury was ablaze, but his voice was calm. "Well, it's a great thing he kept it such a goddamn secret all those years, and it took this long for you to let me know how he felt. Thanks for that, by the way."

"But, Artie—"

She looked sad, and it killed him. He took a deep breath. "Mom, look, I'm sorry. I know you're just trying to help me out, and I'm glad you let me know this." He smiled at her. "I'll think about what you've said; really I will. I'll see you later." And with that, he retrieved his laptop bag from his bedroom, went out the door and got into his car.

He used to wait for you.

He headed north toward the shopping center in the middle of town, where he knew of a dreary coffeehouse whose only draw was its free Internet access; he figured he could set up his computer, slug some caffeine, and see if there was anything promising on the community message boards. Maybe he'd even ask for a job application; that would be great, being a forty-year-old man filling coffee orders for teenagers. *Hooray!*

But what sort of job would he look for? Under what category would he find his next opportunity for disaster?

Then the truth hit him:

He had no college degree, he had no references from his last jobs, but what he did have was a dishonorable discharge from the U.S. Marines.

Should he go back to the FBI and try to get a desk job, so he wouldn't be able to screw up any more cases? He could try, but since his superiors had censured him after discovering he'd omitted critical information about having been Jonathan's lover, thus accepting an assignment with his security clearance in jeopardy, then had accepted Katharine's employment offer without leaving the bureau after the customary one month's notice, there was little chance they'd ever hire him back.

Yes, he'd burned that bridge, and it was such a short time ago that the wood was probably still smoking.

A startling thought occurred to him: what was the use of trying to jump-start his life when there was absolutely nothing to salvage—no lover, no home, no career, no friends—and at almost forty, if he hadn't made it happen by now, would he ever?

He was sick of starting over.

He'd done it more times than he cared to remember.

And each time had ended with failure.

He remembered how depressed he'd been as a teenager, and his plan to smash his van into that tree in front of his house; he'd really only joined the Marines because there was nothing else to do, but there was always the chance he could die a hero. And joining the FBI after Danny's death was really just "military lite"; it wasn't anything he'd ever really aspired to.

In fact, he'd never discovered what he was destined for.

Could it be that underneath whatever uniform he chose for himself, there would always be the same aimless man wandering around naked underneath it, just waiting to fail?

All I ever do is fuck up, so what's the point in starting over? No one will miss me, except maybe Jeremy, and now he's gone because I made the wrong decision again.

I'm so tired of feeling sad and lonely....

Katharine was right.

I should just get it over with.

A great heaviness overcame him, and he pulled the car to the side of the road and bowed his head.

He could feel the knife twisting in his soul, but who was shoving the hilt?

After a few moments, he knew:

I am.

Because as much as he hated himself for it, he would never be able to see himself through eyes other than his father's.

He used to wait for you.

You need to forgive him.

So was this it? He scanned his surroundings and saw there was a short pier a block away that he could drive his car off.

No drowning. Anything but drowning.

An overdose? His mother, most likely, had a stockpile of meds he could swallow a couple handfuls of, along with some Southern Comfort— just like Jonathan's mom had.

But what if she didn't have anything stronger than Advil? And what if it didn't work? He'd heard that trying to overdose was probably one of the least reliable methods of suicide, because if you're revived, you may have to live with permanent organ and brain damage.

No, thanks.

A gun? Could he actually put a barrel to his temple, or in his throat, and pull the trigger? That would be over quickly, but then there'd be such a mess. He remembered seeing a video of some congressman who'd been charged with corruption, and the man had very calmly stuck a gun into his mouth and pulled the trigger at a press conference, in front of staffers and the media and anyone in America who'd been unfortunate enough to be watching. And it was a mess: He'd been haunted by the image of the fat old guy staring blankly from where he'd slid down onto the floor, with a river of blood pouring out of his nostrils and down his shirt. That blood, it never seemed to stop as the cameras kept rolling and people screamed in the background. Gallons of it. Everywhere. It must have taken them days to clean it up.

No, shooting it would not be.

So what would be the best way to do it, should he decide it was time?

Check it out on the Internet.

He put the car back in drive, turned around and made his way toward the coffeehouse. Once there, he found a place close by to park, grabbed his computer and walked through the doors.

Thankfully, the place was deserted except for the tiny old lady behind the counter and a sullen teenage girl in goth makeup who slouched on a droopy brown-and-red-plaid sofa, her feet up and twitching atop the battered coffee table.

"Hi," he said to the old lady, while perusing the overhead menu. "Could I please just have the coffee of the day?"

"You'd like the large size, I'll bet," she told him, smiling. "You're a big man."

He looked down at her and smiled back, noticing the tatters on her navy blue visor. "Sure. Large would be fine."

"Comin' right up!" she piped, and went to work.

He looked at the baked goods and decided on a blueberry scone. "Could I get one of those, too?" he asked, pointing to it.

"Try one of the cranberry ones, and if you don't like it I'll still give you the blueberry for free. The cranberries are perfect on a sunny day like today—tart 'n' sweet."

He shrugged. "Sure, I was hedging between the two anyway."

She gave him his order and he paid; then he sat down at the seat farthest from the glowering young lady, who held an empty cup in front of her while perusing an old *Us Weekly* magazine.

He popped open his laptop, waited for it to start, then Googled *best ways to kill yourself.*

The search netted more than four million results.

Guess I'm not the only one who feels like this.

He began clicking on the various links and found that many of them were facetious, but some did offer practical advice. And others were message boards with pleas from strangers to believe in Jesus, or to seek counseling.

Not a bad idea—the counseling, that is.

Then he hit on a site run by survivors of abuse and began reading the list of reasons *not* to kill yourself:

You will never again feel the thrill of even a small accomplishment.
Your life has value, whether or not you believe it.
You didn't choose to be abused.
You are in control of both your destiny and your pain.

All good arguments, he thought, but they still didn't address the profound, utter sadness and grief—*or was it anger?*—he was trying not to feel.

Grief for losing Jeremy...Danny...Jonathan...my job...of never having had a real father or a son or any real self-esteem...of only having this anger inside—equal parts anger and all of this useless, frustrating, unrequited love.

Would he ever have anything to look forward to again? He couldn't ever imagine loving anyone as much as he did Jeremy. And without love, what was the point?

What harm would it do to forgive him? He can't hurt you anymore—unless you let him...

He used to wait for you.

"You young people spend so much time on those things," squeaked a voice from behind him. He turned and saw the little lady from the counter, wiping down a nearby table.

"Yeah, it seems like we can't live without 'em now."

"Seems like a sorry excuse for human interaction, if you ask me. What're you so busy studying there?" She craned her neck to see, and Arthur tried to block her view by leaning sideways in his seat.

"Just a...project I'm researching."

"Oh." She continued wiping the table, then picked up some half-empty cups from the counter, which she dropped into a nearby trash can.

He thought he'd better be sociable. "So do you own this place?" he asked, not caring.

She laughed. "No, but I wish I did. I love it here."

"You do?"

"You bet. I get to meet nice people all day long, different folks every day, and some of the regulars are real good company. And I like making people happy with the coffee and the pastries here. Peps 'em up. They're real good."

He agreed in his head that they were. "How long've you worked here?"

"Four years. Started here just after my husband passed away."

"I'm sorry."

"Thanks. Just needed something to do to keep the blues away," she told him, with big exaggerated blinks of her eyes. "If you don't stay busy, then you find a way to go crazy."

"Isn't that the truth," he agreed, thinking it actually was.

She continued straightening magazines and cleaning up spilled sweetener packets. "Do ya want a refill, young man?" she asked him.

Young man. "I'd love one. Thanks."

She hefted the diner-style coffeepot over to him and carefully filled his cup. "Do ya mind if I take a load off for a second?"

He motioned to the chair next to him. "Please."

She sat herself slowly into the old club chair. "You know, after my Donald died," she began, "I had a really hard time."

"How long were you married?"

"Forty-two years. And we dated for three before that. He was the best man I ever met—never a harsh word, always worked hard, loved our kids. He was as good a husband as a woman ever gets to marry in this life. Only thing, though, was that he smoked."

"My dad died of lung cancer. Donald, too?"

"Oh, no. He used to smoke when he'd take the dog out for a walk; I wouldn't let him do it in the house. Then one evening he never came back—some teenager in a BMW mowed them both down in a crosswalk."

Arthur closed his eyes reverently, then met her gaze. "Oh, God, I'm sorry."

Her eyes softened behind her glasses. "And to think I was angry at him that night because his dinner was gettin' cold; because you know he loved to chat with folks they met on their walks, so they was always coming back kinda late," she said, fiddling with the wet cloth in her hand. "Pot roast and rice pilaf with peas. I can still see it warmin' on the stove under the foil."

She pushed herself up from the chair. "Sorry to burden you with this."

"No burden…but I do have a question, if you don't mind."

She smiled brightly, and he saw she wore dentures. "I don't mind."

"What kept you going?" He blinked at her, and looked over to see that the glum teenager was also listening.

She rested one hand on the chair and cocked the other hand on her hip, still clutching her wet rag. "I s'pose I had some long times feeling sorry for myself, of course. And the kids already moved away and had the little ones in school, so there was no point havin' 'em come back here. But I had one friend o' mine left at the time—Ruthie, and she's gone now, too, of course—she told me, 'You need someone who needs you.' And o' course she was right…everyone needs to be needed."

"And who did you find who needed you?"

"Well, that's the funny part," she said, her eyes sparkling. "Right after I hung up from talkin' to her, I stepped outside to take out the trash, and there was a dog, a beautiful red dog sniffin' around my yard. No collar, needed a bath somethin' fierce. And when she saw me she came runnin' to me like I was her best friend in the world. 'Course I took her in and put up signs and all, but no one ever called for her. Named her Emma Lou, after my little sister who used to look up to me so."

"So where's Emma Lou now?" he asked, afraid to hear the answer.

She whistled, and a white-faced golden retriever came trotting out from behind the counter, went up to Arthur and stuck her nose in his crotch. "Hi, Emma Lou," Arthur cooed. "What a sweet girl you are."

Emma's wagging tail almost knocked over his coffee, but he grabbed it in time.

The feel of her soft, red-velvet head in his hand choked him up; he hadn't realized how much he'd been on the verge of tears since everything happened.

"You're hurtin', young man."

He let go of the dog's head. "I'm sorry."

"No, you're not hurtin' *her*; you're just hurtin'. I can see it on you."

He looked up. *How did you know?*

"Don't do anything you won't live to regret." She laughed. "That's my motto. And go find yourself someone, or something, that needs you. That's my five-cent advice."

He nodded and wiped the tears from his eyes. "Is Emma Lou here available?" He laughed, taking in the dog's sweet brown eyes and generous grin and lolling tongue and hot breath on his chest.

"Oh, no; no one's gonna take her away," she said, with a laugh. "Except maybe for God, but then again, he's gonna have a hell of a fight from me."

"Thank you," he told her.

"I'm here every day," she replied. "And so's my little girlie."

CHAPTER 51

He drove back down Pacific Coast Highway at a reckless speed, weaving in and out of traffic, and flooring the poor old Taurus's accelerator anytime the signal ahead switched from green to yellow, or from red to green. But when he passed Zumirez Road he kept flying south, until he saw the familiar wall of immense granite boulders—placed there years ago by the county's tractors—that marked his destination.

After his tires slid to a stop on the sandy asphalt, he jumped out, slammed shut the door, then picked his way down quickly, with arms extended for balance like a child playing airplane, through the huge rocks to the shoreline. Once his feet hit the sand, he turned north and began running toward the wealthy private enclaves that hovered on the cliffs beyond Boulder Creek, whose feeble stream and arid, rocky banks still served as Ballena Beach's unofficial *No Trespassing* sign.

He continued running in the sand, on the firmest meandering strip of dark beige next to the water line, for twenty or so minutes, before rounding the final bend and seeing it: the familiar red-tiled roof of the Tyler mansion, and its stout metal staircase that zigzagged up from the pristine beach and its thundering waves, through the lumpy rugs of ice plant and cliff-hugging prickly pear cactus, to the white wooden gazebo offset from the crest.

But the base of the stairs had been fitted recently with a security door, and he'd surrendered his keys earlier in the day.

So he bent his knees and jumped up from the sand, and his hands had barely grasped the edge over the doorway before losing their grip, sending him ass over teakettle back into the sand. He tried a second time and gripped the metal tighter. Then he pulled and lifted his body in a gravity-defying chin-up over the top of the high barrier, where he balanced in a crouch until he could drop safely onto the stairway.

At once he began taking the risers two at a time, while pulling at the handrail as if in a frantic game of tug-of-war, until he reached the top, panting like a marathoner. His eyes scanned the expansive grounds and saw that everything looked status quo: The lawn was pristine and the roses were jaunty and the grounds looked characteristically maintained—except for the fancy stone fountain, which was in need of another refill.

Then he heard a strange noise behind him, so he turned...

The familiar silhouette in the gazebo was bent over, head down, his elbows locked against the banister.

Jeremy!

He hurried across the flagstone path toward him, knowing *she* might have even spotted him already from inside her lair. Then as he drew closer he slowed and began padding softly, not wanting to intrude on this private moment of his, and not certain exactly what he was going to say.

He heard the noise again.

"*Uh-hu-hu-hnnn,*" Jeremy sobbed. Arthur heard him draw in another deep breath before continuing. "*Uh-hu-hu-hu-hnnn.*"

Upon hearing his grief, Arthur felt like a wooden stake had been hammered into his heart. He drew up next to the gazebo and stopped, then placed his hand on the nearest post. "Jeremy?" he asked softly.

At the sound of his name's first syllable he whipped around, gasping. "What?" His eyes blinked unbelievingly. "*What?*" His eyelids looked beestung and his cheeks were blotched scarlet and white, and snot glistened equally from both nostrils; he'd even drooled a little down the front of his white polo shirt.

I did this to him.

Fighting his own tears, he held his arms wide, in perfect Cristo fashion.

Jeremy fell into his embrace.

"I'm so sorry I hurt you," Arthur whispered at last.

"Don't," Jeremy replied, as his hands smoothed the familiar granite of Arthur's back. "Just don't leave."

"I won't," Arthur said, and squeezed him tighter, breathing him in. "Promise?"

Arthur reached up to smooth the back of his head, as his mouth slid down to kiss the crook of his neck. "Promise," he whispered.

Jeremy pulled away from him and their eyes met. "Your e-mail," he said, and his face screwed up and he began crying again. "I got...your e-mail and I read it and then I...wrote you one back but it got...bounced back to—"

A sudden clapping of frantic footsteps along the flagstone walk startled them. *"YOU!"* she shrieked, jogging toward the pair, pointing at Arthur with her cell phone. *"Get out of here! GET OUT OF HERE!"* She turned to Jeremy. *"And you get back into the house. NOW!"*

She drew in almost close enough to make a grab for Jeremy's wrist, when Arthur stepped in front of him, shielding him. "Stop!" he barked into her face, his eyelids peeled back and his mouth twisted into a snarl. "Stop, or I'll do something we're both gonna regret!"

She threw back her head and halted, wholly alarmed by the rabid animal he'd become. Then she stepped backward half a dozen paces while holding up the phone so they both could see her dial *911*.

She pressed the contraption to her ear.

"Police?" Her voice belied a panic that was not registering on her placid features. "This is Katharine Tyler, down on Morning View! An intruder has breached our security and is threatening my life, as well as my nephew's! He's a former employee, Arthur Blauefee. Please hurry—he's a trained soldier and is very dangerous and I don't know what he's capable of!" Then she screamed and heaved the phone over the cliff.

"Have you completely lost your mind?" Arthur asked her, laughing.

"I was about to ask you the same," she sneered. "You made the decision to leave him, to abandon him. And now you're back, within hours?" She turned to Jeremy. "This man you're so 'in love with' has all of the emotional maturity of a retarded twelve-year-old."

"Back down, Katharine," Arthur growled. "I've listened to enough of your poison for one day."

"You're on private property, little man, but you still have time to flee before the police show up. By the way, do you happen to know what the statute of limitations is on child molestation?"

"You're going to shut your mouth and listen," he began. "I don't know what's wrong with me, listening to you castrate me in there before." He tossed his head toward the house. "And I'm not gonna stand here and outline all of your personal shortcomings for you, or the horrible, *horrible* mistakes you've made, because I'm too much of a gentleman to beat up a lady—even with words. But I will say this: You're a selfish, pigheaded bully, and I've spent a lifetime trying to live with myself for not standing up to the biggest bully I ever knew, until now. I'm also not gonna spend the rest of my life wishing I'd told you to your face that you're dead wrong about me, and about him." He put his arm around Jeremy and pulled him close. "You almost had me, Katharine." He narrowed his eyes and stared her down. "You even had me believing that things like social class and age and 'breeding' have more to do with happiness than just plain old love, and laughter, and respect. But you're wrong." He pointed his finger accusingly at her. "And where did it ever get you? What kind of happiness did you ever have, married to that monster, to that *murderer?*" He laughed. "You got a pretty house and a lot of filthy money, more than you'll probably ever spend or need, but you also got a lot of grief. Grief that's gonna stick around for decades, *and maybe even for the rest of your pathetic life.*"

She glared at him, her eyes glazed over with sheer hatred. "I told you what I'd do to him if you didn't leave quietly." She turned and began trudging toward the house. "And now you've given me no choice!"

"Neither have you," he yelled after her. "Either you tell him or I will!"

She froze in midstep, and then pivoted slowly. "You wouldn't. It would destroy him."

"No!" he hollered. "It'll destroy you!"

He put both hands on Jeremy's sagging shoulders and pushed him gently in front of himself. "Look at him now, Katharine! Just look at what you've done to this person who you supposedly love! Doesn't your one living relative—this wonderful, innocent creature—look destroyed already?" Tears began streaming down his own face now, as he felt the gentle warmth of Jeremy's shoulders under the palms of his hands. "And who do you think is responsible for this destruction, for his tears and his misery? Whose *greed* did this to him?" His voice was a roar now, as he fought to be heard over the sudden thrash of the waves below. "By all of the gods in heaven, you know it wasn't mine!"

"You will live to regret this!" she cried. "I promise you that I'll use every resource at my disposal to ruin you. How dare you try to turn him against me!"

"I'm already living with the regret of what I did this morning, and that's why I'm here. But everyone who makes mistakes has to pay for them. I'm willing to pay for mine, but why make me, or worse yet, Jeremy, pay for yours? Hasn't he paid enough already? Hasn't *everyone* paid for your mistakes—*but you?*"

"You're mistaken." She shook her head emphatically. "I only did what was in our best interest. His and mine. You can't fault me for that."

"But you gambled, and it went very, very wrong," he reminded her. "And Jeremy, who trusted you, almost died. Don't you at least owe him the truth, and then let him make the decision about what to do next? It's about redemption, Katharine. You need to redeem yourself, or it'll destroy you; I promise you it will, just like Tiffany's mistakes ruined her. You, of all people, should know you can't bury your secrets forever."

She began marching toward the house again, but stopped. Then she continued walking away, more slowly. "I don't even know what you're speaking of!" she shot back feebly over her shoulder.

The overlapping wails of approaching sirens caught their ears, as did the flapping of a helicopter's rotor.

"What're you both talking about?" Jeremy asked, wiping his eyes and nose with his wrist.

The sirens, as well as the chopper, were getting louder.

"Aunt Katharine!" Jeremy called out to her. "Tell me what he's talking about!"

Time stopped—until she turned.

And took one step toward them.

Then another.

And another.

When she drew in, a long arm's distance away, she looked from one man to the other. She opened her mouth to speak, but no sounds came out. Then she squeezed shut her eyes and sudden tears spilled down her cheeks.

"I've done something terrible," she said to Jeremy at last.

CHAPTER 52

Although the news had predicted rain, they decided to dine on the deck, as it was Arthur's first time at the Lake Estrella chalet, and he was entranced by the tranquil alpine setting the back of the home presented. And because the storm was tardy, the slivered moon, like a giant glow-in-the-dark fingernail clipping, was visible riding up over the eastern mountain ridge, while a sage-scented zephyr made the redwoods whisper and the darkened water wrinkle as it fluttered through the nestled cove before soaring out to the broad main channel.

"Do you think the police thought she was crazy?" Jeremy asked him over the lapping of the waves below.

"No, they're probably used to going out on calls like that. But it's good that she got herself together in time—so at least she *looked* rational." He looked him up and down. "Where'd you get that red sweatshirt? I've never seen it before."

"Yeah, one of my friends left it up here," Jeremy answered mysteriously. "Anyways, I'm just glad they went away so soon, so we were still able to come up here."

"So am I." Arthur gazed across the rough-hewn table at him and saw that the twilight had thickened just enough that Jeremy's thoughtful features were illuminated now from the flickering citronella candle instead of the fading sky. "I figured you didn't want to spend the night there with her any more than I wanted to be back at my folks' house, and my mom was fine with putting off dinner for later this week. Want some more?" he asked.

"Sure," Jeremy replied, so Arthur scooped more of the mac 'n' cheese from the steaming bowl and dropped it onto his plate next to the mostly untouched heap of broccoli. "Just let me know what night you're gonna see her, so I can see Carlo at the same time; in fact, Babalu's coming up next week for a visit, and I don't want to miss him." He popped a forkful into his mouth. "Jesus, this is hot."

"You always forget." Arthur snickered. "I want to see Babalu then too, so let's go together." He paused. "So what was it you were going to tell me, that you wouldn't in the car on the way up?"

"I'm still saving that for later. Aren't you gonna ask me more about Carlo?"

"How *was* that whole thing? You never really told me that, either."

He shrugged. "It went so much better than I ever thought it would. I mean, we were having problems from the start, like we were arguing too much, but it's like we were both sort of forcing it because we thought we *should* be together, that it was crazy not to be—and of course because the gay sex was good, too." He laughed. "I love him, Arthur; you know that. He's my best, best, best friend in the world, and nothing's gonna ever change that. But I don't think I was ever *in* love with him; he never made my panties wet."

"What did he say to you when you brought it up, if you don't mind me asking?"

"He said it was better that I was breaking up with him, because I wouldn't be able to take him breaking up with me, because he's so much stronger than me."

"Sounds just like him." Arthur laughed. "He's such a strong young man with so much to offer—and he deserves to be with someone who gets wet panties around him. He's a hot little dude."

"Don't I know it," Jeremy agreed, then scooped his spoon into the half-empty Pyrex bowl and drew out some cheesy noodles for Arthur.

"Thanks, old buddy. So are you gonna tell me now?"

"Tell you what?" Jeremy grinned mysteriously.

Arthur glared threateningly at him.

"OK, OK." He chewed some more and swallowed. "That e-mail I sent you. Remember I mentioned it, right before she attacked us at the gazebo?"

Arthur cocked his head to one side. "Yeah?"

"I sent you one, a reply to yours, and it got bounced back."

"I'd deleted my account." He shrugged. "I'm sorry, but I thought it'd be best, under the horrible circumstances."

He took a bite. "I know you did, it's just that…I was writing to you to say that I already knew about everything. Then when it got returned with 'fatal errors,' I went outside to try and think of how I could reach you." He stabbed more of his dinner with his fork, and popped it into his mouth. "After that, when I was standing in the gazebo looking out at the ocean, I thought about you being gone, and my mom and dad being dead, and that I'd just ended it all with Carlo, and all I had was awful old Katharine for the rest of my life, so I started crying. And I couldn't stop—it was like I had no future anymore; there was no one anywhere that I could laugh with, and I looked at the big house and the beach out there and thought 'even though this looks cool, this place sucks just as much as Fresno.' And then—just then—you walked up out of nowhere and I almost peed my pants."

"What do you mean, you knew?" Arthur asked, leaning forward. *"Knew about what?"*

He smiled mischievously. "Does it bug you when I talk with my mouth full?"

"Jeremy..."

He giggled. "I was standing outside her office doors listening when she told you everything." He took a casual swig of his soda and gulped it down. "I followed you over there; I was right behind you, but you were too pissed off to notice. So by the time you'd agreed to her evil terms, I already knew the whole story, but I ran upstairs before either of you came out of the office. And I tried to tell you I knew about everything when I answered your e-mail—and I also told you I didn't care about her money, or my trust, or 'returning to the gutter from whence I came.' She'd never even thought for a second that because I was raised how I was, I didn't need the same things she needs, you know?"

"What do you mean?"

He looked skyward for a moment, then his eyes found Arthur's again. "It's like, I've already been through boot camp like you were, so I'll always know what I actually need to survive—like my dad told me in that old dream, where he said that in order to be a 'real man' I should learn the difference between what I need and what I want."

Arthur beamed happily across the table at him, and reached over to nudge his chin with his knuckle. "I can't believe I ever doubted you."

He shrugged. "You did what you thought I wanted—and I appreciate that—but it was totally manipulative of her because...she brainwashed you, or at least she tried to make you believe she'd been able to brainwash me, you know?"

"Yeah, I think I do. And I think you're right."

"And she was being such a total, wailing bitch to you; it's like she cut off your nuts and was jumping up and down on them in her Chanel pumps. I had to stop myself from running in there to scream at her, but I also…"

"You also what?"

"I guess I wanted to see what you'd do, how you'd react to what she was saying."

"I'm glad you did, because it gave me a chance to figure out everything, too."

Jeremy downed more of his soda. "So anyway, all I wanted to do after you left was leave the house and find you and run away somewhere, but I didn't know where you were."

Arthur fell back into his chair, remembering his Internet search. "If only I'd known."

"And I tried calling your cell, but I forgot they took yours back in Brazil and I didn't have the number for your new one programmed into mine, so I couldn't call you."

Arthur thought for a moment. "But you acted like…like you didn't know *anything* about her conversation with me in front of her, like you'd no idea at all that she tried to be the evil puppet master."

"I wanted to make her squirm," he said flatly. "After everything she did and the way she talked to you, I wanted to see her suffer while I played dumb; she needed to be humble, for once. It just would've been too easy on her if I'd said, 'Yeah, I knew it all already, you scheming Nazi.'"

"You devil." Arthur chuckled. "But you know, she was right about some of what she said."

"Like what?"

"Like that I need to do something with my life. Find a real job. Have a successful career. And here's the funny part: You know that agent who called me? Carl Singer, the one I told you about that gave me all that info on Katharine?"

"Yeah?"

"He left me another voice mail today saying there's an opening in his department. And maybe I should consider applying for it."

"So are you?" Jeremy asked, shivering as a sudden wind whipped by. He looked up and saw that a silver-edged blanket of clouds had slid over the moon.

"I don't know." He shrugged. "I guess I should, and God knows I need the work now, but I'd like to do something different. Something I feel passionate about."

"Like what?"

"Honestly, old buddy, I just don't know. Maybe I should go back to school and finish my BA."

"Then what?"

"Teach, maybe. Or study business."

"Are those things you'd really like?"

He grimaced. "Not really. My mom was a teacher, and most days, she hated it."

"Then why would you want to do that, when you could do something you're hot about?"

"That's the thing. I really don't know what I'm excited by. I guess I'm just gonna have to think about it some more. Especially now."

"I'm sure you'll—or we'll—figure it out," Jeremy said, and reached over to smooth his wrist from across the table.

Arthur considered making his announcement now but decided to wait. "Hey, when we get back, there's this really nice lady I want you to meet. She works at this little coffee place up at the edge of town."

"Sure." He nodded. "What's so great about her?"

"She's just this amazing person who loves working at this seemingly insignificant job; it's like she lives just to talk to people and make them feel better with her magical coffee and heavenly scones. She's actually living her life in the here and now, and she's *happy* with what she has."

"Sounds like somebody my aunt should get to know," Jeremy said, laughing. "Do you know if they're hiring? 'Cause I hear that Tyler, Inc., isn't doing so hot right now."

They both laughed, picturing Katharine scowling behind the muffins.

"But she's got this dog," Arthur continued, "this gorgeous golden retriever that goes with her to the shop every day, and sleeps behind the counter. You'll absolutely fall in love with her. Her name's Emma Lou, and she's this perfect rust-colored angel with a snow-white face."

"Emma Lou?" Jeremy giggled, grinning. "It sounds like an old hillbilly lady."

"It fits her perfectly. You'll see."

He thought for a moment. "I want a dog, Arthur."

"Me, too. I've never had one, not even as a kid. My dad wouldn't let us."

"My aunt and mom wouldn't let me have one, either," he said, hugging his shoulders against the sudden cold. "What kind would you get?"

"There's this really beautiful breed called a flat-coated retriever; they look just like goldens, but they're coal black. And they're supposed to be amazingly smart, really friendly dogs."

"Let's look for one when we get back," Jeremy suggested, suddenly excited. "We could take it for runs on the beach, and then we could bring it up here!"

"But nothing from a breeder, OK? Let's see if we can rescue one; there's something called 'black-dog syndrome,' and they're usually the last ones rescued from shelters."

He nodded enthusiastically. "I'd love that. What could we name it?"

"If it's a boy, I'd name him Bingham."

"What if it's a girl?"

"Probably Bingham, too."

Jeremy laughed. "Then Bingham it is. But why?"

"After a hero of mine. He died the same day as Danny." Another gust of wind kicked up, and Arthur shivered. "But there's something we haven't talked about, and even though I've been thinking a lot about this…I still don't know how to say it."

Jeremy's eyebrows scrunched together. "What?"

Arthur sighed. It was now or never. "You know this'll never work. It can't—as much as I love you and you love me. It's just not meant to be."

"What—?"

"Let me finish," he said, grasping Jeremy's hand. "OK? Let me just put this out there so you can hear me out."

"But—"

He held up his free hand, and the young man stopped midsentence.

Arthur closed his eyes and began. "Never in my life have I been more flattered—no, more *honored*—to have someone like you interested in me."

"Don't do this Arthur," Jeremy pleaded. "Don't leave me. Everybody leaves me."

"And that's exactly why we need to end this...*this part of it.* Before the inevitable happens. I know that if we tried to make this work, it would end in disaster: hurt feelings, unfulfilled expectations, resentment, disappointment, second-guessing ourselves. And I could never live with myself knowing I had a chance to head all of that off before it happened; that if I'd listened to my head instead of my...my desperation and my ego and my cock, that we could've been in each other's lives until the very end. Because that's what I want. And I think that's what you want, too."

"But it'll be perfect, Arthur. You and me and Bingham."

"You're right. It would be perfect for a year, maybe two—if we're really lucky, then maybe even five. But now it's going to stay perfect for a lot longer than that because we're going to do *our very goddamned best* to go back to the way things were before."

"But we've had the hot gay sex."

Arthur laughed. "And it was great. But the hot gay sex can be just as good or better with the one you're really supposed to be with—or maybe it's not quite as hot, but there are other trade-offs that make up for it." He thought for a moment. "That's one of the things about being gay that you still don't really know about. Because we're outside of mainstream society, we don't have to follow their rules, so you're pretty much free to experience it the way you want to—so long as you're safe and you don't hurt anyone or do anything illegal; in other words, we're already square pegs, so we don't have to kick ourselves for not fitting into round holes, so to speak. And besides, you're off to school in the spring, so that's going to be a great learning experience for you—sexually, and otherwise. And it's going to take up a lot of your time. What would you do with this old man pining after you, wondering why you were out so late and why you're not coming home this weekend?"

"But I'm not living on campus," Jeremy reminded him. "I'm gonna commute."

"Well, maybe you shouldn't. Maybe you should have that once-in-a-lifetime American college experience, where you live in a dorm and do stupid things and cram for tests and hang out with your buddies and talk about life until the sun comes up. And"—he hesitated—"I really don't want to ask you this, but you've never really told me why you wanted to be with me. I mean, any idiot can see why I would be in love with you, because...God must have been horny the day he made you, but why do you want to make this into something more? Why aren't you out there trying to find another guy your own age?"

Jeremy looked down at the table for a moment, then lifted his eyes. "All my life, as long as I can remember, it's been just me. Me with no dad. Me with my drunk mom. Me thinking I'm the only fag at school. And then I come to Ballena Beach and it's still just me, but now it's with Katharine ordering me around, or Bill the psycho figuring out how to murder me. But then, through all of that, there was you."

Arthur shrugged. "What did I do?"

"You didn't want anything from me," he said. "You were just there to smooth out everything, to be my protector, my dad, my big brother, my bud, even my boyfriend. I mean, we've never had to fight about anything, because you'd never do anything to hurt me."

"Not knowingly I wouldn't."

"But that's what's so important, Arthur. Everybody except you has let me down, has disappointed me. But you wouldn't. That's why we should be together."

"So even Carlo's disappointed you?" Arthur asked, eyeing him suspiciously.

Jeremy's eyes drifted out to the darkened cove. "No, he hasn't. But I know if we stayed together, he will, or I'll disappoint him. You know?"

"That's exactly what I'm talking about. But Carlo and you seem so great with each other most of the time."

"Yeah, but it's like...Carlo has this expectation of me, just like Katharine does; he expects me to be the perfect boyfriend and I'm not, just like I'm not Katharine's preppy little robot. And it's almost as frustrating sometimes living up to his expectations as it is living up to hers. But you; your only expectation for me is to be Jeremy Tyler— whatever that means." He smoothed the map of veins in Arthur's forearm. "Understand?"

"But I don't expect things of you because I always knew we shouldn't be together," Arthur muttered. "And that's the way it has to be. It has to—and I think you know it, you feel it too." He smoothed the long wrinkled bandage on Jeremy's arm, and had a momentary flash of him lying in that creepy glass coffin. "I'm doing this because I want to be there for you, *forever*. I want to be there at your commitment ceremony or wedding or whatever, weeping uncontrollably in the front row; then sitting proudly at the county courthouse when the child you and your partner adopt becomes yours forever." He looked up at the sky and felt a wet drop land on his nose. "Then I want to listen to you bitch and moan about your partner's maddening idiosyncrasies, all the while knowing you two are perfect for each other. And I want you to be there for me when I find someone, and later when he's driving me crazy, or when either of us finally gets that big promotion. But whether or not I ever find someone again has nothing to do with wanting you to always be a part of my life, because as I get older I want you to help me smooth out those coming bumps in the road like I try to do for you, and then maybe even…maybe when that time comes you'll be with me…you know…at the end."

"I'm not gonna think about things like that," Jeremy grumbled, looking away.

"But that's really what matters in this life, Jeremy: If we love each other, we need to be totally realistic and look down the road, then lay the foundation for that long haul—because there's going to be a million distractions and frustrations and triumphs and failures along the way. As for sex, well, that matters too, but then sometimes it really doesn't. You need to trust me about this. And we'll get over the fact that we crossed that line but then we came right back, and that'll just be a part of our weird little history—no big deal."

"I guess I get what you're saying," Jeremy said, his voice heavy with resignation. "But do you remember what you told me right after I came to Ballena Beach, when we were in the conservatory once watching the sunset?"

"I remember the conversation, but I don't remember the specifics."

"I never forgot one thing you said to me, when we were talking about relationships. I asked how you knew when you were in love, and you said it's like knowing the difference between when you're hungry and when you're full."

"I said that?"

He nodded. "And then you said that trying to make yourself fall in love with the wrong person is like trying to make yourself hungry when you've just eaten too much, or trying to convince yourself that you're not hungry when you're starving. Remember now?"

"Vaguely," Arthur mumbled. "I can't believe you remember all that."

"It stuck with me, Arthur. I've never forgotten that. And I'm sad now because I was just starting to feel full—without convincing myself."

Arthur smiled and closed his eyes. No wonder he loved him so dearly!

"Jeremy, I know—just as much as I know that I'm sitting here right now—that there's another delicious meal somewhere being prepared for you as we speak—whether it's Mexican or Italian or Brazilian or Asian or Ethiopian or from Kansas. You're gonna love it, more than these old leftovers. Trust me." He pushed back his chair to stand, then reached across the table to pull Jeremy up. "It's gettin' cold. Do you want to go in? We can make a big fire..."

Jeremy grinned at him, nodding. He pushed his chair back and stood, just as the first sprinkles began speckling the deck.

Then they walked up the stairs to the chalet with their arms around each other, and their empty dishes hugged to their sated bellies.

EPILOGUE

Good, I'm so sorry—I usually keep him on a leash. He's friendly, don't worry."

"Not a problem." Arthur allowed the leash in his own hand some slack, and the dogs circled each other comfortably, each sniffing under the other's tail. "He's a beautiful spaniel. What's his name?"

"Bingham. After—"

"*Mark Bingham?*" Arthur grinned at him unbelievingly. "Believe me, I know the reference; if you can believe it, I almost named my dog that."

"Yeah, he's kind of the martyred saint of guys like...me."

"Guys like *us*," Arthur added with a smile.

His eyes flashed bashfully at him. "So, what about yours?"

"He's a flat-coated retriever. His name's Spot."

"*Spot?*" The man laughed. "That's hilarious, considering he's pitch black."

"My dad had a dog once named Spot; he loved him a lot. So I named him after him. The dog, that is." He held out his hand. "I'm Arthur, by the way."

"Jess. Good to meet you."

They shook hands, and Arthur sized him up: black hair, flawless skin, intelligent dark eyes, firm handshake...

Very nice.

"Do you live around here?" Jess asked.

"I'm here every day around this same time. Otherwise he barks at me until I can't hear myself think; I swear he can tell time. How about you?"

"This is my first time bringing him to the park. I just moved here. New job."

"Well, welcome." He bent down and rubbed Bingham's soft head, and his pink tongue lolled happily from his panting mouth. "What do you do?"

"I'm a finish carpenter."

"You're from Finland?" Arthur deadpanned.

He laughed. "That's good. Actually, I'm Mexican. And Irish. How about you?"

"I sell boats, down at the Marina; actually, they were stupid enough to make me the manager recently. And I'm Irish-German. Very boring."

"Well, it's a small world, after all." He crouched down to scratch behind Spot's ears, and the big dog cocked his head to the side and closed his eyes. "Hey, I love boats." He looked up at Arthur. "I should...come down there to see you sometime; I could even pretend like I'm rich, and go for a test drive—"

"Anytime."

They smiled into each other's eyes. "It's funny, but you look familiar somehow," Jess told him. "Have we met before?"

"I was just about to ask you the same."

***

The rain soothed his ears, even as it called him gently from his sleep. He opened his eyes.

Had it really happened? He didn't need to look over at the sleeping form next to him to know it had. He'd been dreaming about it even before he'd awakened; his mind had been running it over and over the same way it did a beautiful song while it's playing, and then even after it ends, with a melody so sweet that you can't let it go—you keep humming and humming it until you get tired of it.

But he knew he wouldn't get tired of this.

Tired of him.

He was a song he'd been singing all his life, even before he knew the melody. Before he knew the words.

For so long now, he'd been harmonizing with silence.

Until tonight.

He smiled in the darkness, then reached over to smooth his warm, muscled shoulder.

His lover shifted, and rolled onto his back.

Then he sighed.

A sigh of contentment is what it sounded like.

No, a sigh of *elation*—like the sigh you make when you see the grand finale at a fireworks show. Or maybe it was the kind of sigh like wind winding through a cave...the sound of emptiness filled with God's breath.

He'd never heard a sigh like that before.
Or had he?
Yes, he had.

Once, a long time ago.

TRANSLATIONS

Excerpts from the mass of San Januário are in Latin, and the translation is somewhat irrelevant to this story.

"Quien engaña no gana."   Deceivers never win.

menino.   Young man.

mijo.   My son, used loosely as a term of endearment.

chanklas.   Sandals

huaraches Peasant's shoes

hermano Brother

maricón Derogatory term for homosexual

Cariocas Natives to Rio de Janeiro

Churrascarias   Barbecue restaurants

guapo.   Handsome.

puto.   Derogatory term for male whore.

dinheiro.   Money.

Cale a boca e dirija.   Shut your mouth and drive.

avó Grandmother

Eu entendo mais do que posso falar.   I understand much more than I can speak.

Gostaria?   Do you want some?

vinte reais Twenty real, or about about sixteen dollars

cola de sapato.   Shoemaker's glue.

sim, sim.   Yes, yes.

obrigado.   Thanks.

Com licenca, estou procurando por Afonso Peres. Sabe onde posso encontra-lo?   Excuse me, I'm looking for Afonso Perez. Do you know where I can find him?

pendejos.   Idiots, assholes.

meu primo.   My cousin.

Entré   Come in.

meu amor.   My love.

muito forte.   Very strong.

amante.   Lover.

chorizo Spicy sausage dish

Ela não está aqui.   He's not here.

Sabe onde ele foi?   Do you know where he went?

Dois homens. Ele saiu com dois homens.   Two men. He left with two men.

Eles estavam armadas?   Did they have guns?

Maos pra cima!   Get your hands in the air!

Senão bou atirar!   If you don't we'll kill you!

novia Girlfriend

Que escándalo!   What a scandal!

Cai fora, macacada!   Get out of here, you monkeys!

Cale a boca puta velha!   Shut up, you old whore!

Tire a roupa. Faz o que ele quer. Qual e o seu problema? Vire-se.   Get your clothes off. Do whatever he wants. What's wrong with you? Turn around.

Made in the USA